THE TRIBULATION

Book 2 of the Messiah Chronicles

by

Theodore J. Nottingham

Nottingham Publishing
Indianapolis

Dedication

To my beloved Rebecca, without whose love nothing would have been possible, and to our daughter Ashley, child of the new millenium. For a brighter future.

THE TRIBULATION
By Theodore J. Nottingham

Book design: Robert Coalson
Cover art: Dale O'Dell

ISBN 0-9664960-1-9

Library of Congress Catalog Card Number: 98-68006

Nottingham Publishing
Indianapolis, Indiana
http://tedn.hypermart.net

Printed in the United States of America

PROLOGUE

A Prophet had appeared in the early part of the twenty-first century, the last in a long line of healers, visionaries and mystics down through the ages. People around the world heard his message of oncoming devastation and his warning that the only shelter that would save them would be their own inner strength and nobility of spirit.

In response to his mission of compassion, the Prophet was beaten to death by an angry mob. No one wanted to face reality, not until it slammed into them in all its fury.

A handful of the Prophet's followers were left behind with instructions from their beloved teacher to survive the cataclysms ahead as best they could and start again. Religions and technologies had failed humanity. Only these few men and women inspired by the wisdom transmitted to them by the Final Prophet could offer desperate people a path to sanity and renewal.

But the odds were amassed against them. Not only was the planet facing utter destruction from wild weather changes, earthquakes, volcanoes, floods and a dreaded pole shift, but the world government considered them their most fearsome enemies. These humble few were carriers of truth that defied all the illusions which the iron-fisted Federation had instilled in the minds of the masses. Such persons were as dangerous as the storms gathering across the globe.

The time of reckoning was here. Everyone would have to face this age of transition in one of two ways—in utter horror and despair or with the slim hope that renewal lay on the other side of catastrophic earth changes. The second option would vanish entirely if it was known what forces were at the heart of the destruction, forces that were darker and more savage than Nature's mightiest upheavals.

* * *

The lights had gone out in the human soul. Every aspect of life was drenched in the most primitive, subanimal forms of behavior. Relationships, education, religion, politics, entertainment—all were seeping into a black hole of meaninglessness and despair.

Not even the newly formed mammoth military-political complex that transcended former national boundaries could stamp out the ever-present threat of fanatic and bloodthirsty terrorist cell groups hidden away on all parts of the globe. The killing of the innocent had become a hobby of the disenchanted and marginalized who measured their worth according to the volume of gore spread on city streets. The skills of these shadowy groups rivaled the sophistication of the Assassin sects of Medieval Arabia. In the new century, terrorism was a tool that belonged to all races and religions. It was the means of choice for venting rage, despair, and madness. Such feelings were everywhere among a species that had lost its conscience and any traces of meaning as to its purpose in the cosmos. The law of the jungle reigned supreme even in this high-tech global civilization.

The Federation was forever on search and destroy missions against these elusive groups, facing hopeless odds against stamping them all out. The population simply had to accept the risk of living in these times. Personal safety was no longer guaranteed, not by the dynasties of insurance companies nor multinational medical corporations who ruled the economies of the world and the lives of each person. Everyone was trapped in a colossal system that was not designed for personal welfare. Every human life was an unstable pressure cooker held down by an ever more oppressive world government that knew everything there was to know about each person. This was the very reason why entertainment was now the drug of choice. It numbed the pain and absurdity of living in such a world. But entertainment was the most invasive and insidious oppressive force of all. It stole a greater freedom than the military forces could hope to accomplish. It stole the freedom to think for oneself and make some sense out of life in the twenty-first century.

A highly toxic influence had slipped into the international media culture that dominated the human mind in the first quarter of the twenty-first century. How it had gotten there, taking center stage in the hearts and souls of people across the globe, could not be tracked. It had simply appeared as though overnight. In its wake lay a hundred years of slow development leading to the current state of affairs. In less than a century—the blink of an eye—everything had changed.

Young children were now bred on the most horrific displays of violence masquerading as harmless entertainment. Every child on every continent was influenced to the very roots of his soul by the all pervasive presence of the media. Subliminally or overtly, the great masses of humanity were shaped, brainwashed, manipulated through the powers hidden behind seemingly innocent entertainment. The technology originally developed to project a satisfying stimulus meant to generate ticket sales had reached a level of sophistication undreamt of by its creators. Neither Thomas Edison nor Charlie Chaplin had ever imagined that flickering images could mutate into spiritual vampires. Little boys built their identity on models spoon-fed from earliest childhood by their electronic mother, the television set. Little girls were told how to look and behave in songs and fashion by idolized and vacuous movie stars.

For years it was only the greedy heads of movie studios and crafty corporate executives who orchestrated these irresponsible assaults on the human soul. But now the media had become a precise tool in the hands of another power whose agenda was far more complex than retrieving money from the bored masses. Whether comedy or drama, everything had a common underlying thread. The same assumptions and prejudices were hidden behind the spell of imagery and myth-making. Only the very few could see it, and none of them lived long once they tried to speak up. The world government had a crucial stake in controlling the thought processes of a dangerously overpopulated planet on the verge of self-destruction.

An invading alien army could not have more thoroughly conquered the people of earth. The battle did not require bombs and generals. The invasion was from within, through the psyche of each individual.

These forces which now dominated the international media were unknown even to the producers of this toxic material. Behind the cameras, glamorous personalities, and obscene mountains of money was the hideous face of demonic power whose mission was known only to lone visionaries and prophets.

In the first decades of the twenty-first century, individual thinking had nearly vanished. But no one would believe that they were not originators of their own ideas. The illusion was overwhelming and yet nearly invisible. It was as though an all-powerful hypnotist had waved his hand across the sight of humanity and magically taken over the will, mind, and heart of countless millions. The question was, what kind of magician held this control?

The human body was desecrated into a marketing commodity, an object of lust to sell trinkets. The international sex trade had reinvented slavery for a new millennium, herding daughters and sons of the desperately poor into whorehouses on every continent where businessmen indulged themselves on company credit cards.

The mythic heroes of the day were techno-barbarians, wielding the latest weaponry with the same savagery that hurled Europe into the dark ages at another turning point of history. But this time the cruelty of these Neanderthal gods was praised and glorified rather than reviled and condemned. The dignity of being human was now mutilated beyond recognition, if not utterly forgotten.

An ancient saying from pre-sand Egypt echoed down the halls of human wisdom: "As above so below." The latest insights of quantum physics confirmed this intuitive vision of the nature of reality. The same dynamics found in the Macrocosmos—the vast expanses of the universe—could also be witnessed in the core of the Microcosmos, within the most infinitesimal particle. So it was with the human drama. Weather crises were reflected in psychological turmoil. Planetary catastrophes mirrored themselves in conflict across the globe, whether in the intimacy of human relations or in the political clashes between nations.

The onset of the great Tribulation was manifesting at every level of life. The oceans of the world stirred with storms and bizarre changes in temperatures. Human hearts and minds did the same, desecrating the last shreds of civilized behavior. Never had chaos reigned so supreme in the soul of men, women, and children. It was as though humanity were being hurled toward a vortex of destruction by powers utterly intent on that result.

CHAPTER ONE

The stench of cigarette smoke mixed with car fumes filled his nostrils and made him sick to his stomach. He'd only been in the city one day and he was desperate to get out of it. Life in the desert had given him a taste for an environment ruled by Nature and not by human beings.

Jeremy walked quickly along the city sidewalks. They were so thick with people that every step of the way someone's elbow poked him. He'd look back, but everybody was in a hurry or in some kind of trance-like state and hardly took notice.

Car horns echoed raucously against the steeples of power looming above the scurrying masses. Mounds of trash had taken the place of flower pots and trees that once attempted to beautify the concrete jungle which was the legacy of the twentieth century. The new millennium hadn't put a dent into the disintegration of urban life. Technology had continued to soar and conquer, yet it hadn't managed to clean up the garbage from the sidewalk nor out of the human soul.

Grey clouds were passing overhead, keeping the sun away from the filth and crime of the big city. A month in the barren purity of the desert had made Jeremy allergic to urban pollution. He found himself hoping that a thunderstorm would crash down upon them all and wash away the layers of scum that covered everything in sight.

An explosion nearly threw him out of his shoes. The synchronicity of his thought and its physical manifestation caused a tingle of vertigo to shoot through his nervous system. But he had too much to worry about to wrestle with the strange coincidence. Heavy raindrops struck the sidewalk, warning of more to come.

He barely made it to a doorway when the belly of the clouds opened up and a torrent of water blasted the city streets. Within moments, the sky turned nearly black as night. Lights came on even though it was only midday. Angry winds had swept in a strange storm indeed, just one in a series of bizarre occurrences that were plaguing the entire planet. This was no surprise to Jeremy. Adam Hawthorn had prophesied the oncoming devastation and Jeremy, as his first and most devoted disciple, had seen too much to have any doubts left, even for a rational, educated man. The mysteries of the cosmos so far outweighed human knowledge that it wasn't worth pretending anymore that he had any idea of what was at the heart of human existence.

In his late thirties, chiselled features framed by thick reddish hair and deeply inset eyes of emerald green on fire with vigilant awareness, Jeremy Taylor Wilkes stood out from the other passersby. There was a light on inside, just as clear as from a cabin's window in the deep of night. A light that was conscious of itself and generating itself as though creating its own world.

The strangely intense man looked older than his years. A deep wisdom emanated from his face, even though it was unsettled, interrupted with flashes of still unmastered emotions. His pale skin and sparsely freckled features added an aura of being 'different', even slightly unearthly. Anyone who could maintain any degree of inner calm and balance in these dangerous, tormented times was extremely rare. Self-mastery was a forgotten part of human development. Self-indulgence, instant gratification, disregard for any greater purpose in life had inundated human behavior and nearly conquered it.

Only infinitesimal pockets of individuals retained some link with deeper meaning, a link more life-giving than the ever more poisonous air that enveloped the globe. Deeper thought, ancient teachings, even some aspects of quantum physics had gone underground in the wake of quickly spreading global strife.

Just thirteen years into the millennium, under a highly sophisticated and intrusive but effective world government known as the Federation, the international political, religious, and economic scenes were boiling out of control. A lid had been kept over them during the first decade of the new unified government that held the world's military might at its disposal. Paranoia, invasion of privacy, arbitrary laws were leading the overcrowded and crime-ridden populations of the world into a gigantic police state more effective than any tyrant had hoped for in the previous fifteen thousand years of gore and mayhem which characterized much of human history.

Technological wizardry had betrayed the dreams of its original creators. Or had it? The immense speed at which globalization and interdependence evolved at the end of the second millennium had kept the race from perceiving the inevitable. Whoever controlled the information channels, controlled the minds of the great masses. Millions upon millions of all former nationalities could be compelled to emote, to rejoice, fear, rage, forget, buy with every flicker passing before their hypnotized senses.

Jeremy Taylor Wilkes, child of university professors, lifelong seeker of meaning, having briefly become an ordained minister in a desperate effort to live out in the world what he believed and felt in his inner world, was the unexpected principal leader of the most luminous of those pockets of outsiders whose beliefs were not molded by the Federation. He was the right hand man and trusted friend of the one known to the world as "the Final Prophet". The visionary messenger from above had come and gone like a whirlwind. The world had been warned, in every corner, all at once.

The Final Prophet's extraordinary live global broadcast had rung the last note. Then he was dead, torn to pieces for offering a last cosmic helping hand. His dying words to his friends would haunt them to the end of their days. More than haunting, they would compel them to fulfill the mission entrusted to them by the prophet—" Survive the oncoming world calamities, and rebuild a humanity of the future with the teachings I have imparted to you."

This was the fire in Jeremy's dark green piercing eyes. Everything was at stake at every moment.

Beneath the five inches of shelter that kept him from being soaked, he watched the scene around him turn into loud and messy chaos. Fender benders took place just feet away from him as the wet streets turned into ice-skating rinks and drivers just got mad instead of careful.

"What insanity!" he thought to himself. If people couldn't handle a rain shower without rage and havoc, what were they going to do when everything caved in?

"Die gruesome deaths!"

The words struck him like a two by four across the head. He turned to see who had answered his private thoughts. He found himself confronted by a wretched homeless man, as dirty as a human being could get and completely out of his mind.

"What did you say?" Jeremy asked as thunder shook

the windows.

The wretched man laughed and skipped off into the rain like a child dancing in mud puddles.

"Wait a minute!" Jeremy called out. But his voice was lost beneath a curtain of rainfall that blocked out all other sounds.

Leaning back against the wall, he tried to digest what just happened. The man had clearly read his mind. But what difference did the gift of telepathy make in the ruins of this human being who couldn't even take care of himself anymore? On the heels of the previous synchronistic event—his thought of thunder right before the strike—he sensed some larger phenomenon taking place that his mind just couldn't bring into focus.

He shook off his inner confusion and looked out once again at the world around him. People raced to and fro and sirens wailed over the downpour. The stench of the city gave way to a cleansing scent of purifying rain. He couldn't tell if he was imagining the smell of wet grass or whether some drifting aroma of real nature was coming around the corner to reach him. It soothed his tormented soul and gave him a moment of peace. But his tranquility was quickly shattered again as his eyes fell upon a large silhouette standing directly across the street in another doorway, staring at him with vicious, glowing eyes.

Jeremy knew instantly who the man was. How could he forget, though he'd only caught sight of him for a split second once before. How could anyone forget the grizzly bear shape and evil aura of Stefan Zorn? The most famous warlock of the underworld had visited the Prophet's little community only three months before. He'd come to test the man of light and had lost. But now that the Prophet was dead, there was no one to stop him and the man of darkness was unrestricted. This was his world and he was master of it.

Jeremy shivered, not because of the cold dampness that came from the rain shower, but from icy terror that gripped him from his toes to the top of his head. He could feel the man's hate a hundred yards away. Jeremy suddenly understood that the strange mental events that had occurred just a moment before were linked with the presence of the evil man, as though he emanated a magnetic field of psychic phenomena.

Jeremy chose to follow his intuition rather than wait for his rational mind to catch up. He took off into the wall of rain and was immediately soaked to the bone, but felt nothing except raw fear snapping at him like a thousand piranhas assaulting a carcass in their waters.

Somehow he knew he was being followed, even though he couldn't bring himself to look back. He hurried through the crowd, pushing people aside with the skill of a lifelong city dweller. His hurried steps turned into a jog and finally into a fast run as he made his way through side streets. Before long, he found himself in back alleyways within the bowels of the city. He slowed his pace realizing that there was no one to be seen anywhere in this wasteland of condemned buildings and permanent garbage dumps.

The rain still fell hard, whipping at him as though telling him to hurry on. But he came to a stop, sensing a new fear in the eerie no man's land into which he had wandered. For the first time, he longed for the overpopulated sidewalks where at least there was some security, even among unfriendly strangers. Now he was alone and utterly vulnerable.

He turned around. The skeletons of abandoned houses rose up around him like the guardians of some infernal territory. He knew he had to get out of there fast before new dangers just as deadly as Stefan Zorn came after him. But it was too late. Four young men appeared from under the ruins of the city. Carrying chains, tire irons, and knives, they headed toward him with the aggressive glare of predatory animals hunting down their victim.

Jeremy turned to run in the other direction. Two other youths came out of a building. One of them pulled out a switchblade. The gang members approached and circled him, eyes sparkling with blood-lust in anticipation of what they were about to do to the unfortunate man who had entered their world.

At that moment, Jeremy could only think of one thing. His beloved Lynn, the one person he loved more than his own life. He was suddenly overwhelmed with the realization that he hadn't told her how deeply he loved her when he kissed her good-bye that morning on his way to the city.

The rattle of the chain brought him back with gruesome vividness to the situation at hand. He had never seen such brutal desire for violence in human faces before. These were creatures without a drop of conscience, like zombies fresh from the grave. Their only link with humanity was a superficial resemblance. But even that vanished behind the savagery in their features.

Every fiber in his body went into high alert. He knew he was going to have to fight for his life even if there was no chance of saving himself. Jeremy had trained to be a minister, a caretaker of human beings. He knew nothing about self-defense. Yet some primeval part of his nature came up from cellular memory and readied him to tear and break and claw like a wild man in order to survive.

He watched them like a trapped animal as they came closer and closer. He could now see the color of their eyes and the vile grins on their faces. He was outraged by the realization that they wanted to see him suffer. They had no idea who he was—one of the few who, if he ever had the opportunity to help any of them, would have gladly given them his last dollar. But they wanted to maim and destroy in some futile attempt to claim some power and control over their hopeless circumstances.

His eyes darted about looking for a weapon. He saw a three foot lead pipe lying on a pile of debris nearby. In a flash, the pipe was in his hands without his thinking consciously of picking it up. The young men stopped ten feet from him, surrounding him.

"Why don't you just put that down like a good boy and save yourself a lot of trouble!" one of them said. He looked to be no more than sixteen years old.

Jeremy tightened his grip around the pipe, prepared to crush the skull of the first one who moved. He could see the two others in his peripheral vision. He knew he would have to act at the slightest movement. Sweat poured from his body in streams. But he wasn't shivering anymore. Something had taken over in the recesses of his ancestry. The adrenaline flowing through his muscles was so intense that he couldn't even feel his fear. He was enraged that they wanted to take him away from Lynn merely for their entertainment.

"Put it down, man," one said. "We're gonna cut you either way."

Wild-eyed and silent, Jeremy waited for the first move. One of the young men behind him leaped forward. Jeremy swung with all his might. The youth ducked and jumped aside. Before Jeremy could regain his balance, he heard a whistle and was struck by heavy chains across the ribs. He found himself on his knees. The pipe was torn from his hands. He looked up. One of his attackers stood over him with the pipe raised high, about to bring it down over his head.

"Stop!"

The voice exploded through the alleyway, freezing the

young man's arms in the air. They all looked into the shadows.

"Get outta here before you get hurt!" one of them shouted to the newcomer.

A silhouette moved forward.

"Did you hear what I said?" the youth yelled again as he stepped toward the stranger.

"Get rid of him!" one of his companions called out.

"The more the merrier!" another one added, shifting the knife in his hand.

The youth moved forward to confront the figure in the shadows. Suddenly, he let out a horrific, high-pitched scream. Jeremy turned his head as the other gang members shouted in shock. Their companion was on fire from head to foot. They raced over to help him as he threw himself on the ground, desperately trying to put the flames out. The silhouette stepped into the pale light. Jeremy recognized Stefan Zorn.

One of the youths let out a roar of animal rage and leaped at the large man. He caught himself, virtually in midair. It wasn't the six foot five, three hundred and fifty pounds size that terrified him, but the glare from the man's eyes. Framed in a finely cut black beard, shadowed by thick eyebrows, the man's bulldog features looked like the incarnation of Lucifer himself. It was the utter lack of fear and the intensity of power coming out of the man's small, gleaming eyes that frightened the youth.

Before the assailant could react, Zorn's big hand reached out and grabbed his throat. A crunching sound was heard and he threw the boy down like a broken rag doll. The three other punks jumped up and attacked him, letting out savage war cries.

With stunning agility, Zorn struck the first one in the eyes with his fingers and sent him to the ground screaming. The second assailant swung the chains at him. They wrapped around the big man's arm. Zorn let out a fearful laugh and tore the chains out of the youth's hand. He smashed him in the face with his forearm and swept his foot out from under him with a kick behind his ankle. The youth fell. Before he could get up, Zorn raised his foot and brought it down on his head with incredible power, crushing it like a spoiled egg.

The last youth stood in front of him, eyes wide with shock. Zorn looked at him and grinned with the very same blood-lust they had turned on Jeremy. Dressed in black, wearing gold necklaces covered with amulets and four rings on each hand, Zorn was a frightful sight. The young man turned to run, but Zorn pointed a finger at him and focused an unearthly energy on his back. The thug was frozen still and couldn't move, except for his eyes that turned back in sheer terror as Zorn approached him.

"You dare mess with me, Boy?" the man muttered in a guttural sound, full of hate and violence.

He teased his prey's terror, walking around him. The youth tried to move.

"You're gonna find out where you belong, son. It's not a pretty place."

He smashed his two open hands on either side of his head, bursting the youth's eardrums. Blood shot out of his ears and nose.

"This is nothing compared to what's waiting for you. It's just the appetizer. You're gonna be the main course for something much worse. And you asked for it."

He pressed his finger against the boy's forehead. His skin ripped across the length of his skull. By this time, Jeremy was standing.

"Don't do this!" he cried out.

The dark man looked over at him with an evil grin.

"You do-gooders are all alike. This slime was about to cut you to pieces. Now you want to be his friend?"

"Don't torture him!" Jeremy insisted. "You came for me, not for him."

"True enough!" Zorn muttered. "But you ought to be more grateful to me for getting these maggots off your back."

"Just leave him be."

"I can't do that," Zorn said as he looked back at his victim. The boy shivered in his frozen position, blood streaming down his face from the cut on his forehead.

"Don't you get any satisfaction from seeing your enemy suffer, Mr. Wilkes?" Stefan Zorn asked as he eyed his victim.

"No I don't," Jeremy answered. "Let him go."

"Oh, all right," the big man said sarcastically. He raised his hand. The young man's body suddenly flew across the alley and smashed against a wall like a ripe tomato. He slid down to the ground, lifeless.

Zorn turned his vicious features upon Jeremy.

"There, I let him go like you wanted," he said with a laugh that chilled Jeremy to the bone.

Stefan Zorn looked over at the bodies littering the ground. The one he had set on fire was now dead, burnt beyond recognition. The other one, whom he had struck in the eyes, was curled up in fetal position, moaning.

"Just for you, pastor," the big man said cynically, "I'll let that one live. He'll spend the rest of his days as a blind beggar. That'll teach him, don't you think?"

"Why did you protect me?" Jeremy asked grimly.

Zorn approached him until he stood inches from his face, looking down at him with disdain. Jeremy instinctively took a step back, unable to bear his oppressive presence.

"Don't think I did you any favors by keeping you alive. I've got my own use for you."

"What do you want from me?" Jeremy asked defiantly, outraged by this savage manifestation of evil.

"You were the Prophet's right hand man, weren't you? I want you to witness who has the ultimate power now and what foolishness it was to think that he spoke the truth."

"You'll never convince me otherwise."

"We'll see about that," Zorn said menacingly. "As long as you're alive, I have a link to the man who dared to defy me. I'll get my vengeance through you and those like you. If you survive what is to come, I'll make you my disciple instead of his."

"Never!"

Zorn raised his hand to strike him. His eyes were filled with a look of unbounded rage. But he managed to control himself and smiled mockingly.

"Either way, I'm gonna get you, Wilkes. And you'll see who the real master is. You will do my bidding some day."

"Go to hell!" Jeremy responded fearlessly.

Zorn let out a big laugh. "Look around you, fool! We're already there!"

He turned his back on him and walked off into the shadows. Jeremy watched him, overwhelmed with disgust. Zorn turned back one last time.

"Give my best to your lovely wife," he said with a snicker.

Jeremy wanted to run after him and strike him, but he remembered the teaching of the Prophet and realized that this was just another trick Zorn was playing on his psyche, proving how easy it was to make him his servant.

The man disappeared. Jeremy took a deep breath to calm himself. He looked up at the dark clouds above and noticed for the first time that the rain had stopped. He became aware of the whimpering youth whose eyes had been damaged. Instinctively, Jeremy went over to him and kneeled at his side.

He moved the youth's hands away from his face. His eyes were swollen and bloody.

"Help me!" he whimpered desperately.

Without thinking, Jeremy placed his hands upon the youth's eyes as he had seen the Prophet do many times. At first, he felt awkward, wondering why he was reaching out to this thug who had intended to brain him with the lead pipe, but the desire to heal brought back his memory of the Prophet with an intensity that overwhelmed everything else.

Jeremy had committed himself to the mission of the one who was the herald of the age of transition and the great Tribulation that was to strike all living things on this planet. He had told Jeremy many times that he had to make a decision from which there was no going back if he sought any kind of enlightenment and wanted to make himself useful to the forces of light.

It had taken Jeremy a long time to understand the full impact of that teaching, but it was becoming clear to him now. He had to choose again and again not to be a child of darkness despite all the horrors that surrounded him.

Now he held his hand on the youth's blinded eyes simply wishing to emulate the unconditional goodness he had seen manifested in the Prophet. Perhaps it was as much to honor his friend and teacher as it was for the sake of the wounded youth that he found himself kneeling there in the mud trying to help him. Whatever his reasons, in that moment of healing there were no thoughts, just the wish to be a channel of goodness.

He said a silent prayer for the lost soul moaning in agony. Then he felt his hand suddenly heat up and tingle. His desire for right action opened the floodgates of his heart and the vision of his beloved Lynn came into his mind. Now his chest warmed just like his hand. For an instant, he was no longer in a grim ghetto surrounded by dead bodies, but in an oasis of peace and joy that seemed to be the very apex of the purpose of life.

He basked in the inner sunlight of this spiritual tranquility and gave thanks to the mysterious forces that had kept him alive. He realized in that moment that he owed his gratitude not to the beast Stefan Zorn but to the higher powers that moved humans about like chess pieces on the table of destiny.

He became aware of his body again and realized that his face was wet, not with raindrops but with tears. He opened his eyes. He couldn't even feel his hand. It seemed to have turned into a wave of warmth like a sun-drenched beach where sun and sand become one. He looked down. His hand was swollen and reddish. It felt like a mass of hot vibration rather than flesh and bone.

Through his tears he noticed something and blinked several times to bring his sight into focus. He moved his hand away from the youth's face. The young man was staring at him, eyes wide with amazement and a new found serenity. It was as though he'd absorbed something of the state in which Jeremy had entered, and in that contact had become transformed from a vicious brute into the human being he was meant to be.

Jeremy couldn't believe it. Nothing like this had ever happened through him before. Not only was the swelling gone, but the youth's eyes were clear and bright. He radiated a new quality, as though he'd become aligned with the self he had lost long ago.

Jeremy stood up, unable to bear the mystery that had happened in the blood-soaked mud. The young man looked at him without a word, stunned by his act of goodness and the miracle that had accompanied it. Jeremy was just as amazed and shook his hand to bring it out of its numb condition as well as to release the pain that he had taken into himself from the wounds.

He was struck with the realization that not only was the Prophet's teaching taking hold in his being but so was his power. Adam Hawthorn had sown seeds that contained miraculous possibilities. Jeremy's absorption of his words were not merely intellectual but transformational.

A ray of sunshine broke through the grey clouds and spotlit the desolate alleyway. Jeremy looked up, almost expecting to see the face of the Prophet gazing down upon him. A golden light shimmered above him. In this dreary place, it was the very image of the angelic realm.

He looked back at the young man who was still staring at him. Tears were rushing down his cheeks as well. The power of unconditional love was performing its magic in his heart. Jeremy heard himself say: "Don't hurt people anymore."

Somehow he knew that the youth would remember and abide by those words for the rest of his life. He turned away in a daze and stumbled out of the alley toward the noise and confusion of the city that made him feel safe. Beneath the blanket of activity and distraction, he could soothe his psyche from the world of mystery that had just revealed itself to him.

CHAPTER TWO

The freak storm that had angrily blown over the city vanished as quickly as it had come. The oppressive clouds gave way to clear blue skies. Yet there remained a threatening electricity in the atmosphere. A tinge of green and orange blended with the familiar blue, warning of more to come.

A woman with thick locks of brown hair curled about her face by the hot wind stared out at the vast desert horizon. Her shimmering eyes drank in the view with an intensity that mirrored a powerful, deep soul rich with clairvoyant insight and warmed by a heart of gold. Lynn Wilkes sat at a picnic table behind the desert shack that was now her home. She wore her poverty with regal dignity and no one would have guessed the hardship that she and Jeremy endured.

Lynn had learned to find her way to a measureless peace within that gave her contentment which outer circumstances could not. The pain of life had taught her the hard way, perhaps the only way. She had given herself over to caring for whatever living being came her way, just as the Prophet had done.

This day she was less tranquil than usual. She disliked being separated from Jeremy. The greatest joy in the world for both of them was found in their togetherness and they were rarely apart. But this was one of those times when he had to be away from her side. The trip to the city was critical to them.

They had been living in the desert for nearly a month, hidden away in the rundown reservation under the protection of Stargazer, an Indian elder and friend of the Prophet. This excursion was their first resurfacing into society.

They had been assured safe passage by security agents of the Federation in return for meeting with General MacDaniel himself, the military's chief-of-staff and highest commanding officer in the Federation. The world government was desperate to have them deny the prophecies in order to bring the world back to some semblance of peace. This was their only chance to save themselves from the Federation's wrath.

Lynn stood and walked along the dusty ridge that overlooked the barren plains stretching to all four horizons as far as the eye could see. A few rusty trailers and dilapidated farms dotted the barren landscape, but gave it little sense of life. This was the land of a proud people brought into submission under the yoke of extreme poverty.

In their desert hideaway, Lynn had come to know a number of Native Americans and admired their deep relationship with nature and their instinctive mystical intuition. Religious persons she had known in her past were far removed from the openness to the mysteries of life that she found among these barely educated people.

An old pickup truck bounced along a red trail leading to the isolated home where the friends of the Prophet were hiding. She recognized it as the elder's truck. Stargazer checked on them several times a week even though the journey through the rocky terrain was difficult for his aged body.

But there were no other choices. Lynn and her companions were on the Federation's most wanted list. The fact that one of them, Michelle Blair, was a former security agent enraged the Federation all the more and it was using the full power of its technology and limitless personnel to find and punish them.

Within hours of the Prophet's death, catastrophes had in fact begun to take place. But that didn't matter. The Federation had only one thing in mind. And that was to keep control over the massive hordes of panicked humanity. If cataclysmic earth changes were to occur, the Federation wanted the people of the world to die passively.

Lynn walked up to the ridge and waved at the oncoming truck. A hand appeared out of the window and waved back. Her heart warmed as a wave of gratitude washed through her in reaction to the kindness of the old Indian mystic. The truck pulled up in a cloud of dust. Stargazer painfully stepped out of the vehicle. A young man got out on the other side. He was the very opposite of the old elder, the incarnation of a vibrant Cherokee warrior.

They approached Lynn. "Good morning!" Stargazer said in a tired but resonant voice. "Meet a friend of mine. He's known to our people as Brave Eagle. But on his driver's license it says John Littlebear."

Lynn looked into the brown eyes of the newcomer and drank in the quality of his soul. She understood immediately why he was given that name as a result of his vision quest. A strong, honest presence radiated from him, one she sensed could be trusted.

"I brought him here to meet you and to take over for me. I won't be able to make this trip as often anymore."

Lynn turned to the old mystic, feeling that he was leaving something unsaid.

"You must have Indian blood in you," Stargazer stated with a gentle smile. "You don't need words to understand."

"How soon?" she asked, realizing that he had just informed her of his imminent departure from this life.

"Hard to say. The doctors tell me a few weeks, but their medicine is weak."

She knew that he was the kind of man who, once gone, could never be replaced. He held up his hand, as though putting an end to her sad thoughts.

"I'm at peace. I'm ready. I may be of more use to you in the spirit world than I am here."

She looked into his limpid brown eyes and saw the truth of his statement emanating from deep within.

"I'll be leaving you in good company. Brave Eagle is like my son. He's one of the few of his generation who's chosen to learn the ancient ways."

Lynn saw in the youth's serenity the kind of dignity of spirit and alertness of mind that was the characteristic of one awake and committed to the deeper mysteries of life.

"Where's Jeremy?" Stargazer asked.

"He's gone to the city," she said, knowing that the old man would not be happy at the news. He looked at her sadly. "There was no choice," she added. "We had to consider the Federation's offer."

Stargazer shook his head. "They can't be trusted. We'll need to move you to another place, further into the desert."

"I love these lands," Lynn responded. "But I don't know how much longer we can live out here, so dependent on your assistance. We need other means to take care of ourselves."

"I knew this day would come," Stargazer said somberly. "Maybe it's best in the long run. It's good that Brave Eagle can take over now."

"No one has been a better friend," Lynn said as she

approached the medicine man and took hold of his wrinkled hands. He whispered a blessing for her in his native language.

"As the Prophet said," he spoke slowly, "you will have to live through hard times. Much harder than these."

"I'm ready," Lynn stated with certainty.

She hugged him, sensing that this was the last time she would see him. He patted her gently on the back.

"You must survive, dear Lynn, you must."

A dust-devil cloud suddenly swirled up at their feet and circled them, covering them with a mist of sand as they held onto each other for courage to face what lay ahead.

* * * * *

Michelle Blair sat in a dark restaurant, waiting impatiently for Jeremy's arrival. Her strong, graceful features were marred with anxiety and her forehead glistened with perspiration even though the day had become strangely cold after the storm.

She knew that she had ruined her career by committing the ultimate heresy and choosing the Prophet over the world government. She had brought disgrace upon her family name, but she had no regrets. Her conscience was clear. She had chosen Truth, even at the price of losing everything else.

However, she hadn't planned on returning into the belly of the beast to whom she had once given all her loyalty and talents. Her former colleagues considered her a traitor and the reputation she had reveled in was now one of infamy. Yet she knew she must face this dangerous turn of events if they wanted to save the Prophet's followers from certain death.

This fateful encounter was the last chance for her companions to make a deal with the Federation. Their stay in the desert had been severe and far too demanding for people use to the amenities of twenty-first century living. In this last months of the year 2016, it seemed absurd that they should live like primitive peasants scratching out a living in an unfriendly landscape. And yet something deep within her already knew that this harsh life-style was merely a foretaste of what was to come, not only for them but for the entire population of the planet.

A tall, lanky silhouette appeared in the doorway. Michelle sat up. It was Andrew Bradshaw. His eyes fell upon her immediately, as though attracted by a magnetic current. The instant their eyes locked together, electricity filled the air. These were two people on the verge of discovering that they were meant for each other.

Andrew made his way over to her and sat at the table. He gave her a warm smile.

"How are you holding out?" he asked.

"It's not easy," she answered with sincerity. She saw no point in hiding anything from him.

"I'm not going to let them hurt you," Andrew said, placing his hand on hers. The warmth of his affection was evident to the very marrow of his bones.

Michelle looked at him and received his proclamation of protection with gratitude and a tinge of hopelessness. She knew who they were dealing with. She had been one of them. And even the Prophet's devoted friends couldn't overcome the power of highly-trained, unscrupulous bureaucrats and military personnel.

"Jeremy's not here yet?" Andrew asked.

"He's late. That's not his way," Michelle said, worried.

"He'll be here," Andrew assured her. "It's been awhile since he's had to navigated through the city."

A waiter came up to them. Andrew ordered some coffee, though he hadn't eaten since the night before.

He didn't have the money even to buy a side order. This felt very strange for him, having grown up in lavish wealth. He had never before experienced such severe shortage of the greasy green paper he despised so much. He sure could have used a warm sandwich, but he had nothing left except the shirt on his back. That was the price he paid for financing the Prophet's mission. The Federation had frozen all his assets.

"Have something to eat," Michelle said, reading the look in his face. She put a ten dollar bill on the table. "Come one, it's on me."

He looked at her in utter humiliation.

"Don't be silly. Take it. You have to be able to receive as well as to give, you know."

He nodded in agreement.

"Where are you getting money from?" he asked, still hesitant.

"Oh, I was able to gather some before I lost my job."

"Let's conserve it then."

"You're gonna need your energy for this, Andrew. That's more important." She had become intimate enough with him to know that he was hypoglycemic. He needed to be able to think quickly and sharply in their meeting with General MacDaniel and his cronies.

He looked at her with gratitude in his eyes, a feeling that went much further than the need for a sandwich. She was giving him new life at a time when he had lost everything.

Jeremy found his way to the restaurant and headed straight to the men's room to clean himself up from what he'd been through. He didn't want to frighten his friends with the ordeal.

He splashed cold water on his face, trying to wipe away the trauma of his psyche. He was in a strange condition, one mixed with horror and ecstacy, two opposite states that made for very uncertain emotional stability. He dried his hair with paper towels and combed it, breathing slowly and deeply to calm his jangled nerves. The event he and his companions were facing was dramatic enough by itself without the addition of this incident that had shaken his soul to its core.

He looked at himself in the mirror. He noticed for the first time the signs of wear and tear from the last few months. Dark circles under his clear, green eyes had permanently installed themselves, giving him a virtual mask over his fair and lightly freckled features. Several streaks of white spread through his red curly hair. He was never one to be concerned about the inevitability of aging, hoping that with it would come the kind of inner peace and fulfillment he'd searched and studied for these many years.

He noticed that the crow's feet had deepened and travelled nearly to his temples. Each wrinkle on his face was a scar from the white-hot intensity of the life he now led. As a minister, he had once enjoyed the rather bland and safe existence of a little community. Even hospital visits and funerals were easy compared to the colossal events that whirled around him like a deadly hurricane.

The Prophet had revealed what his generation was in for. Already, the news was screaming with stories of freakish weather and political unrest across the globe. It seemed that the entire planet was exploding with catastrophe, and the worst was yet to come. The fulfillment of the prophecies that had haunted humanity throughout the course of its history had now come to a climax in this age.

Jeremy was at the center of it all, aware of the cosmic struggle involved in this agonizing transition. There were no guarantees that humanity would survive this moment in history. After one last cleansing breath, he stepped out into the restaurant and spotted Michelle and Andrew awaiting at a table in the back corner.

They warmly greeted each other.

"Are you ready?" he asked them as he sat at the table.

"I don't know," Michelle said through gritted teeth, trying to keep the fear down. "I've got a bad feeling about this, Jeremy."

"What do you mean?"

"I know they can't be trusted and I know they want to put us away for good."

"Don't they need us for their propaganda more than they want to bury us?" Andrew asked.

"Sure," Michelle responded. "But if we don't give them what they want, then they don't need us anymore."

"Maybe we'll give them what they want," Jeremy stated flatly.

His friends looked at him in shock. "What's that suppose to mean?" Andrew cried out.

"I've been thinking about this a great deal in the last week, " Jeremy said with hesitation. "Whatever we say won't change the facts. If we satisfy the Federation's requirements, we'll be better able to survive what's about to happen."

"Wouldn't you feel kind of guilty about publicly denying the Prophet's words?" Andrew asked angrily.

"Eventually, they'll find us anyway," Jerry said in return.

"There's no guarantee we'll ever walk out of there. Not all of us."

"Do you think they'll try to keep you, Michelle?" Andrew asked as he put his arm around her. In these last months of common struggle, their nascent affection was coming into full bloom. Lynn and Jeremy had celebrated their developing attraction for each other. But now, in the face of such dangers, it was taking on a bittersweet quality.

"I'm a traitor as far as they're concerned," Michelle continued. "You know what they do with traitors."

"Can't your father influence them in some way?" Andrew asked as he kissed her cheek with a gentleness mixed with desperation.

"My father's retired and no longer has any power."

"They always liked a good deal. Can we bargain with them in some way?"

"That's the reason for this meeting," Jeremy interrupted. "Part of the results will be to free Michelle from their vengeance. Otherwise they'll just hunt us down."

"So how far are you willing to go in order to come to an agreement?" Andrew challenged.

"Like I said, I'll tell them what they want to hear. They can distribute it all over the world for all I care."

"I don't know if I can handle the shame," Andrew responded. "It'll blacken the Prophet's name and wreck his mission."

"He was never interested in his reputation. Whatever we say now won't stop what's taking place. But it might buy us a little time."

"Time to do what?" Andrew, always the pessimist, asked with renewed anger.

"You're not giving up before it starts, are you, friend?" Jeremy challenged.

"No, of course not! But we need to be building some kind of proper shelter for what's ahead."

"I thought the Prophet advised us not to depend on shelters," Michelle remembered with a trembling voice. Every time she thought about the man who had changed her life, deep emotion rose out of the wound in her soul.

"What he said," Jeremy responded, "was that our real security doesn't lie in underground shelters, but in our inner being and our effort to open ourselves to something higher than we are."

"That doesn't mean that we stand around and wait for our destruction," Michelle pointed out.

"Don't you think we should try to warn people so that they can take shelter as well?" Andrew asked, upset by the focus on their own safety when millions of lives were at stake.

"That's what the Prophet did," Jeremy answered. "He said it loud and clear. If people don't want to believe him, that's their problem. They had their opportunity."

"That's mighty cold of you, Jeremy," Michelle scolded.

"There's no more room for sentimentality. Everything's gonna crash and we must take care of ourselves so that we can eventually be useful to others."

"I can't imagine the Prophet saying such a thing," Andrew muttered.

"Damn it!" Jeremy slammed his hand on the table. His two friends were stunned by his violent reaction. But his nerves were still on edge from his earlier experience. "Let's not get caught up in arguing over what he would have wanted us to do or not do according to each one's interpretation. It's happened too many times before with other messengers. Let's not fall into that trap! We need to stay focused on the critical issue."

"And are you the one to tell us what that issue is?" Andrew asked with a scowl.

"Yes I am!" Jeremy replied with a commanding voice. "I paid the price from the beginning. I was his first assistant. And it's crystal clear to me that what the Prophet wants from us is to undergo these trials and carry the seeds for a future that will come after the Tribulation. That's the key."

"The odds are against us," Michelle observed nervously.

"That's right," Jeremy responded. "But some of us must try to make it, not for our own sakes, but because that's what he wants us to do. Remember, he said some day others would come along to help once again."

"Others?" Michelle asked. "What others?"

"Other Messiahs . . . " Jeremy said simply. "Messengers from a higher world."

The three companions sat in silence in the shadows, weighed down by the implications of what Jeremy had just stated.

The restaurant was bustling with activity. The growing fear across the world population was causing a resurgence of need for communal gatherings and the illusion of safety they seemed to provide. Public places were always packed now.

"Are we together on this?"

Michelle and Andrew looked at each other. That brief glimpse carried a lifetime of hopes and dreams. They wanted so much to be together and seek out the quiet joy of a life shared in love. But they were fated to exist in a time where peace would not be found in any corner of the world.

They nodded in unison. There was strength in the single-minded commitment that they shared. Jeremy looked at his watch.

"It's time. Remember, the Federation is not our greatest enemy."

The two lovers turned pale, understanding what he was referring to even though they didn't want to believe it.

"So beware not only of the outside dangers, but of the inner turmoil that will be created to throw us off-track. That's where the most deadly quicksands are to be found."

He stood and look at each of them in turn. "Remember," he whispered, "we carry the teachings of the Prophet that he passed on to us, the Light that must be saved from annihilation and forgetfulness. We have to keep it bright by living it. Then maybe we can share it with others in the future."

"If there is a future . . . " Andrew muttered cynically.

CHAPTER THREE

Frenzy filled the air at the U.S. headquarters of the World Federation. Employees of the Science Division were running about, shouting to each other in hallways, and obsessed with the responses on their computer screens. News of yet another terrifying discovery had exploded among them like a neutron bomb. Their latest sonar cameras were sending back photos of an immense crack on the ocean floor. Careful analysis revealed that it had widened to twice its size in just the last few weeks.

The small earthquakes that had shaken the west coast of the continental shelf were warning signs that the mythic Big One was indeed about to occur. Yet the residents of the coastal states were taking the unstable earth in stride as they had for nearly two centuries. Under the influence of the Federation, the media was required to put the most positive and least alarmist spin on the information. News reports were softened to avoid mass panic.

Now at headquarters, across the continent, there were clear indications that it was not business as usual out in the Pacific.

"How in the hell can the earth crack open all of a sudden like that?" Brad Coglan, head of the Division, growled at three anxious scientists standing in front of him.

"I don't know sir. There's no natural explanation for

it. But the facts are clear," the more courageous assistant stated, holding up the color printouts of radar images. "You can see for yourself."

He pointed to the jagged red line running across the image. "There it is, as clear as day."

Coglan grabbed the paper out of his hand and compared it with one that lay on his desk and was dated several months earlier.

"It's widened out all right. So what are your conclusions?"

"Sir, in my opinion, a killer quake is going to erupt any day now. There is no way the pressure isn't going to split that shelf in half and rip apart all the faults like never before."

"What magnitude are we talking about? Seven, eight?"

"Off the charts, sir. California will float out to sea."

"Get outta here!" Coglan called out.

"And there's another thing," the third scientist pipped up. "A lot more serious than that."

His boss looked at him incredulously.

"What could be more serious than losing a piece of the country and millions of people dropping into the ocean?"

"Well, sir, I believe we've got definite proof that the earth's axis is undergoing a shift."

"A what?" Coglan may have been head of the Federation's Science Division, but he was no scientist. He'd been in the core of engineers, but when it came to things of a cosmic nature, he was utterly ignorant. They had placed him in management for his leadership skills, not for his intellectual abilities.

"A complete lithospheric reorientation of the earth's crust."

Coglan didn't want to reveal his ignorance in front of his underlings. He didn't have to. They already knew his limitations.

"We're talking about a pole shift, sir. It's also known as an earth crust displacement. If you imagine removing the peel of an orange and then reattaching it, you can see how the peel could easily move over the inner layers. We can expect a tilting of the earth's axis, changing the centrifugal balance of the crust and generating massive surfaces changes."

"So what would that result in?" Coglan asked, already knowing the answer.

"Some continents could sink and others rise from the depths. The oceans will back up in their basins at an average velocity of two to three hundred miles an hour. We can expect gigantic tidal waves some three thousand feet high inundating the continental shores."

"Has this ever happened before?" Coglan barely managed to ask as his throat nearly shut down with anxiety.

"Our geological and geomagnetic records suggest that this cataclysm occured nearly fifteen thousand years ago."

"That's why we've found skeletons of sea animals in the Himalayas and tropical coral reefs in the Polar Circle," another man in a white coat offered. "Coal deposits in Antarctica tell us that there was a great forest up there once."

"When you consider the results of the greenhouse effect," another scientist continued, "and the buildup of ice at the South Pole, it makes the globe all the more unstable."

"Are you telling me the climates are going to change?"

"Dramatically!" the scientist responded with enthusiasm. He was fascinated by the geological phenomenon and seemed to have overlooked the damage to the planet's population. "Some of the warmer countries will become ice-covered. And ice-covered lands will thaw."

"That's too strange!" Coglan cried out. "How can you

be sure about this?"

"Well, it's happened before. That's one of the theories about the demise of the continent of Atlantis, you know. Some believe it's hidden under miles of ice in the arctic."

"Don't be talking to me about Atlantis, damn it! Let's stay focused on reality, shall we?"

The scientist held up a six inch thick folder.

"Got the data right here, sir. Six months of research."

"That could explain the fast increase of the fault lines on the ocean floor. The entire globe is under incredible pressure now."

Brad Coglan stepped away from his colleagues and looked out the window, staring at the doomed city beneath them.

"Maybe that man they call the Final Prophet was right after all . . . "

* * * * *

A black limousine, shaped in the latest aerodynamic style, swept around the corner and glided to a halt in front of a dilapidated church. Two men got out, obviously highly-trained bodyguards, and scanned the area for any trouble. They nodded to each other and opened the passenger door. The glistening dome of a bald head appeared from the car. A man of medium build stepped out, covered in a large raincoat. Beneath the flaps of the coat appeared shiny medals.

Under thick black eyebrows, steely eyes darted about searching the environs for potential enemies. General MacDaniel was the hero of the turn of the century Syrian war and feared nothing, expect perhaps renegade holy men. At his side, he wore the latest heat-seeking, laser driven pistol. Despite his years, he moved about with catlike grace and vitality.

He checked his watch and motioned for the men to open the old church door. This abandoned sanctuary in a forgotten corner of the city was a perfect rendezvous. Close to the waterfront, surrounded by discarded factories of another era, it was a no man's land. Not even the homeless and dope dealers ventured into this landscape.

The men muscled their way through the door into the dark room. They were greeted by giant cobwebs and an overwhelming wave of musty aroma. The old orthodox church had once been home to a thousand worshipers. Now it was more like a rotting cadaver than a place of reverence. Left to disintegrate soon after the beginning of the third millennium, no one had ever come to revive it. The angelic hymns and mystical chants that had once resonated in its walls had given way to a deep silence that in some ways was even more mysterious and compelling. Its very desolation spoke volumes about the times.

Educated people no longer thought about getting on their knees, unless it was to work with the latest technological wizardry. This gutted church was a symbol of a death at the heart of civilization which, like a black hole, sucked in all the dislocated pieces of societies into its barren vortex.

The general stepped into the cool shadows of the old sanctuary. He coughed as the dust choked him. For a man who hadn't had a spiritual thought in forty years, this place was very irritating. Irritation, in fact, was his antidote. He buried any intuitive feelings that might have opened his eyes to another dimension of reality deep in the morass of negative energy which stirred within him where they were sure to be swallowed up and forgotten. At least for now.

He smiled at the paradox of being a man of darkness in this "hallowed" ground. The blasphemy tickled his atheism.

It took him a few moments to adjust to the darkness of the Gothic setting. The heavy aroma of mildew filled his nostrils, further confirming the fact that religion had been defeated long ago by men like him. Impatience burned through his veins as he sought out the man he had come to see. "Where the hell are you?" he finally called out, after bumping into several columns of cold stone. The electricity was out. An orange, flickering glow came from a few newly lit candles beneath a disintegrating statue of the "Mother of God."

"Turn on a flashlight," he ordered angrily. One of his men lit a high-powered lantern and aimed it around the room. A beam of light shot through the darkness, illuminating icons, candles, crosses and broken pews.

"What the hell do they want to meet here for?" the general muttered as he looked upon the religious objects with disdain. "I guess they can't let go of the old fantasies of the race. They haven't entered the modern world yet. That's their whole problem."

The general took off his raincoat and tossed it to one of his men. He wore a carefully tailored military uniform. Tight riding pants, shiny boots, a sharply creased shirt with insignias of his four-star rank. An expert horseman, he liked to wear the clothes that came with the sport even though the animals were as anachronistic as this ancient church in an age where nothing mattered but high speed and efficient control. He wandered about the large space, looking at the ruins of another time.

"This all died out with the last millennium," he said arrogantly, looking up at an icon of a mother and child whose gaze were warmer than his. "We've entered more enlightened times. Do you know how many wars were fought over these myths?" he asked his men without expecting any answers. "At least our wars have a rational purpose."

The purpose was straightforward indeed: the destruction of maverick rulers and political terrorists, and the domination of the world population. For a planet on the brink of collapse, the strategy made a lot of sense. Especially to a man whose only insight on human beings was to crush them into submission.

The general stumbled over an object and kicked it away from him, cursing. It was a porcelain angel wing. It shattered against the wall.

"It's all junk!" he said angrily. "I don't know why anyone ever fell for it. It sure didn't do him any good," he added as he paused below a crucifix.

But he quickly turned away, disturbed by the sensation he felt gazing upon the face of one who was called the savior of the world. He moved off abruptly.

"I can't believe I'm wasting my time with these fools."

He looked at his watch again. "I have to be in Paris in a few hours."

"Sir, I think I see them coming," one of his men called out as he looked through the crack in the door.

"You two disappear. We agreed to a one on one. Needless to say, shoot anything that looks suspicious. And I mean shoot to kill!"

The men vanished in the shadows as they pulled out their weapons. The general leaned back against an old wooden table that had once been a holy altar where the sacraments were distributed to the faithful. The door opened, sending a ray of light into the room which immediately filled with a myriad dancing dust particles. The silhouette of Jeremy Wilkes appeared in the doorway. He stepped into the sanctuary.

At first he didn't notice the presence of the man he was to meet. Jeremy was struck by a memory with the force of a bolt of lightning. His early spiritual encounters as a child in an old church swept through him like a tidal wave crashing on the shores of his consciousness, rekindling all the feelings that had changed his life and put him on this path. In the next instant, it was lost again. He was back in the dangerous present.

His eyes first saw the shiny leather boots, so terribly out of place in the old sanctuary.

"General MacDaniel?" he asked in a voice strengthened by the remembrance of his commitment.

The general said nothing, still leaning on the altar as though it were a bar.

"You'd be Jeremy Wilkes."

"That's right. Are we alone?"

The general stood up straight and stepped forward. "I'm here. Isn't that enough for you?"

"I've got two friends waiting outside who are prepared to speak with you as well."

"The deal was one on one."

Both men knew that his friends were there to witness any possible betrayal.

"I take it one of them would be Michelle Blair," the general muttered hatefully.

This time it was Jeremy who didn't answer.

"I'd like to see her again," he added with an evil grin.

He approached Jeremy swaggering with the confidence of an all-powerful, merciless leader.

"I'd like to look into her eyes and ask her if she's happy with the decision she made."

He was now just a few feet from Jeremy. They could see each other's features well. Jeremy was disgusted by what he witnessed in the cold eyes, and he stared back defiantly at the bravado of the arrogant military man.

"So you're the Prophet's right hand man, eh?" he asked almost mockingly.

Jeremy let the insulting tone slip by and studied the angular features of his adversary. This man had seen more dead bodies than Dante had described in his gruesome vision of the inferno. He was in the highest echelons of a world government that controlled the planet more effectively than any empire before it. And yet it was teetering on the brink of utter collapse despite the increasing military control.

Jeremy smiled to himself at the irony. This man so full of pride had to lower himself to meet an ordinary person. That alone was an admission of the underlying weakness and fear within the Federation.

"Let's get straight to it, shall we!" the bald warrior said impatiently. "You've heard the terms of the deal. You declare the prophecies untrue and we let you live in peace."

"How can you guarantee us safe passage?"

The general's little eyes caught fire with rage. "You're talkin' to a four-star general, son, the commander of the western military branch of the World Federation! My orders are sacred. When I give a command, it's obeyed without question."

"Are you a man of honor?" Jeremy dared to ask.

The general's jaws clenched tight. He did his best to maintain his composure, unwilling to let himself be thrown off balance by this nobody.

"Are you?" he shot back.

"That's why I'm here, general," Jeremy said fearlessly. "So what exactly would you have me do?"

"We want to call a news conference and have you make a statement to the world press. We want you to say that the Prophet was wrong."

"And what do you think that will accomplish?"

"It will keep the world population from utter panic."

"What if his words aren't wrong?"

The two men glared at each other through the shadows of the silent sanctuary.

"Then it will keep them content," he said with a subtle smile. The man might as well have told him that the

Federation was the wizard of Oz. More illusion than power.

"But he is wrong!" the general continued. "I don't see the earth caving in under our feet."

"Not yet . . . But I know you've seen other reports from across the globe. There's no denying that geological and political unrest are coming to a climax."

"We've handled difficult situations before."

"I'm sure you have. But this one is even beyond your powers, general. There's going to be a clean sweep and men like you will have no authority."

The general winced as though he'd been hit in the face.

"How dare you?" he responded. "I could splatter you against the wall right now with my bare hands."

For a moment, it seemed as though he was going to follow through with his threat. But Jeremy was no longer worried. He understood that his work was to step into the lion's den and say what he must.

"So what's your proposition?" Jeremy asked coldly.

The general paced back and forth, moving away from Jeremy, trying to control his desire to kill him.

"I'll set up a news conference tomorrow morning. It will be the largest ever assembled. I want you there with whomever else will stand at your side. I want you to state that the prophecies are—at best—disturbed imaginations and not to be taken seriously."

He glanced over at Jeremy, knowing how much he was demanding. "You can qualify that however you wish. Tell the world that your friend was under stress, ill, or whatever. Just give people something else to think about besides total destruction."

"And what will you do for us?" Jeremy asked, biting his lip, forcing himself to continue forward with this bargain.

"As soon as the news conference is over, if you have

achieved what we require, my soldiers will escort you to the edge of the city. No one will harm you. All you have to do is never show yourself in public again."

"This would include all those who are with me?"

"That's right."

"Even Michelle Blair?"

The general flashed a hate-filled glare at him. "Even Michelle Blair," he said through gritted teeth.

"I thought the Federation never forgave its rogue agents. Isn't that official policy?"

The general's dome glistened with sweat as his emotions roared within him again. He walked up to Jeremy and tried to stare him down.

"We'll make an exception for this case. There's too much at stake to waste our time with one traitor."

Jeremy peered into the fierce light coming from his eyes, seeking to detect what he was really thinking. The general relaxed his facial muscles, as though backing off from a frontal assault.

"Look, Wilkes," he said in a calmer voice, "we're trying to keep the world from annihilation, don't you understand? For all our military strength and surveillance capacities, we're at the mercy of madmen and terrorists, some of whom have uranium in their possession. One spark could ignite a war that would kill us all. Your Prophet has just raised the odds that we're not going to make it. So now it's up to you," he said, sticking his finger against Jeremy's chest, "you're the one who can make the difference. If it wasn't so, I wouldn't be wasting my time with you. I deal with world leaders, not bohemians and religious fruitcakes."

Jeremy had to repress his instinctive reaction to the man's poking finger. He had learned the hard way not to let himself be victimized by his every response. This effort was at the heart of the Prophet's teaching.

The man was so close to him that he could smell his

cigar-laden breath and could sense his inner violence.

"It's up to you, Jeremy Wilkes, to keep us from a disaster from which we cannot recover. You don't even have to condemn your friend, just give people another option besides the total devastation which the Prophet predicted."

"I repeat, general. What if there is no stopping what he said was on its way? I can't blind them to what's before their eyes."

"Young man, I've been in the business of world government for twenty years. I've learned that reality is not the issue—perception is. If some kind of end of the world is coming, I want to avoid the hundred revolutions that will explode before its onset. At least we can limit the bloodbath."

"Since when were you concerned with human life?" Jeremy asked in a challenging voice.

General MacDaniel studied him from beneath his thick eyebrows. His angular face tightened again into a knot of disdain. "Son, I deal with the things of this world. You may be interested in another, but my feet are planted solidly on the ground here below. If I have to take lives to save other lives, then that's how it's gotta be."

"Aren't you just repeating what has always been the curse of human history?"

This time the general lost control. He grabbed hold of Jeremy's collar and choked him.

"You bastard! How dare you judge me? What have you ever done for your country? I stood in front of enemy fire. Where have you shown your courage? Don't you dare judge me! What have you done for your fellow human beings?"

"I've never tried to choke them!"

The general released his grip and walked away from him.

"Are we agreed?" he asked in a loud, angry voice.

"What if I don't agree?"

The general turned around and pulled out his pistol.

"Then I'll waste you right here, son. You're of no use to me."

Jeremy didn't flinch. This would be the easy way out to end it all right here in this old sanctuary.

"You've now given me the experience of facing enemy fire," he said serenely.

"How does it feel?" the man asked, arming his weapon. A red light came on and projected against Jeremy's heart.

"You have no power over me, general. Go ahead, shoot!"

"Is that really how you feel about it?"

The general held his weapon with both hands and aimed at him.

"Do you want your wife Lynn to come here and mop you off the floor?"

Jeremy was stunned at hearing his beloved's name come from the vicious man's lips.

"Don't you think we know all about you, Wilkes? Who do you think you're dealing with? We know what time you go to bed at night. We know you're hiding in the desert somewhere and we're going to smoke you out like rats. Every one of you. So think of your friends before you play the hero."

Jeremy's mind went into hyperspeed. The faces of his companions appeared before him beginning with his soul mate, Lynn, and followed by Stargazer and his people who had protected them. And beyond the welfare of his friends, the mission that the Prophet had bequeathed upon them—to stay alive and survive the Tribulation in order to help the race begin again.

"It's a deal, general," Jeremy said, his heart sinking, knowing there was no other way.

CHAPTER FOUR

The phone rang in the Indian elder's shack. It was one of those old touch tone phones from the previous century, predating the era of satellite transmitted calls, even before the use of fiber optics. Very few such phones were still in operation, except in rural areas and among the marginalized.

Stargazer sat in a gutted sofa with a cup of water in his hand. He looked over at Lynn who was sitting on a tattered couch across from him. The old man studied her, eyes sparkling with concern. He nodded for her to pick up the phone. She did so with a trembling hand.

"Hello?"

"Lynn?"

Jeremy's voice reassured her.

"Are you safe?" she asked breathlessly.

"I am."

She detected a grim tone to his voice. "Tell me," she said, not sure she wanted to hear.

"We've made a deal. But it's going to be costly."

"What do you mean?"

"They're going to leave us be, all of us."

"That's great! What do we have to do in return?"

There was silence at the end of the line.

"Jeremy?"

"They want us to publicly reject the Prophet's words."

Lynn's face turned ghostly pale.

"We can't do that!"

"Not all his teachings, just his statements concerning the predictions of global disaster."

"What predictions? They're already here!" Lynn cried out.

"They don't want to know that. They believe there's security in ignorance."

"We can't deny his words!"

"Do you remember what his first requirement was from us?"

"Of course I do."

"That's what this is about—survival."

"Not at the cost of rejecting him publicly. I can't do that. I didn't think you could either."

"Damn it, I feel bad enough as it is, Lynn! Don't make it any harder! This is the only way out. Otherwise, they'll slaughter every last one of us and bury us in some mass grave in the desert."

Lynn turned and looked at little Angel, the six months old infant who had been saved from death by the Prophet's mysterious powers. Her mother, barely fourteen years old, had also found new life through him.

Lynn turned to Stargazer. The old man was staring out the window, but listening intently. He too was suffering from the desperation of their situation.

"Lynn, we've got to do it. It's the only card we can play."

"What makes you think we can trust them?" she asked, trying to find a way out of the unthinkable.

"I spoke directly with MacDaniel. You can't get higher than that. The Federation is ready to do anything to calm the world population."

"Don't they realize that people can see for themselves what's taking place? You can't very well overlook earthquakes and giant storms!"

"They've been manipulating people's minds for so long, they believe they can keep them from seeing what's in front of their faces. In any case, it's only temporary. They're buying time just to keep control."

"Jeremy, I can't believe you would do this."

"What the hell do you want from me, Lynn?" he shouted through the phone line. It was the first time he had spoken such angry words to his beloved wife. She was shocked, speechless.

"I'm doing this to save our lives!" he said more calmly.

"I don't want my life saved at that price."

"All right then," he responded with irritation. "Don't think about your life, think about the mission we've been given. We've got to make it through this for the sake of the future."

"I don't want to carry that kind of responsibility on my shoulders, Jeremy. I just want to be true to what I believe in."

"It's too late to back out now, Lynn! You were right there when we made our promise to him. If we give up now, he will have died for nothing."

His last words struck her in the chest like a sledge hammer. Nothing could get her to betray the Prophet, except his own legacy. She knew her husband spoke the truth. If they were destroyed, nothing would be left of what the Prophet had brought to humanity. His mysterious mission, which was still so unclear to them, could vanish like dew at sunrise and be lost for all time.

"Lynn, darling," Jeremy said gently, "people are becoming more insane than ever. They have no idea of the madness taking over their own souls. They're easy victims of deception. The Federation knows this all too well."

"So we'll participate in the deception?"

"No," he answered, no longer angry, but feeling her

pain. "We'll create an oasis of sanity for those who can find us."

"When must this happen?" Lynn asked in a weary voice, resigned to what had to be.

"Tomorrow morning."

"Tomorrow?"

"The sooner the better."

"Don't you realize what tomorrow is?"

"No."

"It's the anniversary of our first encounter with Adam Hawthorn."

Another silence came over the phone line.

"I'll be back by the weekend," Jeremy finally stated.

* * * * *

A gigantic bank of fog had fallen upon the city during the night. It drifted through the streets like some lost ghostly monster. By daybreak, nothing could be seen more than ten feet away. The world appeared captured by a thick mist that wandered over it unhindered. Clouds of fog seemed to rise from the ground like puffs of smoke exhaled by some unseen creature.

An eerie silence hung over the vast jungle of buildings as though all life were crushed by the mammoth clouds dragging their bellies across concrete pavement.

A black car, headlights beaming bright, made its way through the empty streets. It came to a halt in front of a television studio. Three security agents jumped out and scanned the area for safety. A limousine swept around the corner and pulled up in front of the building. Four bodyguards exited the car, followed by General MacDaniel who was dressed in a colorful, fully decorated uniform. He adjusted his cap on the shiny dome of his head and approached the entrance.

Suddenly, a light tremor shook the ground beneath

his feet. He caught himself on the stair railing as the building shuttered. The men looked at each other, trying to conceal their fear generated by this interference of nature's instability. This was especially difficult for the general. He was heading to a news conference that would assure the world population that there were no imminent catastrophes ahead.

The tremors stopped after a few seconds. Everyone stood still. No one breathed. Each man remembered the dire warnings of the Prophet, despite their denial of them. The general was the first to break out of the fearful trance that held them all in its grip.

"Let's take care of business, shall we!" he said gruffly. They headed into the building.

One of the bodyguards looked back before closing the door behind him. The streets were quiet as the strange fog wound its way between the buildings. There was something threatening in the air, something ominous. The man could sense it like a jungle animal knowing that it was being watched but unable to detect the presence of its adversaries.

Jeremy, Andrew and Michelle were already waiting in the conference room, along with a crowd of reporters summoned there by the Federation.

The trio sat at a table covered with microphones. Their faces were grim, but determined. The tremor had made them even more uneasy about what they were doing, and yet Jeremy was certain of the necessity for pushing onward. They could barely hide their nervousness, however, as military men—some with weapons strapped to their sides—filled the back of the room.

General MacDaniel entered and gestured to an assistant. Immediately, everything went into motion. Lights came on, reporters opened their notepads, cameras rolled.

An army officer pointed to a reporter, ordering him

to ask the first question.

"Reverend Wilkes, you were a key associate to Adam Hawthorn, better known around the world as the 'Final Prophet.' You were with him from the beginning."

"That's right," Jeremy replied solemnly.

"Why have you called this news conference today?"

"We're here as friends of the Prophet to dispel misunderstandings concerning his announcement to the world prior to his death."

Jeremy paused. The room was utterly silent. Andrew looked over at him, tense and worried.

"The Prophet was here for more reasons than forecasting oncoming calamities. He taught us in very specific ways how to live with meaning and purpose."

General MacDaniel leaned against the wall in the back of the room, grimacing impatiently at Jeremy's delay in getting to the point.

The reporter, coached by the Federation, pressed on. "What are you trying to tell us?"

"The reason for this news conference," Jeremy continued grimly, "is to let people know that the prophecies they heard broadcast around the world which have caused such panic are not the central purpose of the Prophet's mission."

General MacDaniel barely managed to keep himself from smacking the wall with his fist. The military men in the room looked at their superior with concern. The man hated double talk.

"What are you saying about the prophecies then?" another reporter asked.

"We are here to tell you that they should be disregarded because, whether they are true or not, they are not the point of his teaching."

"Are you telling us that you do not believe in the prophecies?"

Jeremy swallowed hard. He felt as though his heart

was being pulled out of him. He glanced over at the general who eyed him fiercely.

"I'm saying that they are metaphors rather than statements of fact."

"What do you mean by metaphors?" the reporter insisted.

"The Prophet did not merely warn us of oncoming natural catastrophes. He saw them only as reflections of the spiritual devastation of humanity. We should be more concerned about the death of conscience among us than about dramatic weather changes.

"He told us of the invasion of the walking dead among us, people so alienated from their spiritual identity that they are devoid of all feeling and reason. Such legions of pathological individuals are capable of every kind of atrocity. This is the real disaster. Not whether the earth shifts on its axis.

"The Prophet spoke of demonic predators seeking to destroy the very dignity of being human. His emphasis was placed on each individual's personal effort to avoid sinking into the endless night of human degeneration.

"What I'm saying is that people have focused on the wrong issues. It doesn't matter whether or not we're destroyed by wars and natural cataclysms if our souls are lost to greed, selfishness, and perversion."

Jeremy leaned forward toward the microphone.

"The real tribulation that is coming stems more from the cataclysms within the human soul than from wars and weather conditions. The most dangerous battles will not be conducted with bombs and bullets but with unseen forces pitted against each other whose battleground is at the center of every human being."

"What kind of mumbo jumbo is that?" someone cried out.

Jeremy didn't blink. A new serenity had suddenly

taken over where uncertainty and confusion previously ran rampant.

"Everything is connected. We know that by now. Our physicists have told us that each of us is at the center of the expansion of the universe. Each of us is also the center of the destruction of the universe. And everyone of us must become aware of the real struggle before we can do anything to protect ourselves and change what is coming. Our own inner demons are the cause of what we see around us. Either we exorcise them through new awareness and effort or we're all going down in flames."

"How are your statements different from the Prophet's message?" a reporter asked, taking the words right out of General MacDaniel's mind.

"Don't look without, look within," Jeremy said simply. A strange silence fell over the room, as though his words had jolted his listeners into that very experience..

"People around the world are making the mistake of seeking shelter from external danger because of the Prophet's words," Jeremy continued. "But his true message has to do with the dangers within us."

"So you're saying that the world population is not in such imminent danger. It's more of a spiritual thing, eh?" a reporter asked with a mocking grin.

Jeremy did not answer, letting people draw their own conclusions. In the back of the room, General MacDaniel shook his head in anger and disgust. He was entirely unsatisfied with the direction of the news conference.

"Do you take any responsibility for what the Prophet has unleashed across the globe? The panic, the suicides, the general mayhem that is upon us? Could the world have been saved from this if his words had not been broadcast on television?" another journalist asked.

Jeremy leaned into the microphone again. "I'm sorry that people have suffered unnecessarily by making wrong decisions based on their misunderstanding of the call that he sent out. But I'm not surprised that his message was reduced to such limited interpretation."

"You people ought to be thrown in jail!" someone called out. "Somebody's gotta be held responsible for the anarchy that's so rampant now!"

"It would be absurd to blame the messenger for the message," Andrew responded angrily. "The natural cataclysms that we witness everywhere around us are certainly not of his doing!"

"But you did kill the messenger, didn't you!" Michelle suddenly blurted out.

Jeremy looked at his companion whose emotions were bubbling to the surface. Andrew took her hand, worried. But she couldn't contain herself.

"You beat him to death! Now you suffer the consequences. This man could have changed everything! Now we're left with the results of your rejection!"

The general leapt like a tiger from his position at the far end of the room and shouted an order as he personally tore the microphone's cable out of the wall.

"You're under arrest!" he cried out.

"What are you doing?" Andrew exclaimed, his face turning scarlet with anger.

"This news conference is over!" the general shouted, motioning for his men to rush the cameras and shut them down. He called for two soldiers nearby to draw their weapons.

"Arrest her! Your irresponsible accusations are treachery!"

"You promised us free passage!" Andrew yelled as he jumped between Michelle and the approaching soldiers.

"False accusations are tantamount to betrayal!" the old warrior thundered.

Jeremy jumped up and came face to face with the general.

"This is not going to look good at all for the Federation to be seen as untrustworthy. Not in these times!"

His words stopped the general cold.

"It was a live feed," Jeremy continued, "just like we agreed. The whole idea was to show your magnanimity, wasn't it? And quiet the fears that are threatening the entire civilized world. Arresting her won't help meet those goals."

The general held up his hand, stopping the soldiers.

"Get outta here now," he whispered between his teeth. "Don't ever let me see your face again, or I'll shoot you myself!"

Jeremy looked into the steely grey eyes and sensed that he meant exactly what he said.

"Good luck," Jeremy whispered back sincerely. He knew the man was going to need it to keep civilization afloat against all odds.

CHAPTER FIVE

The companions hurried out of the building. A black van was double parked next to their car, surrounded by a dozen heavily-armed soldiers. The friends looked at each other as a feeling of terror shot through them.

"They've betrayed their promise!" Michelle whispered hoarsely. "Just like I knew they would."

"We've got to make a run for it!" Andrew said as every muscle in his body tightened in fear.

"Don't panic!" Jeremy ordered. He slowly moved down the steps ahead of them. "I think they're going to let us go."

Excitement made his heart beat wildly as a feeling of certainty filled him with new hope. Andrew and Michelle followed, suddenly struck with the same sensation.

They came to the bottom of the stairs and stopped in front of the van and the ring of soldiers. Jeremy unlocked the doors to his car with his remote control and motioned for his friends to get in.

"Now what?" Andrew muttered under his breath once inside the vehicle.

Jeremy looked back at the building in expectation. The doors opened and General MacDaniel appeared at the top of the steps. His face was distorted with a fierce anger as he motioned to the soldiers to follow their orders.

Several men opened the back of the van, revealing a group of men carrying submachine guns.

"I don't believe it!" Michelle whispered in horror. "Hurry!" she suddenly cried out.

Jeremy looked up in time to see the general command his soldiers to fire.

"Get us out of here!" Andrew shouted.

Jeremy threw all his weight onto the accelerator. The car hurled forward, slamming into the soldiers who had appeared from the van and were preparing to shoot. Jeremy managed to maintain control of the vehicle as it flew around a corner under a hail of gunfire.

The car raced toward the outskirts of the city. Just as they reached the highway, an old trailer truck appeared on the road directly ahead of them.

"We're done for!" Andrew shouted.

The truck stopped in the middle of the road. Someone jumped out of the passenger seat and waved them down. It was Lynn.

"Is that who I think it is?" Michelle cried out.

Jeremy slammed on the breaks, barely avoiding a collision with the huge vehicle. At the wheel of the truck was young Brave Eagle, motioning for them to get into the trailer.

Jeremy pulled the car off the road and came to a screeching halt behind a clump of trees that would provide camouflage from their pursuers.

"Come on, let's go!" Jeremy said nervously as he jumped out of the car and hurried toward Lynn. He took her in his arms.

"What a woman you are! You'll never cease to amaze me!"

"I hope not!" she responded with a big smile.

They jumped into the truck and headed into the countryside.

Jeremy put his arm around Lynn and kissed her gently on the forehead. They sat on thick layers of Indian blankets that padded the inside of the vehicle.

"How did you know where to find us?" Jeremy asked as he caught his breath.

"We've been following the news conference on the radio. Stargazer told us to be ready to meet you by the highway. He had another one of his visions. This time, I knew better than to question it."

Jeremy pressed his lips against her warm forehead.

"We're going to be all right," he whispered.

"As long as we're together," she said, "I don't care what happens."

* * * * *

That night, colossal storm clouds thundered all around the world. Gigantic lightning crackled across the skies, terrifying animals and humans alike. Fires broke out everywhere. Transformer plants exploded beneath the electrical bolts. The stratosphere seemed to be retching violently upon the blue planet and its inhabitants that had so polluted their own nest.

Power outages created immense blackouts that shut down entire states across the North American continent. Computers crashed by the millions, television screens went blank, cars crashed into each other on every highway. The lightning looked like monstrous arms slamming down upon the earth as cosmic sledge hammers savagely assaulting their helpless victims. Armies were mobilized to prevent the population from massive looting. The World Federation declared a global state of emergency as communication systems failed all across the planet.

In the national office for Scientific Research, Brad Coglan stared in stunned silence at the reports coming through their emergency backup system. The high tech computers they had taken so for granted were as useless as empty beer cans. Hundreds of power transformers had been put out of commission.

"Has anybody ever seen anything like this?" he shouted out with uncharacteristic frenzy.

Several colleagues gathered around him, hair and clothing askew from the frantic work they had been doing for the last few hours.

"Never! Not in forty years on the job," one of the scientists said.

Another associate took off his glasses and cleaned them pensively on his disheveled shirt.

"There's never been such a thing in the annals of weather history. I don't even know what to call this phenomenon. It's as though the entire magnetic field of the planet has been disrupted."

"Maybe it's that axis shift you were talking about," Coglan suggested in spite of his disbelief.

"It may well be," James Fuller, the oldest scientist on staff responded as he joined the group.

"What can we expect next if that's the case?" Coglan asked, uncertain that he wanted an answer.

"That's a hard one," the old man stated, scratching the grey nubs on his chin. "It's never happened before. But if I were to guess . . . "

"Go ahead, guess!" Coglan said with irritation.

"Well, I suppose the plates would shift."

"You mean the continental shelves?" Coglan asked with a new rush of fear.

"That's right," Fuller said sadly.

"We're talking earthquakes all around the globe on top of this?"

"Probably."

"Under these conditions, no one can be rescued!"

"That would be a correct deduction," Fuller said in a low, somber tone.

"Thousands, millions maybe, are gonna die!" Coglan cried out as he wiped the sweat from his brow.

"Yep."

"What can we do?" Coglan asked in a voice that was now trembling.

James Fuller looked at him with mournful eyes. He was tormented by the fact that his vast knowledge and experience were useless.

"Pray . . . " the old man said in spite of himself.

* * * * *

Thunder echoed across the vast Southwestern desert and slammed into parched earth that hadn't seen a drop of water in months. But still the skies were barren. No rain fell despite the storm.

Young Brave Eagle stood by his mentor Stargazer at the entrance of a deep cave and watched the dangerous lightning crash all around them. The elder shook his head as he studied the strange sight with great intensity.

"This is a sign . . . I've never seen such manifestations before."

"What is it saying to us?" the young man asked in frightened awe at the freak cosmic event displayed before him.

Stargazer listened to the crackle and explosions shattering the great silence of the desert, as though seeking to hear what the spirits had to tell him.

"He said this would happen . . . " the old man whispered.

"Who did?" Brave Eagle asked.

"The one they call the Prophet. He spoke of oncoming devastation, the end of the age."

"Our seers have also spoken of this, haven't they?"

"Yes, but what they did not say was that these events

would come about because of the darkened souls of human beings."

"But this is nature's doing!" the young Cherokee warrior said to him.

Jeremy came up behind them from the back of the cave, leaving the shelter where his friends were huddled.

"He said that poison emitted by wrong action and the spiritual death of people everywhere would alter the magnetic field of the planet," Jeremy stated. He looked out at the purple sky furiously hurling thunder to the earth. "This has been building up for centuries and has reached critical mass in this age."

"What you call critical mass," Stargazer said sadly, "my people call the victory of the evil ones."

"It seems that we are the evil ones," Jeremy replied softly.

"All the dark deeds that humanity has committed are preserved in the spheres of the Great Spirit, like dust caught in the folds of a giant cloak."

"So the massacre of our people is part of this downpour of rage?" Brave Eagle asked in a whispered voice.

"That's right," Stargazer responded. "The Spirit World is releasing its fury over the cries of the innocent."

Just then, an explosion of lightning ripped across the horizon and shook the rocks around them. The men were unable to restrain a startled reaction at the great roar that followed upon the mystic Indian's words.

"It has always been said that evil deeds would be remembered. We thought it was our elders who would be the rememberers, through the stories they passed on to us. But maybe it's the cosmos itself that remembers."

"That's what the Prophet told us, Stargazer," Jeremy said. "In the East they call it Karma and it seems that the effects of countless terrible causes are now being played out."

"Must the innocent suffer as well?" the young man

asked, lips trembling with the implications of his question.

"We must all suffer now," Jeremy answered. "Guilty or innocent, we're all in the same boat."

* * * * *

From his office in the headquarters of the World Federation Military Sector, General MacDaniel ordered a state of emergency across the entire North American continent. The unprecedented weather conditions gave him the excuse he'd been waiting for to increase his power over the population. Military control had been hidden just under the surface for years, but now it would come out into the open with full force.

Reports were arriving over secret military satellite systems from every major city describing massive looting and violent anarchy. Vast urban areas were blacked out from the storms. The festering brutality and anger barely under control for the past half century was erupting with vehemence. People who had been reduced to cogs in the great machine of the social structure were now rebelling with insane fervor as they saw the system begin to fall apart. The youth of the day, whose family unit had been broken down since the last century, were without parents or conscience and were eager to destroy the civilization that had given them their miserable lives.

The active black market of weapons and drugs which formed a toxic mix that nothing could contain were now surfacing, adding deadly fuel to the firestorm. The Prophet had warned his friends that the cities would be the most dangerous place to be when the time came.

"Have you found them yet?" General MacDaniel barked as he studied the half dozen monitors on the back wall of his huge office.

"No sir, but we're on their trail," a military officer answered nervously.

"What the hell does that mean?"

"We know they're in the southwest and most likely on an Indian reservation."

"Then what are you waiting for? Bring them all in! Anybody who shelters them is an enemy of the Federation."

"Well, sir, we've been through every shack in that stinking hole. They must be out in the desert somewhere."

General MacDaniel stood up and stared fiercely at his officer.

"I don't care if you have to bulldoze the entire southwest! You find those rebels and you bring them to me dead or alive! This is the wrong time to have people like that on the loose!"

"I thought the Prophet spoke against violence."

"Well, he's not here anymore, is he?" the general shouted. "All his people ever wanted was to cause anarchy and destroy our system of government."

He pointed to the monitors on which news reports from around the world were being piped in, every one of them a picture of devastation from the freak storms across the globe.

"If ever there was an opportunity to take advantage of the situation, this is it!"

"Sir, we've got two regiments out there looking for them. Are you sure we should be using that kind of manpower? They're needed elsewhere."

"You questioning my orders, captain?" he asked as he stepped up to him. The soldier wasn't sure whether his superior officer was going to smash his knuckles into his face. He stood at attention and looked away, hoping for the best.

"Continue to follow my instructions to the letter, is

that clear? I'll let you know when I'm ready to release the men for other purposes. That'll be all!"

The captain saluted stiffly and hurried out of the office, his jaws clenched.

He stepped into the antechamber and took a deep breath to control his anger. He looked around at the secretaries and people waiting for audience with the powerful general. He shook his head, realizing MacDaniel was more of a dictator than a military officer. He'd known for years that the puppet civilian government would eventually disintegrate and give way to the real power which always belonged to the men with the weapons.

The captain felt a strange heat in the right side of his face. Instinctively, he turned and saw in a corner of the room a large silhouette with gleaming eyes boring holes into the side of his head as though reading his mind. The soldier flinched. He'd never felt such a sinister sensation.

"What in the world is this man doing in here?" he wondered to himself as he looked away from the dark, massive figure.

"You'll find out soon enough!" came an answer in his head. The captain's eyes widened in shock. The man had read his mind and responded. He hurried out of the room, unable to deal with the strange phenomenon.

Stefan Zorn smiled slyly as he watched the captain walk away. One of the secretaries approached him.

"The General will see you now, sir."

He stood and adjusted his heavy black coat. He was dressed in a dark suit and tie and had removed the rings from his hand so as to look more like a business man than the occult magician that he was. He entered the general's office.

MacDaniel lit a cigar and watched Zorn approach with steely, suspicious eyes.

"I've heard a lot about you, Mr. Zorn."

"I'm sure you have," the big man said with an evil grin.

"Do you know why I called you here?" the general asked as he sat himself in the manner of an emperor on his throne.

"Of course. You need my skills."

The general did not respond and puffed on his cigar, unwilling to acknowledge his statement.

"Have a seat," the general said coldly as he pointed to one of the comfortable furnishings decorating the room.

"I'd be interested in learning how you came to find me, general."

"Now Mr. Zorn, you should know that the Federation's security forces can find anyone."

"You have a file on me, do you?"

"Certainly."

"What am I identified as?"

"I beg your pardon?"

"Am I under 'W' for warlock?" he asked sarcastically. "I didn't think the Federation had any interest in the supernatural."

"Officially we take no interest in these matters, because they have no reality for us. But the Federation can't be foolish enough to disregard anything completely."

Zorn let out a deep, booming laugh that startled the general.

"I'll bet you've got some department buried in a sub-basement somewhere conducting experiments with the unmentionable."

"You're partially right, Mr. Zorn. We've looked into telepathy, hypnosis and other such things. They can be powerful weapons."

"Indeed!" Zorn responded, sending a glare toward the

general that reduced his own to shame. "So what conclusions have your bureaucrats come to?"

"No conclusions," MacDaniel said coldly, barely hiding the dislike he was developing for his visitor. "But we want to fight fire with fire."

"Aaah . . . fire. I know about that."

"You know that the world government's stability is threatened as never before, particularly because of the unfortunate spectacle that was made by the man they call the Final Prophet. I assume you saw that."

Stefan Zorn shifted in his chair. He was never comfortable talking about his nemesis.

"Did you know him?" the general asked.

"Who?"

"The Prophet."

"I met him once," Zorn replied with a distant look in his eyes, clearly uninterested in pursuing this line of conversation.

"Ever since he appeared on world television warning of dire things to come, we've had a rash of religious fanatics come out from under their rocks."

The men sat in silence. Zorn waited for him to continue. The general studied him carefully.

"How does this concern me?" he finally asked impatiently.

"We need someone who can identify their degree of "power" and then terminate them," MacDaniel said bluntly.

"You've got an army of hired assassins on your bank rolls. You don't need me for that kind of work."

"No, but we don't have a single person at any level of the government who would know how to deal with people with strange powers. We thought that perhaps you could identify these persons. We'll do the rest."

"Let me get this straight. You want me to be like a hunting dog."

"You can call it that if you want. We can't afford to have any more dangerous mystics appear on the world scene. It's worth a lot to us."

"A million dollars a head."

"They told me you had expensive tastes," the general said without flinching.

"Indeed I do. So do you by the look of things," he added as he waved at the decorations that filled the large office.

The general ignored his comment. "For a million dollars, you'd have to convince us that the individual in question was truly a person with dangerous powers."

"That's right."

"Is our information correct? You can detect such things?"

"I can detect them all right. And I'll be happy to tell you all about it for a million dollars. Add another half million and I'll kill them for you."

"We don't use that word around here."

"Ah yes, terminate. Tell me, how do you know you can trust that I'm not the very kind of person you're seeking to "terminate"?"

The general sat back in his chair and let out a circle of smoke.

"My people tell me that you don't care for those religious types anymore than we do."

"This is true."

"They also tell me that you're exclusively devoted to the dark side, as they call it."

Zorn did not respond, but held the general's gaze defiantly.

"You don't believe in such mythology, do you general?"

"No, I don't. The only power I'm interested in is at the end of my laser gun. The rest is irrelevant. But I know what loyalty is. If you're loyal to the enemies of the Prophet, then you're on my side."

Stefan Zorn revealed his big teeth in an evil grin. "If you're looking for the Prophet's archenemy, you've found him all right."

The general looked at him with satisfaction. He knew he had made the right decision by making a pact with the malefic man. One way or the other, he would come out the winner. Whatever it took.

CHAPTER SIX

Jeremy returned deep into the heart of the cave where the storm sounded only like distant canons and the howling of ghosts from ancient wars. He made his way down a narrow corridor that descended into the bowels of the earth. Primitive lanterns hung on the sides of the walls, barely lighting the steep natural stairway created by waters that had once carved their way through the stone.

He descended further and further underground, sometimes having to slide between the wet walls through spaces hardly wide enough for an adult body. After awhile there were fewer lanterns to light his way and he had to grope in the dark. The sound of the freak storms could no longer be heard and a heavy silence, akin to the one heard only in the depths of the ocean or in the infinite vistas of outer space, filled Jeremy's senses. Somewhere in the belly of the earth, the slow drip of underground water echoed loudly, intensifying the eerie impression of intense isolation from the rest of life, a feeling that was comforting under the circumstances.

Flickering light appeared far below at the end of the steep corridor, a vision that would have terrified Medieval painters of a literal Hell. Jeremy came out into a vast chamber whose ceiling was higher than any cathedral ever built by human hands. It was lit up by torchlight on all four sides. The shivering light illumined giant Indian paintings created in primordial times. An overpowering sense of sacredness was given off by the symbols and images that climbed to the very top of the huge chamber. The place had once been a secret ceremonial temple for peoples who had disappeared long ago. Stargazer was the last of the elders to know of its existence. The secret would have died with him had he not chosen to make it a refuge for the friends of the Prophet. Nothing less than the end of civilization would have caused the old mystic to let outsiders into this holy place.

Colorful blankets covered the stone floor throughout the chamber, except in the center where a large fire crackled and warmed the humid walls. A slit in the ceiling served as a chimney, releasing the smoke into the upper rooms of the colossal cave.

In the far corner stood three large tepees, looking strangely out of place. They served as private rooms for the unlikely guests. Jeremy headed for the nearest one. He lifted the flap and peeked in. Blankets and furs made the space cozy and warm. In the midst of them, his beloved slept peacefully. Jeremy smiled at the sight of the woman he loved more than anything in the world.

Lynn moved slightly and opened here eyes as though she'd sensed his presence. She smiled a radiant smile and raised her hands for him to come into her arms. He entered the makeshift home and laid next to her. They hugged warmly, both keenly aware that their embrace was the only peace and joy to be found for them in this doomed world. They kissed passionately.

"Has the storm abated?" Lynn asked as she looked lovingly into Jeremy's bright green eyes and moved his wave of red hair dangling on his forehead back into place.

"Not at all. I've never seen anything like it."

Lynn's cheerful expression darkened. "Then it has begun!"

Jeremy shook his head. No words were necessary.

"My God! He was right!" Lynn whispered in shock.

"You knew he was right all along, Lynn, before any of us really understood what he was saying and how much he knew."

"But it's not the same when it actually happens." She tightened her embrace around Jeremy's strong shoulders. "I'm scared."

"There's reason to be, sweetheart. There's plenty of reason to be scared. Any sane person should be."

"Do they know what's going on out there?" Lynn asked in a trembling voice.

"You mean the Federation and the general public?"

"Does anybody understand what's taking place?"

"I don't think so. Not yet. You know how people are. It's gonna take recurring cataclysmic devastations to get their attention. By then, of course, it will be too late."

"Do you think we can make it through this?" she asked, pressing her warm, soft cheek against his.

"We have to, Lynn. Just like the Prophet wanted us to."

"How can we ever have a family under these conditions?"

He looked deep into her glistening eyes. The light blue of her pupils made him think of a cloudless spring sky in more peaceful times.

"You have to hold onto hope, hold on real tight. That's all we've got."

"Hope for what?" she asked breathlessly.

"For our happiness."

"I can be happy right now with you here in this place."

She kissed him gently on the lips. He felt a thrill

rush through his body at the contact of her wet, quivering touch. They'd been married five years and madly in love every day, yet he'd never felt so loved as in this moment.

"Yes, we can be happy now," he whispered. "Like you said so many times, as long as we've got each other."

"Don't ever leave me, Jeremy. I couldn't handle this without you."

"I won't."

"I mean, never. No more trips away from me. Whatever we do, we do together now. And if we must die, it's gotta be together."

"Don't talk like that, darling. We're gonna make it. We've got to."

"What about the others?"

"You mean Andrew and Michelle?"

"No, all the other students of the Prophet who were dispersed when the security forces overran our community?"

"They'll learn to take care of themselves. You know that some of them have regrouped and are creating little communities all over the world. Think of Max and his people in the Bay area. They're thriving again. More and more people are joining them in response to the Prophet's words. They're better off than we are."

"I wonder why the Federation doesn't go after them?"

"They don't have time for the small fry. They want the ones closest to the source of power. The ones who can influence public opinion most."

"I sure don't feel close to the power right now . . . " Lynn whispered sadly.

Jeremy kissed her passionately and held her tightly in his arms.

"Why did he leave us with this responsibility?" she asked after a moment. "Who are we to carry Light into the future?"

"I guess we just happened to be in the right place at the right time."

"No, it doesn't work that way." She leaned back into the furs and looked up at the sides of the tepee where torchlight moved in a bizarre dance of color and shadow. "It had to take long preparation for us to end up here."

"What do you mean?"

"I don't know . . . Maybe people live many lives. I just feel that this couldn't be sheer accident that we're the ones to be given this awesome task. I can hardly bring myself to think about it."

"Then don't! Live for right now, in the moment like he always told us."

"But we're not him. We don't have any of his powers, and barely a drop of his wisdom. How can we live the way he did?"

"He gave us knowledge. He gave us strength by his example. And, who knows, maybe he'll sustain us even though he's not here."

Tears streamed down Lynn's cheeks. It was like this any time reference was made to the Prophet's death. It was an open wound in her heart that would never heal. Adam Hawthorn had given her a unique vision of unconditional goodness and self-sacrifice.

"Don't cry, Lynn," Jeremy said softly. "He wouldn't want you to keep suffering like this."

"I can't help myself. It hurts too much."

Jeremy had to stop himself from trying to convince her not to feel her pain. He'd learned by now that the intellect was useless as a tool for healing emotions, so he gently caressed her face with his hand and kissed her on the forehead and cheeks. He shielded her with his love. He knew that was the only way to ease her agony.

After a while, the tears slowed and she regained her composure. A muffled groan came from the tent next to theirs which housed Andrew and Michelle. Jeremy and Lynn looked at each other and tried to hold back their reaction. They smiled and broke out in soft laughter.

"Are they at it again?" Jeremy managed to say.

She nodded merrily. "They're as bad as we are." He kissed her full, sensual lips. He'd always loved those lips. They were like the fruit of Paradise—luscious, vibrant, overflowing with love. He knew he would never tire of tasting those lips as long as he lived.

"Privacy is going to be a problem from now on," he said after a moment. "We're gonna have to get used to a lot of new things."

He leaned over her and pressed his cheek against her soft, brown curls. He ran his fingers through them and breathed in her sweet scent. It immediately brought back the memories of the first time he had been that close to her.

They had found each other under strange circumstances, the kind that were suspiciously more than mere accident. At that time, Jeremy was in his mid-twenties, trying to make sense of the insanity around him. He was one of those intense loners who searched high and low for something more than the oppressive, materialistic society that dictated its version of reality to all its citizens.

He had landed in some sprawling urban setting after having traveled the continents like a bohemian wanderer searching for meaning. Coming out of a subway one day on his way to some menial job he had managed to acquire, he noticed a poster advertising a lecture on the mystical origins of Christianity. Upon closer inspection, he saw that it was to be given by a Dr. Hogrogian, professor at some seminary in the Southwest. Jeremy didn't have much use for academics and their vain mind games, but something seemed familiar about this man's name. Perhaps he'd read an article in some obscure esoteric journal and retained the memory of the author's eastern European name.

That night, Jeremy entered a shabby public hall where the lecture was to be held. Fancy, high-tech meeting rooms were not available to people interested in these matters. Few persons were attracted to such ideas, partly because the world government had so thoroughly purged them from public consciousness. Only the outsiders and outcasts, those with no money or power, supported these events.

Jeremy looked around the room. Two dozen people sat in old metal fold-up chairs from the past century. He was curious about the individuals who would gather for such a lecture and studied their faces as best he could—loners, artists, rejects from the corporate world, all keeping to themselves. They were the laughing stock of the comfortable elite of the world. Most were dressed in wretched clothing, although some of them wore their simple garb with a dignity that transcended their poverty. Nobility of character shone in many of the faces. He observed a few potential sociopaths, the inevitable by-product of any group called together around the word "mystical." But most seemed stable, intelligent people.

No one seemed interested in socializing. They were here for one purpose, to seek knowledge and food for their starving souls.

Jeremy's eyes fell upon thick brown curls hanging over a black cloak which a young woman held around her tightly. Her clothing suggested that she wasn't a street urchin like the others, but came out of a more cultivated and successful world. His curiosity got the best of him and he walked down the aisle until he could catch a glimpse of her profile. He was immediately struck by the graceful lines of her face, the fullness of her lips, and most especially, the brilliance in her eyes.

They emanated a gleam of intelligence and awareness that he had rarely seen before.

Then she turned and looked at him. He knew immediately that she had sensed his gaze and that she was a person with psychic powers. Their eyes locked and he stood mesmerized by the directness and sincerity in those sky blue eyes. He knew in that moment that he'd found his soul mate. Concerned that he was going to lose his balance, he decided to step forward.

"Is this seat taken?" he asked, pointing to an entire row of empty chairs.

A soft smile came across Lynn's features and she shook her head. That was the beginning.

The old professor entered and they were both completely absorbed by his words. He was a man of extraordinary wisdom, and a mysterious capacity to see into the soul of each person he looked upon. Jeremy knew that he would be his student some day, although he had no idea how close they would become.

Afterwards, he and Lynn spent the entire night at a local cafe discussing the radical ideas expounded by Dr. Hogrogian. Higher consciousness, autonomy of spirit, psychological liberation, detachment, awakening, all potent concepts on the evolution of humanity that thrilled their hearts and minds.

From that moment on, they were inseparable. Neither of them could stand being away from the other for very long. As their knowledge of each other grew, it became crystal clear to them that they were destined to be together. Each in their own way understood that they had found their other half, someone who shared mutual understanding, all-consuming affection, and a wondrous harmony in the balancing of each other's nature. They had no other desire but to merge their lives together.

Jeremy and Lynn joined forces in their common

search for the deeper meaning of their existence and were ecstatic that they were no longer alone in their solitary journeys. They were lovers, companions, friends, co-workers in the effort to find meaning and purpose in their allotted time on earth. It wasn't long before Jeremy felt the need to enter seminary in his desire to study the illumined souls of the past. Lynn dropped everything to accompany him on this new path, even though she had grave doubts about the viability of religious institutions that were Federation approved. Nothing was sacred or safe anymore. Every aspect of society was reduced to the purpose of efficiently assisting the world government's effort to keep chaos at bay.

It was in seminary, under the tutelage of Dr. Hogrogian, that they encountered Adam Hawthorn, the man they would come to know as the Final Prophet.

Now they were at a new stage of their journey. And this underground home made it clear how dramatically different life would become for them. The Prophet had made them promise to make every effort to survive the oncoming devastations so that they might carry the seeds of the wisdom he had brought forth in them for that day when a new beginning was possible. But such a time was far off. First they would have to endure the unimaginable. Along with the danger of planetary catastrophes and the Federation Security forces, Jeremy knew that Stefan Zorn would be seeking them out. He chose not to tell Lynn of his encounter in the city, knowing that it would only cause her more distress at a time when he wanted so desperately to find some sort of peace despite the circumstances.

He also knew that it wouldn't be long before she detected his state of mind and uncovered the horrific experience he'd had in the ghetto. But with it would also come the revelation of his strange new ability to heal. He still needed to keep this event to himself until he could confirm that it was not a one time freak occurrence. The opportunity to find out was not far off.

* * * * *

"General MacDaniel, sir, this is Brad Coglan calling." The scientist wiped the sweat from his brow and did his best to keep his voice from shaking.

"What is it, Coglan?" the general asked in his usual bad mood.

"I've got some data that you need to know about."

"Can't you send it through the normal channels?"

"No sir, this is something you need to see before word gets out."

"Talk to me."

The scientist swallowed hard and struggled to find the right words to begin.

"Hurry up, I've got a conference in ten minutes."

"Well, sir, it's like this. We have reason to believe that the planet is going to experience a shift in its axis that will have terrible repercussions for the world population."

"What do you mean a shift?"

"It's happened before in the planet's history, and it seems that it's in process as we speak."

"Tell me in plain English what this means."

"Well, the weather patterns are going to change drastically. We can expect major earthquakes, volcanoes, and tidal waves, some of which may cross over entire continents."

General MacDaniel was speechless, perhaps for the first time in his life. For a moment, he couldn't think. This was an enemy that he didn't know how to combat.

"Keep me informed on a priority one basis." He hung up the phone and looked over at Stefan Zorn who was still sitting in his office, smoking one of the general's expensive cigars.

"Do you know anything about this?"

"Of course I do, general. It's been predicted for centuries by every warlock and visionary I know of."

"You're kidding!"

"I don't do that, general. You should have been reading those books you banned."

"I never had time for that supernatural crap."

"Well, now you'll have to deal with the consequences."

"There's not anything you can do about this problem, is there?"

"I'm afraid not. I can conjure up a few things for you, but I can't keep a cosmic event from taking place. You'd better get the Federation's leadership in underground shelters and plan on total anarchy spreading across the globe."

He smiled with evil glee. The general was disgusted.

"But you've got a great opportunity now, general. You can clamp down with your military might like never before. Get rid of a lot of people you don't want opening their mouths. Declare martial law in every country."

"This is unbelievable! How can the earth change so drastically and so quickly?"

"It's not just the earth that's changing."

"What do you mean?" the general asked, placing a hand on the back of his chair to steady himself for more bad news.

"Not only is the planet mutating, but so are the creatures who live on it."

"Go on . . . "

"The electromagnetic transformations that are occurring as the magnetic poles shift and reverse are having an impact on the subatomic levels of our physical being. We are nothing other than organic energy transformers.

The increased energy in the atmosphere will cause our molecular structure to vibrate at higher frequencies. Our cells will be infused with new electromagnetic impulses. There is information encoded in our DNA that is now being activated. We can expect an acceleration of the nervous system which will also trigger a temporary weakening of the immune system."

"What does all this mean?"

"For one thing, you can count on a greater level of aggressive agitation. People are going to be overloaded with such energy that they won't know how to channel it. These greater frequencies will diminish the boundaries of the physical self. There will be more out-of-body experiences, and greater contact with beings from other realms."

"That's insane!" General MacDaniel cried out. He couldn't take anymore of this kind of talk. Or perhaps he couldn't bare to hear anything that didn't fit into the rationally constructed world that he helped to govern.

"The electromagnetic fields in the solar system are shifting and we little organic creatures are going to be profoundly affected by those forces," Zorn said slowly in a voice heavy with warning.

The general sat down and took a reflective puff on his cigar. "What are you telling me, Mister Zorn?"

"Our species is undergoing a transformation at the cellular level."

MacDaniel coughed on his cigar and poured himself a shot of cognac.

"Our DNA will evolve from two helixes to twelve or even fourteen strands which correspond to energy centers, what the ancient East called chakras. I'm sure you know that our cells are light-encoded filaments, threads of energy that carry information. These threads are detaching so that energy flows through us more easily."

"What would that result in?"

"People will experience physical vibrations that are odd and uncomfortable to them. Our endocrine systems may speed up or slow down, impacting our hormonal balance. This will create everything from strong feelings to intensified memory to new psychic abilities. It will depend in part on a person's capacity to consciously receive these new energies."

Zorn inhaled on his cigar and studied the general's reaction. The military man remained poker faced.

"People are going to lose control," he continued with arrogant certainty. "You'll see many cases of what was once called possession. Some will be able to communicate with entities from other dimensions."

"Enough of this nonsense!"

The general slammed his fist on the table. Zorn stared him down with an eerie calm.

"I don't have any more time for this babble!" MacDaniel grumbled. "Our security forces will call on your services when needed. Good day, Mister Zorn."

Zorn did not move from his seat.

The general raised his voice angrily. "I said good day!"

Zorn slowly put out the cigar in the ashtray and stood without taking his eyes from the powerful military man.

"You're making a big mistake, General MacDaniel. People in your position can't afford to make these kinds of errors in judgment."

"I want you out of my office right now!"

"You're going to regret not paying more attention to what I'm telling you, sir. Even your blind scientists who think the world is only what their senses can perceive will be reporting on these matters. They won't have any choice. You'll be hearing from hospitals and psychiatric wards. You'll see it in the streets, in every city and town across the globe."

"I told you to get out!" the general roared.

"And then you'll come looking for me, sir, but it'll be

too late. Because by then you'll realize that I'll be the one with the power!"

He turned abruptly and headed toward the door.

"Is that a threat, Zorn?" the general cried out.

He turned back as he opened the door. A sinister grin twisted his features. He said nothing and turned away.

"I asked you a question!"

The door slammed behind the dark man.

* * * * *

The storms finally abated and the sun broke through the clouds only to reveal massive floods on every continent. Engorged rivers everywhere spilled out across the land. The Hopi tribes had prophesied the cleansing of the earth in this age, but as the natural disasters increased, the earth began to rumble deep in its core and corruption surfaced as never before, not only on the mineral level but among the peoples of the planet.

Beneath the thin veneer of civilization held up by the world government, the wretched disintegration of the human spirit had continued its free fall that had accelerated in the last century and was now on an unalterable course. The vilest pornography was now available everywhere, anytime to everyone. The vast ocean of television viewers had gone from fantasy gore at the movies to the viewing of real deaths on their living room screens watched with a perverse lust that was sub-animal.

The market in child prostitution was one of the largest industries in the East, second only to opium and heroin. The illegal drugs that gave people an escape from the meaninglessness of their lives made up only a fraction of the drug market. The rest was generated by the international medical community that had no answers to the physical and mental troubles of the great hordes of humanity knocking on their doors. The majority of people were on some kind of tranquilizer or antidepressant. The men and women in white coats were doing their best to keep their patients as numb as possible.

Tension between the races was at an all time high as people searched for excuses to release their rage and frustration at a life that had lost its natural foundations. The work place was a giant oppressive force where everyone was terrified of being thrown out into the outer darkness of unemployment and hopeless misery. The streets were teeming with abandoned children who were quickly turned into super-predators by their ugly life of survival. There were miles and miles of concrete jungle, cemeteries of prosperous days gone by where no one ventured, not even the well-armed police forces. Savagery lurked around every corner.

It was a world that only the likes of Stefan Zorn found appealing. Evil was emperor. Only a very few still held onto some kind of faith in the goodness at the heart of the universe. But they were so marginalized that no one ever heard a word from them. History had come full circle. The Dark Ages had returned, even in the midst of extraordinary technological developments. Now that the foundations of human decency had been utterly eroded, those of nature itself were collapsing. Chaos and terror were creeping across the planet like the great shadow of a meteorite about to slam into the earth.

As the military branch of the World Federation expected, it took no time at all for guerilla leaders and warlords to emerge and take advantage of the destabilized societies. Like rats scurrying in the darkness, they felt safe under the cloak of catastrophes and mass confusion. Many of these new leaders had no intention of making the world a better place. Like most everyone, they'd given up hope on that a long time ago. They were from a generation that wanted to urge forward the degeneration of their societies. They wanted to insure the destruction of the world, not save it from its terrible fate. Like vultures circling a body near death, most of these troublemakers were lovers of death and corruption. What they did, they did with an insane zeal for self-annihilation. And they had no trouble finding followers. People were so emptied of meaning and purpose that any cause would do to wring out some kind of momentary satisfaction.

Hordes of youths who had never known a family hearth were eager to throw themselves into the furnace of self-destruction as long as they could take somebody with them. The world religions had reached their ultimate failure and left the species without any sense of direction.

Religious leaders began to appear with the speed of poisonous mushrooms after a spring shower, spouting the wildest brands of teachings ever brought forth by the human imagination. It had been so long since the world population had any exposure to the deeper truths of religion that anything was acceptable and worth considering. People wanted to be told what to do and become submissive to someone else's fantasy of deliverance from a world sterilized by greed and materialism. Underground cults that had been hidden for decades from public view now began to surface, revealing that a vast undercurrent of subcultures and separate societies had grown in the shadows of the dominant civilization. Some of them had stockpiled weapons for half a century. Among these obscure figures claiming some sort of divine knowledge was one man in particular who embodied both revolutionary furor and religious zeal. He lived in both worlds—the hidden realm of believers in metaphysics and in the very earthy world of assassins and paramilitary organizations. This unholy alliance gave him a power that few of the other self-proclaimed leaders could summon up. Stefan Zorn thrived on the wretchedness of the times.

CHAPTER SEVEN

"What's wrong with this thing?"

Oliver Lance studied the homemade satellite receiver with an expert's eye. In his mid-thirties, he was at the height of his physical and mental powers. Rugged good looks, wild and thick hair flying in all directions, somehow never clean-shaven, Lance was the very incarnation of a maverick guerilla fighter. Hard bodied, weather-beaten skin, and intense dark eyes got him attention wherever he went. With the animal magnetism of a leopard and the single-minded devotion of a crusader, no one questioned who was in charge when he entered a room.

Lance braided several strands of wire and turned the system on again. This time, an image came through the static on the ten inch screen.

"We got him!" Loretta cried out as she adjusted her headphones. She shot a twinkling smile at Lance and turned up the volume on the sound board. Hardly into her twenties, Loretta looked nothing like an electronics engineer. She could have been a model, with her sunshine curls and harmonious features. But her devotion to the cause sent her off-course into the underworld of dangerous revolutionaries like the man standing at her side.

Loretta would have been accepted into the best of the international corporations who preyed on multi-talented, highly-trained graduates with relentless tenacity. Now she sat in a dingy, poorly lit room somewhere in the desert of New Mexico, following Oliver Lance on his one way path.

"Talk to him," she said enthusiastically.

Lance grabbed the microphone. "This is Omega One. Come in Master Zorn. Come in."

A faraway voice echoed out of the homemade loud speakers.

"This is Stefan Zorn. I read you."

Lance leaned toward the monitor and examined the unfocused figure. Despite the dim light source, there was no mistaking the hulking, powerful frame of the warlock. His coal-black hair and haughty features gave him a demonic look.

"Is it him?" he asked softly.

"He's too close to the camera," Loretta whispered.

"Looks like the photo they faxed us."

"You can't trust those things. Not with the new scanners. His face could be made out of four different people."

"You'd better talk to him before the connection breaks down again," Loretta insisted.

"I'll just have to risk it," Lance mumbled to himself.

Loretta smiled. How many times had he said that line before? Risk was what they did on a daily basis. It wasn't simply that they were so recklessly daring, or so devoted to their cause. There simply was no other way. Either they stepped out into the insanity of international social upheaval or they stayed home and watched reruns.

"Commander, we have completed our task. The time and place are set."

The little image in the monitor stared blankly at the camera as though digesting the meaning of those words crossing over the continent.

"Very well. Let us proceed to stage two."

They glanced at each other as a surge of adrenaline sent their hearts pounding in unison.

"Do you copy?" the voice came crackling through the speakers.

"We copy," Lance responded. "I will set things in motion immediately."

"Good. Until next time . . . "

The image vanished into a tiny dot of metallic light and the screen went dark.

"Next time? He's optimistic," Lance observed with a strange smile.

Loretta tried to mask her nervousness. But her companion knew the signs only too well. He took her in his arms and kissed her aggressively. Danger was a powerful aphrodisiac for this mercenary. She pulled away, disturbed by the violence of his passion.

"It'll all work out fine. What could go wrong?" he said as he studied the fear on her lovely features.

"You're kidding!" she cried out, finding it hard to control her growing uncertainty over both the mission and the man she worked for.

"Look at it this way. The worst that could happen is that we get killed."

"And you don't have a problem with that?"

Lance sat next to her and gazed into her large brown eyes.

"What's the alternative? To go on living in this madness? Without freedom or privacy? Civilization is only an excuse for powers-that-be to control us all the way to the grave. So why not take out as many as we can when it's our time to get outta here?"

"Is that what this is about? Some kind of cynical death-wish?"

Lance pulled out a crumpled pack of cigarettes from his shirt pocket. He fished out a bent cigarette and placed it between his lips.

"If we don't make something happen, everything will just stay the same. And this "sameness" is not static. It's heading downhill fast."

"I know that," Loretta said with a twinge of guilt for her hesitation.

"So we help shake things up a bit. At least we'll show we care."

"By killing dozens of people?"

Lance took her face in his hands. "This is not the time to get the jitters, baby doll. You've been with us, what, three years now? You knew this was planned all along."

His gaze darkened as he studied her closely. "I can still count on you, can't I?"

She tried to keep herself from shaking. Whether it was the look in his eyes or the upcoming event, she wasn't sure.

"Of course you can. I'm sorry."

"That's better," he said with strained warmth as he stood up. "Are you clear about your next step?"

He could see her mind racing, probably imagining the gory devastation that would soon be on all the newscasts around the world. He grabbed her by the shoulders to snap her out of it.

"Think of the result. We're lighting the spark that will bring on the shift in power. The Master will take over and the Federation itself will become his puppet. We just have to clear the way by liquidating the only people who could stand in the way."

"I've never been responsible for the death of innocent people before."

"You haven't?"

She looked up at him, horrified by his implication.

"What the hell do you think we've been doing all along? You don't think those diplomats were innocent?"

"They were part of a repressive coalition . . . "

"They were sacrificial victims on the altar of destabilization."

Loretta's breath caught in her throat and her face turned a scarlet red. Oliver leaned over and touched her cheek with unusual tenderness.

"Am I not the one who pulled you out of your meaningless little life and gave you the kind of excitement that made it all worthwhile? Hasn't it been really good?"

She nodded hesitantly, unable to speak.

"Who else would you want to have by your side when everything crashes? Who's the best protector you could ever hope for?"

She raised a finger and pointed at him.

"Then trust me. Trust Master Zorn. We'll take you places you've never dreamt of, not in the wildest throws of ecstacy."

Her fear vanished beneath a growing smile as she recalled all that they had shared together. He took her in his arms again, knowing that this would be the quickest way for her to conquer her fears. And after he'd satisfied himself, he had a bullet with her name on it when the time came. He wasn't taking any chances. No one, not even a pretty face, would interfere with the job he'd been hired to do.

* * * * *

A death-like silence weighed heavily over the dark seacoast. Across the bay, the famous silhouette of the San Francisco skyline sparkled like jewels in the moonlight. But on the other side of the waters, a strange motionlessness held the landscape in its grip. Something cataclysmic was about to happen.

In the midst of this nowhere land, where only seagulls and a few seals wandered by, a car suddenly appeared on the dirt road. Its headlights were out but the dim moonlight glimmered on silver designs revealing a Rolls Royce.

The elegant car pulled off into the grass. It sat there strangely out of place, engine running, waiting. Within moments, another car crawled quietly over the gravel. The Mercedes Benz also moved in the dark, lights out. It came up behind the Rolls and waited.

Then a line of cars appeared from the shadows—three, four, five, all without lights. They gathered around the Rolls. A tinted back window slid down into the innards of the door. A gloved hand appeared and pointed upward toward the top of a cliff. An old manor overlooked the ocean. A porch light illumined the nineteenth century home like a fragile candle soon to be snuffed out. The gloved hand abruptly gestured forward with regal authority.

The cars moved off toward the solitary home. A face looked out from the Rolls. The vicious eyes of Stefan Zorn sparkled with eager anticipation in the pale haze of moonlight. His face radiated power, strength, and most of all, hatred.

A silhouette detached itself from the tree line at the bottom of the cliff. Dressed in black, Oliver Lance was ready for battle.

* * * * *

It was in all the headlines: "Bizarre Bloodbath" . . . "Grotesque Massacre." Reporters bested each other on adjectives to describe the indescribable. Something had happened that had never been seen before. Those who had the misfortune to go to the scene were in shock. Forty-five bodies lay in and around the old mansion on the remote slopes of the mountain, each one more unrecognizable than the other.

Doctors argued among themselves as to what exactly had taken place. Bodies were exploded, not like victims of war struck by bombs but from within. Corpses were splattered on walls, dripping down staircases, split to pieces. Something, a power never seen before had destroyed an entire community. The fact that the dead were followers of the man who was called the Final Prophet only intensified the imaginings of the local inhabitants. Police felt incapable of dealing with such an abnormal atrocity and the Federation's security forces were called in immediately. But the best of them could not come up with any theory. What had happened was unearthly, unholy and unknown. The only question that could be dealt with was: would this happen again?

Detective Ernest Sloane was first at the scene, having gotten a call on his radio on his way home from work. By the time his colleagues joined him, he was knee deep in blood and knew he wouldn't be eating for a week. Nor would he ever order a rare steak again. Detective Sloane was a twenty-five year veteran, at the top of his game. A large, muscular man who had played pro football before a lineman ripped the cartilage out of his knee, Sloane lacked manners but made up for it with an unusual dose of common sense.

"What do you make of this, detective?"

Sloane turned from the grisly sight and studied his questioner. A young man, thirty-something, stood before him.

"Looks like a tornado passed through here."

"The lab boys are looking for explosives. We're also checking the wiring," Sloane mumbled with a mix of fatigue and disgust.

"You think it could be a short circuit, eh?" the young man said, a smirk on his face.

"What's so funny?" the detective responded with irritation.

"How 'bout a gas leak?" the young man suggested sarcastically.

"Who are you?" the detective asked suspiciously as he stood and looked down upon the man whose humor seemed so out of place..

"Name's Tom Wells."

"Who are you with?"

"Uuh, the Times . . . "

"Let me see your press card."

Tom pulled out a card, swallowing nervously. Sloane studied it closely and gave it back to him.

"How did you get in here? This is a crime scene. Official police business."

"You haven't put up the demarcations yet, so I thought . . . "

"We will any minute. Get out before I throw you out."

"I might be able to help you, detective."

"I don't think so," the detective said as he turned his back on him.

"Have you seen this?"

Sloane turned around and looked at the object Tom was holding up. It was a medallion.

"Where'd you get that?"

"Right by those steps over there."

"You mean you picked up evidence? You wanna go to jail?"

"Nobody'd found it."

Sloane tore it out of his hand. "You might have covered up finger prints!"

"Sir, I believe I can help you. I can assist in identifying the symbolism of this medallion."

"What are you, some kind of expert?"

"As a matter of fact I am. I have been studying occult sciences for fifteen years."

"Anybody can look into an encyclopedia."

"Sir, there are no encyclopedias with this kind of

information in them. That's a three thousand year old symbol that comes out of ancient Egypt. I'd date it around the Nineteenth Dynasty, in the reign of Amenhotep. "

"You're not expert enough to know not to pick up evidence at a crime scene. Get outta here!"

"You don't think this is the work of your neighborhood syndicate, do you?"

"Maybe, maybe not. A little analysis will tell."

"Analysis?" Tom responded, amazed at the man's blindness. "I think you're going to be in for a surprise, inspector."

"How's that?"

"There are no bullet holes or knife slashes on the corpses. You just might have to look in another direction."

"What other direction?"

"The realm of dark forces," Tom whispered with a gloomy look in his eyes.

The big detective studied him for a moment with a look of disdain.

"Get outta here!"

"You're not dealing with your average maniacs here, inspector. There is something . . . demonic about these killings."

"Don't bother me anymore!" the man growled as he turned back to the grisly mess around them.

"When was the last time you saw a body smashed against a wall like a ripe tomato? What do you plan to do? Look for fingerprints?"

"That's right! And take pictures and measurements, and those things I've done for twenty-five years to put these puzzles together. And I've been highly successful at it, thank you very much. Now get outta here and don't waste my time!"

Tom didn't move. He watched the detective search

through the gore.

"With all due respect, sir, your narrow mind is going to get a lot more people killed. And you're going to keep walking through these massacres with your head up . . ."

The detective turned around and grabbed Tom by the collar.

"You push me any farther, bigmouth, and I'm gonna have you arrested!"

"I'm not the enemy, inspector," Tom said as calmly as he could.

Sloane let him go and walked away. Tom shook his head at the man's stubbornness. The stench of death was beginning to make him sick to his stomach. But his curiosity would not let him turn away from the gruesome sights. He walked over to his rusty Oldsmobile and leaned against it. From this distance he could survey the activities of the investigators. Personnel from the coroner's office were invading the premises with loads of body bags.

Tom knew that the media would be here soon with their cameras and remote trucks. In no time there would be a wall of people and equipment between him and the old mansion. Television sets and newspapers across the world would package the story and fit it into a framework that might be understandable: Victims and villains, weird religions and violence . . . Nothing new, really. There were more bodies at Jonestown.

But Tom was certain that there was something radically new about the horrid event. It wasn't only the inexplicable manner of death and the vicious slaughter of everyone in the house without exception, but the fact that such carnage was signed with a symbol lost to humanity for eight hundred years. Tom felt goosebumps raise the skin from this bones. Something very big was surfacing, something that did not belong to this plane of reality.

Tom had been a writer for over a decade but had only published two books. The material he researched was too esoteric for the marketplace. Few wanted to hear about secret orders and ancient teachings when, for the same price, they could acquire pornography and brutality as food for their imaginations. The young man knew that his path would keep him in poverty, but he was committed to that direction. Whether out of choice or because of the hypnotic attraction he had for mysteries that transcended human reasoning, he did not know. He studied sages, mystic knights, and obscure communities separated from the bulk of humanity because of their experience of transcendent realms. He knew more about these things than most professors. Unfortunately, it kept him eating pasta and soup. But he was adapting to his fate, unwilling to waste his time on more trivial things like satisfying the public taste. Now that his isolated love affair with arcane matters was blending with front page news, he felt that perhaps he was living a relevant life after all.

His dark auburn hair and bright eyes wrapped in a face that could have been in the movies made him a potential catch for the opposite sex. But he hadn't been very successful in that area either. In fact, his relations with all humans, male or female, was reduced to small talk with the waiter in the coffee shop where he did his writing and with the owner of a used bookstore. He didn't have time for anything else. There was so much to learn from the buried wisdom of humanity that he scarcely noticed the world of the twenty-first century. And it returned the compliment.

So his treatment at the hands of detective Sloane was no surprise to him. He smiled sadly at the trouble his sight gave him in the land of the blind. He pictured the symbol to himself: the sun with rays extending all around and ending in human hands. He knew that its origin came from the time of Amenhotep, also known as Ikhnaton. The pharaoh had so shaken up his times, that at his death, the stones of his monuments were buried beneath new constructions so that the world might forget him altogether.

There was one thing that Tom knew for certain: The people who had been massacred in this ungodly display of mysterious forces were clearly connected to a group with great knowledge. He'd given up years ago finding people with such interests. It wasn't until he saw the Prophet on that infamous international broadcast that he dared to hope that others were drawn to the deeper mysteries of life as he was, instead of being chained to the wretched treadmill of this age. He had searched in vain for the Prophet's followers. When he learned of his death, he gave up in despair and returned to his melancholic reflections.

But the medallion had stirred his hopes again. Perhaps what had happened here was related to the Prophet's mission. He remembered that while he sat mesmerized in front of the TV set listening to the Prophet's searing words, something he said made him think of the ancient pharaoh. He had been one of those few people in human history who had attempted to unite religious teachings in a deeper synthesis that lifted the veil from the uncreated One behind all forms. Now in the twenty-first century, another man had raised his voice for that cause and been killed for it as others had before him. The Prophet had warned of dramatic changes that would shift world history off of its tracks, just as Ikhnaton had done in his day. He had torn down all the idols of his people that had reigned over them for three thousand years. For one brief shining moment, he offered them a greater understanding that might enlighten their short journey through time and space. He worshiped a formless being, the energetic form that acted through the sun, the divinity immanent in all things, Aton the intangible essence of all creation.

Another man grasped his vision and carried it to another people—the former Egyptian prince known as Moses. Tom's studies had clearly shown him that there was a link between the mystic pharaoh and the man who took the Hebrews to the Promised Land and opened the way for the tradition of the universal Messiah.

It made perfect sense to the lonely writer that in the Final Prophet's lightning streak through history, there should reappear signs of past visionaries, reminding the world of the roots of his message. Tom had heard about the followers of the one called Adam Hawthorn. He had eagerly sought them out and would have been thrilled to speak with the least of them. Anyone who was privileged enough to be around such a man must have worked hard for it. It would be among such people that these treasures of humanity's lost wisdom would be found.

The amateur sleuth wandered around the parameters of the crime scene, looking at every detail with intense attention. He felt in his gut that there was something for him to find. The sense that this atrocity was related to the man called the Final Prophet kept growing within him with irrational zeal. Suddenly, he became aware of the gravel beneath his feet on the far edge of the property. He looked down and found that he was standing in front of tire marks. Discreetly, he followed the tracks which were visible for just a few feet before they vanished onto the paved road. The Federation security forces were too busy walking through the slaughter in the mansion to have examined this area. His heart began to beat to the cadence of a tribal drum. He knew he was going to find something. His eyes scanned the ground with an eagle's beam. That's when he saw it.

The dim sunlight partially hidden behind incoming fog from the bay created a sparkle that revealed an object in the gravel. Tom look around to make sure no one was paying attention to him. He quickly kneeled down and grabbed a handful of gravel that surrounded the shiny object. He stood, walked off toward the trees lining the road and stepped into the shadows. He closed his eyes, took a deep breath and then opened his hand. In the middle of his palm was a tiny diamond pin, an ornament for expensive glasses. It had apparently fallen from the rim unnoticed by its owner.

Tom brought it to eye level. The hair thin golden pin was topped by a small diamond-encrusted shape. There was no doubt as to what the symbol was. Fifteen years of study had trained Tom's eye to recognize it instantly. It was an upside down cross, the sign of the beast, the Antichrist as history had once called him in days when people believed in deeper mysteries than the senses revealed.

Sweat broke out over his entire body and a wave of nausea sparked by unspeakable terror shot through him. For the first time in his life, he realized that the mythology that had fascinated him all these years was no fantasy.

The sound of a car screeching to a halt nearby pulled him out of his state of shock.

Tom looked up, instinctively wrapping his fist around the pin and slipping it in his pocket. A shiny Mercedes Benz with dark tinted windows was stopped next to him. He couldn't see any of the passengers but he immediately sensed the presence of evil. Though he was more of an intellectual than a mystic, there was no denying what his intuition was telling him.

With a slight electronic buzz, the window slowly rolled down and the face of a striking older woman stared out at him. She had strong aristocratic features and her piercing green eyes were set wide apart and shaped at an angle, giving her an unsettling feline look. She stared at him like a tiger studying its prey.

"May I help you?" Tom heard himself say.

The woman peered into his eyes as though trying to read his mind. Tom froze, seeking to keep any thought from revealing itself to her. He felt his hand tremble in his pocket.

"Did you find something?" she asked in a husky voice deepened by years of cigarette smoking.

"What do you mean?"

The woman's strange eyes narrowed as she studied him carefully, as though she were trying to detect a lie.

"A friend has lost something precious. Have you seen it?" she asked again.

"I don't know what you're talking about," Tom said, giving the best performance of his life.

The woman did not respond and suddenly rolled the window up. The car took off and quickly vanished around the steep corner. Tom stood there for a few moments, uncertain as to whether he was going to collapse from fear. He had just looked into the face of unspeakable darkness. And it had stared back at him with fierce hatred. He had seen a practitioner of the occult who had most likely been part of the horror that had taken place in the mansion. He would have been less mortified had he stared down a hungry lion on the prowl.

Somehow he knew that this was not the end of the affair. He sensed that she recognized his lie. He hurried away toward his dilapidated car and headed back to the city, wishing this had just been a bad dream.

CHAPTER 8

Jeremy walked along the ridge of a dusty cliff just as the golden orb of the sun rose above the razor-sharp edge of the desert horizon. His loyal friend Andrew Bradshaw walked alongside him, a tall melancholic silhouette contrasting sharply with the intensity of his companion

"We can't stay here," Jeremy whispered as he looked at the glorious sunrise spread out before him.

"What do you mean? This is a perfect hideout."

"They'll kill everybody on the reservation to locate us. We can't do this to Stargazer's people."

"There's no place for us to go. As soon as the authorities spot us, they'll put us away for good."

"It's not just the Federation that is looking for us," Jeremy said almost unwillingly.

"What do you mean?" Andrew responded, stopping dead in his tracks. Jeremy turned around and looked at him sadly.

"Don't you get it, Andrew? We've taken sides."

"Sides?"

"By choosing to go the way of the Prophet, we've made some terrible enemies, some of whom are much more dangerous than the Federation. Even with all its surveillance gadgets and deadly weapons."

"Are you talking about some kind of force of evil?"

Jeremy shook his head. He couldn't bring himself to acknowledge it out loud.

"Don't you remember Adam telling us about it?"

"Only in the vaguest terms!" Andrew said angrily. "I thought it was more philosophical than literal."

"It's literal all right. I've looked in its eyes."

"What are you talking about? Demons?"

"They're human beings who have devoted themselves to very different powers than those of light and evolution. They're now the servants of destruction and degeneration."

"I thought that kind of thinking went out with the last millennium."

"That doesn't take away the reality of the matter. There's so much that we don't know that what we do know is either irrelevant or so fragmentary that it has to be wrong! But you can be sure of this. By choosing to support the Prophet's mission, we have made enemies in high places. They won't waste any time coming after us. And there won't be any deals like we had with General MacDaniel. What they want is our death, physical and spiritual."

"I wish we'd been warned about this early on."

"Why? Would you have backed out? To do what? Wander around in chaos and confusion like you had before? Don't be ridiculous, Andrew. There was only one way for us. We're the lucky ones. We've found some kind of meaning in this madness. Whenever our lives end on this plane, we'll have found some kind of purpose."

Andrew turned red, embarrassed by his reaction. He looked across the desert wasteland toward the mountains to the north.

"What can we expect?"

"I don't have the answers. But we'll have to be watching our backs every moment. Not only that, we'll have to be attentive inwardly, because they may come at us in more ways than one."

"How's that possible?"

"They'll attack us in our thoughts, our imagination, our feelings. They'll confuse us, stir us up emotionally."

"How are we suppose to cope with this?" Andrew asked in terror.

"We'll definitely need all the help we can get from the higher regions. And I think we can expect to receive it. The Prophet has not left us alone."

"It sure feels like it!"

Andrew kicked at the sand, still feeling betrayed and abandoned.

"Jeremy!"

Lynn's voice echoed across the ridge. He looked up, immediately concerned. He raced back toward the entrance of the cave and found Lynn standing there, arms wrapped around herself to keep from shivering.

"What happened?" he cried out.

"A horrible premonition . . . "

She was as pale as a ghost. Her lower lip trembled like a child about to weep. Jeremy took her in his arms.

"Tell me. Was it a dream?"

"I was stirring the fire. I thought I saw something in the coals. A vision came to me."

"What did you see?"

"Our friends . . . Max and the others . . . "

"What about them?" he asked as he tried to comfort her.

"I think they've been killed!"

Jeremy pulled back and studied her. He knew better than to reject her intuition. He'd learned over the years that, when she intuited something in this way, it was no fantasy.

"What did you see?" he asked again.

"Something terrible . . . Something not of this world.

Everybody's dead. The coals glowed like devil eyes. The hiss of the wood was like evil laughter. The eyes were full of hate and violence. Then they seemed to turn on me!"

She looked at her beloved, eyes glistening with tears.

"They're coming after us, Jeremy! They killed our friends, but it's us they want! They seek to wipe out all traces of the Prophet's presence among us."

Jeremy flinched. The synchronicity of his conversation with Andrew and Lynn's vision only intensified his feeling that she was right. A thought came to him.

"We should tell this to Stargazer. Maybe he knows a way to shield us from this kind of evil."

"We've got to warn all the others before it's too late! If they could find the teaching house in San Francisco, they'll locate all our other friends!"

"They're scattered about everywhere."

"We can't just let them all die like sheep sent to the slaughterhouse!"

"Andrew can reach a few of them on the WorldNet, but that'll expose us to the Federation's scanning devices."

"Our people would be better off in prison than left vulnerable to these creatures!"

The sky suddenly rumbled with a powerful roar of thunder. Jeremy looked across the horizon to see a pitch black mountain of violent clouds headed their way. It struck him that these dark forces were rising out of the earth's agony, as though the instability of the planet opened the way to the entrance of infernal powers.

* * * * *

Oliver Lance came out of the basement where he'd been hiding out and stepped into the light of day for the first time in two months. He took a deep breath and felt immediately invigorated. The subtle scent of sea breeze coming in off the bay gave him a thrill he didn't expect. Oliver wasn't a sentimental type. He'd had his emotions crushed years ago by a disinterested mother, a broken family, and a dreary career in the corpse of some mega-corporation. When he finally rebelled against a society that had never given him any value or attention, he sold his soul to a wretched cause that turned him from a disenchanted citizen into a cold-blooded mass murderer.

The joy of nature's sweetness was a rare experience for him. But even to one as dead as he was toward the beauty of life, two months in a windowless concrete basement was enough to entice his need for contact with the world around him. The sun had not yet burned through the fog that covered the area since morning. He liked it that way—grey and overcast. He had no use for sunshine and blue skies that reflected a happiness and lightheartedness which would never be his.

Oliver Lance walked down the sidewalk heading toward famed Union Street where he could mingle through the crowd undetected. He felt exhilarated by the success of the operation for which he'd been a key point person. He was the one who had located the Prophet's followers and he could take a good share of the credit for the destruction that had occured at dawn. In his twisted mind and frozen conscience, this was a good thing. He was a success in the eyes of people he admired. People like this Master Zorn, the most mysterious figure he'd ever encountered. And also the most powerful. Oliver was proud to be a trusted member of his elite secret organization.

He didn't even know what his leader's objectives were or who it was that he worked for. He just knew that this was a man of action who could make big things happen. That was good enough for him. It seemed that his boss's agenda was primarily death and devastation, something he had lusted for since his teens. It was the only thing that could get him up in the morning. Life had no purpose, so he'd chosen to find it in death.

He still enjoyed the taste of good food and the company of women. But even those sensations couldn't justify a life that had no direction. Now he had a cause, even if it was in opposition to everything good.

Oliver wandered by the shops and studied the crowd. He glanced at the passing faces. Some of these people could be his future victims. That thought gave him a power he'd never felt before. He entered a shop for no particular reason and found himself in a bookstore. Oliver hadn't picked up a book in ten years. But he was drawn by the obscurity of the atmosphere and the smell of coffee that came from a small reading area.

He ordered a strong coffee, grabbed a newspaper, and sat at a small table in the shadows of the room. Several intellectual types sat at the other tables. He looked at them with disdain. He had no use for people who used only their minds. He was a man who lived by his muscles and instincts. Oliver's athletic prowess had always been his greatest asset. In his teen years, he was the best of his generation across the entire state. No one was as strong, as quick, as graceful in the use of his limbs as he was. He didn't know why his body was so good at throwing footballs or combination punches. He'd never met his father so he couldn't trace it back to ancestral genes. But it was the only gift that came with the package. His mind was ordinary, his imagination mediocre. But his hands and feet were amazingly coordinated.

Unfortunately, he was too small to make a career out of these skills. He had hoped to enter the elite world of the Federation's security forces, but he failed too many tests. The world government had no place for powerful bodies with limited intelligence. Their agents had to combine top engineering education with physical ability. The days of dull-witted tough guys had vanished with the previous century. Degrees in computer science had to go with sharp shooting skills.

So Oliver was left at loose ends with no prospects but the most menial manual labor. His ego had been far too aroused by cheering crowds in high school to accept such a fate. It was at his lowest point that he came across an underground figure who introduced him to the world of terrorism. Oliver realized that behind the name of Stefan Zorn was more than a military renegade or political anarchist. He knew there was something else motivating him, something supernatural. But like virtually everyone else in this age, he had no capacity to grasp what that could mean, so he dismissed it from his mind.

His eyes wandered across the shelves of books surrounding him. The very thought of reading fatigued him. As far as he was concerned, the Nazis of the last century had the right idea when they made bonfires of all that intellectual babble. It had too much influence on gullible minds. He looked at the readers sitting around him, sipping their expensive coffees. He stared at them with disgust. It made no sense to him that the human body should sit motionless absorbing something that didn't strengthen tendons or exercise circulation. He was a true product of a society focused on the surface of life. People were judged and measured according to the flesh and bones that were visible. The depths of their mind, heart and soul—that invisible realm where the vaster part of life resided—was utterly closed to the general consensus on what constituted reality. Oliver had swallowed the government approved version of truth hook, line and sinker, even though he rebelled against the oppression of the Federation's tentacles.

His eyes fell on a young man who was furiously writing in a notebook. Oliver realized that he was looking at a producer of books. He imagined pulling out his hidden weapon and blowing off the top of that overworked head. That would make clear which one of them was the superior man. Raw power was the only yardstick he had for proving his worth.

Suddenly Tom Wells looked up and their eyes locked. Oliver was caught in the glare of Tom's vision with his disgust and hatred revealed in their primal ugliness. Tom was stunned and then angered by what he saw in the man's face. What right did that unshaven, ragged-looking character have to despise him like that? Hatred and anger mingled together like toxic energies and before they knew it both men were on their feet.

"What is your problem?" the young writer asked between clenched teeth.

"Why don't you step outside and I'll show you!" Oliver responded, losing all control of whatever reason he had.

Tom realized that he was dealing with a completely irrational creature, as dangerous as a wild dog who had torn himself free from his chain.

"What did I do to you?" Tom asked more calmly.

"I don't like your kind!"

"What kind would that be?"

"Are you man enough to come out on the sidewalk?"

By this time, the other customers in the bookstore were watching the scene, horrified.

"I don't want to fight you," Tom said quietly, trying to ease the tension.

"I knew it. You're all talk and no action. It's up to my kind to make things happen."

Tom said nothing. He glanced over at the employee who served coffee and noticed that he was already on the phone to the police.

"You don't like me because I write? Is that it?"

"That's right!" Oliver spit out. His hatred of all life shot through him like acid. He looked at the other faces staring at him.

"I don't like any of you! You're all a waste of space on this planet! You'd be better off as fertilizer!"

Oliver suddenly grabbed Tom's collar. Tom's adrenaline burst through his veins and he pulled himself free, jumping back and landed in a karate stance.

Oliver snickered. "You've had some training, have you?"

Tom didn't answer, waiting for his adversary's next move. A police siren reverberated down the street. Oliver froze and came to himself. The last thing he wanted was trouble with the authorities. Not on this day. Stefan Zorn would never forgive him. He unclenched his fists and looked around for a quick exit.

His eyes fell on the newspaper headlines that screamed in giant bold letters of the predawn massacre. Tom watched his adversary's face change colors. Oliver looked up quickly. Their eyes met. In that split second, Tom saw that Oliver was connected to those terrible headlines. The glare in Oliver's dark eyes revealed that he also perceived Tom's recognition. He was about to reach for his gun when a police squad car screeched to a halt in front of the store.

Oliver suddenly dashed toward the back door and was gone before the officers entered. A shiver shot up Tom's spine. He knew that he had made a deadly enemy. The man would kill him if they ever encountered each other again. Yet his fear was tempered by the excitement that roared through his veins. He had unwittingly been given a clue to the occult murders that had taken place only hours ago.

Before his mind had a chance to stop him, Tom ran out of the store on Oliver's heels. He'd never followed anyone before, although he had written many pages carefully describing the experience. Now he had to live his fantasy into action.

He caught sight of Oliver racing toward the end of the alley and turning onto Gough Street. His eardrums pounding with the frantic thump of his heart, Tom hurried through the shadows keeping his eyes on Oliver's vanishing silhouette.

Sliding against the wall, he tripped over a garbage can and fell in a heap on the ground. He turned rigid with fear, expecting the dark-eyed man to come around the corner with a pistol aimed at his head. But no one came. Beyond his shuddering heartbeat, he could hear the man's hurried footsteps moving off in the distance.

Tom scrambled to his feet and carefully looked out onto the steeply inclined street. He saw Oliver turn toward a house at the top of the hill and descend a set of stairs leading to a lower level entrance. Tom fell back against the wall and slid to the ground.

"I must be totally nuts!" he muttered to himself. He wasn't in the habit of talking out loud when no one was around, except when he was in the heat of inspiration for one of those novels that he couldn't get published. But he was beside himself with a schizophrenic combination of bloodcurdling fear and ecstatic excitement.

The last thing he wanted to do was to tangle with the likes of Oliver Wells. Until a few moments before, he had only met that kind of individual in his darker fantasies as they spilled out onto paper. Never before had he been threatened like that. But the very intensity of the threat convinced him that he had stumbled onto the trail of an extraordinary story, the like of which he had never dreamt up, not even in his overactive imagination. Moreover, he sensed that the immensity of evil he had encountered across the bay hinted at the other side of the equation. Such dark forces could only be out to crush a manifestation from the higher realms. And who else but the one called the Final Prophet could fit that bill in this day and age?

Twenty years of studying metaphysical texts made this conclusion as clear and solid as crystal.

It was rumored in the underground of spiritual outsiders that the Federation was hunting down all the Prophet's followers. They had dispersed almost immediately after his murder, scattering in all directions. It made sense that one of those directions would be the west coast. A number of the Prophet's disciples had come from Asia and the Pacific rim was a perfect stopover for those who needed to vanish into obscurity at a moment's notice. Besides, the Bay Area was still the last refuge of maverick thinkers despite the long years of intellectual drought inflicted on society by the world government.

Tom now had the opportunity to not only resolve the mystery of the massacre at the old mansion, but to also be brought into contact with those who had been close to the Prophet. They would surely reflect something of his influence. A man with that kind of power and enlightenment hadn't appeared on earth for nearly a century. Tom didn't expect to be around for the next "visit" from the celestial realm, so he considered this chance his one shot at coming face to face with a wisdom not of this world.

He stood up and dusted himself off. He knew he couldn't just walk into the house that Oliver had entered. It would mean certain death. First he would have to find some of the Prophet's students, not only to warn them but also to call for reinforcements. This was not a conflict he wanted to tackle alone.

* * * * *

Andrew tapped away on his keyboard, sending urgent messages out over the WorldNet. He sat in Stargazer's shack, his laptop plugged into the only outlet within five miles. Michelle stood by the window, keeping a vigilant eye on the horizon. Any sign of approaching vehicles and they would rush back to their more secure hideout. In the back of the room, Lynn and Jeremy were engaged in whispered conversation with the old Indian mystic. Tension filled the small, cluttered space. They all knew that change was in the air. After three months buried in the soothing silence of the desert, they were being compelled to step out into the madness of a world in chaos and before the all-seeing eye of the Federation's security forces.

But they had no choice. Within moments of logging on, Andrew had found the gruesome news flash of the killings on the west coast. There was no time to mourn the dead. As the leaders of the Prophet's former community, they had to assist those in immediate danger regardless of the risk to their own safety.

After sending a general word of alarm across the globe to whomever might receive it and relay it onto friends of the Prophet, the first order of business was to contact those who were left in the Bay Area. Andrew's genius with computer communication would not be enough to fly under the radar of the Federation's constant scan of the WorldNet. Nothing was private anymore in cyberspace, but the sheer volume of global business and babble might give them a few precious moments to make vital contact.

They could only hope that someone out there happened to be online at the time. E-mail would be detected by Federation agents before it was ever retrieved from in-boxes. Technology had become as much an oppressive force as it was a producer of ease and efficiency. The pioneers of the last century would be turning over in their graves or wandering the halls of their nursing homes in misery and despair. What had been unleashed on humanity was not a gateway to new opportunities but an enslavement to the powers of international dictatorship. There was no room for individuality on a planet that was ablaze with anarchy and terror.

"Marla's on!" Andrew cried out.

The others turned to see little yellow letters forming on the blue screen.

"All dead . . . Except for Juanita, the baby, and Maxim Ivanovitch. They were staying with us overnight because the baby was sick. Can you get us out?"

Andrew looked up at Jeremy, despair in his eyes. Juanita was a thirteen year old whose life and that of her baby Angel had been saved by the Prophet. Marla and Ivanovitch were loyal members of their former community who had joined the Prophet in the early days.

"Answer yes!" Jeremy stated with determination. "Tell her we're on our way."

CHAPTER NINE

Jeremy looked into the rearview mirror as the car roared down the highway. A white car travelled at a certain distance behind them. His stomach suddenly tightened as he realized that he had seen this same vehicle just to his left for the last half hour. It seemed obstinately stuck behind him at a constant hundred yards away. A wave of hot adrenaline shot through him from head to foot, pouring out of some primeval instinct telling him that he was being hunted. Once, the white car had come close enough for him to catch a glimpse of the driver's features. He saw a bulky, powerful silhouette with a crewcut that suggested military training.

If his suspicions were right, the man was good at his job, seeming distracted and completely uninterested in giving his attention to the car ahead of him. Jeremy tried to convince himself that he was being paranoid, that the car was merely traveling in the same direction. The vehicle looked at least ten years old, although it clearly had an aerodynamic structure that could move at great speeds.

By now he'd lost tract of the conversation his friends were having. He suddenly realized that he was hearing Lynn's raised voice calling out to him.

"What's going on, Jeremy?" she asked, worried.

"What do you mean?"

"I called you twice. You didn't respond."

"Sorry, I guess I'm a little tired. I was daydreaming," Jeremy said, swallowing hard. He knew he couldn't lie to Lynn for a moment. But he had to try anyway. At least for a little while, until he was sure that they were being tracked by a Federation agent, and probably many more who were not within view.

Jeremy drove on for some time along the isolated stretches of the desert highway. Few cars were on the road, except for that white vehicle, tracking him relentlessly. His mind started racing. Should he pull off the road, confirming whether the car was indeed following him? Should he try to lose him somehow? Or should he continue to pretend that he was unaware of the threat that hung over him? The more he studied the car behind him, the more he realized that the Federation was too skilled to have such an obvious plant. The security forces were not merely following them, but closing in on them.

"Do you want me to drive for awhile?" Andrew asked, jolting Jeremy out of his intense watch of the enemy.

"No!" he responded louder than necessary. "I'm fine, thank you."

The highway curved up ahead and forked off into an exit toward some community nearby. Jeremy watched the white car pull off toward the right lane and head off the ramp. His momentary sense of relief was interrupted by another car appearing in the far distance and rapidly approaching. The high-powered vehicle slipped into place with professional ease.

Jeremy understood then that things were worse than he had imagined. Undoubtedly a helicopter lurked somewhere in the distance, and perhaps a jet's surveillance equipment was focused on them high in the stratosphere. The Federation spared no expense against those it considered a danger. Jeremy and his friends were listed as public enemy number one on the world government's list. The Prophet's dark predictions of the future had so shaken the world population that no more influence from his followers could be tolerated. Every word was sedition and betrayal. Even the simplest wisdom teaching was a political matter. How could it be different when the Federation's only real power was in the distraction and sedation of the great hordes of humanity, keeping mass attention focused on its priorities and view of the world?

This time the car followed them even closer, more brazen than the previous one. He could clearly see the figures in the front seat, both large, stocky men with close cropped hair and features that reflected a violent past. Still he didn't want to tell the others yet. Nothing could be done, except to try not to be overwhelmed by fear. He knew they'd angered one of the most powerful men in the organization and there would be no mercy, and certainly no safe passage for them now.

"Have you noticed the sky?" Lynn asked.

Jeremy switched his gaze from the little car behind them and leaned forward to look at the heavens. The familiar soothing light blue had turned a strange translucent orange.

"What is that?" Michelle wondered as she stared out the window. "I've never seen anything like it!"

"It's too early for sunset, isn't it?" Andrew asked.

"We're hours away from that," Jeremy responded, conscious now not only of time but of each passing second.

"Some bizarre weather phenomenon, I guess," Michelle whispered.

"Maybe it's going to storm again," Jeremy suggested.

"But there hasn't been a cloud on the horizon," Michelle observed.

Jeremy looked back at the car following them, only ten feet away now. He could see that one of the men had a cell phone against his ear and was relaying information. The tension of the moment seemed to fire an inspired idea into his mind. Though it wasn't in Jeremy's nature to think like a survivalist, he knew it was their only chance.

"Start looking for paths coming off the highway!" he ordered.

His friends looked at him, instantly cognizant that danger was imminent.

"Don't look back but we're being followed, and they're about to close in on us. If there's a strong downpour and visibility goes down, we might be able to lose them in the canyons."

Just them a rumble of thunder echoed across the vast desert sky, promising a hard rain.

"It's going to come down hard!" Andrew announced, familiar with the southwestern weather's temperament.

Michelle, being the highest trained among them for these conditions, quickly calculated their situation.

"They also know the rain will make things more difficult, which means they're going to move quicker. We need to outsmart them. Our only chance is surprise. They undoubtedly have reinforcements up ahead along with air surveillance. Don't take a road that ends in someone's homestead. We need to get into the wilds where there'll be lots of dust and mud."

"They've got small, thick wheels, front drive probably . . . "Jeremy muttered. "Their vehicle is at least twice as powerful as ours."

"How close are they?"

"I can see the whites of their eyes."

"Then we must act in the next thirty seconds or it'll be too late. We're about to run into a road block."

Without any warning, light vanished from the sky and the strange translucent glow turned a violent purple. A massive explosion ripped open the sudden darkness.

Jeremy switched on the car's lights, disoriented by the appearance of night in the middle of the day. A curtain of rain crashed onto the ground, drilling holes into the cracked dirt. The precipitation looked like steel rods connecting heaven and earth.

"There!" Michelle yelled, pointing to a path leading off the highway. Jeremy turned the wheel with brute force. The car swerved off the road, nearly falling on its side. But it worked. The vehicle behind them was unable to slow down in order to follow them. It took their pursuers several hundred feet to come a halt, turn around and head off in hot pursuit.

Dust on the surrounding rocks rose like steam as the rain slammed upon them. A foggy veil overtook the landscape and within moments visibility was nearly gone.

"Keep moving!" Andrew cried out as Jeremy checked his rearview mirror while trying to keep the vehicle on the dirt path. "Can you see them?"

"No, but that doesn't mean anything. I can hardly see anything at all back there. Look for another path heading off this road. If we can get up into those hills before they find us, we'll lose them for sure."

The friends held on tight as the car bounced and swerved along the increasingly slippery path.

"Do you see anything up ahead?" Lynn asked as she peered through the blinding shower.

"There's a farm on the right slope on the other side of the ridge," Michelle noted. "I think this road will lead us right by it."

Lynn saw Michelle retrieve a small pistol from her coat pocket.

"Put that away!" she said angrily. "We can't shoot at security agents!"

"Why not?" Michelle retorted. "They're going to shoot us if they catch us."

Lynn looked into Michelle's eyes which glared with

an energy that was ready for battle.

"We don't want to be like them," Lynn said softly, "otherwise, what's the point to all this?"

"The point is to stay alive!" Andrew interrupted. "Whatever it takes. Isn't that what the Prophet said?"

"Not at the cost of compromising everything that we believe in!" Lynn insisted.

"Stay focused!" Jeremy yelled. "Keep an eye out for another path. If we don't get off of this road they'll be on our tail any second."

"Too late!" Michelle cried out as the little car appeared out of the mist at high speed. It nearly crashed into the back of their car. Michelle could see a laser guided weapon in the hands of the passenger. She knew what would come next.

"Damn it, they're not taking me alive!" she roared, cocking her pistol. "I know what they do in the subbasement of the Federation headquarters!"

She leaned out the window and fired, striking the passenger right between the eyes.

"My God, you killed him!" Lynn shouted in horror.

"Yep, and I'm gonna kill the other one too!" Michelle responded with eerie calm as she carefully aimed her pistol.

The driver veered off the path trying to avoid her skilled aim. But he was going too fast. The vehicle smashed into the rocky hillside rising up at the edge of the road. The car was thrown across the road, crashing into the other wall of granite. It burst into flames. The twisted metal kept barreling down upon its prey.

"Faster!" Andrew shouted. "It's gonna hit us and we'll all blow up!"

Lynn held her face in her hands, more horrified by Michelle's act than by the danger that was bearing down on them. Jeremy slammed the accelerator into the floor. The car jumped forward just as the out of control vehicle swung past them and exploded into the hillside. A jet of twisted metal struck the car and cracked the two side windows.

Jeremy took his foot off the accelerator and held on tight to the wheel as the car slowed to a more controllable speed.

"We're in for it now," he said grimly. "They'll come after us with everything they've got."

"That's already what they're doing," Michelle said. "This won't make any difference."

"Of course it will!" Lynn cried out, her outrage boiling to the surface. "How could you do that?"

"This is war, Lynn. We have no other choices. It was us or them."

Jeremy pulled off the road onto another path heading deep into the desolate landscape. They all stared in silence at the violent skies shedding tears upon the ground, echoing the feelings within them. Lynn began to weep. Jeremy took her hand as he drove along.

"The Prophet's mission was to bring life, not take it!" she said, choking on her agony.

"I know," Jeremy whispered. "But everything's gone helter-skelter. If those men had stopped us, that would be the end of the Prophet's legacy."

Michelle leaned forward and put her hand on Lynn's shoulder. Lynn pulled away, disgusted. A look of great sadness came over Michelle.

"Please Lynn, don't hate me for this."

"I won't have anything to do with violence and death. I'd rather be dead myself."

Michelle looked over at Andrew, silently asking for help. He leaned forward in turn.

"You have to accept the situation we're in, Lynn. Be realistic. The last thing the Prophet told us was to stay alive. We've got work to do."

"Not that kind of work," she said.

Michelle sat back, heartsick. Lynn was the best friend she'd ever known. She couldn't stand the rejection. A feeling of guilt began to creep into her soul, even though she'd acted for the welfare of her friends. In her days as a security agent for the Federation, she had seen death up close and had shot government enemies in self-defense. But now she was experiencing the killing in all its ugliness, apart from any justification. It was as though Lynn's feelings had invaded her being. She bitterly understood the horror that her friend was experiencing—the horror of extinguishing a human life. There was something cosmically blasphemous about it.

Andrew took her in his arms, seeing her emotional faltering.

"It's okay," he whispered in her ear. "You did what you had to do."

Michelle wept quietly. She was no longer the person she once was. The military mindset she'd grown up in was evaporating rapidly. The memory of the Prophet's serene presence was the strongest source of this transformation.

"Where are we headed?" Andrew asked, trying to break the tension.

"I'm not sure. I think we're going north again," Jeremy replied. "We'd better find some other entryway onto that highway so we can get ourselves on the right direction. If the Federation's reinforcements track us down out here, we're done for. They'll have a tougher time in the cities."

Andrew opened a map and tried to get his bearings. One way or the other they would reach the coast and locate their friends.

* * * * *

A fourteen year old girl of Mexican descent walked

up the steep sidewalk of an old San Francisco street, pushing her six month old baby in a carriage. There was something about her carriage and her luminous dark eyes that made her immensely more mature than children her age. She was the miracle child whom the Prophet had brought back from death, saving both her and her baby. They named the infant Angel, even though she was the product of incestuous rape. The mystery of her birth had transcended the conditions of her conception. Juanita loved her with her whole heart and never failed to remember the features of the man who had saved them both and brought a new spirit of joy and hope into her life.

Though he was dead now, his spirit remained with her, surrounding her with a glow of protection. She was as confidant in the reality of this invisible protection as she was sure of the existence of the buildings alongside the sidewalk. With the fear of the great earthquake looming in everyone's mind, the structures were more unstable than the reality she believed in but could not see.

She looked down at her child and smiled at her lovingly. The Prophet's friends, especially Lynn, had assisted Juanita in her first steps as a new mother. She had been a quick learner and developed the skills of a woman twice her age. She was privately tutored by other members of the Prophet's community and took classes every day with her mentor Ivanovitch with whom she and several other disciples lived. Ivanovitch was a Russian immigrant in his mid seventies who had been trained as an educator and a philosopher. He had been fired from several universities for his old fashioned mystical ideas which were unacceptable to the world government in its obsessive effort to control the population. When word of the Prophet's appearance reached him, he dropped everything, sold all he had, and came to join him in the Southwestern desert. The Prophet had charged him with Juanita and Angel's care and Ivanovitch took this responsibility with the utmost seriousness. The charge which the holy man had left him helped him stay in touch with the mystical presence that had graced his life.

After the Prophet's death, the community had been raided by the Federation's soldiers. Ivanovitch returned to his home near his old alma mater, Berkeley. He gave shelter to several other students. There were three such homes in the Bay Area where the Prophet's disciples had found refuge from the Federation and lived in quiet seclusion. Unfortunately, none of them paid much attention to the news broadcast across the media. They studied together, read the notes they had kept from the Prophet's teachings and tried to apply them to their daily lives. They had no time for the interference of a world gone mad. They knew nothing of the massacre and went about their lives in the usual manner—serene, peaceful, attentive to the things of the spirit. The earth changes were no surprise to them. The Prophet had said they were oncoming and they expected colossal destruction to sweep civilization away. They accepted their fate with courage and dignity, their greatest hope being that of living out the Prophet's message of spiritual transformation in the midst of chaos.

Ivanovitch poured a can of soup into a bowl and stirred it. At seventy-five, he was the senior student of the Prophet's community. Half of his life had been spent in the twentieth century, at a time when searching for meaning was still a viable option for human beings. Already past his prime by the time of the Mideastern wars in the early part of the third millennium, he watched society's total transformation at the hands of the world government. The very nature of reality had been redesigned by the centralized powers of the media.

He had seen a gradual snuffing out of interest in the intangible things that were not in the order of consumer goods or fiscal improvement. Much like the Bolchevic strategy in the Russia of the previous century, the leadership managed to block the masses from their own perceptions and intuitions of reality. People's minds were shaped by the dominant forces of world culture. The razzle-dazzle of celebrities and of stimulating entertainment was all they needed to keep the reins tight.

Ivanovitch had seen the complete demise of individual freedom for the sake of the collective security. Surveillance was everywhere, privacy was inundated through every channel, and the dreams of unity had yielded to a world military state. He had seen the tragic end of his generation's fantasies for a better world. Despite radical efforts to get control of the global situation, things couldn't be worse. Not only had the earth and its resources been throttled, but the human spirit itself seem to hang lifeless on the gallows of materialism and secularism. There was nothing anyone could do about it. Not until the appearance of the Prophet.

Ivanovitch had lost hope long ago of coming across such a luminous human being. He had given up on the possibility of gaining a wisdom that would save him from despair. Not even nature was around anymore to provide some transcendent pleasure and bear witness to a world that was not dominated by human ignorance. There were very few parks left in the cities. Whatever bit of nature was to be found in the hinterlands was private or government property.

Ivanovitch was an unhappy man. Most of his life had been spent depressed over the lost dreams of the former century. He was one of the very last from that other time when the hopes of humanity had been renewed with the transition to a new millennium. Then everything happened very quickly. The complete disintegration of the so-called "New Age" philosophies, world economic collapse, global instability dragged the human psyche back to its most basic survival mode. All things of a higher order were put aside in a frantic attempt to stay alive.

Ivanovitch was among the few to hold on at all cost to the ideas and teachings that had given his life meaning. But all around him everything else fell into ruin. The tidal wave of spiritual hunger that had swept across the second half of the twentieth century crashed on the shores of a harsh realism that could see nothing but the bleak law of eat or be eaten.

By the time the World Federation was set in place, there was nothing left of the idealism of former times. Once again, humanity was lost in the dull work of day to day living without any reference to a higher purpose. For people like Ivanovitch this was unlivable. He had longed to die years ago. Somehow some primeval will to live kept him plodding along until the day when the Prophet appeared.

He had almost not survived the Prophet's death. But the teaching had empowered him with a new sense of purpose and responsibility. Now the attention that he gave to those placed in his care by the Teacher himself was enough to satisfy his need to contribute to the universe. He knew that in the wake of the Final Prophet's mission, he was now aligned with an event of great significance. Ordinary tasks were no longer ordinary. He was especially honored by the gift of caring for Juanita and Angel. It was clear to everyone that they were very special to the Prophet, the first signs of his powers. Ivanovitch was devoted to them as though they were his own grandchildren, and he lived to protect and nurture them along with the other students who had come West with him.

Despite their age differences, Ivanovitch had accepted

Jeremy Wilkes' leadership, recognizing in him an utterly devoted soul, the first one picked by the Prophet. That was enough to qualify him as far as Ivanovitch was concerned. When word reached him that Jeremy, Lynn and the others were on their way to his home, he was filled with a joy and lightness of being that he had not felt for most of his adult life. It kept him rushing about like a man half his age. He was particularly fond of Lynn, whose sensitive spirit reflected the very mysticism that he had witnessed in the Prophet's eyes.

He pensively stirred the meal boiling on the stove, then checked his loaf of bread in the oven. The man still made his own bread even though it had gone out of style more than half a century ago. Electronic gadgetry now made everything, but he hung on stubbornly to a former way of life that kept human beings closer to nature. He loved the sight of earth's bounty transformed into nutrition for the organism that housed the human spirit.

The large loaf was golden brown, just about perfect. He thought he'd give it another few seconds so that his special guests could enjoy it all the more. His busyness kept him from considering the feeling that disturbed him somewhere in the recesses of his being. He felt that something was wrong, terribly wrong, for the most wanted members of the Prophet's community to come out into the open. Perhaps they needed to flee to Asia as some had already done. Of greatest concern to Ivanovitch was the fact that the sudden announcement of their trip came on the heels of the horrific massacre that had taken place the day before. He did his best to keep himself from thinking about it. If such forces were after them, then all was lost.

It was one thing to hide from Federation agents and their tinker toys of surveillance, but there was no hiding from occult powers bent on total destruction.

Ivanovitch had been around metaphysical circles long enough to know better than to imagine that there was no such thing as evil. It was more than merely human ignorance and selfishness. It was more than bad habits and tempers, and perverse behavior. There was something ancient, relentless and all-consuming about it. Humans were mere puppets in its hands, though each one was capable of choosing to become a willing slave of its demonic desires. Even before the Prophet, he had learned to keep a close watch on his impulses and thoughts. He guided the ship of his psyche with the sure hand of a captain committed to making it to his destination without wrecking on unseen rocks.

It was one of the few works he had accomplished in his life—control over himself and devotion to a higher purpose than satisfying his every desires. Now the payoff was upon him. He had developed a gift of discernment and he could tell when some external force was seeking entrance into his heart and soul, attempting to pollute his efforts toward a purer life and throw him off the path of awakening to his true purpose.

When he first came across the news of the horrific murders of his friends across the Bay, he sensed immediately that his household was in grave danger. But he chose not to tell anyone for fear of causing a panic that would make things worse for them. So he kept a close eye on his companions. But the contact with Andrew in cyberspace had suddenly confirmed his fears.

Ivanovitch moved to the window and looked past the little enclosed garden toward the steep streets over which the home was perched. His aged eyes encased in layers of wrinkles sparkled when he spotted the graceful teenager wandering along the sidewalk, pushing a baby carriage ahead of her. With the back of his hand, he brushed a wave of snow-white hair that had fallen from the striking mane that he wore long but carefully controlled. The natural regal dignity that accompanied him at all times was his last refuge from inevitable disintegration. He would be taking nothing with him except his stalwart and honest spirit.

Too many of his old friends had died in utter despair, damning a world that had purged all mystery and wonder from its essence.

Ivanovitch's square jaw, aquiline nose, and high forehead added to the impression that he was some mysterious count who had lost his estate. But it was the quiet serenity of his energy that was most captivating about his presence. Long practiced in the art of continual awareness and the bodily harmony of Tai-Chi, he was a silent witness to the peaceful centeredness that was possible for everyone—if they would only reject the crush of their frantic life-styles.

But few people were given the privilege of his company. Only the Prophet's disciples shared his time and attention. Most of his days were spent indoors, reading long-forgotten books or doing domestic work for the sake of his friends. His forays into the outside world were limited to the garden, that little piece of planet Earth not covered by concrete. He often sat in the shade of an oak tree engaged in deep conversation with a student or offering advice to Juanita.

Ivanovitch removed the bread from the oven. The mouth-watering aroma filled the kitchen and drifted out the open window. A passerby looked up, shocked by the smell of homemade bread. Tom Wells stopped in front of the house and noticed Ivanovitch's silhouette in the midday light.

His amateur sleuth's imagination had led him to this neighborhood. It was one of the last strongholds of artists and independent thinkers. They were left undisturbed by the Federation despite its phobia of free spirits. No rebel leader could come out of this caricature of the past and lead an uprising against government-approved reality. No one would take seriously individuals stamped with the stigma of west coast foolishness. Three generations of media-fed children had been trained to mock any new trend coming out of California. Too many "original thinkers" had been revealed as frauds and neurotic megalomaniacs. The overburdened world had lost patience with the descendants of the flower children.

In his urgent search for remnants of the Prophet's following, Tom had learned of a group of people characterized by a strange peacefulness completely out of step with the fear and anguish that burned through the city like wildfire. For Tom, this was a sure clue that these people were in touch with a living wisdom teaching. Self-transcendence and inner peace at a time of global catastrophe were no accident. These people were applying specialized information that had transforming power on their daily behavior. There wasn't a guru on the coast who could generate such knowledge. Not anymore.

The golden age of "New Age" philosophies had gone down the drain with the ideals of world peace and environmental rehabilitation. A cynicism had settled in that melded comfortably with the atheism of the dominators. The wretched ghosts of Mao, Lenin, and Stalin were giddy with victory. The world had fallen into step behind their march to nowhere without even trying. No more speeches, propaganda, or secret death squads were necessary to turn people's minds toward the cattle barn of serving the state.

A grocery clerk had further informed Tom of an aristocratic old man who never spoke and bought supplies for a large family. Tom noticed that the elderly gentleman who at the window had taken notice of him and slipped discreetly out of sight. That was all the mystery writer needed to convince him that he had found what he was looking for.

His mind went into overdrive. How could he communicate with these reclusive people? How could he tell them that he was a friend at a time when the whole world was their enemy?

"Hi there."

Tom nearly jumped out of his skin. He turned around to find a sweet face with wide dark eyes staring at him. Juanita was returning from her stroll with Angel.

"Hello," Tom replied as best he could. He felt like he'd been caught doing something wrong. He sensed the flush of embarrassment turn his face red.

"I need to get by," Juanita said softly. Tom realized that he was standing between her and the gate of the house where he'd seen the mysterious old man.

"You live here?" he asked as casually as he could.

She nodded. Her bright, happy features suddenly became overcast with worry. She had been taught to distrust snoopy individuals. Tome felt certain that he stood in the presence of someone who had known the Final Prophet.

"I'm a friend," he whispered. "Don't be afraid."

Her face turned sunny again.

"I need to talk to your leader," he stated more boldly. "I've got important information . . . "

"How can I help you?"

The voice was a rich baritone booming just behind Tom's head. He turned to find Ivanovitch standing over him with the wrath of God in his eyes. If ever there was a lion protecting his pride, this was it. Tom tried to gather his wits as quickly as he could.

"I'm a friend," he said nervously.

"I heard you say that already. What does it mean?"

"We shouldn't be standing in the street," Tom suggested. "Can we talk indoors?"

"Only as far as the garden," Ivanovitch ordered. He motioned for Juanita to enter the property ahead of them, all the while keeping his eagle glare on the young man. "Don't try any funny business. I may be aged, but I know how to use this."

He held up a thick oak cane sculpted in intricate designs. "And I don't use it just for walking."

"I understand," Tom said, swallowing hard. He knew the old gentleman had the power to brain him before he could turn to run.

"I'll let you in the garden," Ivanovitch said sternly, "because it is clear to me that you are not a security agent."

He motioned for Tom to step into the garden.

"How can you tell?" Tom asked as he walked past him through the gate, hoping to ease the tension.

"You obviously don't know what you're doing."

Tom's face turned a deep red. "This is true," he admitted as Ivanovitch locked the heavy brass doors behind them, sealing them off from the outside world.

Ivanovitch pointed to a chair and sat in his favorite one beneath the tree. He proceeded to study Tom from head to foot. The young man felt stripped of all masks. At the same time, a state of euphoria began to rise within him as he realized that he was in the presence of an advanced student of spiritual matters. His knowing eyes, gazing out from beneath white eyebrows, were the ultimate proof that this man had learned from the Prophet himself.

"I'm looking for the friends of the Prophet."

The old man did not so much as blink. His noble features betrayed nothing of his mind's activity.

"Why look here?" he finally questioned.

"It's a matter of life and death. I had to take a wild guess."

"Sheer accident brings you here?" the old man asked suspiciously.

"I like to think of it as intuitive deduction."

"Where did you develop such skills?"

"I've been a student of the paranormal for years."

"What do you do for a living?"

"I write works of fiction."

"Books? No one reads books anymore. They went out when I was your age."

"So I'm a writer with no money. I also create interactive cd-rom stories for education and entertainment companies."

"How do your studies fit into those products?"

"They don't. Strictly bread and butter. Although my interest in history and literature help me out."

Ivanovitch stared at him as though weighing his soul in the palm of his hand. Tom twitched with discomfort.

"So what makes you think that you've come to the right place?"

Tom smiled. "I can see that you are different."

"Different than what?"

"Different than the assembly line produced masses so effectively developed by the Federation."

"That's dangerous talk."

"Maybe."

"You're playing with fire, son," Ivanovitch stated in a strong voice full of warning.

"Sir, I've been playing with fire all my adult life. Now I want to burn."

The trace of a smile came and went across the old man's face. He knew about burning. Burning for the need to find something all-consuming which alone could feed the soul. But he was still on his guard.

"How do I know you're not a spy working for the Federation.

Tom's eyes widened, as though exposing his soul to Ivanovitch's seeing eyes.

"See me . . . Know me. That will be your answer."

A tense silence ensued as the old man pierced into the heart of the youthful visitor. He peered deep into the core of his being. A breeze fluttered through the burgeoning branches overhead, the only sound in the garden. For a moment, the intensity of their encounter silenced even the traffic in the distance.

"Son, if you walk across this bridge, there's no going back."

A shiver shot through Tom's body and caused his features to twitch. "I've got nothing to lose."

"You've got everything to lose."

"I've got nothing holding me back."

"Really?"

"The world doesn't buy my writing anyway. I'm ready."

"For what?"

"To take the plunge."

"There are no guarantees."

"I know that."

"Everything must all be paid for up front."

Tom knew that the man was not speaking about cash, but about hopes, dreams, fantasies, ambitions. If he was to step into the inner circle of the Prophet's followers, he would have to step out of society's version of comfortable living.

"Can you use me?" Tom asked with deep sincerity.

Ivanovitch smiled. "We can always use an honest, devoted seeker of truth."

"You have found one."

"Apparently, you've found us."

Tom beamed at the admission that his intuition was indeed correct. He was looking into the face of one who had been close to the Final Prophet. The old man stood with unusual grace and dignity and approached him. Tom rose from the chair in time to grasp the extended hand.

"You are welcome among us. I hope you don't regret the decision you've made today."

"No sir, I . . . "

Ivanovitch raised his hand to silence him.

"Don't be so certain. None of us are unified enough to be so certain. There will be days when parts of you will feel very differently."

Tom realized that he was looking at a man who had climbed the treacherous mountain of self-mastery and paid a heavy price for it. He understood that there was no getting around the long, hard labor involved. He couldn't expect to conquer himself overnight, no matter how committed he was, no matter how much he longed for the deeper truth of his being.

Ivanovitch escorted him into the house. Soon Tom was surrounded by half a dozen men and women listening with full attention to his concerns. He told them what he had found at the sight of the massacre, of his encounter with Oliver, and of his intuitions that this was an intentional attack on the Prophet's followers. When he finished talking, there was a long silence as everyone digested the implications and realized the danger they were in. Finally, Ivanovitch spoke.

"Friends, I'm not surprised at this news. I believe that is why Jeremy and the others are on their way. They should be here by tomorrow evening. We'll figure out then what to do next. In the meantime, everyone needs to stay in the house. I don't want anyone to answer the door."

"A locked door is not going to keep these creatures of darkness away," a man said in a trembling voice.

"No, that's for sure," the old man responded. "But until we talk to the others, we're stuck."

"You mean, we're sitting ducks, deer caught in the headlights," another said.

"Not quite," Tom stated firmly. "There's another

option. We can be proactive. If some of you will help me, we can check out this man who threatened me in the restaurant. I can tell you this. He may be dangerous but he's an ordinary mortal."

"What would this accomplish, besides exposing us to danger?" Ivanovitch asked.

"We might get a headstart on the adversaries. Find out more about who they are. Get a clue on their activities," Tom suggested.

"I'll go," a tall man with a powerful frame and bright, intelligent eyes said.

"Me too!" another man standing next to him said. Allan was the very opposite of his friend John. Shabbily dressed and unshaven, his hair hadn't seen a comb in several days, his eyes lit by some erratic energy that never seemed to calm down, he was one of those outsiders who had wandered in the more bizarre realms of the occult searching for something to give purpose to his life. Allan was a man who had seen it all—drugs, cults, perversion. He had made some terrible mistakes until the day he came across the Prophet's community.

Ivanovitch raised his hand before anyone else could talk.

"Friends, you are considering something completely irrational and possibly fatal. As Tom describes this man who assaulted him, it seems that we're dealing with some sort of mercenary. Those men shoot before they ask questions, you may be sure of that. They've made a craft out of killing other people."

"What choices do we have, Ivanovitch?" Allan pressed on. "I don't want to sit here and passively be slaughtered like happened to William and the others in Marin County."

"If we were to run," John added, "they will simply chase us and overtake us. If they take my life in this effort to help my friends, I will consider it well spent."

"Let's wait until Jeremy and Lynn get here," Ivanovitch insisted. "They may have another perspective on the matter."

"We cannot wait, sir," Tom stated boldly. "If you value your lives at all, we've got to counter attack right away. The scientists tell us that we're about to get hit by the Big One any day with the polar shift taking place. I'm sure these people will take advantage of the chaos and finish their work."

"Friends, remember this man is a writer of fantasy," the old man said sternly.

"He may also be saving our lives," Juanita spoke out in a calm, serene voice.

"He's a Godsend," another woman agreed.

"I think the Prophet sent him," Juanita added. "From the place where he protects us."

They all turned and looked at the young woman who had been brought back from the dead by their Teacher. The certainty in her innocent face left no room for argument. There was something so ethereal about the look in her eyes that they took her words as a message from the higher realms. Ivanovitch finally lowered his head.

"You have my blessing to pursue this course of action. But please be very careful. You can only help us if you stay alive."

* * * * *

Tom drove his two companions past the house and slowed down as they approached. The sun had set and the moon was hidden behind a bank of growling clouds. The streets were barren. In the darkness, the ghetto was more fierce and grim than in the light of day. Ruined buildings, boarded up homes that weren't fit for human habitation, rose out of the concrete for miles on end.

The emptiness of the streets added to the feeling of the death of civilization. Every once and awhile, a few silhouettes moved furtively in and out of the shadows, obviously up to no good.

A stray dog wandered through the rumble, searching for some place to spend the night. The feeling of desolation and gloom was overwhelming. Tom had never been so deep into the heart of disintegrated society. He felt his mouth turn dry and his muscles tighten with nervousness. The threatening figures were hardly more disturbing than the remains of buildings from another century rising as disfigured monuments to the failure of the past. The acrid tinge of danger raced through his nerves. He took a deep breath in a useless attempt to relax. This was a place where no one should venture, especially after the midnight hour.

Every square foot of this ugly landscape screamed pain and misery. Tom found himself longing for the comfortable neighborhoods that had been his world until now. This third world country was just down the road from the other sights and sounds he had known. It was terribly unsettling to him. How could such a gruesome world be in such proximity to the seeming security that he took for solid ground. It struck him that a whole lot more of the planet looked like this dark, mean ghetto than like the suburbs of his middle class acquaintances.

A shiver rushed through him as he considered the possibility that further economic decay could turn every place on earth into this sunken underworld. The brokenness of the ghetto could become a way of life for everyone. He saw a man walking down an empty street and was astonished that he seemed so uncaring of the dangers lurking in every shadow. Within moments, he could be lying in a pool of his own blood, split open for pocket change. Apparently, human beings could get used to anything and overlook the reality of their situation.

They drove around in circles, studying the house in every detail. They drove down streets that looked more like a nightmare than arteries of a twenty-first century city. A strange terror began to eat at Tom's insides. He suddenly felt caught in the web of some monstrous spider seeking to suck the life force out of him. Every street was worse than the next.

Soon Tom and his two colleagues were in the shadows across the street from the house that Oliver had entered. They had worked out a daring plan with the help of Ivanovitch and the others. Allan would keep watch across the street while John and Tom attempted to enter the house. It was decided that the only way to deal with this situation was directly, that John should knock at the door and draw Oliver out. Tom would then enter and see what he could find.

"Allan, you'll wait here. Be sure you stay against the wall so you can't be seen. Are you ready?" Tom asked.

The men nodded.

"Not too nervous?"

"I gave my life up when I joined the Prophet and his mission," John stated calmly. "There's nothing for me to lose. I've found what I needed."

Tom smiled sadly as he looked into the determined eyes of his new friend. The man had encountered something that was still out of his grasp. He was ready to die and he would be at peace with himself. Tom envied him.

John crossed the street and approached the house. It was agreed that he would first try the front door and claim to be looking for someone else.

A half hour later, John had not yet reappeared. Tom decided that they couldn't wait any longer.

"If I'm not back in ten minutes, return without me," he told Allan solemnly.

"I can't do that!" Allan responded, horrified.

"Don't argue with me. We can't risk any more lives!"

Tom crossed the street, leaving Allan trembling in the shadows. He knocked at the door aggressively, pumped up with adrenaline.

A young woman dressed in a strange combination of Hindu attire and homemade designs answered the door.

"What do you want?"

"I'm here to see a friend . . . "

She tried to close the door in his face, but he blocked it and pushed his way in. She flattened herself against the wall, terrified. Tom spotted a stairway leading to a large door and headed in that direction.

"You can't go up there!" she cried out. "This is a temple!"

"Why don't you call the police!" he shouted back

"Amir!" the young man shrieked. "Amir! Help!"

As Tom reached the top of the stairs, the door opened and a man appeared, blocking his way. His dress was also mid-eastern, but more authentic than the woman's clothing. His skin was olive colored and his eyes flashed with dark intensity.

"You cannot enter, sir!" he said angrily.

"I don't want any trouble. I just want to find my brother who was here a little while ago."

"There is no one that you would know here."

"Who are you people?"

"We are the children of Anavirn, followers of his Holiness Shri Halameh."

"What religion is that?" Tom asked, trying to look over the man's shoulder suspiciously.

"It is the unifying Path to ultimate Truth, gathering the heart of all other teachings brought down by the true masters," Amir responded with artificial serenity.

"And my brother believes in this?"

"If he is, he's no longer your brother. We are his true brothers in the spirit."

"So you won't let me see him?"

"This is sacred ground. You cannot enter without being purified."

Suddenly, Tom pushed him out of the way and dashed into the room. Persian blankets covered the large room and incense burners filled the air with smoke. Candles illuminated the exotic decor. Long curtains hung down from the ceiling, covering the walls. Tom frantically searched for a door behind the heavy colorful cloth.

Within moments, he'd found a small entrance. He entered quickly and found himself in an obscure chamber. An old man with a long white beard and dressed in eastern garb, sat in lotus position at the far end, surrounded by mesmerized students. No one reacted to Tom's sudden entrance. Tom was momentarily taken aback by the immobile forms sitting in the shadows. Amir entered behind him and threw him back into the main room, closing the door tightly.

Tom scrambled to his feet as Amir approached him, his whole body tense with rage. He flung off one of his long shawls and took a karate stance. Tom backed away just as Amir kicked him in the side of the head with lightning speed. Tom quickly regained his balance and dashed for the door. The young woman blocked his way, holding a switchblade in her hand.

Tom grabbed an incense burner and threw it at her. She evaded it, but Tom took hold of her arm and sent her flying into Amir as he charged him. Tom raced through the front door, down the stairs and out of the house. He ran toward the back of the building and found himself in the garden of the cult house. Breathing frantically, he searched the area and found an iron bar near the garbage cans. He broke a basement window and entered.

He found himself in a dark room filled with crates. The eerie sound of chanting echoed from the floor above. Tom searched for a door and entered into a narrow hallway. He heard footsteps up ahead and hurried to another door. He entered quickly and leaned against it, trying to catch his breath. The footsteps passed him by and faded away down the hall. Tom moved forward and stumbled over a large object which he caught just as it went crashing to the floor. He set the expensive vase back on its pedestal just as a dim lightbulb came on, illuminating the room.

In the corner of the room, an emaciated man in his late twenties, head shaved and clothes tattered, stared at Tom with eyes of doom. A drug overdose kept him in a near comatose state.

"Who are you?" he mumbled.

Tom did not answer, terrified that the man would reveal his presence.

"Are you a student? Did you also find out?"

Tom approached him cautiously.

"Find out what?"

"God, I came here to find answers . . . and I found more lies!" the broken youth cried out.

Then he snickered tragically. "Maybe that's the answer. It's all lies. What do you think?"

Tom realized the man's mind was nearly gone. He studied the room to find a way out.

"I thought if I put on a robe and listened to a guy with a big white beard that I'd be enlightened . . . I'm not even sure his beard is real now!"

The man started flaying his hands about, unable to move his legs. Tom noticed that he'd been severely beaten.

"I came out here looking for a true teacher . . . Let me tell ya, nobody gives nothin' for free. Especially Truth. Hell, I'd go to India tomorrow if I thought I could find God there. But you know what? He isn't. He isn't in the pockets of some wrinkled old guru or priest or inside some shrine . . . "

Tom had stopped listening. In one of the crates, he had found large plastic bags. He sniffed them and was stunned to discover that they contained hashish and heroin. The man continued to talk to himself, tears welling up in his eyes.

"This is the fourth group I've joined to find God . . . And it's another caravan to nowhere. I'm through looking on the outside, man."

He grabbed Tom's leg as he stepped near him. Tom pulled away and continued his search of the room.

"You know, I've spent a year and a half working two jobs seven days a week to pay for the privilege of receiving crumbs of knowledge from these people. There's about twenty-five other poor fools doing the same thing in this house alone. And they've got centers in five other cities . . . They've got a lot of competition in the secret initiation business. It's open season year round for desperate seekers . . . "

The door suddenly burst open. Amir entered with five other students.

"Get him!" he barked angrily.

The men leaped on Tom and beat him savagely. Horrified, the young man in the corner managed to stand up in spite of his condition.

"What the hell are you doing?" he cried out.

"He's a danger to our family," Amir said angrily.

"But surely his Holiness didn't order this treatment!"

"He asked me to question him, in whatever manner necessary," the fanatic follower replied coldly.

"Question him about what?"

Amir turned a glare full of fire upon the sickly youth. "This is not your affair, brother. Remember your vows. You have renounced the maya of this world!"

"Is that maya I'm looking at?" he raged, full of a righteous indignation. "Is this cowardly beating an illusion?"

"Don't be swept away by negative energies, brother

Massu. Try to remain objective. This is a test for you. Use it to your spiritual advantage."

"But this isn't right!"

Amir took hold of his arm and pulled him out into the hallway as the others continued to beat Tom mercilessly.

"You've chosen to follow the path of enlightenment as given to us by our teacher. Things are not what they seem for those of us who follow him. Each experience is for the growth of your understanding, regardless of its seeming appearance of wrong. You must absorb the energy of this scene and separate yourself from your subjective attitude. This will strengthen your internal work."

Amir shut the door so that the ugly sounds were less overwhelming to the young student.

But brother Massu shook uncontrollably.

"I've been here eight months, Amir. I was really hoping to learn from you people. So I've done what I was told, and I never questioned your knowledge. But this . . . this is not acceptable."

"It's a great test for you," Amir said with exaggerated theatrics.

"Why don't you just let him go?"

"He can't go home. He's desecrated our temple. Besides, our master wishes him to stay."

"What for?"

"He could be injurious to our family. That's what master says."

"How?"

"Don't question his holiness!" Amir shouted with fury.

"But he's not a threat . . . "

"How dare you resist the will of our teacher?"

"If you kill this man, I'll go to the authorities!"

Amir suddenly slapped him hard across the face. Brother Massu turned back, eyes gleaming with a new determination.

"Is this an example of your spiritual awareness, brother Amir?"

"You're still attached to the outer world. Can't you see that? You must learn to lift yourself above those illusory ties."

"Check out this illusion, you freak!" Massu shouted as he lunged at him. They fell back against the wall and the frenzied young man pounded his fists into the man who had dominated him for so long.

The young woman who had let Tom into the house appeared in the hallway. Her graceful facial features turned grotesque as a villainous expression came over them. Out of her cloth belt she pulled a razor-sharp knife curved in the Arabic fashion. She hurried to the battling men and took hold of the long hair of the one they called brother Massu. Without blinking, she slit his throat in one quick and deadly motion. Amir jumped away as the blood shot out and sprayed the wall with red designs.

CHAPTER TEN

It was almost three in the morning when Jeremy and his friends pulled up in front of the house. They checked the address and confirmed that they had reached their destination. Lynn was the first one out of the car. She looked up at a lit window on the second floor of the old mansion. The curtain moved slightly and Ivanovitch's silhouette appeared in the frame. He held up his hand in a loving sign of greeting to the woman he admired so much.

Lynn smiled with great joy. She hadn't felt such a rush of happiness in a long time. The thought of seeing people she loved and cared for during their communal experience under the Prophet's leadership was an unhoped-for gift. Her heart beat faster at the thought of embracing Juanita and Angel, the children first put under her wing. Every time she saw them, she perceived the presence of her beloved Teacher. Within moments, Ivanovitch was unlocking the gates. Other lights appeared in windows as the house awoke and word of their arrival spread.

Lynn was the first to stand before the old man.

"Lynn . . . " he whispered in a voice weighty with unspoken affection.

"I didn't think I'd see you again, Ivanovitch," she said as her eyes sparkled with tears.

Their hands clasped warmly. He kissed her forehead with a serenity and unconditional love worthy of a sage.

"Are you surviving?" he asked with paternal concern.

"We're managing so far," Lynn responded. "We've been well-cared for by Stargazer and his people."

"I'm sure," he said, recalling the wise Indian elder who had come to visit the community and shared his confirmation of the Prophet's mission.

Jeremy came up behind Lynn.

"Are you well?" he asked his elderly friend. Ivanovitch moved his gaze from Lynn's radiant features to the strong, thoughtful eyes of her husband, the Prophet's right-hand man.

They looked at each other without speaking. A nonverbal contact, more powerful than any words they could express, filled the space between them. They peered into each other's souls and communed in brotherly affection.

Both men had developed a level of awareness that could see deeper than most people. They also shared unshakable commitment to the higher realm that had sent them a messenger who pointed out the way the rest of their lives should be lived.

Lynn observed the silent communion between her two favorite people. The sheer power of their presence to each other allowed them to empathize in a telepathic manner. Ivanovitch saw in the features of the dynamic young man before him a pioneer of future times. He sensed the weight of the world on his shoulders and the awesome responsibility with which the Prophet had charged him. His curly red hair, lightly freckled face and intense green eyes presented the unmistakable image of the peaceful warrior. He had given himself heart and soul to a higher cause and lived a life of unconquerable integrity. In the shadowy light, the old man who stood at the summit of his own existence perceived a clairvoyant vision of this strong, vital face in the distant future. The same eyes would be there, perhaps a bit more at peace, but all the more penetrating, and framed in white hair and a beard worthy of the hermits of old.

His heart leapt. He realized that he was the sudden recipient of a gift from the angelic realm where such timeless vision was commonplace. He sensed that the momentary glimpse was a message for him. What he had finally found at the end of his life would blossom and seed the future in a way that was of ultimate importance to the human race. In knowing that, Ivanovitch was given the gift of seeing the value of his contribution to this sacred cause. For the first time in nearly eight decades, he felt a profound sense of fulfillment. He had achieved the goal of his lifelong search. His presence among these special people had brought him the wisdom, enlightenment and purpose that had eluded him for many tormented years.

Lynn looked up at the profile of the dignified old man and saw in the light of his eyes the timeless inner vision that overwhelmed him. She turned to Jeremy and witnessed the same light in his face. A new quality of depth and knowing scintillated in those intense emerald eyes that she had looked into so often.

Behind those eyes, Jeremy was also seeing a flash of insight. He perceived that the old man who was so close to the grave would not become dust in the wind. The soul that Jeremy could see coming at him through those aged eyes would be part of his life in the future after the body that encased it was left behind. At the same time, he realized that an entire ocean of conscious souls was present in this moment, surrounding them like the darkness of space, shimmering with awareness like the stars above and the sparkle in the pupils looking at each other. They were not two men standing in the night air, but centers of awareness linked to the continuum of the vaster awareness that lived in a nonmaterial dimension and somehow interpenetrated the reality of the five senses.

In the old man's face, soon to leave this world, Jeremy witnessed the immortality of the spirit, especially of a spirit awakened during the life of the body. Jeremy realized that if he could sense the continued presence of this man after his death, then the infinitely vaster soul of the Prophet was also with him somehow, linked to him in the invisible world and aware of his hopes and fears.

The old man in turn saw in Jeremy's vital features the undying hope for the victory of light over the darkness of human ignorance. As long as someone carried the torch and passed it on, the Prophet's living teaching—itself a summation of all the enlightened teachings of the past—would continue to feed human beings of the future. It was not a lost cause despite the hardships of the presence, and neither the Federation nor the evil ones could extinguish it altogether. He could die in peace, saved from the despair of hopeless.

Soon, they were in the comfort of the old house, being offered tea and lemonade. Ivanovitch quickly brought them up to date. He told the newcomers of Tom's appearance among them and of their effort to gather information on the group that had massacred their friends.

"We've got to get all of you out of here immediately!" Jeremy said. "It's far too dangerous to stay in the area. How soon can you pack up?"

The dozen friends responded as one. "By sunrise."

"You can only take what's necessary. Do you have enough vehicles to accommodate everyone?"

"We've got two vans and several cars," Ivanovitch responded.

"That should do it," Andrew stated. "Why don't you start packing now since everybody's awake."

"What about the three who are out in the city?" Michelle asked with concern. "How do we get them back here safely?"

"They're due to call in at six a.m.," Ivanovitch said. "If we haven't heard from them by then, we'll have to go look for them."

"I wish they hadn't done that," Jeremy muttered. "It complicates matters greatly."

"What happens if they don't show up by the time we're ready to leave?" Lynn asked.

"We'll have to go without them."

"No!" Juanita cried out. "We can't leave without John and Allan."

"We've got to consider everyone's safety," Lynn said gently as she caressed her cheek. "Time is critical."

"We've got to get you out of here without delay," Michelle stated in the commanding voice of one who had been in dangerous circumstances before. "Anything could happen at any moment. There's no time to lose."

"We can't abandon them!" the frightened girl insisted.

"We won't!" Ivanovitch replied. "I'll go find them myself. I allowed them to go in the first place."

Jeremy looked at the old man with worried eyes. "We'll need to send someone else."

"You mean a younger person? I'm perfectly capable of driving around the North Beach area."

"What about the danger?"

"No matter what we do, that's going to be unavoidable as you know so well. Please don't argue this point with me. It's my responsibility. I want to handle it."

"Andrew," Jeremy said as he turned to his friend. "How about if you go with Ivanovitch?"

"No, I insist," the old man responded. "You need him

with you. You'll need all the help you can get. Don't disperse your forces. Let me handle this alone."

Jeremy looked at the frightened faces around him. He had known all these people in a better time, when the Prophet was among them, and the possibility of peaceful living seemed at hand.

"Where will we go?" one of the students asked.

"We'll have to head north," Michelle suggested. "Find some isolated community where we can discreetly hide out. We'll need to stay away from earthquake and volcanic activity as best we can. It'll have to be away from the west coast."

"One of those barren places like Wyoming or Montana?"

"Someplace like that where we are less likely to come under surveillance."

"What about Stargazer's cave?" Lynn asked.

"Not for awhile," Jeremy answered. "The place will be crawling with agents, especially after our little encounter on the way here."

"We can't possibly stay unnoticed by the Federation," an older woman with a European accent stated. "There is no place isolated enough."

"Besides, the earth changes will affect everything everywhere," an Asian man spoke out.

"Friends," Jeremy said calmly, "there is no safe haven. But if we're together, at least we can use our minds to stay a step ahead of the next catastrophe."

Some of the people began to weep, faced with the harsh facts of the uncertainty of their lives now.

"We knew this was coming," Jeremy added. "The Prophet told us loud and clear. He also told us to weather the storm. We do this not for ourselves but for whatever purpose we might serve in the future."

* * * * *

Ivanovitch drove into the neighborhood where his friends had gone. He drove past the house several times and noticed that all the lights were out. No sign of anyone. On the third time around, he spotted a silhouette coming out of the basement door and furtively moving into the shadows. He turned off his headlights and pulled the car against the sidewalk where he couldn't be seen.

The moonlight illuminated the features of a muscular man. For Ivanovitch there was no doubt that this was the individual who had assaulted Tom in the bookstore. Everything about him revealed a soldier of fortune—the arrogant swagger, the careful scanning of his surroundings. Ivanovitch took his car out of neutral and followed at a distance. As they approached the center of town, he saw the man duck into a bar whose crude neon lights blended with the shimmering colors of the city.

Ivanovitch drove past the bar and noticed that it was some sort of strip joint. He had never been into one of those places and he sure didn't want to start now. But he had no choice. Too much was at stake. He pulled into the overcrowded parking lot and stepped out of his car.

It was dark and noisy inside. Low-lifes of all kinds littered the place, drowning whatever was left of their souls in poison that was sure to finish the job. It was the kind of place that generated violence and criminal activity like some unholy nest of vipers.

The old man immediately spotted Oliver at the main bar, ordering himself a drink. It was clear that he had no idea he'd been followed, especially by an old gentleman who sat himself several tables away from him. A buxom woman with too much makeup appeared before him, her body hanging out of her clothes as part of the titillation that made their clients pour their money out faster than the liquor was flowing.

Ivanovitch was sick to his stomach. He hadn't seen the low end of humanity up close for a long time. He couldn't believe how degenerate it had become since the turn of the century when he was last exposed to it. Both men and women were brazen about their animal instincts, grabbing each other publicly, exposing their lust without any conscience or natural dignity. A pigsty had more formality over the mating ritual than this place.

He looked over toward the far corner of the room and immediately turned away. On a small stage, a woman was gyrating with hardly an ounce of clothing on. The last thing he wanted to see was a human being humiliating herself with masochistic verve. Unlike all the other men in the room, he didn't see breasts and thighs, but rather a lost soul—someone's daughter, someone's mother, someone's sister—destroying herself in order to pay the rent.

He turned his back on the ugly scene and took a sip of the soda he'd ordered. He glanced up at Oliver. He could now see his unshaven profile. There was no question this was the man who had confronted Tom. His face looked like war itself—aggressive, merciless, violent. The old man felt terribly out of place among these people. He wished he hadn't made the decision to follow him here. But what else could he do? There was no more time. Either he found his friends, or they would be left to survive on their own. He could stand that idea even less than putting up with the grotesque atmosphere of this human destitution.

On a giant TV screen at both sides of the bar, a bloody boxing match was under way, fitting in just right with the ugliness of the place.

"You here for some action, grandpa?" a female voice said right behind him. He turned his serene features upon the young woman who leaning toward him, seeking to display her merchandise. She reacted as though she'd been struck by a baseball bat between the eyes. The calm, penetrating eyes of the old man completely threw her off her professional persona. She felt as though her own father was peering into her soul.

For an instant, she was utterly ashamed. In the next second, she regained control and turned her shock into rage.

"What the hell's the matter with you, old man? Lost interest in women, have you?"

The insult didn't even make him blink. She wanted to yell and scream at him for revealing to her who she was and what she was doing, but his silence was too overwhelming. She turned away and hurried into the crowd. Ivanovitch watched her go with deep sorrow bubbling up from his soul. How humanity had disintegrated! He thought the previous century had hit rock bottom, but it was clear to him that the twenty-first century was even worse. For all the wizardry that humans had created, there was nothing left of deeper values. A great black hole was at the center of the human soul, sucking out all that was valuable about being human. Self-gratification and greed were the order of the day, especially now that things had become so uncertain.

He scanned the room with his sharp eyes and remembered the ancient Persian saying: "Eat, drink, and be merry for tomorrow . . . " What a tragic way to use one's days on this wretched planet, he thought to himself. It struck him that all of the great wisdom teachings the world over had fallen on deaf ears. People were as barbaric as ever. It didn't matter that prophets, philosophers, poets and martyrs of all stripes had sought to kindle an awakening to humanity's true potential. It had all gone down the drain and now he sat in the spiritual sewage of his fellow man, each one more lost and pathetic than the other.

He turned back to look upon the reason for his being in this cesspool. Oliver was on his second drink, and beginning to loosen up. Ivanovitch knew this was not a good thing. It was all important that he have no sense of being watched. For once, being old and physically weakened would be useful to him. He checked his watch. Jeremy and the others would be leaving within two hours. He couldn't just sit here and watch time evaporate. Three lives were at stake. He would gladly give his to save theirs. Living had become exceedingly tiresome to him. He had learned from the Prophet what he needed to know and he could die happy now.

A large, burly man entered the bar. His fierce energy drew Ivanovitch's attention immediately. Without question this was a merciless warrior hidden in civilian clothes. Tattoos crawled up and down his arms and his bone mass was the heaviest he'd ever seen. The man must have been a professional sportsman prior to developing the skills for hunting humans. The man spotted Oliver and walked straight over to him, paying no attention to anyone else. He stood next to him until Oliver became aware of the mass of muscle behind him. Ivanovitch was close enough to hear them talk to each other.

"What the hell are you doing here?" Oliver asked, doing his best to hide the fact that the man's appearance disturbed him.

"What are you doing here?" the big man responded. "You were told not to do this anymore."

"I do whatever the hell I want to!" Oliver replied, partly inebriated.

"No you can't, not anymore! Come with me."

"I just got here."

The burly man's features spread into a vicious smile.

"Am I going to have to convince you?"

The words fell on Oliver's arrogant ego, instead of on his common sense.

"Don't you dare threaten me!"

"You've got an obligation to your boss now," the man stated, every muscle preparing for combat. "Either you cooperate, or you don't. Those are your choices."

"I'll show you my choices!" Oliver said in a louder voice than he should have. He suddenly tossed the rest of his drink into the man's face.

Ivanovitch felt his adrenaline rush through him. He knew what was coming next. The big man took hold of Oliver by the neck and tore him off the bar stool. People immediately scattered in all directions. Oliver responded by swinging his elbow into the man's temple with professional skill. The blow loosened his grip and Oliver pulled away, turning around to face his adversary.

"You're a damn fool!" the man said.

"You're the fool!"

Oliver's foot shot out and struck the man in the abdomen. He fell back against the bar, sending glass flying across the room. Cursing and roaring with fury, he leaped at Oliver whose blows bounced off of him as though they didn't phase him at all. Despite Oliver's training, he was no match for the brute force of his adversary. Within moments, the man had twisted an arm behind his victim and wrapped his own powerful arm around the man's neck.

"You just made a big mistake!" he whispered in his ear as he pushed through the crowd toward the exit. No one dared say a word. The fierce glare in the man's eyes was enough to keep everyone at bay.

Ivanovitch followed them out of the bar, leaving behind the startled crowd that had stopped all activity. People knew when greater forces—such as the Federation's security agents—were involved in mayhem. They were more frightened by the obvious military training of the two men than by their brawn. The ordinary citizen was used to stepping aside when these powers manifested in their lives. Everyone wanted to remain safe, or at least out of the spotlight of the Federation and its legions of cronies.

Ivanovitch stepped outside into the shadows. He scanned the alley where he expected to see the two men pounding on each other, but there was no one there. An emergency bell went off in his mind, bypassing his logical reasoning and telling him loud and clear that something was terribly wrong. How could the men have suddenly vanished?

He looked the other way and felt his heart shoot up into his throat. The two men were standing next to him, staring at him. They shared in common an evil glare that could kill. Without taking his eyes off of him, the big man said to Oliver:

"I told you you had a tail!"

"We flushed him out all right," Oliver muttered between gritted teeth.

Before Ivanovitch could react, powerful hands grabbed each of his arms and forced him into the back of a van waiting nearby. The old man fell to the floor of the vehicle. He immediately tried to sit up, but a fist struck him in the side of the temple and knocked him across the seat where he lost consciousness. His age made no difference to these thugs. The van took off with squealing tires.

* * * * *

Juanita strapped the baby in the car seat as Jeremy placed the last bag in the trunk. Three cars, a van, and a pickup truck formed a caravan. The drivers stood around Jeremy and an open map, studying the road that would be taken. They were to head northeast to the heartland, as far from civilization as possible. Lynn watched on nervously, her whole being resonating with a dark intuition. She sensed that some great calamity was looming over them, like a tidal wave rising to its peek and about to crash down upon them.

She had already urged Jeremy to hurry and get the caravan moving. It had been delayed several hours, awaiting the return of Ivanovitch and the others. There could be no more delays now. Jeremy felt her gaze and looked over at her. The tense, glassy look in her eyes worried him. He knew she didn't get that way very often, that something momentous must be on its way for her to feel it so strongly. He folded up the map, gave final instructions. Just as the drivers stepped into their vehicles, the earth began to shake.

It wasn't like any quake they had ever felt before. It started as a shiver along the surface, causing loose objects to clang like ominous drum beats. Then all of a sudden, a powerful sensation jerked the ground back and forth. It felt like a gigantic whiplash. People screamed in terror.

"Let's go!" Jeremy shouted over the rising noise of shattering glass and tumbling debris.

"We can't drive under these conditions!" Andrew cried out.

"We've got to!" Lynn said urgently. "We've got to get out of here before it gets any worse."

"Worse?" Michelle asked in horror as she watched the old mansion shake like a palm tree in a strong wind. "We can't get on the highways. Take the back roads!"

"Follow me!" Jeremy ordered.

He started the car and headed past the gates. The others followed, terrified, as the entire city shivered in the grip of a monster quake.

"It's got to be a seven or an eight!" one of the passengers who'd lived a lifetime on the coast said. "This is not just a tremor!"

"What are you saying?" Michelle cried out as she held on to the dash board.

"This is the big one!"

"No!"

"Look over there!"

Through the shaking houses, they could see the Golden Gate bridge sway back and forth, sending cars flying off the edge to the waters below.

"Oh my God!" Michelle shouted out.

All around them, buildings began to collapse with frightful noise. The vehicles raced down the side streets inland, away from the turbulent waters of the bay.

"Make sure everyone's behind us!" Jeremy called out as he held on tight to the wheel.

The car danced over the unstable pavement as debris flew through the air. The shaking became more intense. Sidewalks buckled and cracked around them.

"We can't drive through this!" Michelle insisted again. Even her warrior spirit was terrified by this sudden cataclysm.

"We've got to! We've got to get away from the epicenter!" Jeremy insisted.

Sirens wailed as smoke rose all around them. Fires broke out, gas lines cracked, people ran into the streets in utter panic. Shards of glass, metal, and brick flew through the air. Structures collapsed everywhere.

The little caravan rushed away from the city, heading for the countryside where the danger was less intense. After a moment, the shaking stopped. Jeremy gunned his engine.

"It's just the beginning," Melissa said somberly.

"How do you know?"

"Believe me, I know. I've lived here too long not to know. This is just the appetizer."

They dodged debris in the street and the cars that had crashed into each other when the shaking started. They drove by crowds wandering about in a daze. Thick black smoke drifted over the city.

"Stay off the highways!" another woman stated emphatically as she pointed to a shattered overpass where cars had fallen into an abyss of death, crashing on top of each other three layers thick.

"Can we get out of here without the highways?" Jeremy cried out.

"Take a left here."

"Better slow down. The others won't be able to keep up," Michelle suggested as perspiration rolled down her face.

"Watch out!" one of the passengers yelled as an old telephone poll fell ahead of them.

Jeremy swerved and barely missed it, flying up onto the broken sidewalk, scrapping the side of the car against the ruins of a building that had fallen forward. He pulled the car back out onto the road and came to a halt. He turned to make sure the other cars were avoiding the obstacle and joining them. He looked at the terrified faces of his friends crowded in the vehicle.

"We'll make it! We'll make it. We didn't come this far to fail."

He put the car back into drive. "Failure is not an option!"

He took off at high speed as the second shock began to rumble across the doomed city.

* * * * *

At the Scientific Headquarters, panic had set in. Brad Coglan and his colleagues stared at the information coming over the computers. There was no question that a catastrophic earthquake was ripping open the San Andreas fault like never before.

"It's the tension of the axis shift, I'm telling you!" an assistant whispered in a trembling voice. "It's gonna cause the Big One."

"What are you talking about!" Coglan said, hardly able to bear any more bad news.

"It's gonna crack the Bay Area right off the continent."

"Let's not get carried away!"

"Look at this! Shocks are coming in one after the other, and getting worse in intensity."

"Get hold of the military!" Coglan ordered. "I'll call the general."

"Look at this!" the assistant exclaimed, staring intently at his computer screen.

The group of scientists hurried to his cubicle in time to see a graph appear full screen.

"My God, it's an eight point five!" one of them said. "We've gotta airlift people out of there!"

"There are eight million people in that area alone. There's no way!"

"We can't watch them all get crushed to death!"

Coglan picked up the phone. The ghostly pale face of a scientist on the west coast came on the screen.

"Help us! Everything's coming down! Get us outta here!"

Coglan hurried to the terminal and picked up a microphone.

"Give me a report, Jim."

The man was in tears. "Entire neighborhoods are sliding down the hills! Fires everywhere! Lakes of fire in the streets from broken gas mains. A third of the downtown buildings are down! We're not going to make it, we're trapped! Get us out!"

"I'll see what I can do," Coglan said grimly.

"Do better than that, Brad! You know damn well what the emergency plan is! Federation people get top priority!"

"I can't control the military in a situation like this!"

"What do you mean?" the man yelled, eyes wide in horror. "This was always the plan!"

"You really think they're going to save the scientists before the politicians and the CEOs?"

"I thought level three personnel were top security and priority one!"

"Just on paper, Jim."

"What the hell are you telling me, Brad?"

"I don't know what's going to happen. We never really expected anything like this. You're on your own for now."

"On our own? There's suppose to be a helicopter here within ten minutes of such an emergency, according to our contract!"

"I'll remind General MacDaniel."

The picture started fading in and out.

"Oh God, there goes our backup system!" the scientist shouted. "You know we're perched on top of a hill. The whole laboratory's gonna head for the ocean! Help me, Brad! You know my family!"

"I'll do what I can, Jim," he said as his throat tightened with guilt.

Suddenly, a terrible sound came through the speakers.

"Oh my God!" the scientist screamed.

Then the screen went black. Coglan stared at the empty screen in shock. An assistant approached him.

"Mr. Coglan, what is it?"

"It wasn't suppose to happen like this."

He dropped the microphone. "Our technology was suppose to withstand this kind of thing."

"No one planned on the impact of an axis shift, Mr.

Coglan."

"All this stuff is useless!" he said as he waved his hand across the vast array of technological wizardry surrounding them. "It's all useless!"

He dropped into a chair, thunderstruck with despair.

CHAPTER ELEVEN

An old secluded house stood alone on a cliff overlooking a desolate seashore. A dozen people wandered around the unkempt grounds. With their grim expressions, cold eyes and absolute silence, they looked like the walking dead.

The sound of a violin echoed from one of the many barren rooms in the crumbling home, strangely out of place in this abandoned setting.

Tom wandered through the dark hallways, lost and confused. He was still in a haze from some narcotic with which he had been injected after the beating. He vaguely remembered having been driven through the night to this new location. He'd been deposited in an empty room of this isolated mansion, unguarded and seemingly left to himself.

A silhouette appeared before him. He blinked, uncertain as to whether he was hallucinating or seeing a living being. A young woman of rare beauty and of rarer intensity, studied him curiously. She was dressed in a simple, full length dress that had gone out of fashion two centuries ago.

"Would you come with me, please," she told him in a commanding tone.

He followed her in a virtually hypnotized daze. They walked through chambers decorated by old works of art that looked like orphaned children hidden away in these barren rooms.

Tom stopped in front of a huge Medieval tapestry depicting a unicorn hunted down by knights.

"Beautiful, isn't it?" she stated simply.

"That it is," he whispered, awestruck.

"A true work of art. Have you noticed the expressions on those faces? They're full of vitality and emotion, unlike most medieval works."

"Yes indeed . . . " Tom said, surprised by her obvious education.

"The earliest historical accounts of the unicorn are handed down to us by the Greek philosopher Ctseias who visited India in the fourth century B.C. Have you seen the others in the series?"

"No, I haven't," he said, mesmerized by his mysterious hostess.

"The unicorn was one of the strongest metaphysical analogies of the Middle Ages. He had to be sacrificed, or killed, in order to be tamed. It was said that the unicorn could only be caught by a maiden upon whose lap he would rest his head and thereby be easily taken by hunters."

"You haven't told me your name," Tom whispered breathlessly.

The young woman turned her striking violet eyes upon him. For an instant, he thought he detected a glimmer of warmth. But it vanished beneath a glare of suspicion.

"Oriana," she said coquettishly after deciding that the information was safe to share. She swiftly turned back to the tapestry in order to avoid his admiring smile.

"It captures the spirit of the times, doesn't it? Truly an image of darkness. With an ominous feel . . . Notice the castle in the distance. A man stands on the ramparts. He looks like some sort of mystic, calling down doom upon the merciless hunters."

"What makes you say that?"

"Look at his clothing. Mideastern, I'd say. Despite the Dark Ages, rays of light seeped through to individuals and secret sects who were forced to remain invisible—or in this case, at a distance—for fear of being burned at the stake."

"That's very perceptive," Tom said, genuinely impressed.

"See the knight in the foreground?" she continued, as though swept up in the power of the ancient work of art. "You see the scars of many battles on his face and arms. He exudes a strong, physical sense of life. He likes to fight and gallop and hunt . . . but all the while there is this sword at his side with the symbol of the crucifix—the vertical or spiritual dimension of life—at his side."

"A mighty paradox . . . " Tom observed, enthralled by her sensitive reading of the symbols.

"His zest for the sensual life drives him away from a spiritual quest, yet carries with it the sign of what he is escaping."

She stepped back and examined the painting from another perspective, eyes glowing with a mysterious fascination.

"The very instrument of destruction which directs his way of life—and which is about to kill the unicorn—denotes the path of regeneration that directs the journey of his soul. Instead of raising the blade, he raises the hilt. He's turning his life around, confronted by the purity of the unicorn."

Tom was no longer looking at the artwork. His eyes were focused on the young woman before him whose beauty was more than skin deep. She felt his gaze and turned her back to him.

"Come with me."

They made their way to a patio overlooking a rocky precipice that fell straight into a turbulent ocean. They approached a table, carefully set with plates and food. The young woman motioned for him to sit down.

"Eat. It's not poisoned."

"Would you mind telling me where I am?" Tom asked as he seated himself and proceeded to satisfy his ravenous hunger.

"No."

"Who are you people?" he asked again with a full mouth. "What do you want from me?"

"You're the bait."

Tom stopped eating.

"The what?"

"The bait," the woman said with a coy smile. "We're going to catch our fish with your help."

"What is that suppose to mean?"

She approached the edge of the patio and looked out at the sea.

"See the ocean out there? It comes and goes and comes back again . . . We're like the ocean. We come and we go. And sometimes, we leave unfinished work behind. Or we leave certain "valuables" that we have to find again."

She looked back at Tom who was suddenly no longer hungry.

"That's what we're doing. We're looking for something."

"What's that got to do with me?"

"You'd have an answer to that question if you knew what you were."

"Do you know what I am?" he asked sarcastically.

She nodded. "You're what is called . . . a finder."

"A finder?"

"You will lead us to the people we need to find in

order to accomplish our mission."

"Are you suggesting that I'm not here by accident?"

"Of course you're not. We've been waiting for you."

"That's ridiculous."

"You may think so, but the masters don't."

"Who?"

"You wouldn't know them. They don't show themselves, except to those who know what to look for."

"Are you talking about spiritual beings or what?"

"The masters are a form of energy that can manifest through various channels, generating new degrees of consciousness in certain receptive witnesses. The masters are a bridge between human beings and a higher metaphysical intelligence. Most people are only capable of receiving certain kinds of impressions that are beyond the visibility range of our senses. The masters can only be perceived by more conscious receptors. Sometimes they send a shock through otherwise ordinary experiences, stimulating new insight on the part of the one who can detect their presence."

"I don't understand . . . "

"They are comparable to a powerful voltage of electricity running through ordinary life, giving to whatever they touch a new quality and purpose. They can add an otherwise imperceptible energy to circumstances that someone with the right knowledged will perceive. Then one senses that a higher intelligence is present."

"What is their purpose?"

"What they might be trying to express is sometimes very obvious, especially when their appearance, so to speak, takes place in synchronicity with moments of enlightened perception. Sometimes they 'speak' through others."

"Are they good or evil?"

"I . . . It depends on your definition of those words,"

Oriana hesitated. Tom noticed tht she trembled slightly.

"They seem pretty black and white to me."

"We don't look at reality that way. We know there is a larger picture than our senses deliver to us."

"Who's we?"

"The Fellowship."

"The Fellowship?" he asked with his writer's curiosity suddenly peaking.

"Enough!" a voice cried out from the house.

They turned to find a fierce older woman standing in the doorway. Tom instantly recognized her as the woman he had seen in the mercedes the morning of the massacre.

"Who gave you permission to speak with him?"

"I thought . . . "

"Don't think! Just do what you're told! Keep your mouth shut and make sure he doesn't try to leave before we're done with him."

She turned around and walked away quickly. The young woman's feature turned red with humiliation.

"Eat," she ordered with the same anger expressed by the older woman.

"I'm a writer, Oriana. I've spent years observing people, sensing their energies, their emotional states. I notice things. And you're a neon sign, Oriana."

"Don't analyze me!" the young woman responded angrily. "You think you can slap quick labels on human beings and have them all figured out in one blink of your all-seeing eyes? Who do you think you are?"

"You're laboring under terrible tension," Tom continued calmly as though he hadn't even heard her criticism. "You're one of the most tormented individuals I've ever met. You intrigue me."

"I'm not a character for one of your books! I'm not a

plaything to titillate your scrutiny! I'm not interested in your theories of what I am!"

"This volatile energy only supports what I sense about you."

"Stop this!"

"I want to be your friend, Oriana. I want to help you. You're surrounded by some mysterious tragedy and you're drowning in it. Let me throw you a lifeline."

"You're in no position to help anyone!"

Oriana stood up and hurried onto the patio. Tom followed her.

"What is so terrifying to you?" Tom asked softly.

She stopped at the edge of the patio and stared out at the vast expanse of barren countryside.

"Do you believe in Fate, Tom?"

He was surprised by her sudden question. "Why certainly. It drives us forward, just like it makes the planets rotate. In fact, I think that's a perfect analogy. I believe Fate creates circles. We return to the same points, in different periods of time."

"How can you feel so certain about these things? It all sounds theoretical to me."

"I can only trust the deepest whispers of my soul. Where else are we going to find confirmation?"

He stood at her side and looked out at the quiet scenery. Almost unconsciously, he put his arm around her. She received his comforting touch as though it were a familiar, natural feeling that they had shared forever.

"We humans are such tiny creatures in this universe," he said in a dreamy voice. "Not much at all really. We're born, we love and struggle and feed ourselves. Then we die. We can't possibly conceive of the larger side of life, that infinite ocean of space and consciousness. But we can look out of our eyes and marvel . . . "

"Marvel at what?" she asked in a shy tone.

"This aspect of reality. The birds, the sky, your

smile . . . "

She turned to him as her lips spread into the first happy expression he had seen on her features. He held her closer. The heat of their bodies intensified and merged.

"You know, I decided not to be conquered by the tragedies of this earthly existence. I refuse to forfeit my birthright to find contentment, if not out-and-out happiness."

He took her face in his hands and looked deep into her eyes.

"Live your life fully, Oriana. Don't smother it with melancholy and fear."

Their lips met and they kissed.

"What the hell do you think you're doing?"

The voice rang out across the patio like thunder. Oriana and Tom instantly separated and turned to the newcomer. A shock wave nearly knocked Tom off his feet. In the doorway stood Oliver, the man who had confronted him at the bookstore.

The same shock registered on the violent man's face.

"You!" he cried out. His mind seemed to shut down as his instincts took over. He lunged toward Tom. Oriana stepped between the two men.

"Stop this!" she shouted as she blocked Oliver's way. "He's here because the master wishes it."

"Does he wish you to kiss him also?" he asked venomously.

Tom immediately understood that his adversary was completely under the spell of Oriana's dark beauty.

"That's my business!" she answered angrily.

"Get out of my way!" Oliver muttered through his teeth, unable to contain the rage that boiled in his limbs. "I'm gonna teach him a lesson!"

"You're not going to touch him!" Oriana ordered angrily.

"Oh yeah? Does everybody think they can boss me around?"

"You'd better control yourself, Oliver. You've been warned before."

"I've told you what my feelings were for you, Oriana."

"You have no feelings, Oliver! You're not that kind of a man."

"I'll show you feelings!"

He suddenly pushed her aside and faced Tom. It was now the writer's turn to burn with fury. Seeing Oriana tossed aside like a rag doll was more than he could bear.

"You son of a bitch!" he yelled as he took a swing at Oliver.

The man blocked it with expert force, nearly breaking Tom's wrist, then slammed a vertical push directly into Tom's chin. Tom fell back against the balcony, almost toppling over it into the ocean. Oliver grabbed him and held him up.

"I'm not done with you yet."

Wild-eyed, the brutal man struck Tom with hammer fists that would break a board.

"Stop it!" Oriana cried.

Tom valiantly tried to fight back. He landed several punches even though he was blinded by his broken nose. Oliver didn't even blink at receiving the blows. Oriana grabbed hold of his arm just as he held it up to send a mighty blow against Tom's temple. Insane with anger, Oliver turned around and slapped Oriana across the face. She fell in a heap on the patio. Just then, a bone-thin, cadaver-like creature dressed in a suit that had gone out of style two hundred years ago, stepped through the doorway.

Oliver froze upon seeing the hideous looking man. Dr. Tagore stared with imperious outrage at Oliver for a moment that seemed like forever.

Tom fell to his knees, blood flowing from his face.

"You're through," the strange man grumbled as he raised his hand and pointed a crooked finger at the mercenary.

Oliver's hand shot to his side, grabbing a hidden pistol. But it was too late. A current of energy from Dr. Tagore's finger snapped between them like a lightning bolt, lifting up Oliver's body with extraordinary force and hurling it over the balcony. The man's scream could be heard all the way down the steep cliff until his body smashed against the rocks below.

Dr. Tagore helped Oriana to her feet.

"Are you all right, my child?"

She nodded, placing her hand against her red cheek. He turned to Tom.

"Is he responsible for this?" he asked as he pointed a finger at the writer. Oriana grabbed his hand and moved it away.

"It's not his fault."

"Are you sure?" the gruesome man asked, turning his shark-like eyes upon her.

"I'm sure. The master wants him alive."

Tagore looked back at Tom who was holding his bloody nose. He grimaced with disdain.

"Don't make any more mistakes, Oriana," he whispered hoarsely. "There is no more time for delays."

He promptly walked back into the house. Oriana hurried to Tom's side. She helped him raise his head back to stop the flow of blood.

"I'm so sorry," she said.

"It's okay," Tom whispered. "It'll make good descriptive material for my next book," he added with a painful snicker.

She grabbed a napkin from the table and cleaned his face.

"How bad is it?" he asked, still barely able to see.

"The bone is cracked. You'll probably never have the

same profile. But it will heal by itself."

"I didn't care much for its previous position," he said, trying to be cavalier. "Was that the man I saw playing the violin?"

"Yes, that was Dr. Tagore."

"What did he do to Oliver?"

"It's a skill that certain people develop. Very efficient."

"I guess. It's also what killed the Prophet's disciples."

Oriana looked at him coldly and said nothing.

"What's a beautiful girl doing in the company of people like that?"

"You ask too many questions."

"That's what a writer does. Why would you want to destroy followers of the Prophet?"

"It's been ordained for a long time. You wouldn't understand."

"Try me," he said as he leaned his head back to stop the bleeding.

"There's nothing more I can tell you."

"Answer me this, Oriana. Are you human?"

She looked at him strangely.

"Of course, Tom. What else would I be?"

"I don't know, but what just happened here on this patio wasn't human."

"Paranormal powers, that's all."

"Do you have such powers?"

"No, I do not . . . But a number of people do possess them. This is a turning point in human history. There are great forces at work."

He touched her cheek and felt her soft flesh.

"Oriana, are you evil?"

"Why do you ask me this?"

"The people around you are servants of darkness."

"They work for other purposes," she corrected him.

"How can someone like you be among them?"

"You don't know anything about me."

"I know that your lips are soft and warm. So must be your heart."

"You talk too much."

"Why would you seek to destroy good?"

"Some of us don't have choices, Tom."

"We all have choices."

"Some of us are not like others."

"So you're not human?"

"I couldn't have kissed you if I wasn't."

He took her in his arms again, despite the pain, and kissed her passionately. Her warm response convinced him that she was indeed human.

"I don't want to see you get hurt, Tom. The Fellowship is merciless with those who interfere with the mission."

Oriana lifted a necklace she wore and revealed the ornament on its end that was hidden by her clothing. Tom's eyes widened as he recognized the upside down cross he had found near the mansion.

"Do you know what this is?"

"I've seen it in books . . . "

He wanted to grill her with more questions, but understood from the dark look on her features that he could get no more information from her.

* * * * *

The sun dipped behind the ocean's horizon, taking with it the last golden shades of the day. Tom witnessed the cosmic phenomenon, eagerly awaiting the oncoming darkness. He knew he had to escape this night. It was his last chance.

He hurried to the door that he had taped open, listened for any sound on the other side, and stepped into the hallway. He hurried through the large house, searching for a way out. The deep silence disoriented him. Everyone seemed to have vanished.

Then he heard a low hum rising from the floor below. He stopped to listen and recognized the sound as some kind of chanting. His curiosity took control of him. He had to see what was going on before leaving this strange place. He followed the sound. It led him to the basement.

Tom quietly made his way down the stairs. The further he descended, the more the surroundings changed from a shabby, disintegrating mansion into an underground cathedral.

He made his way toward a large, dark room from which the morbid sound emanated. He peered through a crack in the wall. The whole group was gathered there, dressed in dark ceremonial robes. They hummed a chant unlike any Tom had ever heard before. It carried a Mideastern tonality, but seemed more ancient than the melodies that came from the land of Islam.

In the center of the room, the large figure of Stefan Zorn stood like a great dolman, hovering over his disciples, controlling them with magnetic power.

"The time is here . . . " he proclaimed dramatically in his deep, gravely voice. The stars are aligned to open the way. The stage is set. The actors are in place. We who have dedicated our lives to the destruction of the enemy are now worthy of completing our mission. Remember the ancient saying of our forebears: "When Oros will have returned from His long journey round the throne of Osiris, then shall the days of desolation dawn again with the souls of men, and the child of Baphomet will be born from the flames of wickedness!"

Tom listened intently. Under the spell of the mysterious scene, he lost all sense of personal safety. The name Baphomet stirred a faint memory from his vast studies of the occult. But he was too fascinated with the scene before him to reflect upon it. What he saw in the dim light was part Gothic theater and part nightmare, much like a recurring dream that had plagued him all his life. The familiarity of the sight hypnotized and terrorized him at the same time

Stefan Zorn looked at the strange assortment of faces staring at him with total devotion and fanatic zeal. They were young and old, of all races, and their eyes gleamed with a common intensity.

"You know that for centuries the Fellowship has been preparing for this event. The Grand Masters have guided us to this moment and we are the generation that will carry out the Mission. The forces that have brought us together have made it abundantly clear that the long awaited moment is here. Everywhere across the world, we are making entryways into the halls of power. It won't be long before the World Federation itself will be fully infiltrated.

"You know the signs by which we recognize each other. Some day they will become the code of all who are in positions of power. In the meantime, let us maintain absolute secrecy. Above all, we must not fail. The Prophet nearly derailed our work and we will not let it happen again. Victory is within our reach."

"What will be the sign of the time to act?" someone asked.

"When the planet's upheavals have reached their apex."

"What can we anticipate in the days ahead?" another follower asked.

"We are entering the era of a new cosmic process, one of disease, corruption, and crime," Zorn responded. "In this process, form breaks loose from its natural subservience, and reduces the whole to dead matter. What is taking place on a planetary scale can be seen in the same way as disease in the human body.

The comparable condition on the planet would be for one segment of nature to step out of its role and destroy the general balance. Humankind has been doing this throughout its history and that is why we find ourselves at this moment of cosmic revenge.

"This process represents the rebellion of the part against the whole or, more simply put, crime, cosmic crime. Hence our presence here as . . . jailors if you will."

"Could this have been prevented, master, or was it ordained from the beginning?"

Zorn moved pensively to a large throne-like chair and sat.

"As I said, it is a natural process, the result of many causes. Could it have been prevented? Yes, if another process had been initiated, which is what the so-called Final Prophet was here to accomplish. The process of healing and renewal. It represents the rediscovery of spirit by matter, through the mediation of our enemies, those who come from the places of light."

"You are referring to the intervention of solar forces," Dr. Tagore muttered hoarsely.

"That's right," Zorn responded. "This is the counteractivity to disease and crime that has plagued our Fellowship throughout the centuries. By creating an order similar to that created by a higher power, people can acquire in little the nature of that power. Saints and great teachers, emulate the solar source of light and themselves achieve it.

"But as most of you know, any process of regeneration of natural or human forms must consist in unlocking more and more of the matter of the body from mineral first into molecular and then into electronic state. In such a condition, a being could, as with light, exist in all parts of the Solar System simultaneously.

And this is entirely unacceptable to the Forces that we serve."

"Tell us why, Master Zorn," a follower called out, eager for the dark knowledge.

"It's very simple. such unlocking of energy runs counter to all natural growth, to the whole process of creation, which consists in the locking up of solar energy into complex forms. The process of regeneration is against nature and against creation!"

Zorn turned to Dr. Tagore, his first lieutenant, and motioned for him to step forward.

"Tagore, you're our metaphysical expert. Explain this to them once and for all."

Tagore stepped into the middle of the room and looked about with a stern expression. Then he closed his eyes and began to speak like a professor to his class.

"What is the Sun in relation to humans? As we descend the scale of worlds, on each level the number of possibilities contained in matter diminishes. When we come to this level of earthly elements, the possibilities are already clearly defined and limited. Atoms of carbon, oxygen, nitrogen and hydrogen contain the possibilities of all living matter. But they do not contain the possibility of becoming each other.

"At a still lower level, the world of the moon, nothing can change into anything else and is condemned to remain eternally what it is. This is the antithesis of the absolute, the end of creation. And it is as it should be. In a sense, we are the guardians of the right order of created existence. Those who seek to rise to higher levels are seeking to destroy our ways and the very laws of our world.

"At the level of the sun, however, one element can change into another. A carbon-atom one moment is a nitrogen-atom the next. One element contains in itself the possibility of another element. A hydrogen atom contains within itself the possibility of all other elements."

A man stepped forward from the crowd of onlookers.

"I'm not interested in physics! I gave my life over to this Fellowship for in the name of the Dark Ones!"

Tagore smiled coldly at him and continued calmly.

"In splitting the atom, humans succeeded in chipping one electron off to release an energy never seen before. They introduced to this realm of creation a phenomenon which does not belong here, but rather is from the world of the Sun. The hydrogen bomb involved the actual creation on earth of a miniature sun. In other words, humans compromised solar force to produce death."

Tagore turned a dark glare upon the man who had stepped forward.

"What do you think they will do if they achieve such transformation at a spiritual level?"

The man turned pale beneath the fire of his gaze and moved back among his colleagues.

"Our Grand Masters have taught us that the universe is divided into several major planes of matter or consciousness," Tagore said in a haughty voice. "Humans are endowed with subtle bodies that interpenetrate each of these planes of matter. And even though spiritual writings and teachings that have emerged from every culture contain this concept, the vast majority of people have failed to discover these entryways into other dimensions. We must keep it that way!"

"Is this the violation of dark matter that our teachers have spoken of?" a woman asked.

"Dark matter is associated with mystical matter from other planes, the matter that also constitutes the subtle bodies of humankind. Our teachers have revealed to us that this dark matter was present before—and thus responsible for the Big Bang which created visible matter. It therefore has consciousness, primeval consciousness."

Tagore noticed the puzzled look on several faces.

"The explanation of "dark matter" is not so mysterious. It is matter which is not composed of electrically charged particles. This simple property makes this matter invisible to our normal vision, and also would give "dark matter" the ability to pass right through visible matter . . . ," he added with a sinister twinkle.

Zorn leaped impatiently from his great chair.

"Enough! There is no more time for lessons. Now is the time for action! If you haven't understood the big picture, then just obey orders and leave the rest to your leaders!"

Zorn motioned for someone to begin the chant again and the group resumed its mind-numbing activity.

Tom listened in a trance of fascination. Until a hand fell on his shoulder. He nearly jumped out of his skin and turned around to find Oriana staring at him sternly. She motioned for him to follow her upstairs.

He followed her sheepishly, feeling like a little boy who'd been caught with his hand in the cooky jar. It irritated him that she would have such an effect on him. But he couldn't help it.

As they walked down the hallway, they heard the group coming out of the basement. In a near panic, Oriana grabbed his arm and they slipped behind a curtain decorating the otherwise dark and dreary home. Dr. Tagore and Madame de Belmar walked past her.

"What do we do with this Tom Wells when he's fulfilled his purpose?" the odious doctor asked in his gravely voice.

"We hand him over to you, doctor."

Oriana peeked out from the shadows in time to see an evil grin spread across the man's gruesome features.

She turned to Tom and whispered in his ear. The sensation of her breath on his earlobe startled him.

"You've got to get out of here immediately."

"What?"

"I can't let them turn you over to Dr. Tagore! Come with me."

She pushed him forward into a nearby empty room and hurried to the windows. She unlocked the steel shutters and opened them wide.

"What's going to happen to you?" Tom asked nervously.

"Don't worry about me. This is the first decent thing I've done with my life. Let's go!"

They slipped out the window and hurried through the darkness.

Oriana took his hand and they ran to a tall fence on the edge of the property. The faint sound of Dr. Tagore's melancholic violin floated toward them on a cold breeze. Tom thought he heard the music become menacing, as though the freakish man knew what they were doing.

They managed to climb the fence and jumped to the other side. Dashing across the rocky cliff, they ran toward the ruins of a deserted seaside resort.

Tom stopped her just before entering the ruins. "Stay here. I'm going to take a look around."

She hid in the shadows as Tom investigated the area. He spotted a fisherman making his way up the beach toward a car parked near the road. Tom hurried back to Oriana. As he came around the disintegrating walls, the figure of Dr. Tagore appeared before him, a savage look in his eyes. The fiendish man aimed his finger at him and hurled him through the wall.

Oriana jumped up from her hiding place at the sound of the crash and raced toward them. She came between the two men.

"Run, Tom, run!" she cried out.

"I can't leave you," he responded as he rose from the debris.

"For the future!" she shouted as she sent a beam of light straight into her adversary's face.

Tom raced wildly for the beach as several silhouettes hurried toward them from the mansion, led by Madame de Belmar.

Dr. Tagore wiped the burning flesh from his features and laughed at the brave young woman. He swung his arm and an entire side of the resort came crashing down on her in a great cloud of dust. Oriana barely escaped the tumbling debris and fell to her knees in terror and despair. Tagore gave her a disdainful look and headed off into the darkness in search of Tom.

The desperate young man made his way to the road and saw the fisherman gathering his gear from the trunk of his car.

"Please help me! Help me!"

The man turned around, frightened by the terrified pleas. Tom came up to him, drenched in sweat.

"Take me into town."

"Do what?"

"I have to get to the police!"

"Hey, I don't want no trouble."

"Then give me your keys!" Tom shouted as he approached him.

"Hold on now!"

Dr. Tagore appeared on the road and walked calmly toward them. Tom grabbed the keys from the trunk lock and hurried to the driver's side.

"What's the big idea?" the fisherman cried out.

As Tom started the car, he suddenly realized that it was already moving. The vehicle began to pick up speed as it weaved down the road, pushed on by Dr. Tagore's mysterious powers. Tom jumped out just as the car was lifted into the air and hurled down the hillside.

He tried to run but stumbled in pain from a twisted ankle. He fell and helplessly watched the evil man approach. The fisherman hurried to Dr. Tagore.

"What the hell is going on here?"

The vicious man slowly turned and looked at the fisherman. Horror filled his victim's eyes as he saw clearly the evil nature of the creature he was confronting. Dr. Tagore waved his hand and the man exploded into bloody pieces. He turned to Tom, snickering. But the young man was nowhere in sight.

CHAPTER TWELVE

Within twenty-four hours, the cult on Gough Street in San Francisco had vacated the house and stripped it bare of any signs of their activities. Everyone was moved to the property further north where Tom had been taken.

It was here that they brought their new prisoner.

A dozen students were sitting at a long table for lunch while others served them. They all looked up at the old man limping alongside Amir who watched him closely. Ivanovitch was stunned by their expressions. They each had vacant eyes and quietly went about their chores like hypnotized people. The entrance of the stranger seemed to disturb their routine, temporarily jolting them out of their odd state of somnambulance.

"Return to your chores!" Amir ordered. He turned to the old man and looked at him haughtily. "One of our teachers will see you now."

"Who?" the old man asked, disoriented.

"Our teacher. You should be grateful that he respects your age."

The student escorted him up the stairs. Ivanovitch followed passively, knowing that they were seeking to manipulate his mind and throw him into confusion.

Ivanovitch was brought into the hidden inner temple. The "teacher" sat on a small ornate sofa. He stared at the newcomer intently. Amir motioned for the old man to sit in a chair across from the sofa.

"I welcome you to our home," the teacher said slowly.

"Thank you," Ivanovitch responded with suspicion.

"You have questions for me?"

"I do," the old man said, playing along. "I suppose everyone does. What do you teach your students about God?"

"God . . . " the theatrical teacher whispered. "The power of the universe. The power within you."

"The power of the universe is in me?" Ivanovitch questioned, trying to draw out the man's opinions.

"We are all the center of the universe."

"Is this power love?"

"Love? This power is power. It is objective."

"Isn't there objective love as well that is both impersonal and unconditional?"

"Love as we know it is merely a sentiment. And sentiment is frailty and illusion."

"But humans are frail. "

"We seek release from frailty."

"I see . . . " Ivanovitch responded, studying the man closely.

"My teacher and his teacher's teacher bring to humanity a message that is concrete, practical. A message that makes sense: Discover your latent powers and develop them with all the discipline and consciousness available to you."

"Why develop them?" Ivanovitch asked suspiciously.

"In order to reach your ultimate destiny."

"Is our destiny to end in God?"

Our destiny is to find our higher selves, and thus immortality."

"Are our higher selves the same as God?"

"There are many theologies," the man answered evasively.

"What do you believe?"

"I believe nothing. In time you will know."

"That's an evasive answer if I ever heard one. So I'll ask you another question: When do your students get to think for themselves?"

"When they have a self."

"Is there any room for compassion in your teachings?" Ivanovitch wondered sadly.

"There is room for knowledge."

"You don't concern yourself with the human needs of your followers?"

"We concern ourselves with that which is more than human."

"But isn't the divine spirit everywhere, even in the most ordinary, the most human? Isn't the spirit present in that which is most human?"

"I don't know what the divine spirit concerns itself with. I know what I concern myself with."

"And what would that be?"

"The achievement of powers that are not available to the ordinary person."

"They call you the teacher. Are you the master here?" Ivanovitch asked, suddenly suspicious. He studied the man carefully. He was of Indian decent and had the ideal look for an exotic guru, along with the right words and voice intonation for the part. The very perfection of the presentation struck Ivanovitch with a feeling that came deep from his belly and shot up into his brain with the thundering power of insight.

"You're not the master here, are you!"

The soft-spoken, bronze-colored man was taken aback by the statement. His serenity lost its balance. For a split second, Ivanovitch saw in his eyes a look of absolute terror. The mysterious brown pupils soon regain their outer calm, revealing the powerful control the man had over himself. But it was too late. The Final Prophet's disciple had seen enough.

"You are a front for something else, aren't you?"

The guru was back in his seat of stability and was able to play his part to perfection again.

"I don't understand what you mean."

"Sure you do," the old man said, sick and tired of the abuse he had undergone and distressed that he'd missed his chance to leave with Jeremy and his friends. The fact that his life was in danger made no difference to him at all.

"Someone else is in charge. You're not the teacher. You're just a smoke and mirror trick."

"I don't understand why you are insulting me, sir," the man said, keeping control as best he could over his heart rate.

"You may be a knowledgeable man," Ivanovitch continued, his eyes burning into those of the guru, "but you're no teacher of higher wisdom. I've met a true Teacher. I've seen a great soul. You're just a servant of something . . . evil."

This time he'd gotten through. The guru was losing his cool.

"I am Swami Saravida! I abhor evil!"

"You may hate it, but it pays your bills!"

"That's absurd!"

"Either you're completely disconnected with reality or you have powerful buffers in place, Mister Swami. You're looking at a nearly eighty year old man who was roughed up by two brutes, driven face down in the back seat of a car for hours and brought here by men who just as soon cut my heart out as look at me. How dare you lie to my face when evil is all around you!"

The dark brown eyes twitched. They turned wet. The man tried so hard to stay in control that he couldn't speak.

"How did they get you to sell out? Surely not the cheap gimmicks of indulging your weaknesses," Ivanovitch whispered as he looked around.

A look of profound sadness shifted the musculature in the man's features. His posture slumped slightly. The guru looked away.

"I won't divulge your secret," Ivanovitch said softly. "I'm a dead man. They won't let me out of here alive."

The Indian swami looked back at him, eyes filled to the brim with tears.

"I too am a dead man . . . "

"Then we are brothers!" Ivanovitch said with an ironic smirk. "Why not speak the truth to each other?"

"They captured my soul," the man said in a whisper. "Not with money, not with the flesh . . . They gave me passive students, and a position of authority that I always wanted. Back in my village, I admired the great swamis of the previous century that had gone to America and were surrounded by adoring students for sharing the simplest crumbs of our teachings. You Westerners were so starved that anything from the East was gold, even the weeds. I would have made a good teacher. But I was a farmer's son, stuck where I was born. They came and lifted me from my outcast position and answered my prayers."

"Who is they?" Ivanovitch asked.

"Don't you know?"

"Enemies of the Prophet, that I know!"

The swami uncrossed his legs and his body curved downward, overwhelmed with the weight of his inner misery. "I thought they were merely rich Europeans who would take care of me and let me teach what I had learned from my culture. I never meant to hurt anyone."

Ivanovitch's anger receded as he observed the broken man before him whose mask of detachment and wisdom had cracked open.

"So who are they?"

The Hindu looked up, a wild look in his eyes.

"The Dark Ones!"

Ivanovitch was struck by the answer as by a spear. His mind didn't know what to do with it. The guru who had fallen into line with the wrong masters began to weep like a child. Ivanovitch knew better than to ask him anymore questions. Besides, he had the information he needed. He had already sensed the forces of evil in this house and knew that they were more than human, even though incarnated in transient form.

A door suddenly opened, tearing through the moment with a sinister creak. Ivanovitch looked up in time to see the very manifestation of what he had just been sensing. The hideous figure of Dr. Tagore stood in the shadows, eyes gleaming like a savage wolf. The guru immediately brought himself back into his facade of serene disinterest. Ivanovitch felt his muscles tense with anger and disgust, knowing that he was in the presence of all that was hateful.

"So we have another of the prophet's devotees, do we?" Tagore said in a sadistic tone.

Ivanovitch stood up. "Who else have you brought here?"

Tagore stepped forward and eyed the old man intensely.

"You're in way over your head, old man. You should be watching television in a nursing home, waiting to die comfortably instead of how you're going to die now."

"What have you done to my friends?"

"I'll be frank with you out of respect for the fact that you're not going to live much longer. One of them is splattered in a back alley off of Gough Street. The other has just gotten away from us, temporarily."

Ivanovitch's throat tightened in agony. "Which one?"

"I didn't check his identification papers. I believe

Oriana called him Tom."

Ivanovitch did his best not to smile. If anyone could get away from these monsters, it would be the daring young writer who had appeared in their lives from out of nowhere. He felt certain that Tom would somehow reunite with the others. His heart ached for John and Allan, but he also knew that his friends' troubles were over, unlike his own.

"What are you going to do with me?"

"That depends on what you're going to do for us," Tagore said with an evil grin revealing his rotting teeth.

"I can answer that for you right now," Ivanovitch responded defiantly. "I'm not going to do anything for you." He would die a thousand deaths before serving the wishes of his murderous captors. He felt a new energy rush through him, a youthful vigor that hadn't run through his veins for decades.

A strange sensation came to him. Like a strong wind in his solar plexus, he suddenly felt the presence of the Prophet and his heart was filled with courage and strength. The experience covered his body with goose bumps. Despite looking into the eyes of death, he rejoiced in the feeling that the spirit of the man who had so changed his life was in this room.

"I wouldn't speak so quickly, old man," Dr. Tagore said menacingly. "You don't know who you're dealing with."

"Oh yes I do!" Ivanovitch stated as he stared him in the eyes. "I've fought you all my life!"

Tagore was taken aback by his answer.

"You knew the man they call the Final Prophet, did you not?" Tagore asked between gritted teeth.

"I did."

"And you know his leading disciples?"

"I do."

"And you know where they're headed at this moment."

Ivanovitch nodded, almost daring the man to tear the information out of him. A grin spread over Tagore's gruesome features. He knew that no torture would get it out of the loyal elder.

"We flushed them out, you know."

"How do you mean?" Ivanovitch asked with sudden fear from his companions.

"We killed your friends by the bay knowing that it would bring the leaders to your aid. The plan worked."

Ivanovitch did his best to repress his outrage.

"Shall I describe to you how your friends died?" Tagore asked, taunting him. "Those still living will suffer the same fate."

"No they won't!"

"You seem awfully sure of yourself, old man, for one who is about to die."

"I know that evil will not be victorious in the end."

Dr. Tagore burst out in a high-pitched laugh that sent shivers through Ivanovitch.

"A true believer, eh? What a fantasy! Look around you, old man. I'm sure you felt the earth shaking on your way up here. Tidal waves are headed this way as we speak. The city by the bay will be under water within a few days. This is the end. We've already won."

"You haven't won anything!"

Tagore slapped him across the cheek with incredible power, virtually shattering his jawbone.

"You fool! You have no idea what you're saying. The human race is done for. It's a failed experiment. Whatever is left of it will be under our power. It is written!"

"Not in the books I read it isn't!"

"Not only will we conquer your world, but we'll have the full assistance of your fellow human beings. Don't you understand?"

Tagore leaned toward him, exhaling a vile breath in

his face. "Humanity has wished this fate upon itself! Humanity is the vessel of evil."

"This specimen is not!"

With the force of a volcano about to erupt, a boiling rage filled the old man's soul. He'd never been this furious in his life. It was taking over his mind and body like a hurricane tearing everything down in its path. He felt his hands turn into fists. Just as he realized he was losing control of himself, the face of the Prophet appeared to his inner eye, as sharp and clear as though he were standing in front of him.

"Remember who you are!"

The words echoed in his mind like thunder blasting across mountain peaks. He was flooded with the Prophet's teachings, as though remembering them all at once. Every idea was summed up in those four words: Remember who you are.

In that instant, Ivanovitch understood that if he gave way to his murderous outrage, he would descend into the outer darkness where Dr. Tagore and his legions awaited him. With a supreme act of will power, the old man held back his rage and unclenched his fists. The very act of making that choice had an alchemical effect on the energy shooting through him. The violence and hate of an instant ago was now neutralized into pure consciousness. All of that power was channeled by his memories of the Prophet and now reinforced his highest potential, keeping him from falling into the gutter with his enemies.

Everything around him became more clear and bright. He was aware that he could hear better. Aromas were more intense. And the horrific figure of the beast before him faded from the center of his focus, becoming just a dot in the reality around him. He could hear the birds outside and the choppy, disturbed waters of the ocean crashing against the rocks below.

He sensed a cool breeze coming through the window, and with that feeling he knew that he had been blessed by the Prophet and saved from madness.

Ivanovitch was taken to the basement, into an empty room made of concrete walls where bloodstains were the only decoration. Dr. Tagore promised him a dreadful end if he did not cooperate. Ivanovitch accepted his fate. Nothing could shake the transcendent experience he'd just undergone and the undeniable encounter with the presence of the Prophet.

As he sat on the cold floor in a corner of the room, his only regret was that he could not tell his friends about what he had discovered. Though the Final Prophet's body was no longer with them, he was alive in spirit!

A rumble shook the ground beneath him. Ivanovitch was aware that something cataclysmic was taking place. He had felt the car bounce across the road hours before on his way to the cult mansion. But this time the vibrations of the earthquake made it clear to him that some unprecedented catastrophe was in the works. The old mansion rattled and cracked beneath the strain. Dust clouds entered beneath the locked door. As one who'd lived his life on the west coast, Ivanovitch understood that the structure would not remain standing. Perhaps it was a blessing that he would die crushed rather than tortured. Either way, he had accepted the end of his life and was content to leave.

* * * * *

Tom ran along the side of the road as it quivered like a living thing convulsing in the death grip of continental shelves slamming into each other. He fell several times but got back up and kept on his frantic race away from the horrid place. He had no idea where he was or where he was going. The world around him seemed to be crashing in, a perfect expression of his own inner world. He was completely thrown off-balance by what he had encountered over the last few days.

Despite dodging rocks sliding down the hillside toward the road and pavement cracking under his feet, he couldn't get Oriana's features out of his mind. At thirty two years of age, he hadn't really been in love yet, and this strange woman mesmerized him utterly. He couldn't believe he would never see her again. At the same time he realized that there were terrible things in her life that were leading her down a path of no return. He wanted to save her, and bring her into his own life, guiding her into light instead of darkness. How she had gotten herself involved with such evil was a mystery that burned him with intense curiosity. No story he had ever dreamed up could hold a candle to this one.

He stopped running, completely out of breath. He'd quit jogging ten years ago and couldn't sustain the physical effort, even with death at his heels. He looked around. A hundred feet from the road, the ocean waves were rising to heights he'd never seen before, crashing beyond the beaches onto land that had never tasted sea water. The sight was virtually psychedelic. The waters seemed like furies rising up in outrage, seeking to break out of their confines and attack the people of earth. The ground vibrated as though in the grip of some cosmic python squeezing the life out of it. The sky turned a bizarre color—purple and green.

No drug he'd taken in his younger years had ever given him such a vision. He looked back toward the mansion on the distant hill and cried out involuntarily.

"No!"

The roof had already caved in. The walls shuddered as though about to explode. Tom's mind went blank. He lost all contact with his reason. He could only think of the young woman who had stolen her way into his heart. Before he knew it, he was running back toward the mansion. It didn't matter if the beasts inside could kill him in a heartbeat. He didn't care that he had no weapon and no means of defending himself. He knew that if he didn't try to save Oriana, he would never be able to live with himself. He'd rather die at the hands of the evil doctor.

By the time he reached the property, the old mansion was collapsing in on itself. People ran out in panic, hurrying away from the cliff that was on the verge of plunging into the hungry waters. Tom hid behind a clump of trees and kept a close eye on all the people exiting the house. He recognized Madame de Belmar and Dr. Tagore who headed with a few students to their Mercedes and dashed off without looking back. Everyone seemed to be on his own. No surprise for such dead souls, Tom thought to himself.

As the house emptied of its inhabitants, he rushed forward, staying low behind bushes and shrubs. He reached the side of the mansion. The old walls cracked and whined with the terrible stress ripping through the structure. The ground shook like a tight drum skin relentlessly pounded on by a mad drummer. The door frame had slipped off the foundation and the door hung open like a dead limb. Tom ran in without any concern for his safety. He was certain that they had abandoned Oriana to her fate. He ran through large rooms and hallways that were filled with dust, sacrificial victims about to be consumed by the devastation.

He hurried toward the main stairway and came face to face with the guru who was slowly descending the stairs, oblivious of the danger. Tom was taken aback by the desolate, empty look in his eyes.

"Where's Oriana?"

"Have they abandoned her as well?" the man asked in a somber voice.

"Where is she?" Tom yelled.

"I saw her head toward the basement . . . "

"Why isn't she getting out of the house?" Tom cried out, looking up at the huge beams shaking back and forth above his head, rattling like old bones.

"There's an old man down there. She probably wants to save his life."

"Which way to the basement?"

"Over there," the guru said as he pointed. "But you won't make it out alive if you do this, young man."

Tom hurried away and called back. "Don't worry about me. You'd better get out of here yourself!"

"I'm not going anywhere."

Tom looked back, shocked at the answer. The look of despair in the Indian man's eyes said it all. He was anxious to escape the wrong that he had done and to find peace and forgiveness in another dimension. Tom hurried to the stairs just as the first beam came crashing down on the very spot where the guru stood, burying the man beneath its mammoth weight.

Tom made his way with great difficulty down the stairway that shook back and forth brutally, slamming him against the wall several times.

"Oriana!" he shouted. "Oriana, where are you?"

An ear-shattering rumble overwhelmed his senses as he stumbled about in the dark labyrinth of the vast basement. He couldn't tell whether it came from the crashing down of the house or from beneath the earth as the continental shift created havoc along the coastline. He knew it was useless to call her name now. Nothing could be heard above the roar of nature's agony.

He pushed his way through several doors leading into empty chambers, his heartbeat pounding in his head. Any moment now, the entire structure would cave in and bury them alive. At the same time, a new energy filled him with the ecstacy of learning that the woman with whom he'd fallen in love had a good spirit after all and was sacrificing herself for the sake of someone else. Nothing could better express the goodness at the heart of the spiritual teachings that he loved so much.

Dust blinded him as both the floor and the ceiling shook wildly. He could barely hold himself up anymore. He turned down a dark hallway and headed toward one last door. It was locked down by the twisted frame. He would have to break his shoulder on it to open it, perhaps for nothing. This was his last shot. He knew there was no more time to search.

He stepped back and rushed at the door like a mad bull, releasing a war cry as he crashed through it. He landed in a barren room. He didn't notice the pain in his damaged shoulder as his eyes fell upon the most amazing sight he'd ever seen. In the far corner, lit by a single ray of light coming through the window, stood a serene Ivanovitch face to face with Oriana. They held hands and spoke to each other silently, no longer aware of the devastation around them. Tom instantly recognized that the old man was, out of gratitude, feeding her spirit with his wisdom in a manner that was telepathic.

Tom's entrance caused them to break away from their hypnotized attention.

"Tom!" they both cried out at the same time.

"Mister Ivanovitch! What are you doing here?" he said as he scrambled to his feet and hurried to them.

"I was looking for you," the old man said with a half-smile.

"Well, I guess you found me," Tom responded as he took hold of both them. "Let's get out of here!"

"It's too late!" Ivanovitch insisted.

"No, it isn't! It's never too late to try."

He helped them through the broken doorway and led them down the hallway.

"This young woman came to save me, Tom. She

doesn't even know me. She just knew I'd been left here to die."

Tom looked back at Oriana's strangely quiet features and smiled at her.

"I knew you were one of us."

The ceiling cracked overhead and tumbled down behind them, burying the chamber in a mound of debris. Tom took hold of Oriana's hand and pulled her to his side, intending to push her up the stairway.

"Wait for him!" she said as she reached the first step.

Tom turned back. What he saw cut him short. Only Ivanovitch's head and shoulders could be seen beneath a pile of heavy concrete. The old man looked up at him. The peace in his eyes was a mind-bending contrast to his circumstances.

"Go!" he whispered. "Find Jeremy! Fulfill the Prophet's mission!"

Tom stopped dead in his tracks in spite of the shattered debris flying all around him.

"I can't let you die here!" Tom shouted.

"My time is up! Find the Prophet!"

"What do you mean? He's gone!"

Ivanovitch made a supreme effort to force his crushed body to speak.

"Help him find you!"

"Come on!" Oriana shouted, seeing a glimmer of hope for survival. Above the stairway, a dim flicker of greenish light called to them. There was still a chance to get out this deathtrap. But Tom was in the grip of the old man's dying words.

"What are you saying?" he shouted through the dust and the falling cement blocks.

"Fulfill the Prophet's mission!"

Just then another chunk of concrete crashed down on the old man, ending his time on this earth. Tom turned back to Oriana, hoping she hadn't seen the gruesome sight. But she had and she screamed hysterically. Tom picked her up in his arms and rushed up the shaking stairway. One of the steps cracked under his footing, and his leg fell through, pulling every muscle in his thigh. He shouted in pain and rage, calling forth a force in him that lifted him back up on one leg, still holding Oriana tightly in his arms.

He limped into the hallway. The place was unrecognizable. The floor stood up almost vertically, cracked open by the force of the quake. Tom had no idea where to find an exit.

"Help us!" he cried out in spite of himself, uncertain as to whom he was calling to. His mind harkened back to the old man and his last words—*fulfill the Prophet's mission*.

"I can't do it without your help!" Tom cried out again, watching the rest of the mansion crash around them. "Help us so that we may help you!"

He'd never done this in his life, but it was clear to him that this cry from the depths of the heart was true prayer. They crawled through the shattered remnants of the home, squeezing past huge chunks of flooring and devastated walls. The contents of the second story had buried the first.

"Where's the exit?" Tom shouted through his vertigo. The old man's last words rang through his being like an urgent siren. He knew beyond reason that Ivanovitch had given him a legacy to pass on to the world he was leaving behind.

The debris had shut off all light now. They wandered about blindly, quickly losing hope. They fell hard against shards of material, as though on a ship tossed about in the grip of a mighty storm. Tom suddenly saw a thin golden light pierce through the rubble, revealing a path to the outside.

"Look!" he cried out in a state of wild wonderment.

"That way!"

"What is that?" Oriana shouted. She could tell that this was not ordinary light.

Tom tightened his grip on her hand and pushed his way through the ruins, eyes transfixed on the point of light. Like a magnet, it urged him onward as though some gravitational force gave him strength to tear through toward its mysterious source.

Bloodied and covered with dust, they made their way to a small opening, the remnants of a doorway that was nearly buried by broken masonry. The golden light vanished, giving way to the greenish hue of the outdoors.

"We'll have to squeeze through this!" Tom said. "You go first."

He helped Oriana into the narrow passageway. A piece of glass cut through her shirt and tore a red line across her back. She hardly felt it as she scrambled out. The remains of the house moaned like a dying man as the tension shot through its foundations and lifted it up off the ground. The hillside itself was in convulsions.

Tom noticed that the exit space was diminishing rapidly. The odds were high that he would be crushed trying to slip through it. He took a deep breath and forced himself into the passageway. He had just gotten his leg and arm through when the entire structure shifted and the wall above them came down on him, trapping him like steel jaws. His head and arm were still inside the house. He could hear Oriana shrieking and trying to pull on his limbs that had made it out. He let out a yell of agony.

"Help me, Prophet! Help me reach the future with your message!"

Tom didn't even know where those words came from. Suddenly, out of the ruins a figure appeared. Tom let out a shout of utter terror as he recognized Ivanovitch moving toward him over the mounds of debris. He was bloody from head to foot and broken bones stuck out of his flesh. The corpse approaching him was dead even though something living looked through his eyes. Tom's terror gave way to a state of utter shock that made him virtually catatonic as the dead man came closer to him. A strangely serene look emanated from the shattered features. A light vibrated around the cadaver, providing the supernatural force that moved it forward.

The broken body approached him and placed its bloody hands on the frame that had trapped Tom. In one astonishing motion, the corpse lifted the mammoth weight, causing the walls to quiver and groan above the roar of the earthquake. Tom slipped through, eyes fixed on the gruesome yet radiant sight before him. As he fell to the ground, he saw the old man's corpse lay itself against a chunk of flooring. The light surrounding it evaporated like mist at dawn.

Tom shivered in the wet grass and started losing consciousness. Oriana shook him.

"Tom! We've got to get away!"

He opened his glazed eyes, completely traumatized by the experience he had just undergone. His very soul was in shock from the unnatural phenomenon that had saved his life.

He knew that it was a direct response to his prayer and he knew that he would never be the same. The experience had initiated into a dimension of reality that recreated him at the very roots of his being.

Oriana's striking features came into focus and brought him back to the moment. He found himself admiring a black curl of hair that had fallen on her dust-covered forehead. In spite of the fear in her eyes, he could only see the graceful image of the mysterious woman who had set his heart on fire.

"We've got to get away before the rest of the house falls!"

She helped him to his feet. They limped away over the shaking landscape as the rest of the mansion fell in a great crash, crushing everything within it. They collapsed on the edge of the woods and held each other tightly as they looked out at the quivering countryside. They were alone now. All the members of the cult had vanished, leaving them to their fate, assuming that they were buried in the tomb that had once graced the hillside.

For awhile there were no words, just the sensation of their bodies held tight against each other. Their mutual warmth eased the trauma they had undergone and slowed their racing heartbeats. They examined each other's wounds. Tom had severe gashes on his arms and hands, but he couldn't feel any pain. His experience of being saved by a corpse brought back to life and freed from the rubble for that purpose had sent him into a state that kept him barely attached to the physical world. Oriana's warmth alone kept him linked to the realm of the senses. He felt as though his consciousness was on top of a great mountain summit and that his body was far down in the valley below. He soared in the undiscovered country of his spiritual nature, rocketed there by the astonishing events that had kept him alive for a purpose that transcended his own desires.

CHAPTER THIRTEEN

The small caravan of the Prophet's disciples made its way inland through the agonizing countryside. Everyone was utterly silent in the six vehicles, stunned to have survived the destruction of the city that had literally fallen to its knees all around them just as they headed out into the relative safety of the surrounding golden hills.

The grim faces reflected what each person was thinking. The suffering and death behind them was monumental. Hundreds of thousands, perhaps millions, of bodies would be found some day beneath the rubble. It just so happened that they were packed and ready to leave as the devastation began. Everyone else was caught unprepared. They thought about the friends they had left behind, certain now that they would never see them again. Despite the warnings of the man who had transformed their lives, it was impossible to conceive the scale of the destruction that was at hand. They also knew from the prophecies that this was only the beginning, the first in a terrifying list of cataclysms.

Their destination was unknown. They had to escape the more populated areas, far from skyscrapers and glass buildings that were turning into guillotines for the people below. All the signs of human self-importance and achievement were crashing down upon their builders and vanishing in the wind like the grandiose statues of the Pharaohs of old. Once again, human arrogance would turn to dust, but this time the likelihood of starting over again was uncertain at best.

Jeremy and his passengers remembered the words of their Teacher. Now that the cosmic trauma had begun, they knew that a domino effect would take place and that one disaster would lead to another. It wouldn't simply be the results of the axis shift that would devastate the earth. Terrorists, tyrants and fanatics would take advantage of the chaos and intensify the horror. The glee of demonic forces was already palpable as the earth shook and violent storms gathered overhead. A monster lightning bolt ripped through the sky with an explosion that nearly shattered the car windows. Everyone jumped in terror.

"My God! What was that?"

"Creation itself is mourning in travail, as the writings say," Jeremy uttered grimly.

* * * * *

The shaking finally stopped. Thick smoke filled the sky as a strange silence settled briefly over the catastrophic destruction. Nothing moved, as though Nature itself was in a catatonic state.

Then, all of a sudden, sirens and screams exploded through the momentary peace. Every city along the coast—from Seattle to San Diego—had become a death trap to its citizens. Eighty percent of the structures were in some stage of devastation. The ocean roared like a crazed creature stirred from its lair and taking its rage out on the ragged edges of the continent.

It would be weeks before an approximate body count could be collected and months beyond that before basic necessities were restored. The gold coast had finally reached its inevitable encounter with its geological destiny. It was gold no more. Despair and crime would wander through the rubble for years to come. Not even the World Federation could handle such epic devastation. In a few hours, California had returned to its lawless condition out of which it was born. The wild west was back, this time with neither lawmen nor code of honor. Out of the wreckage of civilization would arise sadistic beings who would put their infamous ancestors to shame. Only the most violent would survive—though not for long.

Those who could band together and reach the desert were more likely to stay alive than those stuck in the ruins of the cities. Instantly, barbarians were in power. Decent people were unfortunate prey sure to be attacked by some roving gang.

A lieutenant colonel hurried into the War Department of the World Federation Headquarters. The vast windowless room was filled with anxious generals and other high ranking officers standing over large computer screens displaying constantly shifting maps of the world.

"Where's General MacDaniel?" the frantic lieutenant-colonel cried out.

"He's on the phone with the President. We're expecting him any moment," an older general answered grimly.

"Have you seen this?" the newly arrived officer asked as he opened a file he was carrying.

The general looked at the colored fax that was handed to him.

"What am I looking at?"

"There's been a catastrophic calamity in Asia. It's bound to send shock waves to the west coast that it will not be able to sustain. I think we're going to lose a chunk of California."

"That's crazy!"

"Sir, as we speak there is an 8.5 earthquake going on out there."

"I know . . . "

"You add to that the Tsinamu on its way and the pressure that will create on the plates, and we're in for something we've never seen in our lifetime."

"Are you guessing here?"

"I'm pretty sure, sir."

"Pretty sure won't do it, soldier. We've got a worldwide catastrophe on our heads. Every continent is in utter chaos. We've sent war planes to the Middle East to survey the danger zones. We expect anarchists to take advantage of these disasters."

Another officer came running up to the two men.

"Sir, we've been tracking a giant storm over West Africa. Our satellites have picked a picture you've got to see."

"Another storm?"

The man handed him a large photograph depicting the coast of Africa.

"Look at the size of those lightning strikes. You can see them on the photograph for God's sakes! It's wiping out entire cities and shows no signs of abating. It's crossing the whole continent."

"Is this the same storm we spotted last week?"

"That's right, sir. It's only gotten more powerful."

"What kind of a storm is that?" the man cried out, horrified at the huge red spots on the satellite images.

"Nobody's ever seen anything like it. Every city it comes through is completely blacked out. There's massive looting and total disorder in its wake. Even Federation posts are under attack."

"Why don't they shoot the bastards?"

"Sir, they've been overrun. There are thousands of panicked people in the streets. There's nothing we can do."

"What do you mean, there's nothing we can do?"

General MacDaniel shouted, red-faced as he approached them. His fellow officers turned to him, sad and silent.

"Send the Air Force out there!"

"They don't have the heavy equipment to dig their way through the mess."

"Then order the Navy's largest ships into every harbor."

"It's not safe. There'll be aftershocks, and that means tidal waves."

"We can't leave millions of our citizens without food and water, or medical attention, or protection!"

"People are gonna be on their own for awhile, sir. There's no way around it," one of the older generals said sternly. "We'd better concentrate on the situations we can do something about."

"Explain yourself!" MacDaniel ordered.

"The storms in the Midwest have created blackouts in at least a dozen cities."

"There's massive looting going on," another officer pointed. "We've got to get the army in there and restore order! There's no telling how long the electrical systems will be done. There are so many transformers blown, the blackouts could last for weeks."

MacDaniel ran his hand across his bald head, removing the beads of sweat that had gathered there. A thought came into his mind. For some reason, the image of the dark man who had visited him recently formed on the screen of his inner eye. Why exactly he would think of Stefan Zorn in this moment was unclear to him. But the thought stuck there, obstinately, refusing to give way to more practical matters in this moment of crisis.

"What are your orders, general?"

MacDaniel turned his back on his officers, trying to rid himself of the image of the big, evil-eyed man that was interfering with his rational mind. He'd never had such a problem before. Then it dawned on him. The occult leader might be in possession of mysterious knowledge regarding the global cataclysms taking place. Perhaps he had some inexplicable way to counteract these overwhelming events.

A surge of anger rushed through the general's nervous system. That was the most ludicrous thought he'd ever had. But it remained nevertheless, unwilling to evaporate and give way to logical reasoning. A cold shiver shot through him as another thought came to his mind. Had the evil man done something hypnotic to him, locking down his capacity to function and forcing him to think in a certain way?

That was too much for him to deal with. He let out a bear-like growl and turned around.

"I want military units dispatched to every city that the storm has passed through. I want you to reestablish contact with all authorities that are still functioning on the west coast. And make arrangements to drop supplies from the air to citizens that can't be reached otherwise. Let's do it now, gentlemen!"

The officers immediately dispersed to their various phone centers. An assistant approached the general with a handful of faxes. MacDaniel waved him away and walked over to a corner near the giant world maps etched on glass that surrounded the room. He took a deep breath and concentrated his mind. His iron will had been his strongest gift throughout his life. Zorn's sinister dark eyes remained stuck in his mind like some ghostly freeze frame that couldn't be removed. He had to confront him and deal with this phenomenon before it interfered with any other executive decisions. He hurried back to his office.

He made no eye contact with anyone along the way. He opened his address book in his computer and found the man's cellular phone number. He clicked on it.

Within moments, the intense features of Stefan Zorn appeared on his computer screen. He was driving his car on a road leading toward the headquarters.

"Hello, general," Zorn said with a knowing smirk.

"How did you know it was me?" MacDaniel asked, more confused then ever.

"I'm already on my way."

"You knew I wanted to see you?"

"Yes I did."

"Don't come to my office. Let's meet in a secure location."

"I have several. I know you do as well."

"There's no safer place than the Corridor."

"The what?"

"Corridor 600. It's long been our most secure military location for high level gatherings. I wouldn't want to take any risks. Not now."

"Very good, general. By the way, don't bring anyone else with you. I wouldn't want to get nervous and do something . . . unnecessary."

"You're not threatening me, are you , Zorn?" the general asked, his face turning beet red with outrage.

"No sir, I just wouldn't want to find out that you're planning on arresting me."

"Can't you foretell that?" the officer asked sarcastically.

"As a matter of fact, I can. But I just wanted you to know that I would know if you made that decision. It wouldn't be the smart thing to do."

"Who the hell do you think you are?" MacDaniel yelled, unable to control himself. "Don't you realize who you're talking to?"

"Yes sir, I do. The man who thinks he's got all the power, but who needs to talk to me because he now knows that he doesn't."

MacDaniel's insides felt like they were melting with

shame. It was the worse defeat of his career. He couldn't argue with the beastly man. He had to resolve this situation before it interfered any further with his self-mastery.

"Don't be late!" MacDaniel said menacingly.

Zorn smiled slyly. "I'm almost there already, general."

MacDaniel shut down his computer. He looked around his office to make sure that no one could have heard that conversation. This was a secret that he couldn't afford to let leak under any circumstances.

Suddenly the room filled with a loud mechanical screech as a dozen seismographs shook back and forth. They were receiving signals that were off the charts, shattering the equipment. The officers jumped in fear as sparks and smoke flew out of the machines as the needles ripped through the paper charts running through them.

"What the hell is that?" MacDaniel yelled over the noise.

"We've got seismic activity that's never been recorded before, sir! It's so intense that it's destroying our measuring equipment."

"Where is it coming from?"

"Everywhere!"

That one word said it all. A strange terror filled the room as the building itself began to shake, confirming the fact that every continental plate on the globe was rattling under the strain of incredible pressure.

"What does this mean?" MacDaniel asked as he held on to a table and watched chairs skip across the floor.

"It's gotta be the axis shift, sir" an officer shouted back over the chaos.

"Is the whole planet gonna explode or what?"

"Nobody knows, sir. This has never happened before," the science officer said as he held on for dear life. Everyone knew that if this uniquely designed building was shaking, structures in every other city were tumbling to the ground.

After a moment that seemed like eternity, the shaking stopped. A grim silence fell over the room. Only one of the seismographs still functioned. The others hung loosely from their boards, shattered beyond repair, witnesses to the mammoth destruction that had just taken place.

The officers gathered around the broken equipment.

"Has anyone every read about anything like this?" MacDaniel asked somberly.

"No sir. This has not happened before in recorded history."

"For all the plates to be affected at once, it can't be anything less than the planet shifting its axis. Nothing else could account for that kind of unilateral stress on the earth's surface," another officer stated.

"I hate to see what it's like outside," a general muttered.

"We've got to get control as best we can," MacDaniel responded the only way he knew how. Tight control and overcoming the enemy were the only solutions he knew how to employ. But this time the enemy was larger than anything he'd ever faced.

* * * * *

Stefan Zorn's black luxury car swerved past huge piles of debris and large cracks in the pavement. Smoke covered the city like a thick mourning veil. Sirens and flashing lights were the only signs of life in this traumatized landscape of twisted metal and broken concrete.

The bulletproof vehicle screeched to a stop in front of a side entrance to the Federation's headquarters. Several officers stood in the doorway awaiting him. They scanned the area to make sure there was no one in sight. The large, evil-looking man got out and surveyed the surrealistic environment. The glow of gas fires could be seen in the distance, but here in this desolate section of the city the atmosphere felt like a cemetery.

He looked up at the huge fortress of concrete, somewhat surprised that it was still standing. The steps leading up to the side doors that were camouflaged as a maintenance entrance were cracked from top to bottom. Zorn could not hide a smile. He was thrilled that he was finally entering the ultimate halls of worldly power. This was the holy of holies for political leaders and military commanders who thought they controlled the world's destiny.

It took him a few moments to adjust to the darkness of the labyrinth of secret hallways and large iron doors. After fifteen minutes of following a silent officer up and down lengthy stairways, irritation started to burned through his veins. Zorn was finally led into a long, darkly lit hallway deep below ground level. The officer opened one of the heavy doors and gestured for him to enter.

Zorn wandered in the shadows of the vast, barren room. After a few moments, General MacDaniel entered. His visitor seemed to have vanished in the darkness.

"Where the hell are you?" the general finally called out, after bumping into several columns of cold stone. The backup electrical system was dim and weak. He heard a noise to his left and turned toward it. The massive frame of Stefan Zorn appeared just a few feet away from him, causing the general's instinctive combat readiness to go for his gun.

"Easy, general. This is not a Syrian battle ground."

The general approached him and stared angrily into his dark eyes. Zorn waited patiently for him to speak, full of arrogance and the certainty of his greater power.

"What have you done to me?" the general whispered hoarsely.

"Whatever do you mean?" Zorn replied with a smirk of disdain.

"You know damn well what I mean, Zorn! You've done some hypnotic trick to my mind."

"Do you think so?" the man asked with a mysterious glint in his eyes.

The general looked away, realizing that if he was right, the man could manipulate him even now without his knowing it.

"I want you to undo what you did so that I can perform my duty unhindered!"

"But I didn't do anything, general."

MacDaniel turned purple with rage and pulled out his weapon with great speed, pressing it against Zorn's thick cheek.

"I'll blow your face off right here and now if you play games with me! Tell me what you've done! Now!"

"Please remove your weapon from my face," Zorn said coldly.

The general cocked his gun and prepared to pull the trigger.

"If you kill me, general, no one will be able to help you."

"So you did do something, you son of a bitch!"

"Nothing serious, general."

"Then undo it immediately!"

"I'd be happy to, but you'll have to remove your gun."

The general pushed it deeper into his flesh. "No tricks Zorn, or I swear I'll drop you right here and leave you for the rats to gnaw on."

"I believe you, general. But I can't help you under these conditions."

MacDaniel reluctantly removed the gun just far enough for Zorn to turn his head toward him.

"How dare you mess with my mind!"

"Believe me, general, it kinda happens automatically

with me. Nothing personal. It sort of comes with the territory."

"What the hell are you talking about?"

"Most people I come across are affected in that way, sir. I don't even have to try."

"This has never happened to me before. Undo it."

Zorn focused his intense glare upon the harsh features of the general. His arrogant smirk turned to ice as he shot of beam of energy into the man's soul. The general did his best to hide a tremble that shook his body. There was none braver in a war zone, but this was too foreign for him. He didn't know how to deal with it. He never had any use for occult matters, but he distinctly felt an uncomfortable energy exchange that left him with a feeling of vertigo. His body went limp and he felt his will power diminish. He tightened his grip on his weapon.

"You're a dead man, Zorn, if you're fooling with me."

"Take it easy, general. I did as you requested," Zorn said with a mysterious smile as he stepped back and the glazed intensity left his pupils.

"How do I know you didn't do something else with your magic tricks?"

"I'm not a fool. I've no desire to have your wrath turned upon me. I wish to be an ally, not an enemy. We can be helpful to each other in these difficult times."

"Why did you mess with my mind in the first place?"

"As I said sir, it was unintentional. Just magnetic effects rather than the hypnotism you're imagining."

"I know I didn't imagine what was happening to me. If it happens again, I'll . . . "

"You've already made that clear, general."

"How did you fix the problem?" he asked as he replaced the gun back in its holster.

"Difficult to explain, general. Sort of a release if you will. I'm sure if you become aware of yourself, sir, you'll find that you're particularly clear-minded and sharply focused."

The general turned his awareness on himself and sensed the truth of his words. He felt rested and was more aware of his surroundings, as though his peripheral vision had expanded. He shook his head in dismay at the strangeness of it all.

"You people are too weird for me," he said in disgust. "But I did learn one thing from this. I do realize that you know things that I do not, Zorn. So I'll ask you again. Is there anything that can be done to alleviate the crisis that is taking place around the globe?"

"As a matter of fact there is, general."

"Tell me, then."

"This will require more than deployment of military personnel."

"I'm ready to try anything."

Zorn did his best to keep a look of victory from spreading across his features. The general waited eagerly for a response.

"You have to understand, general, that the source of these cataclysms is not in the physical world but in the psychic realm."

"Go on."

"The magnetic fields of the earth have been contaminated. I'm referring to a dimension that your scientists know nothing about this even with advanced theories of quantum physics. I'm talking about the electromagnetic influence of the cosmic forces that surround us like the ocean surrounds a fish."

"Tell me more," the general muttered reluctantly.

"You see, general, we humans aren't what we think we are. We are receivers, transformers you might say, of planetary energies."

"What are you talking about?" the general asked disdainfully.

"We're part of the thin slice of organic life that covers this rock and which absorbs the influences which come to us from space. You see, general, we humans are only a coating on the surface of this planet, which is merely an organ buried in the far reaches of the cosmic body which is the universe. We blend with the electrons emitted by the sun, the magnetic waves from the orbiting planets, and the raw minerals of earth. This organic life that we're a part of is nearly seventy percent water so we are obviously under the gravitational power of the moon. And beyond that we are subjected to the different subtle energies from distant star configurations as the earth rotates throughout the year. What we call our history or fate is the result of our cosmic interactions that we know nothing about. Influences from celestial bodies are received by our nerve antennae and stimulate our endocrine glands. These secretions create the overall psychological conditions we find in the people around us."

"How is this possible?" MacDaniel growled impatiently.

"These electromagnetic impulses reach us through our nerve plexuses, which then stimulate our endocrine system. In fact, each planet of the solar system corresponds with our endocrine glands."

"Don't waste my time!" MacDaniel said angrily, confused and disturbed by the strange information.

"Each gland passes its accumulated energy from planetary influences into the bloodstream and therefore into our psychology," Zorn continued, oblivious to the man's dismissal. "The sun itself produces cycles of varying influences on us poor humans. The fluctuation of the amperage, if you will, of the planets' magnetic fields affect our nerve systems and our glandular secretions, thereby impacting our behavior. The glorious history of humanity is a manifestation of these cycles of influence."

A mocking smile wrinkled Zorn's features, as though the man before him was the incarnation of this puppet behavior so arrogantly called history.

"Are you saying that everything we think and do is related to rotating rocks in space?" the general challenged.

"The sun affects the thymus, which stimulates the process of regeneration. The moon influences the pancreas, which directs the process of refinement."

"What do you mean by refinement?"

"This is one of six cosmic processes that form the dynamics of what we call reality. The process known to metaphysicians as refinement is characterized by developments in the quality of human culture. The gradual evolution of technology could be considered refinement, if it hadn't led to this state of affairs. From the first uses of the wheel to travel on the surface of other planets, we can see a process of development that has positive influences on human life. You could also include developments in politics, in the entertainment field, the expansion of our cities. As you can see, we have come to the end of that process."

The general moved away from him, pacing the floor with nervousness and a gnawing uncertainty. This was all too bizarre for his rational mind.

"The thyroid," Zorn stated as though he were tutoring a freshmen, "has an affinity with the planet mercury which stimulates crime. The parathyroid is linked to the planet Venus which stimulates growth. The adrenals stimulate fight or flight and are affected by mars, of course. The posterior lobe of the pituitary has an affinity with Jupiter which, like the sun, stimulates the process of regeneration. The anterior pituitary is affected by Saturn and calls forth the process of invention."

The general stared at him, speechless before this outpour of knowledge.

"What is the bottom line, general? Simply this: the combined electromagnetic irradiation of the planets as they orbit our world directs the general movement of human affairs. Each of these celestial influences carry with them cosmic laws under which we place ourselves according to our degree of consciousness. We are currently under a great density of hydrogen and live in the darkest state of psychological captivity. We've been this way for a long time. That is why we have reached this crisis point, general."

The two men stood in the dark cathedral in somber silence as the general absorbed the information he'd been given.

"How can we influence the situation?" he finally asked in words that he could barely make himself speak. This was a reality he hated to recognize.

"There are methods, general, that have been known for a long time. Rituals, manipulations of energies can alter the atmosphere from which the disturbance is coming. But this requires massive control of the population. We need to harness a critical mass to generate the necessary tone of energy."

"How do we do that?"

"First, you'll have to remove those who might distract people from participating in the mass mind. At the top of the list are the so-called Final Prophet's disciples. They'll throw a monkey wrench in this thing, believe me. As long as they're around, people will consider alternatives and we'll have a lack of unity in the population's focus."

"What will it take to get the population's attention harnessed?"

"Very simple, general. Something you're good at and that will make perfect use of your skills."

"What are you talking about?"

"We need a war, general, a world war in which millions will die. The slaughter and all that goes with the events of war will generate the psychic substance that will balance out the magnetic fields."

"That's the craziest thing I ever heard!" the general grumbled, while at the same time a surge of excitement filled his whole being. He had trained all his life for just this sort of thing. War was something he could understand and accomplish to perfection. He felt back on familiar ground. The relief was palpable. The rest of the mumbo jumbo was irrelevant.

Zorn could read his mind like an open book. He knew he had his man where he wanted him.

"So this release of substance is like a purging of some sort?"

"You might say that. Human beings are simply organic transformers of energy. We serve a purpose like plants, but in a more complex way. Every once in awhile the planetary systems need what we might call mass psychosis for purposes that have nothing to do with the politics that seem to generate it. The universe itself is a series of processes and transformations. The small cells that we represent in the body of the solar system have a function that is far different than we imagine it to be. Death and destruction may not be pleasant to those who undergo it but they have their own value beyond their impact on human beings. We're kind of a compost heap for celestial gardeners."

"Enough of that! You're giving me a headache. Any suggestions on how we go about this?"

"That's your department, general. I'm sure you can find a way."

General MacDaniel looked at his watch.

"We'll stay in touch. Let's be sure to keep this relationship entirely confidential. I'm not interested in your cosmology or metaphysics, but if you can help me get things under control, then I'll take your counsel on these matters."

"You can count on me to assist you in every possible way."

MacDaniel headed for the great door, then turned around. He studied the big man standing silently in the dim light. A wave of suspicion crashed upon his feelings.

"What's your purpose for helping us?"

"I live on this planet too, general. I have no desire to see it wrecked beyond repair. I'm a man of responsibility."

"What's in it for you, Stefan Zorn?" the general asked again, unconvinced.

The dark man stared back at him, an inscrutable look in his eyes. The general took a step back, eager to get away from his overbearing presence.

"You're not wanting to take over the world, or something like that, are you?"

Zorn let out a loud laugh that echoed across the concrete walls surrounding them.

"I leave that kind of power to men like you. I don't need it. I'm not a conqueror of territories. My interests are elswhere."

"That's what I'm asking you, Zorn. Where are your interests?"

"What does it matter to you?"

"If we're going to be allies, I have to have some kind of trust in you. To be honest about it, it's hard to come up with."

"I don't blame you, general. You're a man of war. Everyone's a potential enemy."

"It's not that, Zorn," MacDaniel said impatiently. "You think I'm an idiot. You're not a lamb, you're a wolf. Don't try to pass yourself off as some kind of innocent, patriotic citizen."

"You'd be surprised, general," Zorn responded with a certain melancholy in his voice. "I've been sidelined from mainstream society all of my life because of my interests. But I'm not what people think I am. Everyone has their specialties. Does that mean they can't be good citizens?"

The general stepped forward angrily, sick of his play-acting.

"My spies tell me that you're involved with evil things. They say you drink the blood of the innocent!"

"It's a myth," Zorn stated, looking back at him unblinking. "I'm surprised you fell for that superstition from the Dark Ages. I'm a . . . philosopher."

"Who do you really work for, Zorn?" the general asked, his face contorted with distrust.

"I don't work for anybody. Maybe that's my greatest interest. Personal autonomy."

"Why don't I believe you?"

"I don't know. You're beginning to hurt my feelings, general. I've offered my talents to you in a sincere wish to help an agonizing world. We've desired to help for a long time."

"You've known about this all along?"

"We have information from ancient sources that a crustal slippage of global proportions occured around fourteen thousand and some odd years ago. It's part of a cycle. This may have happened several times in remote antiquity."

"What does this mean for us today?"

"We can expect a complete lithospheric reorientation of the earth's crust. Hudson's Bay could end up where the North Pole is currently located. The Antarctic continent may rotate away from the South Pole Axis as much as forty-five degrees south latitude. If this happens, we can expect the oceans to back up in their basins at an average speed of two to four hundred miles an hour, creating gigantic tidal waves. In a period of eight to twelve hours, Chicago could end up at the North Pole and a three thousand foot wall of water will come down on the empty ocean basins at a velocity of a hundred miles an hour."

The men stood in silence, stunned by the gravity of the future hurdling down upon them.

"It is also said," he continued, "that a huge magma bubble is pushing up beneath the United States."

"A what?" the general cried out, distressed by a new tale of horror.

"A magma bubble. They're caused by ice buildup at the poles. This in turn causes an instability in the earth's rotation, and that creates instability in the earth's magma and core."

"What will be the result?"

"Land fractures. Expect great migrations of people out of California, Oregon, Washington into the deserts of Arizona, Utah, New Mexico, Nevada and Colorado."

"What will happen to the land west of the fractures?"

"They'll break up further, become inundated, and some will turn into islands. There'll be a seaport in Nebraska. Denver will become a seaside resort," he added sarcastically.

"What about the east coast?"

"Half of Manhattan will go under water. Most of Rhode Island and a third of Maine will be submerged as well. Forget about Long Island. We'll lose a good chunk of Florida. There'll be other phenomena as well that you might not expect . . . New land will rise up out of the shifting oceans."

"New lands?"

"Well, not so new. We hope to see part of Atlantis resurface."

"Don't give me that babble!" the general cried out, red-faced.

"You might get to walk among the ruins of its great cities and see for yourself, general. They'll rise out of the water between Florida and the Bahamas. We'll see ruins come up out of the Sargasso Sea and the Gulf of Mexico."

"What about the Midwest?" MacDaniel asked, trying to change the subject.

"The Mississippi will expand into a huge seaway. The Great Lakes will turn into an inland sea due to melting polar ice caps. Changes will also come because of those endless storms and floods we're seeing now."

The general brought his hand to his forehead. The fingers trembled ever so slightly. This was an enemy he had never faced before. Zorn snickered at the man's primal fear. It was the sensation he most enjoyed stimulating in others. It was in fact the source of his power.

The general looked at him, stupefied. He had left himself wide open for Zorn's hypnotic influence to seep deep into his soul. Zorn continued like a boxer smelling the kill.

"We humans are part of a much larger organism which has little interest in our survival. We're created primarily to serve the purpose of digesting energies that cannot be absorbed by the earth and moon. Without us, sunlight simply becomes heat when it penetrates the atmosphere. It's the same with the magnetic rays from other planets. The bare minerals of the moon can't do anything with them without a mechanism that will transform these energies. That's us. The masses are here to produce greenhouse gases that conserve the sun's heat. Most humans are obedient cells, or rather a digestive secretion. Nothing more."

"You're talking nonsense!" MacDaniel shouted, feeling his very essence drained out of him.

"Consider this. Before food can become nourishment, it must be refined. In the earth's early history, the sun fell on swampy forests; as the ferns died they formed thick layers of rotting organic material. The climates changed, the continents moved, the swamps became seas, mountains, deserts. These sedimentary materials that were once sun and water became buried under immense pressure and transformed or digested by the earth. Ages later, they are extracted as coal and oil and turned into gases. In other words, the sun's heat, buried countless centuries ago, is released, just like the storing and burning of fat in hibernating animals. Humans simply serve a purpose. The question is—whom will you serve? The sewage of a growing planet or ethereal forces that belong to another plane of existence?"

The general's face was glistening with sweat. Along with his hands, his lips now trembled. He was entirely at the mercy of the man of darkness. He turned his back on Zorn, unable to bear the unearthly tension.

"I don't want to see you again face to face, unless it's absolutely necessary," MacDaniel said coldly as he walked away. "You know how to reach me. Let's keep our communications to a minimum. When I need your input, I'll contact you. Don't call me first."

He moved into the shadows, his army boots resonating on the cold stone floor. An officer entered and escorted Zorn out of the room and down the secret corridor. His big features broadened in a victorious smile as they walked in silence through the underbelly of the military headquarters. He knew he'd won an important battle for his cause, which was most certainly not that of humanity's well-being.

CHAPTER FOURTEEN

The mega earthquake unleashed tsunamis that wiped out most of the Hawaiian Islands. One thousand miles further east, the first new land mass appeared from under the waves. The ancient continent of Lemuria, covered with incalculable treasures from a primordial history, emerged from the deep for the future and the past to meet, if anything was left after the cataclysms.

Japan's fate was the most dire as it faced being utterly swallowed up by the shifting ocean. The catastrophe was so colossal that the world population could only watch in horror, although most people were too concerned for their own safety to worry about the annihilation of another country. Adding to the rising misery and destabilization was the an odd phenomenon soon detected by the Federation's scientists. A hum, just below the capacity of human hearing, caused by tectonic plates sliding against each other, began to create erratic behavior in animals and a variety of symptoms among the human population. Cases of chest pains, nausea, heart failure increased overnight as millions reacted to the inaudible sound.

Large solar flares announced the certain return of super-mega quakes and the further breakup of the continents. Weather changes were turning dry places into wetlands and wet areas into deserts. Monstrous storms thundered across the face of the earth, increasing the relentless devastation. Ironically water was becoming a rare and valuable commodity as salt water contaminated inland reservoirs. Volcanic activity in the Pacific was sending a giant black cloud across the globe, threatening to turn day into night for months on end.

Food shortages and massive rioting kept the ruined cities in a frenzied state of panic. Plagues appeared out of the destruction, like some toxic poison arising to chase after the survivors. It wasn't long before jammed hospitals detected a new strain of the AIDS virus, one that was transmitted through the air. Electromagnetic disturbances generated great disruptions of the technological world on which civilization relied completely.

Throughout Europe, elevations below three hundred feet were inundated by the seas. All the land from the Mediterranean north to the Baltic Sea was in danger of collapsing. Upheavals in the Arctic and Antarctic created volcanoes and were generating the dreaded pole shift that would utterly transform the planet.

Dense clouds were spreading out over large portions of the globe, the result of increased volcanic activity. In their wake, they carried a sense of gloom as rain fell continuously. The ferocious winds brought forth the tales of ancient peoples. The Mayans spoke of a terrible wind destroying entire forests and leading toward the end of the world. Its name was Hurakan. The Hindu Vedas and the Persian Avesta, as well as the primordial Epic of Gilgamesh told of a cosmic hurricane that would sweep the land, devastating humanity. This same mighty wind was known to the Polynesians as Taafanua, to the Arabs as Tyfoon, and to the Chinese as Ty-fong. The Maoris tribes of New Zealand foretold of a wind that was to descend upon creation and turn ocean waves into high mountains. The Buddhist text Visuddhi-Magga described a world cycle that would destroy the inhabitants of earth by wind.

The sacred book of the Mayans, Popol-Vuh, and the Annals of Cuauhtitlan further detailed an age when the sun of fire-rain fell upon the people. The Voguls of Siberia also knew of the time when a sea of fire would fall upon the earth, along with aboriginal tribes from the East Indies who told of the "water of fire".

At the same time, a bright blue comet appeared in the night sky. At least, observers thought it was a comet for awhile. It wouldn't be long before it was discovered to be a star—a new sun. Ten times brighter than the planets and other stars, this new cosmic presence stirred distant memories of a Hopi legend about a blue star they named Kachina. Other mystics had foretold of its appearance and perceived it as the domain of great spiritual forces. In the daytime, it was visible in the sky as a small white light, similar to the moon. At night, it lit up the skies as one of the brightest lights in the galaxy.

This new and inexplicable phenomenon only added to the chaos and panic. In the first week of the onset of global disasters, the Federation set up relocation centers for the millions made homeless. The roads heading inland were jammed with bumper to bumper traffic. Terrified refugees mingled aimlessly toward some place of security that did not exist. Rich and poor travelled side by side, victims of a colossal catastrophe that had suddenly made everyone truly equal. Money was quickly becoming useless as businesses shut down and the economy grounded to a shuddering halt. People were suddenly on their own to stay alive. The promised security of the world Federation had vanished with the first onslaught of devastation.

* * * * *

Tom and Oriana wandered along the road that led inland from the ocean. They'd been in a daze for hours. The world was no longer the one they had known the day before. The pavement was split in half. Trees were uprooted, laying on their sides like petrified corpses, as though they'd been plucked out like weeds by some colossal giant. The few homes located in this sparsely inhabited area were completely demolished. The people inside were most surely crushed beneath the flattened structures. Thick black smoke covered the horizon, coming from the towns and cities further inland that had been devastated by the terrible quake. Behind them, the ocean swirled angrily, sending twenty-foot waves over the coastline, with the promise of more to come. Seafaring eyes would know that this turbulence was the front edge of a killer Tsunami coming in from the open waters, created by the movement of the continental shelves.

The skies were odd shifting colors of purplish green. Cloud formations carried with them that frightful look of the birthing of tornadoes. Everything was in a state of trauma.

Tom and Oriana were desperately thirsty and couldn't make it much farther on their own. His wounds were still bleeding although Oriana had bound and cleaned them with expert care. They were too tired to talk even though they'd walked side by side for hours. They felt like companions in some terrible nightmare that wouldn't fade away with daylight. Even Tom's insatiable curiosity couldn't stir him to find out more about this strange woman and the stranger circumstances in which he had encountered her. He had only one thing in mind, and that was to survive this ordeal.

They came over the top of a hill and were struck by the panoramic view of a small town below them. Not a building remained standing. Vehicles were scattered everywhere, now worthless heaps of scrap iron. There was no sign of life anywhere. It looked like a ghost town in which some angry poltergeist had vented his wrath for past wrongs.

"There's gotta be somebody alive around here," Tom whispered hoarsely.

"Can you make it down the hill?" Oriana asked, looking at his battered condition.

"I'm not sure, but we've got to get food and water . . . or find a phone."

She took his arm and helped him down the hill. They both knew that one fall and their chances of staying alive were over. It didn't matter that they were such different people. Perhaps they would discover that they could never be together, that their romantic feelings couldn't last, but for now they were stripped down to their essential humanity and nothing else mattered than to take care of each other.

As they came closer to the shattered town, a pack of dogs suddenly appeared ahead of them, barking fiercely. They were an odd assortment of different breeds, formerly domesticated and now suddenly reverted back to their primeval ways. The animals were as disoriented as the humans. The dogs raced toward them, baring their teeth. Tom frantically looked about for some kind of weapon.

"Sit down!" Oriana ordered.

"What? They're gonna rip us to shreds!" he cried out.

"Please do as I ask. I know about these things."

In spite of the energy coursing through his system and his desperate urge to run, Tom followed her instructions. They both sat in the grass as the dogs raced toward them.

"Be very still," she said in a strange calm that contrasted dramatically with the dangerous moment. "Don't let them smell your fear."

He looked into her eyes and was astonished by her courage and self-control. He was ashamed of the terror pounding through his nerves. Her serenity was contagious and he felt himself able to find shelter in her peace even though he could already imagine the fangs tearing into his flesh.

He heard the dogs approach and instinctively turned toward them.

"Don't look at them!" she said in a peaceful voice. "Just look at me."

He turned his gaze on her again and was transported out of the terrifying situation.

The dogs charged at them and stopped suddenly a few feet away. They sniffed about. Some of them barked loudly at them, but none attacked. Tom felt a cold nose against his arm. It took all the self-mastery he could muster not to jump up. Oriana's quiet gaze kept him still.

Soon the dogs turned away and headed off into the woods, searching for other prey.

Tom released his tension by taking Oriana in his arms and hugging her with a gratitude and affection he'd never felt before.

"How did you know to do that?" he asked.

"Just a trick from the old country my grandparents told me about."

"You're one brave lady," he said as he touched her soft cheek. "You never cease to amaze me, whoever you are."

She looked at him oddly, realizing that there was indeed much about her that he did not know and that he might feel quite different about her once he found out. He sensed the turmoil in her heart and struggled to get up in order to escape the implications. With new vigor, generated by the adrenaline rush they had just been through, they descended into the town below.

The rubble was spread all across the street, shattered into piles of wreckage. Here and there an arm stuck out from under the mounts.

"These folks never had a chance," Tom said. "They were too close to the epicenter. The San Andreas fault must have split wide open," he added as he surveyed the disaster.

They hadn't walked far before they saw a restaurant front spread out halfway across the street. A side of the building was still standing. The old luncheonette's floor was covered with smashed dishes. A refrigerator lay on its side.

"Let's try this," Tom suggested. They walked carefully through the twisted chaos, trying to avoid sharp objects and hoping they weren't stepping on bodies.

Tom made his way to the back of the restaurant and looked in a cupboard that stood at a forty-five degree angle. It was filled with loaves of bread and hamburger buns.

"Open sesame!" he cried out. The simple food looked like a lost treasure to him.

Oriana pulled out a couple of plastic bottles from the broken refrigerator.

"Well, we're going to live another day," he said as they stumbled out of the destroyed restaurant.

They made their way to the middle of the street and sat on large blocks of concrete that had once graced the town's courtroom.

"Bon appetit!" he said as he raised his bottle.

They ate ravenously, in a near state of starvation, completely oblivious to the bizarre scene—a picnic in the midst of desolation. Tom noted in his writer's mind how amazing it was that people could adjust to virtually anything. The world had fallen apart, but it was still lunchtime and life had to go on, with or without civilization. That thought caused a feeling of fear to interrupt his meal. He realized that it wouldn't be long before the criminal element ruled over the chaos.

He looked around and was relieved by the absolute stillness of the surroundings. Death weighed heavily over the countryside. Nature itself had to catch its breath after what it had been through. There were no bird whistles coming from the groves around them. That in itself intensified the eerie atmosphere. The silence was unnatural.

Then he heard a distant pounding.

"What's that?" he asked as he stopped chewing.

Oriana listened carefully. "I don't hear anything."

"It's kind of a rhythmic beat."

She put down her food and listened again. "I do hear something."

Before she could say another word, the sound was overhead. They looked up and saw a small military helicopter appear above the tree line. Tom's first instinct was terror. But he thought better of it.

"Maybe they're surveying the destruction."

"I don't think so," Oriana responded in a tone filled with dark premonition.

A voice came over a loud speaker on the helicopter.

"Do not move! We have you in our sights. Repeat, do not move or you will be shot!"

"What the hell..!" Tom whispered with a sudden case of indigestion.

Ropes shot out of the craft and several soldiers swung down, landing in the middle of the street just a few feet away from them. As soon as they hit the ground, they aimed their weapons at them.

"Freeze!"

"What's the matter with these guys?" Tom said angrily, sick of the relentless trauma that kept coming his way. "Is there a problem?" he called out.

"Shut up and raise your hands!" an approaching soldier ordered.

"We haven't done anything!" Tom protested.

A gunshot exploded through the air, whizzing right above his head.

"I said keep quiet!" the soldier said as the four men rushed toward them.

"Better do as he says," Oriana whispered.

Tom quickly pulled out a piece of paper from his pocket which Ivanovitch had given him. On the crumbled paper was scribbled Andrew's email address, the only link left with the Prophet's disciples. He placed it in Oriana's hand, closing her fingers around it.

"If you want to help me, try to contact this person."

His action made no sense to him since he knew they were both being arrested. But somehow he sensed that she would have a greater chance of being set free.

The soldiers violently took hold of them, turning both of them around and handcuffing them. Tom turned to Oriana to see a soldier push her forward brutally.

"What are you doing?" he said angrily.

A rifle butt cracked him in the back of the head. He fell forward unconscious.

CHAPTER FIFTEEN

The caravan pulled into a little town in the foothills of the Sierra Nevada mountains. Marysville was lost in the woods of northern California, a refuge for loners who still believed in the American myth of rugged individualism.

The cars and vans stopped at a gas station to refill their tanks before heading further into the hinterlands away from the faults that were destroying the geography of the continent. Jeremy got out of the lead car and stretched his legs. The earthquake had been felt that far north. Pavement was cracked and several structures were partly shattered, but it was a far cry from what they had left behind.

Lynn escorted Juanita and the baby to the restrooms while Andrew and Michelle came up to confer with Jeremy. They opened a map.

"We can make it to the Oregon state line by nightfall," Andrew said as he studied the mileage.

"We're in luck," Michelle added. "The Federation has its hands full for now. They won't be looking for us until we're in the Montana wilderness. We just might make it."

"Let's find a restaurant and feed everybody before we cross the state line," Jeremy said.

"Do you think there'll be something open after what's happened?" Michelle asked.

"The damage isn't too bad," Andrew observed as he studied the surroundings. "We'll find something. People have to keep making a living no matter what."

They were interrupted by a light beeping sound coming from Andrew's car.

"What's that?" Jeremy asked, surprised.

Andrew was stunned. "It's my computer calling me!"

A frown darkened Jeremy's features.

"Who would know how to reach you?"

"Not many, that's for sure. I changed my address after the community was disbanded. Mr. Ivanovitch would be the only one to know . . . "

"You'd better answer it, then," Jeremy stated. "Just be sure the Federation can't track the location, otherwise we're sunk."

Michelle took Andrew's arm. "Get the identity of the person before you respond. They can track you down in seconds. You can be sure agents are lurking everywhere in cyberspace. It's one of their chief means of surveillance."

Andrew listened to her carefully, knowing that her years of experience as a Federation agent gave her inside information into the wicked oppression that ruled the earth in the name of security. He hurried to the car and pulled out a small laptop from his satchel. A red light was blinking on and off. He pressed a button and his email appeared immediately on the screen.

"Tom. Who's Tom? I don't know any Toms."

"Yes you do," Michelle said as she looked over his shoulder, a worried look on her face.

"I do?"

"That new guy that Ivanovitch told us about. The one who was with Allan. The one we waited for this morning."

"That's right. If Ivanovitch gave him my address, he must really trust him."

"I don't understand that. How could he trust him so much after only a few hours of knowing him? That's awfully quick," Michelle wondered.

Jeremy walked up to them. "Well, I count on Mr. Ivanovitch's perceptions. If he thought it was safe, then open the message."

Andrew moved the tiny arrow to the envelop icon and pressed the key. A few lines of print appeared full screen: *Tom arrested. Charged with looting and aggravated assault on an officer—both outrageous lies. Will be arraigned in court on Thursday. Please help. They intend to put him away and throw away the key. Somehow they know of his connection with you. Oriana.*

"Who the hell's Oriana?" Andrew cried out, adrenaline turning his face red.

"Scroll down, there's a P.S.," Michelle said.

He did so and another line appeared on the screen. *I am a friend of Tom's. We survived the quake together. He saved my life. Gave me your address just before the arrest. You can reach me at the community address below in San Anselmo.*

"What is she doing in Marin County? It's gotta be a total ruin."

"I thought it had fallen into the ocean already," Michelle added.

"The aftershocks will surely take it out," Lynn said as she joined the group around the computer.

"What can we do for him?" Michelle asked.

"We've gotta keep going," Jeremy stated emphatically. "We can't stop for this. We can't do anything about it."

"What do you mean?" Lynn asked, horrified. "We can't let them destroy this person!"

"We don't even know the guy!" Jeremy said irritably. "What we do know is that we can't walk into a Federation courtroom and pull him out."

"What about this Oriana?" Lynn asked again. "She must be in terrible circumstances as well."

"Everybody's in terrible circumstances, Lynn," Michelle stated somberly. "We've got to get our friends to safer ground."

"We cannot let these people be swallowed up by the Federation! Tom was trying to help us. And who knows where Mr. Ivanovitch is? At the very least, he deserves our careful consideration of this matter!" Lynn insisted.

"I don't know what there is to consider!" Jeremy turned to her and looked deeply into her eyes, trying to find something more rational within her. "What is there to consider, Lynn? We can't sacrifice ourselves for one person. Surely you know that. What we have to do is too important. You know what the Prophet expects of us."

"Yes, I do. And what he expects is that we be compassionate human beings first and foremost. Otherwise we're of no use to the future anyway."

"This is true. But it doesn't mean we should be unreasonable."

"If we let this person be destroyed without trying everything we can to help him, we will be guilty of the sin of omission and we will lose our right to represent the Prophet."

"What do you think we can do?"

"Think about this way, Jeremy. What would the Prophet do?"

Jeremy smiled sadly, remembering their mysterious friend and teacher who was so unlike anyone else. "He would probably go sacrifice himself to help him."

"Can we do any less?" Lynn challenged.

"What about the lives of the people in our charge? What about Juanita and the baby? Do you want to sacrifice them to?"

Lynn was stung by the remark. It was very rare that they had bad feelings toward each other. A hurt expression glistened in her eyes, but she controlled the anger that arose from the pain he had caused her. Talk of the Prophet made it difficult to fall into the standard stimulus-response routine that ruled most lives.

Jeremy witnessed the transmutation of energy in her soul. Her resistance to her own response in spite of his impatient irritation filled him with gratitude for her unselfish efforts to reach for her higher potential and not give way to old habits.

"I'm sorry," he whispered. "Let's think this through carefully."

He took her in his arms and hugged her. It took her a few moments to release the tension in her body, but his touch was magic to her, second only to that of the Prophet himself. Their closeness quickly healed the alienation that had risen between them.

"What do you think we should do?" he asked her in a calm, even voice.

"One of us will have to return and find out what they're charging him with and how his relationship to us is involved in all this."

"What if it's a trap?"

"Then we do what we have to do. If they're destroying this person because of his brief contact with us, maybe they'd be willing to trade."

It was Michelle's turn to be irritated now.

"So which one of us do you suggest ought to give himself up as a burnt offering?"

"I'll do it," Lynn answered softly.

"No you won't!" Jeremy stated in a voice that would not tolerate any disagreement. "You've got other work you must do."

"I'll go," Andrew said solemnly.

"What are you talking about?" Michelle cried out.

"I owe it to the Prophet," he said grimly.

"He told you to stop feeling guilty over what you did in the past. Let it go."

"I'm the right person to go," Andrew insisted.

"What about us?" Michelle asked, her anger now mixed with grief. "Can you just walk away from me like that?"

"It's not about us, Michelle. It's about him," Andrew said gently.

"Who, this Tom person, someone nobody knows? We're worth more than that, aren't we?"

"It's about the Prophet. If we run off like cowards and let other people pay the price for us, then we are not worthy of representing him to the future."

Michelle turned away and walked off to hide her feelings. She knew there was nothing she could say to that and the pain was too intense. Lynn hurried after her and took her by the arm. Michelle pulled away angrily.

"Leave me alone! I blame you for this!"

"That's right, it's my fault."

Lynn took hold of Michelle's arm again and forced her to turn around. The former security agent instinctively took a defense stance, ready to strike. Lynn didn't blink.

"I simply reminded us of our mission. Our lives are worth nothing if we can't be what the Prophet has called us to be."

"If Andrew goes to his death, I'll never forgive you!" Michelle hissed, eyes narrowing with hate.

"I thought you were totally committed to the Prophet's cause," Lynn said calmly.

"I am! Don't you dare question it. You know what I've sacrificed already. It's got nothing to do with this. We're wasting a good man for nothing!"

"Justice and truth are not nothing . . . They're everything."

"Don't get high and mighty with me, Lynn. I knew

him also. You weren't the only one who was close to him."

"I'm just trying to remind you of not only what we have to do, but what we have to *be*."

"We can't *be*," Michelle said sarcastically, "if we're dead, now can we? Sending Andrew back into the jaws of the Federation in this moment of crisis is asking him to immolate himself on your lofty principles. Don't you think he'd be much more useful to us in our attempt to survive for the long haul in the wilderness? That's where we need him! Not in some Federation prison cell!"

"That's right, we need him. But it's not worth surviving at all if we can't live rightly."

"So saving this stranger who didn't even know the Prophet is the way to live rightly?"

"You're looking at this so negatively, Michelle. Maybe this can be dealt with quietly without too much trouble. We're just talking about investigating the situation."

"Investigating in the middle of the worst earthquake to hit the coast in recorded history? Don't you know how insane the government is right now? They'll shoot people in the streets for no reason at all. This is the opportunity the Federation's been looking for to turn into a completely fascist organization. General MacDaniel will issue shoot to kill orders for the slightest offence."

"So we let this person die for having gotten in touch with us?"

"He made his choices, just like we all did."

"It seems that Andrew has made his choice as well."

Michelle grit her teeth together, grinding them into her jaws. She had the urge to strike the woman who was taking her lover away from her.

"If he dies, I'll hold you responsible."

"You'd better be responsible for your own behavior,

Michelle," Lynn said coldly. "I thought you'd learned to better control the violence of your nature. You know what the Prophet had to say about that. It's all a waste of time if you're just going to wallow in the ghetto of your nature."

"Wallow?" Michelle cried out. "How dare you?"

"Look at yourself. You're ready to draw blood from me. Isn't there another way? Isn't what this is all about?"

"Don't preach to me, Lynn! You're taking away from me the only thing I've got left. How do you expect me to feel?"

"I expect you to remember what's at stake and what the Prophet died for."

Michelle turned away from her.

"Don't you realize Michelle that behaving this way turns you into one of them?" Lynn continued. "The whole point of the Prophet's mission was to create a remnant that doesn't respond with violence and hate. They're not even considered an option. If we can't do that, there is no chance of renewal after the Tribulation."

"You really think we're going to survive these catastrophes?" Michelle asked as a cynical grimace distorted her features.

"Of course! We must! If we don't, the Prophet's work is wasted!"

"You think a lot of yourself, don't you, Lynn?"

"Why do you say that?"

"We're just ordinary people. Why should we be the ones to somehow renew humanity. That's pretty grandiose thinking!"

"What's happening to you, Michelle? You didn't think that way when the Prophet was among us."

"That's right. He cast a spell over me. Made me think I could be somebody I'm not."

Lynn was horrified by her friend's words. "What's come over you? There's nothing else in life worth doing than to seek your highest potential. Otherwise you're useless to the universe."

"Right now I'm useless to myself and to Andrew. I don't give a damn about the universe or the human race for that matter!"

Lynn took hold of her shoulders and shook her. "What demon has possessed you? Snap out of this!"

Michelle pulled away and pushed Lynn back with a sharp strike of her palms against her chest. Lynn fell back against a tree. Watching from a distance, Jeremy stepped forward but Andrew took hold of him.

"Let them work this out or it will never be resolved."

"She'd better not hit her!" Jeremy said. The words caught in his throat as he realized that the poison polluting Michelle's mind and heart was contagious, taking hold of him as well.

"Let them work it out, Jeremy," Andrew said calmly. "You know it's how it's gotta be."

Jeremy turned away, disgusted at himself and at the alienation that was taking place among close friends.

Lynn stared at Michelle sadly, realizing that she was eagerly awaiting for an excuse to attack. The deep sadness in Lynn's eyes acted as a mirror and Michelle became aware of herself. She looked down at her closed fist.

"What the hell am I doing?" she cried out.

She stepped out of her warrior stance and relaxed her muscles, letting go of the savage energy.

"What am I doing?" she whispered again, on the edge of tears.

"Don't you see that's how the enemy conquers us. It begins inside each one of us. One moment of inattention and we can be bulldozed by these dark forces. We lose our will, our ideals, our knowledge. We become slaves!"

Michelle looked away, shaken to the core of her being. It no longer mattered what the initial stimulus was that had sent her into this abyss of violence.

Andrew came up behind her and put his hand on Lynn's shoulder.

"I'll take care of this, Lynn."

He hurried after Michelle and took her in his arms. She broke down in bitter sobs. Lynn returned to the car where Jeremy awaited her.

"This is too hard," she whispered. "I don't know how he imagined that we could live up to his expectations."

"The Prophet only asked us to stick to our choices. That's what you're doing, Lynn. Let Michelle make her own."

She looked up at her beloved husband. "Do you think I'm making a mistake?" she asked, no longer sure of herself. He shook his head, smiled lovingly at her, and leaned forward to kiss her full, warm lips.

Andrew walked away from Michelle who hurried off further away from the group to hide her pain and shame. He spoke somberly with Jeremy. It was agreed that they would stay in electronic contact and that he would meet them in two weeks outside of the Indian reservation where the secret caves would keep them safe. The men hugged warmly, knowing it could be for the last time. Andrew turned to Lynn and hugged her as well. In so doing, he let her know that he did not hold her responsible for his decision. The burden of his future would not be on her shoulders.

* * * * *

The city of San Francisco was in a condition of utter disaster. Electricity had been out for days and bodies still lay rotting in the rubble. Emergency teams could not put a dent in the gigantic catastrophe. The army had been called in and swarmed down upon the city like an invading force. Platoons moved through the debris, shooting looters on sight. Though the government claimed to still be functioning and some attempt was made at returning to normal procedures as though civilization could limp forward through this cataclysm, details like individual rights were forgotten about. Any kind of semblance of law and order could only be maintained at the point of a gun.

Andrew drove carefully over the shattered roadways winding their way toward the city. The closer he got to the Bay Area, the more catastrophic was the damage he encountered. He felt like he was in some kind of bad dream taking place in a surrealistic set that wasn't even trying to look like the reality he once knew. Cars were turned upside down and abandoned like the carcasses of giant metallic bugs littering the countryside. Houses had slid down cliffs and formed bizarre sculptures of death at the bottom. Even the ocean had changed color into a freakish yellowish tint that was profoundly unsettling. Something was wrong at the very heart of Nature itself.

He had contacted Oriana over the WorldNet and was to meet her in a park on the outskirts of the once luxurious haven in Marin County. From miles away he could hear sirens rising with the smoke that darkened three quarters of the sky, announcing the degree of devastation.

The day was heavily overcast by a mixture of thick smoke and grey clouds weighing heavily over the damaged landscape. A harsh wind whistled ferociously and raced about in all directions, carrying with it the stench of decay and toxic fumes. Some turbulent disturbance in the atmosphere was also traumatizing the air currents.

The Bay Area was still in shock from the catastrophe.

Emergency crews continued their nonstop efforts to save broken bodies from under the rubble. But now people were so tired that they worked mechanically as though going about some ordinary business. Sirens weren't as blaring anymore or were so taken for granted that they no longer pierced through the air as they once did.

The gas fires were pretty much under control. Thousands upon thousands of homeless were gathering in shelters, haggard and disoriented. It was the first day of relative sanity since the monster quake.

Dressed in jeans and a sweatshirt, Oriana waited patiently near a collapsed concession stand in the park. Her features were marred by fatigue and a strange, distant look in her eyes. This young woman whose mysterious past had entangled her with the freakish cult now found herself with one foot in each camp. The extremity of the situation rendered her as displaced as the sea of homeless refugees who surrounded her for miles around.

She raised her melancholic brown eyes upon hearing a car pull up. Andrew appeared in her field of vision—tall, slender, intense. She watched this man, one of the Prophet's key disciples, approach her. This would be the first time she encountered someone from the inner circle of the man who had announced this terrible drama. She stood to let him know that she was the one he had come to find, although there was no one else in the area.

He came within a few feet of her and stopped.

"Oriana?" he asked coolly.

She shook her head and studied his angular features. The former intellectual had been remolded by the shattering experiences of the recent past. There was a quality of sensitive perception shimmering in his eyes, born out of his close encounter with the Final Prophet and the traumatic events that had followed in his wake.

"What do we do now?" he asked.

"Let's talk," she answered, eyes glazed over with an emotionless expression.

Andrew looked around to make sure the area was safe. There was not a soul anywhere. The place was abandoned as people went about the business of meeting their immediate survival needs. Andrew sat down at the concrete picnic table that had survived the upheaval. He studied her carefully as she removed a wave of dark hair wrapped around her face by the angry wind.

"Who are you?" he inquired in a suspicious tone.

"All you need to know is that I'm a friend of Tom."

"I don't know that person."

A surprise look came over her. "Then why are you here?"

"If we can help him, we will, just as he tried to help us. How did you meet him?"

"That's not important," she replied.

"Do you know where he is now?"

"They've got him locked up in the county jail down the road."

"It survived the quake?"

"It did. Frank Lloyd Wright designed it, you know. I guess he knew what he was doing."

"How are you managing to survive?"

"I'm all right. This is not about me."

"Do you have any suggestions as to what we can do for this Tom?"

She removed another strand of hair from her eyes. "You're one of the Prophet's disciples, right?"

Andrew hesitated before responding. His gut told him that it was dangerous to answer that question. But his mind still ruled over him. He hadn't learned yet to give priority to those fleeting intuitions.

"I am."

"And you were traveling with the others before coming here?"

"That's right," he answered, suddenly concerned by her questions. "Why do you ask?"

"I don't understand why you risked coming back," she said sadly. "Where were you headed?"

"With all due respect, that's none of your business."

"I'm sorry . . . I was just curious as to why you came back. Would you like to see Tom?"

"Do you think that's possible?"

"Certainly. You can pose as his lawyer or something."

"You mean the government is still doing business as usual in the midst of all this?"

"That's all they know how to do."

"How can we get him out of there?"

"They've got no charges against him. He's done nothing wrong. I'm sure all they want is to locate your friends."

"Well, that's not gonna happen."

"Maybe we can use the system itself to get him out."

"Not if they've declared martial law. All the rules are suspended."

"We might convince them that a swap is possible?"

"How do you mean?"

"Maybe you can make a deal with them and give them false information for his release."

"Surely they're not that easily fooled."

"You'd be surprised. Especially now that everything's in such chaos."

"I'm prepared to do whatever I can. That's why I'm here."

"Thank you."

Oriana leaned forward and placed her hand on his wrist. He was surprised by her action and unsettled by her soft skin on his. Suddenly her hand squeezed tightly around his wrist and turned into an iron grip.

"What are you doing?" he cried out as he tried to pull

his arm away. But he couldn't escape her grip. Before he could make another move, she rose and twisted his arm inside out, a savage look in her eyes. The motion slammed his head against the concrete table. Adrenaline surged through his body on a wave of rage. He tried to jump to his feet. At that moment, the palm of her hand crashed with full force against his extended elbow. He let out a shout of agony as he felt his cartilage tear.

He attempted to stand again in a wild effort to strike back at this sudden attack on his person. But another pair of hands took hold of his head and pulled him back with brute force. He fell off the bench, slamming to the ground on his back. An army boot came down on his throat, cutting off his ability to breathe. He gasped and looked up to find himself staring at a Federation soldier aiming a machine gun in his face. Completely disoriented by the pain and surprise assault, he turned to see Oriana standing a few feet away. At her side stood several soldiers and the most bizarre looking man he'd ever seen. A sadistic grin creased Dr. Tagore's gruesome features. Then everything turned black as he passed out from lack of oxygen.

* * * * *

Andrew was led into a large room lit by dim, sickly green light. The room's atmosphere had a quality of desolation and hopelessness. Several policemen stood in the far end of the room with sullen expressions on their faces that never changed, almost like androids fulfilling their duty.

Raised high over the chairs and tables was the judge's bench. A stern old woman in black robes lorded it over the fellow humans brought before her. Most of the people there were the scum of the earth, uneducated and poor people whose future had died out long ago. There in the center of this wretched crowd and cold authority stood Andrew. He couldn't feel more out of place. Handcuffed criminals were brought in, men who had committed violent acts for a lifetime. They sat in a chair that he soon would sit in beneath the all-powerful robed representative of the Federation.

Prosecutors and lawyers spoke to each other in a language all their own. The lives of the human beings involved seemed irrelevant. It was all a chess game. In the last few decades, no one had outmaneuvered the rule of law. Prosecutors adhered more and more rigidly to the letter of the law instead of its spirit. People were tossed into tiny cells for endless years, regardless of the severity of their crime. The only way to keep order in these chaotic times was to be merciless. No one seemed to notice that it didn't work. Desperation was such that crime continued to soar, people continued their free-fall into psychotic behavior, and jails were packed beyond capacity.

Andrew realized for the first time that once he entered the cave of this monster, he wouldn't come out the same. They wouldn't let him. All the power belonged to the authorities and their primary interest was to crush any deviance from their requirements. The law had long ago forgotten the philosophy that one was innocent until proven guilty. In this day and age, everyone who walked into these dimly lit warehouses ironically called halls of justice was considered guilty. The old statues of blindfolded justice now had new meaning. Justice was indeed blind, but not as it was once understood. The balance that the goddess held in her hand didn't stand for fairness but for control.

Andrew could smell the stale odor of cigarettes and uncleanliness all around him. He wondered if the judge was raised above this mass of miserable humanity to avoid having to take in its stench. Case after case was processed ahead of him. People were sent off to lives of confinement without expectation of rehabilitation. Punishment was the name of the game.

He watched as desperate criminals were presented to the judge and led through a door in the back of the room toward a fate that made his hair stand on end. How did he get to this point? He thought of the insane series of events that had brought him to this unimaginable moment where he was being handed over to the lions who would devour him for certain. The machine of the law would destroy him more effectively than the punks in the street who lusted for blood.

Files were passed back and forth between the judge and her assistants. People were moved through the system at amazing speed. The woman behaved with a strange condescending attitude toward all who came in her presence, acting the part of a benevolent and impartial observer when in fact she had the power to decide human destinies at the blink of an eye. Andrew knew that behind the mask of smooth control and politeness was a Federation-trained puppet whose only purpose was to protect the state or in this case the world government against people like him who refused to step into line with the rest of the sheep. He knew that the moment she opened his file and saw the charges, she would treat him more vehemently than she had the common criminals who filed past her day after day. He was a choice grist for the mill that crushed those who could not be controlled.

He found himself shaking with fear. He had never felt so completely helpless. Already he could imagine the sensation of cold handcuffs squeezing his wrists and the horrifying walk through that back door to a world where there was neither freedom nor sunlight. He thought of the betrayal that had taken place. How could Oriana have done this to him? The woman had no remorse at all. He could almost accept the fact that the lovely young lady was part of some dark conspiracy with the dominators to destroy whatever good was left in the world. What he couldn't accept was that no help from beyond was pulling him out of the grips of this merciless system. He would be rendered useless to the Prophet's cause and his efforts to do right in this wretched world would come to nothing.

The hope that the Prophet's spirit would be present with some of his follower now stirred intense rage. Why was he left out? Wasn't he the one who had given all his material goods to the Prophet's community and risked his life to help his friends? Now when it was his turn to be in need, he was not only betrayed but abandoned by all and left to a fate that no one deserved, least of all those who sought to be helpers of the human cause.

He looked up at the dull panel walls bathed in green, depressing light and listened to the droning on of the judge's voice and the case numbers called out by the bailiff one after the other. There was no room for human feelings here, only efficient destruction of lives. No one who came through this room would be the same afterward and most would wish they'd never been born. Andrew felt that way now, heartsick that he was being thrown into the abyss for having tried to help his fellow humans. He would have been better off becoming one of the dominators like his father before him, a rich contributor to the status quo and guaranteed a life of comfort and luxury. All he had to do was not care what happened to those who were less fortunate. Even with the world devastation, the super wealthy could find ways to protect themselves and satisfy their bodily needs while others died in the cold.

Andrew dropped his head in his hands, trying to clear his mind. He felt nausea rising from the depths of his soul. It was all so unfair. He had given up on human justice long ago, but he held out hope that some cosmic check and balance was in operation. He remembered the moment this set of circumstances had fallen into alignment. Like dominoes, one thing led to another, each furthering his descent into this place of despair.

CHAPTER SIXTEEN

Andrew was taken into an empty, dimly-lit concrete room in the lower levels of the police station. A wooden table and several chairs were the only furnishings.

"Sit down!" a policeman ordered as he pushed him toward one of the chairs.

Andrew looked back at the brute and shook his head. The man turned red with anger and smacked him in the temple.

"What the hell you looking at? Do what I tell ya!"

He kicked Andrew in the back of the knee, causing him to lose his balance and shoved him into a chair.

"When I tell you to sit, you sit! Is that clear?"

The man abruptly left the room, leaving Andrew in the grim silence of the underground chamber. The contrast to the noise of the courtroom made him dizzy. He was so stunned by the sudden turn of events that he couldn't think straight. He had barely stabilized himself long enough to become aware of his own breathing when footsteps echoed outside the door. A quick pattern of beeps announced the unlocking of the entrance. Two men entered. He was too worn out and distressed to look up.

They sat at the table on either side of him.

"So how are you feeling today, Mister Bradshaw?" a gravely voice asked, full of sarcasm.

Andrew looked up and found himself face to face with the freakish Dr. Tagore. Strands of white hair hung from his skull. The skeletal thinness of his face and grizzled skin from illness or burns gave off an aura of evil. But it was the eyes that especially revealed the reality of his nature. They sparkled with sadistic glee. Andrew had never looked into such perverse energy before. Except perhaps for the fleeting glimpse he'd had of Stefan Zorn when he'd come to their community. He felt certain that the association he had made in his mind between this man and the occult leader was no accident. He sensed that they were linked together, both servants of darkness.

In that moment, he remembered the Prophet's words that they be prepared to face a powerful enemy. It was not until now that Andrew understood what he had meant. His words were more than symbolic. They referred to the very incarnation of evil.

"Do you know what we want?" the strange cadaver-like man asked, eyes sizzling with lust for violence.

Andrew looked over at the other man and saw that he was a high ranking officer in the military. They made a very odd pair. Andrew's mind went into high gear. Obviously, the man of darkness was somehow allied with leaders of the Federation.

"No idea," Andrew said calmly.

Dr. Tagore let out a hoarse chuckle. "Nice try." He turned to the officer.

"Colonel, tell this poor man what he's in for if he doesn't cooperate."

"We've been ordered to apply all available means in order to get the information we need from you," the military man said as though he wished he didn't have to. It was clear that he was under orders and not happy about dealing with the likes of the evil man across the table from him. Strings were being pulled from high up the chain of command.

Andrew looked at the officer. He seemed like a decent sort and he was obviously not looking forward to being turned into a torturer. In that instant, Andrew felt sorry for him.

"Who is this man?" Andrew asked the Colonel, as though he were asking a fellow human about some alien being.

"You don't ask the questions. We do!" Tagore responded.

"Is he part of the government?" Andrew continued, staring directly at the officer, seeking out some kind of humanity in him.

"You're really asking for it, Bradshaw!" Tagore said again, eyes widening as his pockmarked skin turned purple with rage.

"Don't I have a right to know who I'm talking with?" Andrew pressed on, staring at the Colonel. "I'm still a citizen of this country."

"You've got nothing left!" Tagore spouted out venomously.

"Enough!" the Colonel barked, unable to withstand the strange civilian's flaunting of authority. There was only so far he would allow him to invade his territory.

"You're here because you are an enemy of this government and you've confessed it already."

"What do you mean?" Andrew asked, confused.

The Colonel pulled out a small digital tape recorder from his pocket and pressed the play button. Andrew's conversation with Oriana instantly came out loud and clear. It was cued to his words about tricking the government in order to help Tom.

Andrew shook his head. He couldn't believe the immensity of the trap he'd fallen into. His situation was hopeless.

"You have a choice," the Colonel said. Either you give us the information we need and we will provide you with immunity, or you talk to us because you'll want to very badly."

"What are you going to do to me?" Andrew asked defiantly.

"It's gonna hurt real bad," Tagore said, revealing his large brown teeth. He looked more like a demented mummy on the loose than a living human being.

The Colonel looked at him with growing irritation. "We'll fill you with enough truth serum to tell us whatever we want. Surely you know that we have the technology necessary for such purposes."

"I know my rights! I won't say another word until I have a lawyer!"

Dr. Tagore let out a high-pitched cackle. "Everything's changed, Mr. Bradshaw. Nothing is like it used to be. You should know that."

"What do you want with my friends, anyway? We're not going to hurt anybody."

"That's for us to decide," Tagore said, eyes narrowing into slits.

"Who's we?" Andrew asked defiantly.

"Just won't stop asking questions, will he?" Tagore said to the officer. "What are we going to do about this, Colonel?"

"You'd better answer us, mister," the officer muttered coldly, "or we're going to take you downstairs. You don't want to go into the subbasement, believe me."

"This is the United States of America, damn it!"

"This is the world Federation at a time of dangerous chaos," Tagore corrected, "and you and your friends have only added to the instability."

"And *your* friends aren't?" Andrew challenged. He turned to the Colonel. "I'll bet you don't know who this guy is either, do you? Well, I've got a pretty good guess.

He works for the forces of destruction. He's your enemy, not me!"

"Be silent!" Tagore shouted. "You have no power here. Your situation is hopeless. Don't make it worse for yourself. Just take him downstairs, Colonel. This is a waste of my time."

Andrew looked sharply at the military officer. "Are you going to obey this goon from Hell? Is that why you rose up the ranks? To be a slave to evil?"

Tagore jumped up and swung his ivory cane at Andrew's head. With surprising speed, the Colonel leaped up and blocked it with his forearm.

"You don't do that!" the Colonel shouted, his face scarlet red. "Law and order still prevail, regardless of whose strings you're pulling."

Tagore turned an unsettled look upon him. He couldn't afford to lose the man's cooperation. He had to swallow back his hatred of Andrew who had outmaneuvered him, even from his position of weakness. The savage man couldn't tolerate not having absolute power. It was his one and only aphrodisiac. But he was too smart to let whatever emotions he had rule over him.

"Sorry about your arm, Colonel," he said apologetically.

"You'll be a lot sorrier if this happens again! This man is in my custody, and we'll follow the rules of war laid down by the Federation."

"Yes sir," Tagore responded, a sarcastic smile distorting his gruesome features. Andrew thought he was going to salute him in mockery. But the man knew better and sat down, straightening his old-fashioned smock.

"Mr. Bradshaw, I'll give you one more chance to save yourself. We're going to find your friends anyway, so why don't you just make it easier on us and on you. They've got no place to go. There's nowhere they can hide. Not from the world Federation."

A strange thought came to Andrew's numbed mind. It had the flash of sudden inspiration, so he acted on it.

"I'll make a deal with you. You release Tom and let him go free, and I'll do what I can to cooperate."

Tagore looked at him suspiciously.

"Why would you want to do that?"

"That's why I'm here. To let this innocent man go free and take his place."

Tagore focused his gaze deep into Andrew's soul, searching for the strategy he knew had to be there. Andrew stared back at him with a blank look on his face, knowing the man was trying to read his mind. He did his best not to think any thoughts.

"My orders were to free this man. So that's what I'm going to do."

"If you're trying to trick me," Tagore hissed, "I'll have you skinned alive! You have my word on that!"

"You'll do no such thing!" the Colonel responded, outraged. "We'll proceed by the book!" He was getting tired of the freakish man's savage violence.

This time Tagore ignored him and kept staring at Andrew, letting him know silently that his promise would be fulfilled. Unspeakable horror awaited him if he dared to betray him.

"Do you want your information or not?" Andrew said bitterly, wishing he could get his fingers around the evil man's thin throat.

The violent urge struck him like an electric shock. He heard a voice in his head.

"*Violence is contagious*."

A chill ran through him and beads of sweat appeared on his forehead. The voice was that of the Prophet himself. It echoed in his head more vividly than any memory he'd ever recalled. It was as though his beloved teacher had leaned over and whispered in his ear. The message also came through loud and clear. He realized that the desire to kill had been stimulated by the bestial brutality emanating from the wretched creature across the table from him. The toxic energy had penetrated unconsciously into his psyche. He found himself behaving at the level of this creature from the Netherworld.

Dr. Tagore watched him intensely, seeing the disturbance flash in his eyes. He tried to detect what was going on within him.

"*Seal yourself!*" the voice said again imperatively.

Andrew focused all his attention on the benevolent order he had just received. An invisible wall rose up between him and Tagore, cutting off the influence the man was having upon him and shielding his vulnerable soul from the dark energies to which he was exposed. His heart raced within him and a hot flash made him nearly faint. This time he knew that those words were not memory but immediate communication from the man whom he had watched die not long ago. The sense of his presence was so powerful that he felt certain the Prophet's spirit was in the room with him, standing behind him and helping him become hermetically sealed to the evil that confronted him.

It was as though the degree of Dr. Tagore's darkness had beckoned forth a light from beyond where the Prophet now lived.

"Are you all right?" the Colonel asked, noticing the change in skin color as Andrew turned ghostly pale.

Andrew managed to control himself enough to nod his head affirmatively.

"I've been fighting off the flue," he responded.

The Colonel accepted the answer, but Tagore knew better. A fierce glint in his eye revealed the heat of violent hate that burned forever in his black soul. He knew that something mysterious was taking place and that worried him greatly.

* * * * *

Oriana sat in the dark room which was hardly larger than a closet and served as her bedroom. She needed silence and obscurity to cover her shame. On the other side of the wall, she could hear the whispered conversations of the other members of her group, the only family she had ever known.

Now every time she saw them, she was filled with repulsion. They had asked too much of her and her lifelong training in the occult arts was not enough to obliterate the feelings rising out of her heart. She was still a human being, despite all the careful efforts of her teachers and companions who had relentlessly attempted to mold her into the perfect servant of their aims, which were now revealing themselves as darkness and destruction.

From earliest childhood, she remembered participating in mysterious activities and going into trances. Early on, she had become fascinated by the strange tales and rituals that were as much part of her daily life as the making of peanut butter cookies was for other children of her age. Her world was Gothic, grim, and shrouded in secrecy. Madame de Belmar was her aunt, but had been a more of a mother to her since her birth mother had died in a tragic fire that had also taken the life of her father. Dr. Tagore had come in and out of her life at every stage of her development. She had become habituated to his gruesome features long ago, but in the recesses of her soul she was still as frightened of him as when she was child. The evil emanating from him was tangible.

In spite of their bizarre ways and the myths they discussed as though they were headline news, these people nevertheless lived the life of a tightly knit community. They provided her with the basics for survival. She was never in need for food or money. They had taken her to Europe several times where she was treated like a princess by foreign members of the sect. She had adapted well to their secretive life-style and learned all the esoteric texts and teachings that were so important to them. But she had never played with anyone her age or gone to school with her peers. She lived alone like a rare and precious jewel carefully tended and monitored by the dozens of people who made up her family.

Oriana had always been a serious, reflective person. Her inherited clairvoyant gifts were legendary among her companions. Her parents had been key members of the organization, as had their parents before them. They were masters of the more psychic elements of the teachings. Their death had been a terrible loss, even though the details were left unspoken. Among the many ways in which she had been manipulated into becoming a perfect member was the painful fact that they had intentionally distorted her development. Her childhood had been barren of play; her youth was devoid of romance; and now her adult years were entirely focused on the requirements of the group.

Despite their best efforts, tender feelings still bubbled to the surface and the increasingly difficult tasks they gave her only intensified the awakening of that repressed part of her nature. Tom had been the first man to break through the ice of her carefully sculpted facade. The destruction of the Prophet's disciple had served to break in the door completely. Andrew's last tragic look at her before passing out haunted her relentlessly. She couldn't get the image out of her mind. It was stuck there on the screen of her inner eye like some broken monitor that couldn't be turned off.

No book, no tale of ancient fellowships and beings from other realms could overcome the breakthrough of her conscience. All of her training, from advanced self-defense to the study of lost languages, collapsed before that look of agony that pierced her soul. She had never been taught about good and evil, but only about power and weakness. Her companions had fed her subconscious with a sense of duty toward her departed parents. She had to carry on their legacy with this lofty and ancient secret society whose roots reached back into antiquity and whose destiny was finally to be fulfilled in this age.

Never before had she experienced such an encounter with this burning, gut-wrenching sensation of guilt. She'd had nothing to be guilty for prior to these events. Now at the very dawn of her maturing into a full-fledged member of the group, her whole world was collapsing before her. No one had ever told her about right and wrong. All the teachings she had absorbed were couched in the context of warring cosmic forces that titillated the mind but never engaged the heart. There was no avoiding those eyes that had looked upon her and reached into the very depths of her being with one all-consuming question—*why*? Andrew's question was now hers.

Her companions would have given her a quick answer. He was the enemy, interfering with their centuries-old plan, and he had to be destroyed. But that wasn't good enough for her anymore.

She stood up and paced back and forth in the darkness. The makeshift home they had found after the quake was not large enough to provide everyone with private space. This was not the first time that she found herself camping out with the cult members. Life had always been a bohemian journey on the outskirts of society and she had enjoyed the variety that it brought into her life. Until today. Everything had lost its savor. What was once an adventure now felt like a gloomy repetition full of sound and fury signifying nothing. Nothing except the destruction of other people.

If she could question one aspect of their mission, then everything was up for grabs. The look in Andrew's eyes was inescapable. Something was terribly wrong and no brainwashing in the world could keep her from seeing the tortured eyes of the man she had trapped and captured to satisfy the secret goals of the mysterious group. Somehow, the Egyptian symbolism and ritualistic formulas, talismans and antique ornaments now sounded empty and looked old and withered, even absurd.

Pacing in the tiny room, she became aware that the narrow confines surrounding her represented perfectly the condition of her entire life. She had never been let out of the closet. She had lived an inbred existence, fed only what the group wanted her to think and feel. They had never let her out in the light of day where she might form some opinions of her own. Despite her brilliant intelligence and encyclopedic knowledge, she suddenly realized that she had never had a thought of her own. She was a machine full of recordings she had stored away in the libraries of her mind. She could teach postgraduate classes all they'd ever want to know about the sources of Freemasonry and the secrets of the high priests of early Egyptian Dynasties. She could write a whole series of books on occult symbolism and its travels through time, but she couldn't tell simple right from wrong.

Oriana was horrified at the creature she had grown into. She felt like vomiting every time the sensation came back to her of twisting Andrew's arm and cracking his elbow. She was a black belt in Goshu Shorei karate and had long gotten use to physical contact as though it was merely mathematics of the body or some intensified dance. It never penetrated her heart that it was savage and brutal. Even physical abuse was justified by the principles and mission of the arrogant group. When she was younger, she couldn't dare question the wisdom of her ancestors and the awesome figures that were quoted to her on a daily basis—Madame Blavatsky, Jacques De Molay, Pharaoh Sequenenre II, Aldous Huxley and all the rest. They were mythic figures, heroes of her past. She had come to know them in a way that other children enjoyed the heroes sold to them on television. She'd been told that the man known as the Final Prophet was the arch enemy, the one who would interfere with the ultimate purpose of this ancient lineage, a purpose which was nothing less than the domination of humanity.

She'd been given a thousand reasons why higher intelligences needed this work accomplished and what the consequences would be if humans were not brought to their knees in the worship of forces who were said to rule this part of the universe. Gnostics myths and archetypal psychology had taken her so far from simple reality and common sense that she had lost sight of her humanity.

She brought her hands to her face and was surprised to find that her cheeks were soaking wet with salty tears. She couldn't remember the last time she had wept. That again was a clue as to how far she had drifted from her essential self on the current of illusion generated by her leaders. Now Madame de Belmar, Dr. Tagore and the rest of them seemed so ugly, evil, and dark. How was it that she had never seen that before? She remembered how the beady, glimmering eyes of the repulsive doctor had lit up with a perverse joy at Andrew's capture and literally turned her stomach. Madame de

Belmar had taken the place of her mother long ago, but behind her dignified, aristocratic features she was as cold as ice. The high curvature of her eyebrows now revealed the haughtiness of her nature rather than the stamp of nobility Oriana had always attributed to her. In one horrifying shift of scenery, these people were now revealed in all their sordid nakedness—grisly, heartless creatures who served ignoble purposes.

Oriana had never really been told what the great mission was, but she was assured that she would be initiated into the secret when she got older. She had accepted that, patiently and with reverence. Now two men faced possible death because of her naivete and her lack of discernment that had allowed her to betray both of them for some fantasy she no longer even understood.

The door to her room swung open. The tall silhouette of Madame de Belmar stood in the light.

"What's the matter?" she asked in a husky voice.

The woman peered at her with the eyes of a cat on the hunt, searching out the mind of the young woman who wept in the dark.

No words came to Oriana's mind. She spoke four languages, had memorized an entire Thesaurus, but not a single word—not an adverb—came to her mind. This woman whom she had admired all her life, though she'd been distant and unaffectionate, now seemed like a predatory fiend. Her changes in perception were happening so fast that Oriana thought she was losing her mind.

"I asked you a question," the woman stated coldly.

"I'm confused," Oriana finally said.

Lying was foreign to her. She didn't know how to do it, although she had learned to repress her more vulnerable feelings over the years.

"Don't let that man poison your mind."

"What man?"

"The man from the park."

"He's not . . . "

"Yes he is!" Madame de Belmar interrupted. "You're upset with what you had to do, aren't you?"

Oriana nodded, although it was only half the truth. But it was close enough. She realized that lying wasn't that hard after all. It could be very safe.

"His poison is contagious. Beware."

"Why did we have to do this?"

"We've discussed these matters thoroughly! We thought you were mature enough to deal with this. Don't disappoint me, Oriana."

"I don't want to do that," Oriana said, lying again.

"We thought you had the inner strength and skill to be useful to us."

"I did too," Oriana mumbled, finally speaking the truth.

"It certainly doesn't look like it. Why can't you just see it as crushing a nasty bug to protect your garden?"

"He's not a bug, he's a human being."

"He is a bug!" the woman growled. With that sound, all of her feminine beauty vanished, revealing eyes full of hate and violence, a terrain where no beauty could grow.

"This man would enjoy seeing us all shot! Why do you feel sorry for him?"

"I no longer understand why he's our enemy . . . He seemed like a good person."

"Don't be so naive, Oriana!" the woman responded angrily, her features tightening with disdain. "I've told you before. It's a problem you've got to deal with head on. You know nothing about the world and you're easily fooled. Besides," she said pulling out a thin cigar from a gold case which she lit with the expertise of long habit, "being a 'good' person is not something to be admired. It's weakness and foolishness as the masters have said.

Instead of whimpering in the dark, you should be proud of what you've done."

She leaned against the doorway and inhaled the acrid smoke, letting it return into the air through her tight, thin nostrils. "You overcame an adversary with physical force. That was an initiation for you and you succeeded. This behavior you're exhibiting now is very disappointing to me."

She turned her glare upon the young person she had brought up as her own.

"I thought you had reached a new level of strength."

For her entire life, Oriana had submissively accepted the reprimands of this harsh woman. But this time, something struck her as unbearably wrong. She couldn't be passive anymore. She stepped into the dim light in the doorway.

"What is so brave and noble about luring someone into a trap and breaking his arm while having a friendly conversation?"

A slight smile crossed Madame de Belmar's heavily made-up lips. They clashed with her blonde-died hair. Despite her deep beliefs in esoteric philosophies, she was as intent upon delaying the ravages of age as any woman who lived on the surface of her nature where vanity ruled.

"Think of the big picture. Think of our mission and the culmination of generations who are a part of you. You're fulfilling their dream. You're a player in a mighty drama and you took center stage for a moment. We all depended on you and you came through. This whining makes me sick!"

She inhaled the sweet smelling smoke and released it with a long sigh. "Get hold of yourself. I don't want the doctor to find you like this."

She had always referred to Dr. Tagore as "the doctor." After all these years, Oriana still didn't know what kind of doctor he was—medical or academic. Maybe he wasn't a doctor of anything. She had only recently begun to wonder what the history of this strange couple might be. They had been together her whole life, an odd platonic twosome united around common goals. She was a stunning aristocratic beauty while he was a man whose ugliness was unparalleled, except perhaps in burn wards. Now Oriana was being told to shape up in order not to disappoint him also.

"I did what you wanted me to do. Isn't that enough?" she blurted out.

"No, it isn't!" the woman said, looking into her eyes. "We need to count on you still. We can't afford to have any doubts. It's all just beginning. There is a long way to go."

"You expect me to brake someone else's arm?"

Madame de Belmar placed the thin cigar between her teeth and gritted the stem with anger. "I expect you to do whatever we require of you and have no opinion on the matter! Just like everyone else here."

She stepped forward, within inches of Oriana. "Maybe I've spoiled you too much. You think you're different from the rest of us. But you're not. You'll give your all to our mission—your life if you have to—and you won't complain or question ever again!"

The women studied each other defiantly. Oriana knew that their relationship would never be the same. It was the first break with the woman's hold on her soul. Madame de Belmar saw it all in her eyes.

"And if you don't show your total loyalty at all times, I'll turn you over to the doctor."

Her eyes narrowed with a hatred that made Oriana's blood run cold. They had never been close, but she had never seen such venom in the woman's behavior. Nor had she any idea of what the implications were in the threat. But she could sense that much was left unsaid as though the woman was somehow jealous of her. Apparently, she had been standing between Dr. Tagore and Oriana's safety for many years.

"And if that doesn't take care of things, I'll go to the master himself."

The master . . . Oriana had only seen him a few times in her life. But it was all she needed to know about real power and danger. Stefan Zorn had only glanced at her and she'd had nightmares for years afterward.

CHAPTER SEVENTEEN

The jail door slide open with a strange iron hiss and Andrew was pushed into a dark, smelly cell. The force of the policeman's thrust landed him against the humid wall. He heard the heavy door slide back and an electronic lock shut him in like the lid of a coffin.

For a moment, he remained in that position, his cheek pressed against the cold concrete block. He had a sudden urge to weep, to let go and release his emotions in a torrent of angry tears. Instead, he took a deep breath and fought to regain control of himself. He couldn't afford to crack, not now, not after experiencing that extraordinary contact with the Prophet.

With great effort, he turned himself around and faced his situation. It took a moment for his eyes to adjust to the darkness. The small room was lost in shadow, except for the shape of a bed which detached itself from the darkness. He looked for a light source and noticed that there were no lamps anywhere. The cell was intended to remain in darkness. That alone was cruel and unusual punishment. But Andrew was not surprised. He knew in whose hands he was in now. Anything was possible.

The fact that the Federation was somehow in league with the servants of darkness was enough to know that his fate was sealed, as well as that of the planet's inhabitants. If the earth changes didn't destroy everyone, a corrupt world government would. He'd always sensed that there was something rotten at the Federation's core. All its efforts for effective control of the global population were not motivated from care but from the need to dominate. Why should he be surprised to find that they were in league with demonic powers. Wasn't that the fuel of every other world power throughout history, from the Third Reich to the Roman Empire? If such allegiance did not directly involve them with the sons of darkness, as the Essenes named these forces, at least the key leaders were manipulated by these forces. How else could one explain the atrocities inflicted on humankind?

An onslaught of gory visions filled Andrew's mind—thousands of crosses lining the road to Jerusalem, on which victims cried out in a chorus of unbearable moans. Then he saw, in a flash of fire and smoke, countless stakes raised through the centuries to burn people accused of thinking for themselves.

Andrew shook his head, horrified at the sudden appearance of these awful images in his mind. He didn't know where they were coming from. He had the odd feeling that these terrible sights lingered in the wake of Dr. Tagore's aura. The man's very proximity made Andrew frantic with the need to wash himself. He had never been so close to pure evil. It took another breath for him to find stability. He remembered that the Prophet had warned them in no uncertain terms as to the nature of their enemy.

Someone coughed.

Andrew turned with a jolt toward the bed. A form detached itself from the darkness. It was sitting on the bed, staring at him. An intuition struck Andrew again. Ever since the Voice had rung in his ears, he'd been flooded with intuitions passing through his mind like shooting stars.

"You wouldn't be Tom by any chance, would you?"

The silhouette reacted strongly to hearing his name.

"How would you know that? Who are you?"

"I'm the guy who came to help you out!" Andrew said with a twinge of irony in his voice.

Tom approached him. A greyish light leaking in through the door's tiny square window illumined the two men's features as they faced each other. Deep circles were carved in Tom's features beneath his eyes and he hadn't shaved for days. He was as pale as a ghost, although no paler than Andrew. Both men were traumatized by having fallen into the Federation's grip.

"Who are you?" Tom asked.

"That's the question I have for you," Andrew said, trying to see his features in the shadows.

"You must be one of the Prophet's people," Tom responded in a sudden burst of hope.

Andrew shook his head sadly. "I am, but as you see I've failed in my efforts to assist you."

Tom grabbed his shoulders, filled with enthusiasm. "I'm so glad to see you! I had a feeling that I wouldn't be left alone."

"Take it easy, Tom. I'm not gonna do you any good."

But his words had no impact on Tom's joy. "I knew someone would come!" he said again.

"Why would you think that?" Andrew asked, suddenly haunted by another intuition.

"Because the Prophet came to my rescue!"

Now it was Andrew's turn to be filled with energy. "What are you talking about?"

"I heard his voice as clear as I can hear yours!"

Andrew heard his heart pounding in his ears. But he was still suspicious.

"How did you know it was his voice? You never knew the man."

"I knew it was him . . . He brought one of his disciples back from the dead to save me when the quake struck!"

"What are you saying?" Andrew cried out, his face turning a scarlet red.

"This old man, a Mister Ivanovitch . . . "

"What about him?" Andrew asked urgently.

"He was crushed by a huge cement block. I saw him appear out of the wreckage when I was unable to get out of the house. There was no way that he was still alive. A supernatural power held him up . . . as an answer to my prayer."

"How do you know it was the Prophet's power?"

"Because he spoke to me, and I just knew it was him."

Andrew couldn't question him any longer. Having heard the voice himself, he knew that it was more than familiarity and memory that identified it as that of the Prophet. Something about its very presence carried with it the identity of the being who voiced it.

The two men looked at each other for a moment, not knowing what to say. The fact that Andrew had just experienced the same phenomenon made it more difficult for him to reject Tom's statement. He was still in shock himself from his encounter.

"So you came to help me . . . That's a beautiful thing," Tom said, tears glistening in his eyes.

"Doesn't look like I'm going to do you much good," Andrew responded grimly.

"But you found me and have come to my side. That gives me incredible hope . . . "

"Hope for what?"

"Hope that anything might happen."

"Those are pretty thick doors locking us in. And the Federation has a special interest in our case. They won't let us fly away."

"Still, they've put us together. Why would that be, do you think?"

Andrew's mind suddenly came into full focus, as though he'd been kicked awake. There could only be one answer to that question. One that he hadn't caught onto right away. They were being electronically monitored. Every word was carefully recorded. To his horror, Andrew realized that they had already let out the mystery of the Prophet's contact with them. He looked into Tom's eyes and the hardness of his glare quieted the young man. He strained to understand what was being said to him in silence.

After a brief moment, he got the message and he also realized that it was not for his convenience that the two had been put together. Tom swiftly turned around and went to sit on the bed.

"Can you tell me about him?" Tom finally said, unable to restrain his need to know.

Andrew stood in the shadows, listening to his heartbeat pounding in his ears, knowing that someone was listening to his every breath. But he also knew that to describe the kind of man the Prophet was could not possibly hurt anyone. It could only be a comfort to them and of no value to the Federation.

"His eyes were incredible," he said slowly, drifting back into golden memories of his time with the one they called the Final Prophet. "He could see right through you, to the depths of your being. Sometimes I felt like the little boy I'd once been when he looked at me, as though he could see my whole life at once and conjure it forth out of my subconscious. I also felt he could see the future, my future and who I would be. The first time he ever looked at me, he knew me better than I know myself."

Tom smiled. He'd been waiting his whole life to hear about someone like this. He had tried to invent him in his little paperback fictions, but he'd never come close to the real thing.

"When he spoke, his words came out of the deep silence where he lived. They were serene, and brilliant with wisdom. He never spoke too much or too little, just the right words at the right time."

Andrew's throat tightened as he remembered the man who had become more than a teacher, but a friend as well. He slid down to the floor and crossed his legs in half lotus position, resting his body comfortably for the first time in days.

"His calm was palpable. Yet his aura was so intense that it was like feeling an ocean breeze in your face every time you came near him. His peace, stability and goodness were contagious."

They sat in silence, letting the words soak in.

"There was also power, electric, radiant, supernatural power all around him. He was like walking thunder. But it was always kept under control, never used in negative ways although there was the sense that he could fry you alive merely by focusing his attention . . . Maybe that was the most amazing thing of all—his awareness. Every time he came in a room, everybody's consciousness heightened because of his. He was aware of everything all around him. Before such a presence, it was impossible to be in a slumbering, automatic state in which things happened just out of habit and momentum. Every gesture, every instant of time was filled to the brim with this electrifying awareness that absorbed everything and yet was affected by none of it. He was his own universe, though intimately linked with the external one."

A shiver went up Tom's spine and he felt goose pumps cover his body. He'd never thought he would cross paths with such a person in this day and age, even in such an indirect manner.

"He could be full of humor and simple joy, like a child," Andrew continued. "You could tell that he loved colors, flowers, the ordinary things of life. He appreciated them more than anyone I've ever seen. He never missed the aroma of cut grass or of oncoming rain. His senses were more acute than anyone else's. And yet there was always the awareness that there was something there besides his senses, which enjoyed what they received but was also master of them. He told us once that our consciousness was not tied to the body, that even if our brain was dead there could be the presence of consciousness. It is not the result of organic activity, but a magnetic field that surrounds the body and is independent of it.

"He taught us to tap into that field and live there rather than merely in the sense-based world."

"Have you achieve such a state?" Tom asked timidly.

"Just in moments . . . Then I'm dragged back down by anxiety or fear or simple daydreaming. But when I'm in those moments of awareness and remembrance of my higher nature, I enter a peace that passes all understanding. These are the moments that make life worthwhile."

Tom realized that this experience was what he had always sought for. He had intuitively sensed that someday he would find it. Little did he imagine that it would be in a Federation cell, facing his mortality like never before.

"You've spent all your time in fantasy land, Tom," Andrew said firmly, as though reading the young man's mind. "You are now given an opportunity to come face to face with the real thing."

"You mean, this situation?"

"I mean the fact that your life's at stake. The Prophet says that it's only when you're intensely aware of your mortality that your perceptions become cleansed and your priorities clear. No more time to waste. Every moment counts."

"So where does all this work on oneself lead?"

"To the capacity to be useful to the human race and to cosmic plans that we know nothing about."

"That's a rather grandiose assertion."

Andrew peered at him harshly through the shadows.

"At a time like this, when everything's up for grabs, we have to think big, no matter how pathetic we are as individuals. Everyone is needed."

"How do individuals combat the Federation or natural cataclysms?"

"Precisely by living more consciously within themselves. Instead of being terrified creatures seeking only to survive, we can maintain some link with meaning and right action. The Prophet says that's when we become useful."

"Does that mean that I could be useful?" Tom asked in a hushed voice.

"You bet!"

The two men looked at each other in the darkness. Tom sensed a new energy rush through his body. Despite his precarious situation, Andrew's words were a call to arms, a call to join the ranks of the warriors of light where he'd always wanted to be.

"How can we be helpful under these conditions?" Tom wondered, pointing at the walls that stood between them and their freedom.

"We are meant to be instruments of higher forces. They will help us get out of here!" Andrew stated with a faith he had never thought himself capable of. In these dangerous moments, a new confidence arose from a place he'd never encountered within himself and that he didn't know existed.

"We both heard this voice," he continued. "We both have proof that we're not alone!"

"A voice can't break walls down!"

"I wouldn't be so sure about that. I've heard of a primitive Indian tribe who would gather around a tree and shout at it until it fell to the ground. The same thing can happen from the psychic realm."

Andrew suddenly put his hand in front of his mouth. "We're doing it again!" he whispered, waving his arm in the air, motioning to an invisible surveillance system that tracked every word they spoke.

For now, they would have to wait in silence.

* * * * *

Stefan Zorn's garden was a bizarre, Gothic design thick with exotic vegetation and gargoyles. Statues from Greek mythology appeared beneath heavy foliage that was carefully landscaped to look wild and threatening. A small waterfall added the odd impression that nature's sanctuary had been caged in with these dark statues, reflecting the presence of the underworld. The earthquake and storms had shattered a third of the statures, but even in their cracked and dismembered state, the stones fit right in with the ghoulish landscape.

This garden was Zorn's private space where he did much of his nefarious thinking. The home itself was designed according to the finest technological standards and could withstand the earth's most violent shaking. Some shingles and windows were shattered, but the high-tech structure had survived.

Sefan Zorn walked through the greenery, followed by his two faithful servants, Dr. Tagore and Madame de Belmar. He was impeccably dressed in a black satin shirt and tuxedo pants, as though he were preparing for an entrance to some formal engagement. His charcoal locks were greased back away from his massive face and tied into a small pony tail at the top of his thick neck.

He might have been considered a handsome figure by some if it weren't for the hateful glare knotting his heavy eyebrows together and making his eyes black and fierce. He turned around and aimed his toxic gaze at the strange couple.

"Why didn't you tell me this earlier?" he bellowed.

The two aristocratic leaders had lost all their arrogance in the presence of their master. They looked rather like terrified school children, fearing punishment and ashamed of their ignorance.

"We thought you would know," Madame de Belmar ventured, her lower lip trembling in sheer terror.

Stefan Zorn growled, sounding more bearlike than human. "Your job is to inform me of every development, especially when it comes to the cursed Prophet's followers."

"We sent word as soon as he was arrested, sir," Dr. Tagore said in a high-pitched whisper.

"When did it become clear to you that he was being communicate with?"

"I myself did not hear anything. I saw a change in his demeanor and a feeling in the atmosphere."

"What are you talking about?" Zorn asked impatiently.

"Something electric was in the room that had not been there a moment before. I sensed a presence."

"And you waited twenty-four hours to let me know?"

Zorn moved toward him with unleashed fury. Tagore turned more ghostlike than his usual freakish appearance.

"I'm sorry, master."

"That's not good enough!" he shouted, blowing strands of the doctor's hair away from his forehead. He poured his dark glare into Tagore's fearful eyes. "There will not be a next time!"

"No, master."

Zorn turned his violent hate toward the beautiful,

aristocratic woman who now looked like a wilted plant. "When did he inform you?"

"Last evening . . . "

"And you waited twelve hours to get the information to me? Wanted to get your beauty rest, was that it?" Zorn asked with a sneer.

Dr. Tagore cleared his throat to keep his voice from trembling. "Master, we did not realize that this matter required your immediate attention. There is no way to tell if this was imagined or not."

"Since when did you confuse imagination with the spirit realm? I thought you were a more advanced initiate!"

Tagore couldn't answer. He looked down at his feet, humiliated. Zorn stalked away and looked at a pile of debris that had once been an expensive antique statue. Though he was often consumed with rage, he had developed his will power to such a degree that he knew how to stay focused on the priorities at hand. He would deal with his followers' incompetence at a later time. Now he had to confront this unexpected occurrence before it interfered with his plans.

"Here's what I want you to do," the dark man said without turning around. "Bring me this Andrew and we will get the information we need from him, I'll guarantee it!"

CHAPTER EIGHTEEN

Lynn awoke with a frightened cry and bolted upright. Her face was gleaming with sweat and her body convulsed in shivers. As her eyes focused, she looked around in the darkness, completely disoriented. She didn't know where she was. After a moment, she recognized the dreary motel room that they had rented for the night. Its alien shadows and grim surroundings did not comfort her in the least.

Jeremy was pulled out of a deep sleep from her anguished sound and sat up beside her. He placed his arms around her.

"Sweetheart, what is it? Another nightmare?"

She couldn't speak and just shivered in his arms. He tried to soothe her.

"Another nightmare . . . " he said as he pressed his lips on her moist forehead. "Tell me . . . "

"This was more than a nightmare," she finally managed to verbalize.

"Another vision?" he asked, suddenly alarmed. His wife's nocturnal experiences were often brimming with clairvoyant insight. "What was it?" he asked again, hoping that her talking about it would exorcise it from her psyche.

"Andrew . . . " she whispered in horror.

"What about him?" Jeremy asked, a knot tightening in his stomach.

"He's surrounded by evil."

"Tell me more!"

Adrenaline flooded Jeremy's mind and body, awakening him completely. "The Federation?"

"No, worse, much worse."

"What could be worse than that?"

"Evil itself."

It was Jeremy's turn to feel a shiver of terror rush up his spine. The shadows of the room turned menacing for him as well.

"What else?"

"They want something from him. They'll torture him for it. We've got to save him!"

"How?"

"I saw the girl . . . "

"What girl?"

"Oriana, Tom's friend. She'll help us . . . even though she's one of them. My God, we sent him right into a trap!"

An intense shiver shook Lynn's body, this time not from the nightmare but from the guilt she felt. "She can help us!"

"Why would she do that if she's one of them?"

"She didn't want this. I can feel it. She's not like the others. There's some humanity left in her soul."

"How do you know?"

"In the dream, I looked into her eyes and I saw it. More than that, she was calling to us."

"What if this is just fantasy?" Jeremy had to ask.

"I just know," Lynn said firmly. Jeremy understood that when his beloved knew in such a way, it came from a place that couldn't be questioned. He had confirmed this too many times in their life together.

"How will we find this person?"

"She'll find us if we make ourselves available."

"Can we risk endangering all of us?"

"No, just me."

"No way!" Jeremy cried out.

"She's got the gift. We'll find each other. No one else can interfere."

"You're not going anywhere by yourself, that's just not going to happen. Not when the world's crashing in on itself. If you feel you must go back, then I'll go with you. Michelle can take the others to safety."

"She'll insist on joining us. We won't be able to keep her from doing so. And it wouldn't be right to stop her from helping Andrew now."

"She's the only other one who knows the way to the caves."

"Contact Brave Eagle. We're not that far. Have him lead them the rest of the way."

"It's going to take my finder's ability to get to him."

Jeremy shook his head. He hadn't heard her use that word in ages. But he certainly knew what it meant. The gift had manifested several times at crucial moments. Lynn was indeed a finder. Her clairvoyance and intuitions made it possible for her to perceive the path to a certain goal, to find the right person, to be at the right place, to discern the right moment. She was like a magnet, pulled toward what was destined to occur. He knew better than to question that skill. It was the very one that had linked him with the Prophet and their ultimate destiny.

"Just look out there," Lynn said, pointing toward the road winding below the motel and drawing his attention to the bumper to bumper traffic that shut the highway down to a crawl for hundreds of miles. "It'll take us a week to get to the next state."

Desperate people were fleeing the epicenter of the quake, not realizing that the earth changes were occurring everywhere. There was no place to hide.

"Look at the lanes going the other way," she observed.

They're completely free of traffic. No one is heading back to the devastated cities along the coast. "It would be easier for all of us to go back and do what we need to do. By the time we get back to this spot, we won't be far behind where we'd be if we went forward now."

"How do we keep the others out of danger? We can't expose Juanita and the baby to any of this."

"We'll have them stay outside the city limits while we go in."

"Why not let them stay here? We've got enough money to pay for several weeks of rent."

Money was the least of their problems. Andrew's generosity had seen to that. Despite the out of control inflation that was doubling on a daily basis, they had enough to keep themselves going for months.

"You've got to convince me how you're going to find this person before we make the decision."

"She's a seer. I will contact her telepathically."

"That's not much of a guarantee."

"Jeremy, if you'd seen what I saw in my dream, you wouldn't wait another five minutes. Andrew's fallen into the hands of sheer evil. They will destroy his soul as well as his body. We've got to get him out at all cost."

"Just a few days ago you were arguing the other side, saying it was better to sacrifice one for the good of all."

"Not this kind of sacrifice! It would overshadow anything we did in the future."

Jeremy stood up and went to the window. He waited in silence for the decision to make itself known. Strangely, his mind was vacant of all thought. He found himself intensely present to the moment, breathing in the cool night hear seeping through the window. This was a terrible decision to make and it made him feel ten years older. If he were to catch his reflection in a mirror, he wouldn't be surprised to find streaks of white hair on his head. He took a deep breath and listened to the peacefulness. In the distance, countless refugees headed toward a promised land that would not be there.

"All right, we'll go back. I'll leave Robert in charge and we'll stay in touch with our radios as long as our batteries last."

Lynn closed her eyes and said a silent prayer, not for themselves but for Andrew who was caught in the jaws of hell because she had sent him there. She felt better already knowing she might be joining him in that abyss. Fear was less intolerable than remorse.

* * * * *

The giant earthquake seemed to have broken the ice. A domino effect expanded across the globe. Fierce winds whipped over the continents. Volcanoes erupted like never before. The entire country of Japan was swallowed up. Within a week, the world's economy had collapsed. International commerce was interrupted by the cataclysms. Societies crumbled overnight under the weight of the calamities. Hospitals that were still functional were crammed with the wounded and the dying, always packed and serving as temporary morgues.

The Federation's world army turned on its people and tried to save some vestige of control over the absolute chaos that inevitably came with mass destruction. Cities in every country were in ruins and destitute of order. Electricity was cut indefinitely to millions upon millions who had depended on it in every way. The complex technology on which twenty-first century civilization was built revealed itself as a fragile giant with no footing. Once the plug was pulled, two centuries of advancement fell into a black hole, taking humanity back to a dark age, this time without the wherewithal to survive. Nature was now a constant threat, humankind's greatest enemy. Once the cosmic mother of the species, providing for all her children's needs, she now turned against them. Her fury was unquenchable. She had been raped for too long and the time had come for retribution.

As lights went out on world civilization, Nature herself was plunged into a new age of dramatic upheaval. The shifting poles disfigured lands everywhere. Weather turned insane—shattering rains no one had ever seen before, winds whose velocity could snap the necks of people caught in their grip, and thunder that fell on mutilated ground with the ferocity of bombardments from above, as from enemy war planes.

Two thirds of the population were without proper shelter. Nature seemed to take advantage of their exposure to ensure their destruction. If falling debris didn't crush them, then the elements would. People banded together in desperate groups, instantly becoming animal-like in their efforts to stay alive. Along with the shutting down of the computer age, the light in the human soul seemed to go out as well. Humanity had been preparing for a century to enter this age of horror where basic goodness and decency no longer even made sense. Generations of unloved children and even more generations devoid of wisdom regarding their purpose for being, set the stage for the species' self-destruction. The specter of a global death wish had shown itself vividly in the international media that fed the masses like a mother's milk. People who loved to see barbaric acts and violence could now live them out in the shadows of devastated societies. Murder, rape, pillage were a daily occurrence and as ordinary as rush hour traffic had been just a week before.

The gruesome jungle law of the survival of the fittest was all that was left of the wisdom of humanity.

General MacDaniel relished his new role as ruthless dictator. This was the part that he had readied for all his life. There were no boundaries now. Men of war could run rampant over civilians with orders to shoot to kill. They no longer needed to face a specific enemy. Everyone was the enemy. People were shot in the streets for the smallest infraction. Encouraged by Stefan Zorn's suggestions, the general turned the world's nightmare into his private playhouse. The military's emergency communications system was all that was left of the WorldNet. Once people's batteries had died out, there would be no way to communicate except through the secret systems of the Federation. The world was theirs to dominate and plunder. But even this was an illusion. They could never shoot enough people to bring order back. The mayhem was out of control and descending at warp speed into a savagery that would eventually consume the Federation itself. Brutality and madness was contagious and spreading through the military ranks as well as the civilian population.

Corridor 600 became the busiest hallway in the military complex as secret meetings took place. Around the clock, the fate of nations was decided in these back rooms where a dozen high ranking officers and financiers made choices with the stroke of a pen or a phone call. Satellite cameras pumped in live video from the most explosive regions where infantry could not penetrate and where rebel leaders were threatening to engulf other populations. The secret audience simply picked and chose who would be carpet bombed and permanently "stabilized".

General MacDaniel was at the center of it all, and the most influential voice whispering in his ear was Stefan Zorn whose powers had completely locked onto the military man's mind and soul like tentacles from a deadly octopus. Zorn had made himself his most trusted advisor, even satisfying his more private desires with his accomplished devotees, sending the man's soul reeling down into an abyss of perversion that made him the perfect instrument. The arrogant officer went about his gory business certain that he was the only one in charge with the world's power at his fingertips. Yet every day he became more of a puppet to the true beast who was holding the reins of humanity's future.

Zorn not only discovered the general's fetiches and dark fantasies, but instilled, intensified and aroused them to deepen his hold on the man's will. The more the general thought that he was master of himself, the more he became entwined in the web of the dark master.

"Use it, use the bomb . . . " were words that kept recurring in the general's head as he wandered down the super secret corridor of power on his way to another decisive meeting. Zorn had made sure those words were repeated in different ways, under different circumstances until they were burned in the man's mind and would come forth at the right time. Once the first nuclear bomb had been dropped, the second one would be easier, further disintegrating the last shreds of civilization. Zorn knew the key to the complete annihilation of humanity's soul. The more perverse and violent the act, the more its evil would spread and repeat itself through the darkened unconscious of a species gone mad. It was such a simple affair—pull the rug of comfort and security out from under human beings and they became capable of the most horrific behavior. In this theater of blood and destruction, he had found the way to pull the rug out from under every individual on the planet.

* * * * *

The long, narrow hallway bathed in dark shadows looked just like a secret corridor of power would be expected to appear. Lights were dim but sufficient. The silence was tense. Doors of magnificent polished oak were closed to the world. The corridor was guarded twenty-four hours a day by heavily armed soldiers and the best in surveillance equipment

The gigantic figure of Stefan Zorn appeared at the far end of the hall. Zorn's eyes shimmered in the darkness like black pearls, strangely illumined from within. He wore his usual excessively expensive tailored suit which looked out of place in this Spartan, serene atmosphere known only to grim-faced men in dreary uniform.

But Zorn was not here on usual business. This was the day he would do more than consult and advise the men who held access to the world's weaponry. This was the day when he would apply the final coup de grace in his total dominance of their psyches.

He came to one of the unmarked doors and knocked. It opened and he stepped into a large room that looked like a five star hotel suite. It served as a lounge for the elite in power, but this day it was redesigned as a playroom. The lights were low, giving off the sense of a dungeon rather than a modern conference room. Zorn had arranged the redecorating himself. He was providing a special birthday present for the man whom he had bound in invisible strings. This gift would wrap the most valuable string of all around General MacDaniel who still imagined himself one of the most powerful men in the world.

The general stood in the shadows, oddly out of uniform in a silk robe, and hiding his features out of a last sliver of shame. Other top brass with similar tastes stood in the room, awaiting the ringleader who would expose them to forbidden pleasures they had never dared seek out before.

Zorn was a consummate actor and played his part to perfection.

"Are you gentlemen ready for the time of your life?" he asked slyly.

Whispered responses confirmed that they were now in the palm of his hand. This orchestrated perversion would chain them to him forever. Zorn turned his back on them for a moment to conceal a grin of satisfaction.

He stepped back into the hallway and motioned for the guards at the end of the hall to open the door. Six women and young men entered the corridor, dressed in long black coats meant to hide what they were not wearing. They carried bags stocked with toys that would provide pleasure and pain.

They filed past Zorn with strange, deadpan faces, looking like zombies covered in lavish makeup. They were ready for the job for which they were highly trained but had lost all passion for the freak show they put on. These creatures were skilled technicians and had turned human deviance into an art form.

Zorn watched his employees with cold, calculating eyes. They had long ago ceased to please him. His only aphrodisiac was his dark mission which was now finally manifesting in colossal proportions. His former indulgences had melted down into one all-consuming interest.

He stopped the last woman as she entered the room. Decorated with tattoos and pierced with jewelry, she turned savage, feline eyes upon her master.

"Make sure they take their time," he whispered. "Double the doses if you have to. I don't want any of them standing when it's all over."

She nodded with no expression.

"If they want to go beyond fantasy, and take somebody out, you let them have their fun. Understand?"

Her icy trance-like look sparkled for a moment.

"You mean . . . all the way?"

He shot a ferocious glare at her.

"That's right. If death turns them on, then give it to them. Sacrifice somebody. It's for a glorious cause."

A wicked grin turned her face evil as she headed into the room.

Zorn watched as the women unpacked their wares and removed their coats.

"Happy birthday," he said in a voice filled with irony.

He closed the door behind him and walked off into the darkness, past secret rooms where the affairs of the world were being determined. But he knew where the real decisions were being made and what would truly generate the future.

* * * * *

Oriana raised her head from her pillow and listened intently. The crumbling mansion was silent except for a whistling breeze shooting through the cracks in the walls and broken windows. She quietly pulled the covers back and got out of bed, stepped carefully onto the wooden floor, and slowly applied her weight to the creaking planks. She tiptoed to the closet and removed her gown. She quickly changed clothes with jeans and sweater that were waiting for her. She hung up her gown and closed the closet door.

Oriana returned to the bed and placed her pillows under the cover to make it look like a form was asleep there. She moved to the door and held her breath as she slowly opened it. She peered out into the hallway. A cemetery silence filled the dark shadows. She knew that someone had to be awake. There was always a watch. She moved passed the closed bedroom doors toward the stairway. Peaceful snoring sounds came from the rooms. Someone groaned in their sleep, stirred by some dark dreams. Her heart leapt.

She made her way down the stairs. At the bottom, she saw a light seeping below the closed door of the library. She walked passed it and heard a sound from behind the door. She bent down and looked through the keyhole. Dr. Tagore was sitting on the couch in his silk robe, drinking from a large liqueur glass and staring vacantly into the darkness.

Oriana moved on quickly. She knew it was now or never. She made her way to the front door and slipped out into the night. She didn't know where she was going, but she knew she would find what she needed to find. Several hours before, she'd been struck with a strong intuition that the people she needed to discover were nearby. As she had learned to do since childhood, she quieted her mind and followed her intuition. She sensed that the people she was to encounter also had the gift and would find their way to her. This was a first. She'd never met her equal in telepathic insight. But she understood that in this colossal metaphysical crisis, everything was possible.

She found herself walking in the street, alone and without the protection of street lamps. A great instinctive fear swept over her. She'd never been left to herself in this way, had never walked down a city block all alone. The cult had protected her as though she were royalty. She knew now that whatever purpose they had for her could only bring sorrow, and however much she had come to care for some of them, there was no going back now. She had no doubt that if Stefan Zorn, Dr. Tagore, or her stepmother learned of her treachery, she would be dealt with mercilessly. All those years of upbringing and nurturing would mean nothing. Not for the followers of Stefan Zorn.

She wandered into the night like a lost waif, trusting that each passing breeze would lead her to the shelter she had never found. The only thing that balanced her terror was the sense that the people she would encounter might bring something into her life that she had never known—simple kindness which she longed for now more than life itself. She had gone far into occult esoterica and found it all shallow and worthless without the goal of goodness at its heart.

She wandered through the cracked asphalt that rose in frozen waves all around her, creating an unreal stage for her escape. She had no idea where she was headed, but she knew she was not to stay with the cult a moment longer.

She turned a corner and found that she was heading toward the park. Suddenly, out of the shadows, three men in rags appeared before her.

"Where are you going on this dark night, darlin'?"

The man addressing her was at the far end of human destitution. She knew that she had the ability to deal with his frail stature. He stepped toward her. She could smell his breath and decided that he'd come close enough. With lightning speed, she turned her hips and shot out a side kick, striking the man right at the point where his diaphragm met his solar plexus. He let out a groan and fell backwards into the mound of trash he'd come out of.

The second man stepped forward, this one much bigger and stronger. Neither drunk nor weak, he was one of the many brutish predators who were taking over the city as quickly as the rats that had begun to crawl out from the destruction. For an instant, she thought she'd run back to the house, but then realized what would await her there if she drew such attention to the cult. She would be better off dead.

"You're a pretty one," he said with a wicked smile. The other one grunted, already enjoying the rape he expected to commit.

She stepped back to create a fighting space between them. She threw a kick but the bigger man grabbed hold of her ankle. She was suddenly completely helpless, unable to move her legs and position herself.

"You're mine now, girl!" the other man said as he grabbed her arm and twisted it behind her back. He was already unbuckling his belt.

Frozen in terror, she became incapable of thinking. Any training she had received was washed away in a tidal wave of fear. The young naive woman that she was stood helpless before these sadistic criminals. Then she heard it. A voice different from any she'd ever heard before.

"*I am with you. Will you be with me?*"

It was as loud and clear as the snarling sounds coming from her attackers. The voice was filled with a strange tranquility that inexplicably gave her new hope.

"Yes!" she cried out. "Yes, I am with you!"

The men looked at her strangely.

"What did you say?"

She was hardly aware of them as a blinding light spread out before her inner sight. Her entire body was set aflame with the thrill of beauty and goodness that entered her consciousness.

"Who are you?" she cried out.

One of the men thought she was talking to him. "You want to know my name?" he asked stupidly. "So you can tell the cops? They're too busy to take care of your problems, that's for sure."

She looked around as though expecting to see a materialization of the voice. The light was nearly blinding her sight.

"*I am with you*," the voice said again.

Her heart pounded no longer from fear but from the joy of this supernatural encounter, liberating her from everything that had ever hurt her or caused her sorrow. She felt as though cool waters were cleansing her soul from a lifetime of unhappiness and confusion. She blinked her eyes and realized that her sight was crystal clear, despite the darkness, as though the inner experience was intensifying her senses.

"I am with you!" she cried out.

"I know you're with me!" the assailant said as he grabbed her waist.

A car suddenly pulled up alongside them from out of nowhere. Jeremy jumped out.

"Is there a problem here?" he asked angrily as he approached the men.

"You'd better scram boy, or you're gonna get yourself hurt!" the bigger one of the two growled.

"Do you think I'm gonna let you hurt my friend?" Jeremy warned as he looked at the amazed young woman.

"You know her?" the smaller man asked in a hesitating voice.

"That's right! And you'll have to walk over my dead body to touch her! Are you ready to do that?"

The man backed away, but his partner stepped forward.

"If that's what it takes!"

Jeremy stared hard into his adversary's bleary eyes.

"You should be ashamed of yourself, Jim Doyle!" he heard himself say, not knowing how the words came out of his mouth.

The man's eyes widened in shock. "How do you know my name?"

Jeremy had no idea. It had just flashed into his mind.

"You've made your mother suffer over your wrongdoings enough, haven't you?"

Once again, some foreign power had taken control of his vocal cords. The man raised his arm to strike him. Jeremy did not react to protect himself. He heard himself speak again.

"You've done enough damage in your life, Jim Doyle.

It's time to stop."

Jeremy's serene voice struck the man in a place deep in his soul, as though his own buried conscience were talking to him. He turned pale and lowered his arm, backing away from Jeremy. Something was tearing him up inside, bringing forth some primordial remembrance of who he once was. Tears sparkled in his eyes, along with immense, incomprehensible fear. He turned away and ran as fast as he could, followed by his companion.

Jeremy was in shock as well. He had only witnessed this sort of thing once before, when the Prophet had spoken to a darkened soul in such a way. Jeremy was certain that it was his teacher and friend who had spoken through him. His whole body resonated with a sense of his mighty presence. A feeling of exhilaration swept through him.

Lynn hurried from the car and took his hand. Her eyes glittered with tears.

"It was him! He's with us!" she whispered in ecstasy. She turned to Oriana who stared at them wide-eyed.

"You're Oriana, are you not?" Lynn asked, knowing the answer already.

The young woman shook her heard, unable to speak.

"My name is Lynn. I've been looking for you. Or maybe it is you who is looking for us. Come." She took her hand and led her like a child toward the car. Jeremy stood on the sidewalk in a trance. Lynn smiled and grabbed his arm. "You'd better get used to these things. The miracles are just beginning."

They got into the car and drove off into the dark night.

CHAPTER NINETEEN

"You can't just take off with our prisoners!" the general said angrily as he paced his office. Dr. Tagore stood in the shadows like a scarecrow from another time.

"I was told that you would cooperate with us," he said calmly.

"We have some laws and regulations left in spite of the chaos!"

"Mr. Zorn assured me that you would make an exception for this case."

The general reacted oddly to the sound of the name his visitor had mentioned. But he caught himself and turned with anger.

"He can't have everything he wants! No one can."

The doctor smiled slyly, knowing better.

"This is not a request, general, this is an urgent necessity and we will do whatever we must to procure this man."

"What the hell does that mean?" the general asked, sensing a threat.

"General, I don't want to go into embarrassing details . . . "

"What are you talking about?"

"We have tapes from Corridor 600 that you would not want to see broadcast on world television."

The general rushed at him and grabbed him by the collar, ready to tear his throat out.

"Who do you think you are? You can't blackmail me! I'll crush you like a bug, freak! How dare you threaten me?"

Tagore looked at him fearlessly. Though he'd trembled before his master Stefan Zorn, he had absolutely no fear of ordinary human beings, not even those with control of the world's armies.

"General, I mean no disrespect. If you permit me to show you where we stand, perhaps that will make everything clear."

"What?" the general asked suspiciously.

"Mr. Zorn would like you to take a look at our position."

The general winced at the name and released his grip. He uncharacteristically backed away from his adversary and became passive, though his jaws were still clenched. The name of Zorn had hypnotic properties that affected him in spite of his soldier's will power.

"Go on!"

Tagore put his hand in his coat pocket. The general instinctively went for his pistol. Tagore smiled and slowly pulled out a videocassette. MacDaniel let go of his weapon but was no less concerned.

"May I?" Tagore asked as he pointed to the television set in the corner of the room. The general noted reluctantly.

Tagore walked over toward the large set, trying not to snicker. He slipped the tape into the video player and pushed the play button, knowing that by that little motion of his finger he would gain control of the powerful general. On the screen instantly appeared an orgiastic scene from the dark room in Corridor 600. The general was in the foreground, partially undressed and on his knees before two of the women who had been brought to him as a birthday gift from Zorn.

MacDaniel's face turned dark red. His eyes bulged out

of his head. There he was with his perverse sexual predilections exposed for the world to see, and in as humiliating a position as could be imagined.

"Turn it off!" the general cried out.

Before Tagore had pressed the stop button, the general rushed to the video player. He ejected the tape and crushed it under his foot. He looked up at Tagore, ready to kill.

"It's only a copy of course," Tagore said calmly.

"How did you turn my own surveillance system on me?"

"Perhaps you don't understand, sir, that you are not the only man in power."

The general pulled out his weapon with the speed of a gunslinger and pressed it against Tagore's forehead.

"I'll splatter you all over this room! We'll see who's got the power!"

Tagore didn't even blink.

"It would only make things worse for you, general. Don't you think this has all been carefully thought out?"

"Zorn betrayed me!" the general shouted, cocking the weapon and eager to spread blood on the floor.

"I wouldn't say that, general. He provided you with entertainment to your liking and thought perhaps you'd enjoy reliving the moment. The tape was a gift."

"Cut the crap!" the general screamed. "You're trying to blackmail me! What kind of a fool do you think I am?"

Dr. Tagore's silence gave him the answer he didn't want to hear. In spite of a lifetime in the military, he had stepped into a trap that a schoolboy could have recognized.

"What would you do with this?"

"Distribute it by the thousands and put it on international television, or what's left of it."

"You don't have the power to do that!"

"You'd be surprised. You don't seem to realize who we are."

"Who exactly are you?" the general grumbled, keeping his gun pressed against Tagore's head.

"The future."

"What the hell does that mean?"

"We will bring order to this planet . . . with your help. A future of unimaginable wealth awaits you if you cooperate."

"You think you're going to take over the world government?"

"There is no world government now, general."

"How dare you say? I've got millions of soldiers at my command!"

"You must come out of denial, general. The current devastations are only going to get worse and destroy all means of communication. Every society will disintegrate in a very short period of time. Humanity will be reduced to barbarism. No army will keep this from happening."

"So how do your people propose to control things?"

"We have other means."

"What kind of means?"

"From the realm of the occult."

The general holstered his gun and stepped away. "I don't want to hear that nonsense."

Tagore smiled knowingly. "Of course not. But the facts are what they are, regardless of whether you can understand them. As Mr. Zorn has made clear to you, we can work together to our mutual satisfaction."

"How do I get you to destroy the tapes?"

"Cooperate with us. Begin by giving us the prisoner we want."

"Why is he so important to you?"

"No questions."

"Damn it, I'm in charge!"

"Whatever you say, general," Tagore stated, knowing

better. "I can tell you this. The prisoner is a follower of the one they call the Final Prophet who was a personal enemy of ours. We have reason to believe that they seek to harm us, which would not be good for you or the ordained future of humanity."

"How do I know you'll destroy the tapes and not use them against me?"

"We will hand you the master copy for your use only. You have our word of honor."

"That's the last thing I'll count on!"

"Mr. Zorn has no desire to create conflict between us. He would not stoop to blackmailing. My job was merely to give you the tape, not to threaten you with it. We wish to work with you, not against you."

"Do you have the master copy on you?"

"We will deliver it to you this very day, as soon as I leave here."

"You do that and tell Zorn not to pull anymore tricks on me."

"As long as we understand each other. Besides, the tapes only show that you are a lucky man. I never had a birthday party such as that. Next time you should invite me."

The general looked at him in surprise. Tagore gave him a lustful snicker as he left the room.

* * * * *

Andrew and Tom were let out of the jail cell, taken down to a lower level toward an underground garage. They walked in grim silence, knowing that nothing good awaited them. The guards were silent and somber as though they too sensed something of the gruesome fate that awaited these men. Both prisoners looked down at the ground, their eyes seeing nothing, their consciousness buried deeply within, seeking to connect with something from another dimension that would comfort them in their trials ahead. They especially didn't want to be present to the realm of the senses that was soon to be horribly violated.

They came out into the garage area. Great fissures cut through the thick cement walls and ceiling. The earthquake had not managed to tear through the high tech fortress of one of the Federation's most secure prisons. Nevertheless, Andrew came out of the recesses of his being long enough to feel a new terror wash over him. This concrete tomb was the wrong place to be at a time of colossal continental shifts. He suddenly felt an unbearable urge to get out of the garage. He looked at Tom who was lost in his own melancholy. Tom felt his gaze and turned to him. He immediately recognized the worry on Andrew's features. In that instant he was struck with the same intuitive urgency to get out immediately. The two men turned to each other and realized at the same that they were receiving a simultaneous communication. This was not imagination or anxiety, but a message from beyond telling them to get out—now!

Andrew searched for an exit as the guards led them toward the armored van and turned their attention to unlocking its doors. It took both of them to slide back the grill inside the vehicle that caged the prisoners. Andrew spotted a light seeping in from an open maintenance door. He looked at Tom and motioned with his head. Without thinking, they both dashed for the door.

"Hey!" a guard yelled. "Don't be stupid!"

The prisoners ran as fast as they could toward the open exit.

"It only leads to the jail courtyard, fools! You can't get away!"

The guard let out a laugh. "That's going to cost you!" he said, pulling out his club. His motion was arrested by the sudden sound of a low vibration that seemed like a growl from below the earth.

"What the hell is that?" he cried out.

Then the ground jerked fiercely below his feet, throwing him against the van. The other guard went sprawling on his back. He shouted as another jolt shot through the ground with such violence that a slab of concrete cracked open and shot upward toward the ceiling, sending cars flying about like insects.

"Get out!" the guard yelled in terror.

A rumble deafened them as the wall and ceiling began to gyrate wildly in the grip of some savage force field. The guards tried to get to their feet but couldn't maintain their balance. The entire surface of the garage was moving up and down as though it was made of liquid, ripping the structure apart. Vehicles slammed together with such force that they were crushed like beer cans. The prison van flew up to the ceiling and came crashing down on the chest of one of the guards. Dust filled the underground chamber, cutting off all visibility. The noise was such that it seemed a giant train was crashing through the walls at full speed.

The ceiling and upper stories slammed down on the shivering garage floor, instantly flattening everything. Tom and Andrew rolled across the courtyard, bounced like rubber balls by the convulsing earth. All around them, everything loose was flying through the air. A soldier on the watchtower crashed through his window and was thrown to the ground, followed by a third of the wall on which his post was perched. The two men looked up at the building behind them steadily sinking in on itself, one cell block after another flattening into the ground, shooting out fragments of metal, glass, and concrete with the force of a machine gun.

"This way!" Tom shouted over the noise. He managed to get on his feet and staggered like a drunkard toward the large breach in the crumbling wall that revealed the countryside. The prison fortress was on the outskirts of the city.

Andrew followed him. They looked like two sailors on the deck of a ship tossed mercilessly by the ocean waves. They leaped through the ruins of the wall as other sections crashed all around them. They fell in the grass on the other side and rolled down a steep hill that shook like a creature gasping for breath. Behind them, the great structure collapsed with a loud roar as tons of concrete shattered over hundreds of people trapped inside.

At the bottom of the hill, Tom and Andrew continued to bounce on the flat surface. It shook back and forth as some nearly supernatural force uprooted trees and ripped roads in half. Despite being unable to stand, the men were grateful that no structure was nearby to crash over them, unlike the millions in the city on the horizon where giant clouds of smoke rose ominously. Though it was only midday, the sky had turned dark purple as the weather responded with spasms of violent reactions to the earth's agony.

Tom felt wet earth beneath him and realized that the ground was cracking open all around them, plowing up the topsoil. Nature had become as terrifying as being in the hands of their torturers.

"Is it ever going to stop?" Andrew shouted as he tried to get control of his body. He felt he was riding a wild bronco whose only aim was to throw him off.

"Watch out for crevices!" Tom shouted back over the roar.

Andrew didn't quite understand at first until he felt his hand enter a hole that hadn't been there a second before.

"My God!" He shouted. "This is no earthquake!"

The smell of fresh mud filled their nostrils as fractures appeared in the grass. An intense gust of wind suddenly swirled around them, sending an icy breeze whipping across their faces. Debris flew by, wrapped in dust devils. The vicious wind shot down from the west with all the force of El Nino. It was as though the continents had moved several degrees and were entering a new latitude ruled by the winds of the open sea which were sweeping across land.

By now boulders from the destroyed prison were flying down the hill, bouncing about like giant soccer balls.

"We've gotta get outta here!" Andrew shouted.

The shaking shifted direction. The men managed to get to their feet and dashed away from the hill, stumbling further out into a field. That very moment, the heavens turned bright with immense thunderclaps.

"Great!" Andrew shouted as they fell into the dirt.

A heavy downpour burst over them, instantly turning their surroundings into thick mud. The men crawled on all fours into the field, creating more distance between them and the deadly fragments of the once mighty stronghold.

A thought came into Andrew's mind, relieving his terror. At least the Federation would be too busy to hunt them down, for awhile anyway. That is, if anyone survived this freakish cataclysm.

* * * * *

The entire west coast was in the thralls of a shattering force that shook the continental shelf. The dreaded polar shift was under way. For the next eight hours, the crust of the earth shifted from its former position as the magnetic fields pushed the planet's core in the other direction. The cosmic tension was so extreme that ocean basins were emptied of their contents. Formerly dry land became the bottom of a new sea. Lands in the north were shifting toward the Equator. No place would be what it once was. No human being would experience life in the same way again.

Giant waves shot across the lowlands, destroying everything in their path. Millions upon millions drowned. Death and destruction were everywhere. Whatever was left standing would be unsafe, all the rest was rubble. Great dams broke, inundating the population below them. It would take generations for the order and symmetry of humanity's architecture to return, if future generations were to rise again.

By the end of the day, as the sunset—made glorious as it sent streaks of light through mammoth clouds of dust and flames that turned global destruction into a thing of beauty—the shift had come to an end. The ground was stable again, but the weather systems were out of control. The magnetic turbulence had whipped up colossal storms and killer winds that would rage for weeks. Any hope now for the maintenance of order and the continuance of civilized life was lost for the foreseeable future. People would have to group together in small communities to sustain themselves with whatever was left of the ruins of technology. Orbiting satellites could still send images from the Federations world headquarters down to receivers, but a third of the viewing audience was dead and the rest scrambling for shelter and food.

Such devastation had not been seen since the atom bombs over Hiroshima and Nagasaki in the previous century. Worst of all were the oceans, raging wildly as though rebelling against the forced transformation of their home. All coastal areas were inundated. Great walls of water tore through everything in their way. Fires were everywhere, from broken gas pipes and downed electrical wires. Explosions would flare up every few moments all over the globe, causing more trauma and tragedy in a situation that was already impossible and unbearable. The Tribulation, foretold by Prophets of all cultures, was upon humanity in full force.

Only the super-wealthy who had prepared for such a catastrophe were in a position to survive it. None was as ready as Stefan Zorn. Before the first shivers had been felt, he had boarded a private supersonic plane that flew him into the quiet space of the stratosphere. There he watched the world crashed in upon itself. Everything was going according to plan. He sat in a large study in the center of the plane, smoking a cigar and listening to television and radio reports from around the world coming out of a bank of monitors and speakers. His wildest fantasies had come true. The world was crumbling at his feet and he would become its master. Then he would turn it into the kind of place desired by the dark forces—a gruesome work colony serving their purposes.

Zorn was one of the few people to know that pain and suffering were energies which fed certain dimensions of the cosmos. It was his mission to harness vast amounts of this substance and he was eager to do so. He turned to another bank of static monitors near the windows of the plane whose shades were drawn. He pressed a few buttons. After a moment, a middle eastern face appeared on the screen.

"I am here, master," the man said in a thick accent. He had the look of an Islamic imam, with beard and turban. But obviously his god was not that of Mohammed nor of the other revealed religions. He was a priest in the teachings of darkness coming out of antiquity before Moses had taken his sandals off on Mount Sinai. His dark eyes made clear what he worshiped.

"Is everything prepared?" Zorn asked.

"All is as planned."

"How many can we count on?"

"Five thousand strong, grandmaster."

"I was hoping for more, Sa'id."

"Some of our people were either killed or made refugees by the cataclysm."

"Weren't they prepared for it?"

"Most of us were. But some were foolish enough to go about their business as usual."

"What about our friends further east?"

"I've just spoken with Ying Chang. They were more careful. We can count on another ten thousand."

"Very good. Stand by."

"Certainly," the man said, bowing his head in submission.

Zorn pressed a few more buttons. Another monitor lit up. A European aristocrat appeared on the screen.

"Lord Havisham, how are you on this fateful day?" Zorn asked with a sneer. "How do we stand with your people?"

"Our brothers and sisters are at your service, and have been in shelters for over a week. Your predictions were most accurate. There are three thousand of us in the U.K., and another six thousand on the continent"

"Very well. Keep them organized and focused on their mission," Zorn ordered.

"Count on us, sir," the Englishman said respectfully.

A few more buttons were pushed and another image formed on a third monitor. A Russian woman appeared, with the features of a bulldog and eyes of fire.

"Madam Oskya, good to see you again."

"It has been a long time, master," she responded with reverence.

"Is everyone safe over there?"

"Da, we knew what to expect."

"I want to speak to all of you at once so that you know that everything is under control. We have access to the power needed to accomplish our goals. There is, however, one detail you need to know. There seems to be some trouble brewing with the followers of the so-called Final Prophet."

"How do you mean, sir?" the aristocrat asked with concern.

"It appears that they have received some communication."

"What sort of communication?" the mid-eastern man questioned.

"From the spirit realm!" Madame Oskya grumbled.

"Precisely," Zorn answered. "There seems to be some contact being established, perhaps by the Prophet himself."

"This is not good," the mid-eastern man stated angrily. "I thought we had taken steps to avoid this."

"There are some things that cannot be fully controlled," Zorn stated coldly.

"Then we must wipe out the followers as soon as possible," the Englishman suggested forcefully.

"That has been one of our goals all along, and we are beginning to accomplish that. There are only a very few left. However, you need to locate those persons who may be in your countries. Only you can identify them. Search them out and destroy them immediately. Even those who are not susceptible to this kind of contact. Anyone of them can become a vehicle for the Enemy. When you take over the communications systems, I want you to send undercover people in nests of resistance that may be forming and burn the rats out as soon as possible. We don't want any interference when we begin the next phase."

"What kind of powers do you think might be conveyed to the followers?" the Russian woman asked.

"None that we cannot overcome, I'm sure of that. But it will motivate them to continue the struggle and that could be contagious. We need people to give up all hope.

Then they will be ours. Place your key leaders in positions that we've outlined. Make sure that we have control of police forces, local magistrates, and that we can proceed quickly. You know how to reach my people for funds and directions."

All three nodded.

"Be sure to stay in contact with people in your regions and inspire them to intensify their efforts for the Cause."

He abruptly shut off the monitors and leaned back against his large padded chair. He took a puff from his cigar, deep in thought. He knew that the only people who could stand up to him now were those influenced by the spirit of the Prophet. That was the only antidote left to the influence he would spread across the globe. He had to stamp it out before they created a stronghold against him.

"Damn you!" he whispered to himself, remembering the man who had stood up to him and defeated him once before. Even in death, he was a threat that wouldn't go away. But for now, Zorn was the one in control, and he knew how to wield power for his purposes.

He looked out the other windows at the quiet zenith around him.

"It won't be long now," he whispered to himself with great satisfaction.

CHAPTER TWENTY

Mammoth clouds of dust filled the skies all around the globe, veiling the sun's light. Cities around the world smoldered in ruins. Smoke would continue to rise for days on end, like a slow death. Some places were completely devastated.

Destruction was everywhere. Although some buildings had managed to resist the cataclysmic shaking, highways were broken like twigs and the oceans contorted in wild convulsions. Some basins had been completely emptied of water, sending tidal waves across the land, turning green pastures into sea floors. The winds mirrored the frenzied waters and tore across the world mercilessly as weather patterns readjusted to the transformation. Places that had been warm were now cold, and the polar regions were becoming temperate, melting the ice rapidly, which assured new catastrophes.

Oriana, Jeremy, and Lynn had camped out in the safety of the park during the hours of the violent shift, keeping away from crashing buildings. When peace settled upon the land again, they ventured out to the edge of the park. They stared in shock at the devastated landscape. Nuclear bombs could hardly have created worse destruction. They knew that life would never be the same. The last shreds of order and civilization were gone. Everyone was left on their own to survive. The future of the species was uncertain. It would be years before societies would be able to rebuild and recreate a semblance of a familiar way of life.

"We knew this would happen generations ago," Oriana whispered. "The ancient foretold it. I've seen this very image in dreams. This very scene."

Lynn put her arm around her. In the dark moments of the shift, they had become friends holding on to each other as the earth convulsed.

"Who is we?" Lynn asked.

The pale young woman turned her large dark eyes on her new friends. They glistened with tears.

"Those who worship the darkness."

"Were your people looking forward to this?" Jeremy asked, disgusted.

"Oh yes. The masters understood years ago that the crippling of civilization would be their opportunity to gain control."

"For what purpose?" Jeremy wondered, sensing the answer already.

"To be masters of humankind and manipulate their behavior to satisfy certain needs."

"What needs?" Lynn asked, not understanding.

"The creation of death and violence and evil on a mass scale release certain kinds of energies into the magnetic fields that feed other realms of the universe."

"Spiritual realms you mean?" Lynn asked again.

"Something like that," Oriana whispered. "You know the power struggle has always been there between those various forces in the unseen world."

"How is it that you chose the dark forces?" Jeremy wondered cautiously.

"I never had a choice. I was born into it. I was taught the mysterious, grandiose side of the teachings that hid its uglier aspects. It seemed to be more about the development of personal power than about the worship of evil. They had me fooled, me and many others who are still fooled. It actually seemed like the right path to take, entering the arcane mysteries and experiencing new psychic capacities. It took me a long time to realize what the ultimate goals were."

"What are those goals?"

"What seemed like personal empowerment is really servitude to masters like Stefan Zorn."

Jeremy and Lynn both reacted in shock.

"I take it you know the name," Oriana said observing the look on their faces.

"He came to our community once to see the Prophet."

"So you've met him?"

"Just very briefly. Do you know him?" Lynn wondered.

"Oh yes. He has come in and out of my life from my earliest memories. He always terrified me. But for years I thought it was because of his great skills. Now I understand that it was because of his black heart. He is very happy right now at what has taken place. This is the moment he has been waiting for and he will undoubtedly accomplish his aims."

"Not as long as I'm alive," Jeremy said.

Oriana looked at him with a certain pity. "You can't fight a man like him. He's got connections in high places."

"So do I!" Jeremy said with new confidence. "And I'm certain of one thing. Even though humanity is helpless right now, and may play into his hands, there are other realms that will not be passive at his takeover."

"Can you call down legions of angels?" Oriana asked sarcastically.

"No, but I'll be a thorn in his side and will create the opposite of what he's trying to do. That's what the Prophet prepared us for."

"I'll help you however I can," Oriana said, her face radiating with sacrificial courage.

"That means a great deal to us, Oriana," Lynn said. "The first thing we need to do is find Andrew."

"In the midst of this chaos, it will take a miracle," the young woman said sadly.

"We count on miracles," Lynn responded. "We live for them. Be sure of one thing. Stefan Zorn and his minions don't have all the power. There is another source. It's power is even greater!"

* * * * *

Before the giant dust clouds had begun to settle over the land or drifted off into the upper layers of the atmosphere, a convocation of the most powerful individuals in the world was called to order in the bowels of Corridor 600, the only safe place left on the planet.

General MacDaniel stood at the head of a vast oval table around which sat the richest and most influential people across the globe. Each one had been flown in on private jets under military protection. In this one room was gathered the very axis that kept the world's economy in operation—CEOs of international corporations, government dictators, arms dealers, billionaires. Two dozen men and women kept the world population at work, fed it, and fueled the system called civilization, a system that made them richer than kings.

In the midst of this powerful group sat the impassive but magnetic figure of Stefan Zorn. No one but the general knew his identity, yet somehow he fit right in with this group of ultimate dominators. Oddly enough, in the midst of utter global chaos, the reins of power were being pulled tighter than ever.

"I call this emergency meeting to order!" the general said, standing before the group in his dress uniform sparkling with rows of medals across his chest. "I need not tell you why you are here. Whatever country you call home has experienced a devastation unlike any other seen before in recorded history. Had we actually faced each other in another world war, the results could not have been worse."

Several men around the table chuckled at the idea, having attempted for years to create that very war.

"The world's communication systems, agricultural activity, and economies are at a standstill. Millions have died, millions more will soon die, and so it is. It is up to us to start the engine again and save our world from slipping back into a dark age from which it may never recover. We have among us the most powerful leaders in the world gathered together for the first time, thanks to the Federation's military communications system which has not been entirely destroyed. You were all personally chosen to be in this meeting by the executive council of the Federation. You are considered to be in positions to actively participate in keeping our civilization from sinking into annihilation altogether. Each of you is highly respected in his or her field. At this table, ladies and gentlemen, is the power of the world. It is we who will control its destiny."

The general paused for dramatic effect. Stefan Zorn looked around the room, keeping a poker face before these people who knew nothing of him. He had a strong desire to release a mocking smirk. These people only imagined they had power. As he humbly sat there among them, without any of the resources or fame the others held, he knew nevertheless that he would some day control them all. With the patience of a master craftsman, he watched his plan unfold before his very eyes. He knew when his time would come to take over.

"Our first duty is to sustain the food distribution as best we can," the general continued. "We will have to make some hard decisions. There are some parts of the world that we will have to let starve so that others may survive. Our decisions cannot be made politically. That is why you are here, being practical, levelheaded business men and women. What is needed here is the common sense that will keep the majority alive. There can be no room for misplaced compassion that would seek to care for everyone's needs. It is simply impossible and I know without taking a vote that you all agree with me.

"The second order of priority is to gain control of the weapon stocks and nuclear armaments that are so vulnerable right now. Have no doubt that rebel leaders will surface like rats rushing out of the sewers. We must crush such individuals mercilessly before they have a chance to set up power bases that will be counter to our plans. I'm sure you'll agree that the Federation has done a fine job in this past decade unifying the military power of the world. Now we must do more than that. It is necessary to make use of that unification by stamping out all of our detractors."

The general glanced at Stefan Zorn who had masterminded the plan for global martial law and delivered it freely to MacDaniel with his blessing to take credit for it. Zorn watched him steadily, enjoying the precision of his manipulations. The general made a slight motion with his hand and half a dozen officers appeared from the shadows. They placed bound manuscripts before each of the people at the table.

"You will find here a methodology to accomplish our common goals, a systematic breakdown of the ways in which we can ensure control of the population, even under these extreme conditions. Your role is carefully defined in these documents and I believe you will be pleased to see how we have made the best use of your skills."

He watched the people open the manuscripts and scan through the material with great interest.

"Rest assured that your comfort and enjoyment of the life-style to which you are accustomed will be well guarded and increased."

"This is the work of a genius," an Asian man stated enthusiastically, having quickly perceived the thread of the ideas on the pages.

The general acknowledged the compliment with false humility and made sure to keep his eyes averted from Zorn.

"But do you have the will to make these plans a reality?" the man asked in a challenging tone.

MacDaniel hesitated. He wasn't sure what that mysterious Chinese mind was seeking out.

"It will take a great deal of . . . clamping down," a woman with a European accent asked.

"A lot of blood in streets," a large Turkish businessman pointed out bluntly.

"This is a new approach for Federation forces," the Asian man continued. "Can you achieve your desired results?"

The general's face turned hard and cold. He let the assemblage witness the appearance of the killer within him.

"Let there be no mistake! We will wipe out all resistance even if it takes a scorched-earth policy to do so!"

"Your soldiers will be willing to shoot civilians on sight?" an Indian woman wondered suspiciously.

"We will place the officers who fought in the Syrian conflict of the last decade in command of our urban squadrons. They'll be happy to follow these orders, believe me. I've seen them in action. And many of them know how I deal with insubordination."

"The armies of the world turned on their own people . . . "an African leader muttered. "That's not a new idea. However, it could backfire and cause greater conflict."

Some agreed with him and turned to the general for his response.

"When you read the material more closely, you will note that we are preparing a vast program that includes the establishment of detention camps the size of our largest stadiums, the training of special death squads whose sole purpose will be the hunting down and termination of dangerous individuals, the creation of interrogation centers that will rival the fear struck in the hearts of the population in the last century by the Gestapo. Our surveillance networks are still operational for tracking dissident groups. And we will invest all of our armed forces with the power to destroy on sight anyone who poses or seems to pose a threat to them. A zero tolerance policy will be in place. We will quickly show by example that we mean what we say. The people will fall in line or they will end up in ditches by the roadside."

The assemblage sat in silence, satisfied by the general's words. They were unified in the knowledge that only the iron fist of total control could maintain them in power and positions of privilege in a world that had lost all semblance of order.

Stefan Zorn sat back in his chair, content with the direction things were taking. His steady climb to the pinnacle of domination was well underway.

* * * * *

Tom and Andrew wandered through the colossal ruins on the outskirts of the city. The horizon was black with dust and the acrid smoke of thousands of fires. Day was turning to night as the sun was buried from view behind the global clouds of destruction. The Earth vomited its misery into the skies as though sending desperate signals to other worlds. But the belching of smoke and toxic vapors would only serve to further the planet's distress. Stirred up by great winds and shrieking storms, the mountains of dust and debris fell over the wounded landscape like a veil of sorrow.

Muddy, black rain fell on the dead and dying from Bangkok to New York City. Rivers of blood, gasoline, and sewage rushed through the streets of every city, from Istanbul to Paris.

The story of human accomplishment would have to start again from scratch.

Andrew and his new companion were mute with shock. Only the fierce, howling wind broke the stillness, punctuated by explosions in the distance.

The city skyline, already splintered by the recent quake, was a horrific mangle of twisted silhouettes smoldering and groaning like a great beast in a death grip. Andrew wanted to turn away and run back to the countryside where at least they were less likely to find mounds of corpses at every corner. Tom suddenly grabbed his arm and shocked him back into the realization that he had to face and endure the very thing that his beloved Prophet had told him would be coming.

At the far end of the road they traveled on, a group of soldiers were pushing people up against the wall of a building. The two men watched in horror as the soldiers struck the civilians with the butt of their rifles, brutalizing them as they searched through their clothing. Then the soldiers stepped back, one of them shouted, and a burst of machine gun fire tore through the helpless people who convulsed and fell to the ground.

"God in heaven!" Tom shouted, unable to control himself.

"Quiet!" Andrew whispered. But it was too late. One

of the soldiers turned and spotted them. He pointed in their direction and shouted at his companions. The soldiers rushed toward them. Tom and Andrew raced into the jungle of ruins. Shots echoed around them and bullets exploded in the concrete, splattering dust on them.

A strange thought went through Andrew's mind as he stumbled over the debris. Maybe it would be simpler to turn around and let them shoot him. Why should he keep living this nightmare which only seemed to get worse by the hour? He started to turn around and meet his death.

"*What are you doing*?"

He turned to Tom who was scampering over the slabs of shattered buildings. He realized that Tom was too busy saving himself to have spoken to him. Andrew suddenly understood that the voice in his head was *the* voice that had saved him before. It was the voice of the Final Prophet.

"*What are you doing*?" the voice said again.

Andrew felt terribly ashamed and suddenly redoubled his efforts to escape, this time not for himself but for the cause for which he had been chosen.

They ran through back alleys and a labyrinth of destruction that protected them from their pursuers even though every step was treacherous.

Out of breath and faces streaked with sweat and dirt, Tom and Andrew finally made their way to a quiet square that seemed like a clearing in the forest of rubble. The space they came upon was strangely peaceful in the midst of all the destruction, a kind of sanctuary at the heart of the devastation. They made their way through a narrow corridor in the debris and stopped to catch their breath in the old-fashioned square, complete with fountain and storefronts. The fountain was cracked and the water burst out of broken pipes like a wild geyser. Shattered glass covered the streets and all the doors were torn off their hinges, hanging sideways like dead men tied to an execution post.

They leaned against the fountain, splashed water on their faces, and drank deeply. The soldiers had long given up their pursuit in the catacombs of destruction that the city had become.

"Any idea where we are?" Tom asked when his voice returned to him.

"None," Andrew answered, still struggling to catch his breath.

"This place is my hometown and I can't recognize a square inch of it. This must be the Forest Hills district, or what's left of it. I don't see any point in wandering any further into the city. What do you propose we do now?"

"We've got to find a way to contact our friends . . . if they're still alive."

"How do we do that? I'll bet there's not a working phone for fifty miles."

"Cell phones are still operational, at least for awhile. I have the strange feeling that Jeremy and Lynn are looking for us."

"You said they were somewhere north of Marysville."

"That's right. I just feel them close by somehow. It makes no sense. But nothing does anymore."

"At least we're alive," Tom pointed out.

"I'm not sure that's doing us any good," Andrew responded, still unable to find any peace with being alive. It would have been easier if the garage ceiling had crushed him like a bug.

"I heard the voice again," he blurted out.

Tom turned to him eagerly.

"When?"

"Just a little bit ago. The soldiers were right behind us. The voice has saved my life twice in less then twenty-four hours."

"It saved my life as well. What do you make of it?"

"Obviously, there's a new breakthrough between us and the spirit realm. I've never in my life encountered phenomena like this. It could be that the terror of the situation is creating new possibilities."

"It should give us hope anyway."

"Don't forget I saw how the Prophet ended up. I'm not sure what there is to hope for. If he didn't escape a gruesome fate, why should we?"

"Because they need us."

"Who?"

"The higher forces. They can't operate on this plane without human agents, no matter how imperfect we are."

"You've been living too long in a world of fantasy," Andrew retorted sarcastically.

"How strange for you to say that, as one who witnessed the Prophet's miracles up close."

Andrew's face turned red with guilt. Tom had struck him where he was most vulnerable. There was no denying what he had witnessed with the Prophet. He couldn't return to a cynical, secular mind set anymore. He knew too much.

"Sometimes I wish I'd never met him," he heard himself say in spite of his wounded conscience.

"You don't mean that!" Tom barked at him. "It's the greatest privilege you could have hoped for."

"To endure unspeakable hardship and accept it serenely?"

"Don't you realize, Andrew, that you and your friends are perhaps the only people in the world who have any purpose and meaning to cling to now? Everybody else is in state of total despair and wretchedness. You've been prepared. You've got a mission."

Andrew looked at the crushed city around them and held up his arms.

"How can we possibly start again?"

"We're not suppose to rebuild a city. We're suppose to rebuild the human soul."

Andrew turned to Tom with irritation. "Awfully arrogant from someone who wasn't even there to hear the man speak!"

Tom shrugged his shoulders. "I'm just telling you what I feel in my heart of hearts."

Andrew suddenly remembered the words of the Prophet about receiving messages from the humblest sources. Everything could speak to one who had ears to hear and eyes to see. Even a down on his luck writer with no future could be a channel of wisdom. Andrew put his hand on Tom's shoulder.

"I'm sorry. I'm not thinking straight right now."

"I don't blame you," Tom answered. "It's been a rather rocky day."

They laughed sadly at the understatement.

A loud speaker suddenly crackled to life and a booming, authoritarian voice burst through the air.

"Attention! Attention! This is the voice of the Federation. Everyone who is able must report to the nearest relocation center where food and blankets will be provided. Repeat: if you are able to walk, you must report to one of our relocation centers immediately! Anyone found in the streets within an hour of this announcement will be arrested. All able persons must report to the relocation center nearest them. The wounded will be cared for by our medical teams."

The voice died away in a haze of static crackle and the message was heard starting again in the far distance.

"Relocation centers?" Tom cried out. "That doesn't sound right."

"It's not just the earth that's undergone changes, Tom. Our government has changed dramatically as well. Its mask of benevolence has been dropped."

"You don't think what we saw back there with those soldiers was an isolated incident?"

"No, I think it's the order of the day. We'll be next if they find us. We've got to get out of the city. It's one giant prison now."

Andrew closed his eyes and seemed to listen to some inner prompting. Tom looked at his new friend whose haggard features were now radiant with a strange tranquility. He waited patiently even though his survival instincts screamed at him to get going.

After a moment, Andrew opened his eyes.

"They're here!" he said in a whisper with a soft smile.

A shiver went through his companion. He wasn't sure whether that was good or bad news. What he did know was that his friend was manifesting clairvoyant gifts which Tom knew had not been his the day before. Transformation was occurring before his very eyes.

"Who?" Tom finally asked.

"Jeremy and Lynn are nearby. Follow me."

Andrew hurried off to the end of the square that led toward a small wooded park.

"The city limits are that way!" Tom called out, pointing in the other direction. "We've got to get out of here!"

"We need to go this way first!"

"Don't tell me you know what you're doing or where you're going!" Tom cried out.

Andrew looked back at him. "I don't! But I know I'm being guided. That's even better."

CHAPTER TWENTY-ONE

Triage was taking place in the streets. Damaged cities throughout the world were turning into vast tent dwellings as survivors tried to protect themselves from the fierce elements and adapt to a life without any twenty-first century comforts. Hospitals especially were overwhelmed. Many of them were destroyed and there were such great numbers of wounded and dying that only the worst cases could be treated. Everyone else was bandaged up and left to be cared for by relatives, if they had any left. The streets were a permanent jumble of broken glass, twisted metal and junks of concrete. Only military vehicles could get through, crushing everything in their way.

The world had turned into a war zone, and the enemy did not come from another nation, but was the planet itself as it convulsed in the grips of its cosmic trauma.

Highways everywhere were broken up like the partial skeleton of great dinosaurs still hovering over the land they once dominated. Sirens were always screaming somewhere as new fires broke out or a building tumbled over. The countryside seemed to be the only sane place to be after centuries of vacating it. But even there nothing was the same. Bridges that remained standing were unstable, rivers were overflowing their banks and washing into people's living rooms. Those who lived in remote areas were entirely on their own in ways they had never wanted to be.

Gun shots echoed constantly through the urban areas. Battalions armed to the teeth hurried through the rubble, attempting to restore order against all hope. The population was in a frenzy, and crime was rampant everywhere. It seemed to be the only way to stay alive, at least for now. Certain elements took advantage of the situation, looted whatever they could get their hands on and murdered with abandon, finally freed from society's boundaries. It wasn't long before people gathered in groups to organize themselves as the realization sunk in that the government could do little to help them. Secret subcultures had been waiting for this time for decades if not centuries. They were in their element now, with underground shelters, hoarding their precious food and weapons for themselves, and considering all who were not part of their privileged group to simply be out of luck. Compassion was the first victim of the destruction.

No one had time for another person. Children were left to expire under the rubble while adults desperately tried to find a morsel of food or a way to stay warm. Humanity's arrogance and certainty that it could control its destiny and the forces of the planet had received a death blow. It would be a long time before the species could fool itself again.

People huddled around battery-operated television sets and radios, listening to Federation information and commands, feeding on the illusion that if someone was in charge, things would be put back in order some day, even though the terrible reality of this catastrophe was all around them. The death wish of three generations had finally been granted. Around the world, mass suicides were occurring hourly as people gave up all hope. Death rose into the atmosphere with the toxic fumes and surrounded the earth with a gruesome melancholy that hovered in the dark clouds.

Occult leaders, revolutionaries, brigand rulers appeared overnight like mushrooms sprouting in the dark. This was the world that the Prophet had depicted, only to be hated for it. No one wanted to believe, not until it was too late, until they had to live it out in utter misery. This was also the world that Stefan Zorn could harness for his purposes.

The occult societies that paid allegiance to Stefan Zorn and worshiped the same forces of darkness were the most prepared to meet the new conditions on the planet. They quickly began to infiltrate the makeshift centers of power that attempted to create structure out of chaos one community at a time. Along with fulfilling a centuries-old mission, there was another top priority on the agenda. Across the world, word was out to search out and destroy all of the remaining followers of the Final Prophet.

No group was better organized than Zorn's minions to maneuver in the chaos. This was their element and human suffering created a perverse pleasurable atmosphere for them. Around the world, super-secret occult societies were stepping out of the shadows to take charge. They had the greatest resources at their disposal, the most sophisticated underground survival systems, and most of all, a carefully rehearsed plan. Entire regions would soon fall under their well-orchestrated manipulations. Relocation centers, food banks, even police stations would soon be run by members of Stefan Zorn's groups. The lights had gone out on gigantic portions of the globe and virtually all that was good about human civilization. No computer technology could provide a quick fix.

* * * * *

As soon as Tom and Andrew stepped out of the rubble onto a wide street, they spotted a car coming out of the park and heading slowly toward them. At that moment, a ray of sunlight pierced through the thick, unnatural darkness, shot through space, and landed directly on the vehicle.

Andrew's attention turned to the car that seemed to glow in the momentary appearance of the star's light.

"That's them!" he said as his heart pounded like never before. "That's Jeremy and Lynn!"

"It can't be!" Tom cried out.

The car came to a stop a short distance from them. Jeremy jumped out.

"Is that you, Andrew?" he cried out.

"Jeremy!" Andrew shouted in a burst of gratitude, relief, and joy. "Yes, it's me, Andrew!"

The passenger door flew open and Lynn stepped out and raced toward them. Andrew met her halfway. They hugged intensely.

"Thank God! Thank God!" she whispered, "thank God we found you!"

She looked up at him and held his face in her hands. "Are you all right?"

He nodded, tears streaming down his face. She kissed his cheeks fervently.

"Forgive me for putting you through all this!"

"It was meant to be," Andrew responded. "We're just instruments."

Jeremy approached Andrew. They hugged silently with deep emotion. When he was able to speak again, Andrew turned to his companion.

"This would be Tom," Jeremy said as he extended his hand. "Welcome among us!"

"You must be Jeremy," Tom said in a wavering voice. "The Prophet's first disciple."

"We've been looking for you," Jeremy said. "Lynn

insisted that we come to your rescue."

"It didn't have to be so dramatic," Tom responded, gesturing to the devastation around them.

Their laughter was interrupted by the appearance of Oriana who stepped out of the car and stood at its side, shivering with remorse.

"What the hell!" Andrew shouted with sudden rage and totally confused. "What is she doing here?"

Tom's eyes nearly popped out of his head. "Oriana! What a day of wonders!"

Andrew grabbed hold of his arm. "She's the one who entrapped me and got me arrested!"

"That's impossible!" Tom said.

"Believe me, there's no mistake. She assaulted me."

Oriana wept silently. Jeremy stepped between Andrew and the young woman.

"Everything's changing, Andrew. She's with us now."

"How can you possibly trust her after what she's done?"

"I'll explain it to you in the car. But know this. Incredible things are happening, not only in the outside world, but in the spirit realm. She's been touched by the Prophet."

Andrew wanted to argue, but realized that it was all too mysterious for him to understand. It was not up to him to judge what miracles might be granted to people around him, since they were happening within him as well. They got into the car.

"What do we do now, Jeremy?" Andrew asked as he wiped tears from his eyes.

"Don't you realize this is what the Prophet prepared us for, this very moment. We know what we have to salvage and keep alive in spite of everything."

"How do we stay away from those who seek our destruction?"

"Oriana will help us keep one step ahead of them."

"How can she do that?" Andrew asked suspiciously.

"She knows their ultimate plan. That will help us anticipate their next move."

"How will we communicate with the outside world and pull people out of the vortex?"

Lynn took Andrew's hand with the greatest gentleness. "Some will find us. We need only build a place that they can come to and start again."

"Do you think anybody cares anymore about the deeper things of the spirit?" he asked as his voice caught in his throat.

"Now more than ever, Andrew," she said, eyes sparkling with intense certainty. "Everything else they've held onto has crumbled. Some will realize that the only solid ground is not made out of matter. Those who are truly seeking for something other than sheer survival will find their way to us."

Tom and Oriana held each other tightly in the back seat of the car, overwhelmed with the joy of being together again against all odds. Andrew leaned over the front seat and whispered to Jeremy and Lynn.

"I've heard a Voice . . . "

A radiant smile softened the tense features of the two soul mates.

"So have we," Lynn said.

Jeremy turned to his friend. "In ancient times, the Essenes told of the battle between the sons of Light and the sons of Darkness. It was taken as symbol and myth, full of esoteric meaning. Today, it's literally true. We have chosen sides."

"Maybe we've *been* chosen," Lynn said softly.

"That could be. In either case," Jeremy added, his jaw clenching with determination, "now it begins!" He turned to his beloved and kissed her waiting lips to give himself courage and to promise her that his love would never die, whatever might happen to him in this life.

"What's that noise?" Tom said suddenly, turning his attention to the window.

Everyone listened as a growing whirling sound filled the air. The eerie, rhythmic noise sounded like the heavy breathing of some monstrous creature or a huge bird flapping its wings.

As it became louder and louder, Andrew finally cried out:

"A helicopter!"

They looked up to the dark skies just as a huge military helicopter burst out of the clouds right above them. They could see the murderous eyes of the soldiers in the cabin.

"Do not move! Stay where you are! Repeat, do not move!" a voice from a loudspeaker shouted, shaking the car windows. "This is a Federation order. You are wanted for questioning. Step out of the car slowly! You will be shot if you do not cooperate!"

The companions turned to each other, terrified.

"What do we do?" Lynn whispered with dread.

"We have no choice," Andrew responded. "We're sitting ducks!"

Jeremy turned back to the wheel and threw the car in gear. The voice echoed again as the helicopter descended to barely fifteen feet above the vehicle.

"Step out of the car now!"

"Hold on tight!" Jeremy yelled as he floored the accelerator.

The car tore off in a cloud of dust and squealing rubber. It swerved frantically over the cracked pavement littered with rubble, heading toward a ray of light that shot through the black clouds and fell over the distant countryside. The helicopter followed swiftly after them, descending to within five feet of the hood of the car. On the horizon, a dark line suddenly appeared and headed at dizzying speeds toward the scene of the chase.

A dozen helicopters separated out of the line and formed a circle that would soon surround the vehicle.

* * * * *

Pale beams of dying sunlight shot through colossal grey clouds, illuminating the shadows hovering over the ruins of the city. A great silence crept through the empty streets, resisted only by the angry howling of the wind. All life seemed to have vanished. A terrifying tranquility announced the onset of more dangerous storms.

A fierce crash of lightning split through the embers of sunset, echoing across the twisted skyline of the ruined city. Within moments, the bellies of great clouds, pregnant with rain, would spill onto the earth.

An old man, of unusual height, overgrown with wild strands of long snow-white hair and a huge unkempt beard, slowly moved through the barren, sinister landscape of devastated buildings. The clothing beneath his heavy, mud-stained trenchcoat from the previous century was tattered and of coarse material. A silver amulet hung from his neck, fashioned in an emblem of strange geometric design. The old man's eyes shimmered with striking intensity. Deep in their dark caverns, they sparkled like rare stones and pierced the object of their attention with the power of a killer hawk's gaze. Though of great strength for his age, the solitary figure supported himself with an antique cane which gave him the appearance of a desert prophet. Yet to most passersby and to the military police that constantly combed the streets, he seemed like a typical homeless vagabond with not much time left to live.

He stopped in front of a cheap motel and observed the flickering neon lights of a broken sign that partially spelled the words "no vacancy". For an instant, the fiery eyes closed and a whisper escaped from the solemn lips.

"Finally . . . " he whispered with a mixture of relief and exhaustion as he knocked on door number forty-four.

The sound of several locks being opened shot back from the other side.

Michelle peered suspiciously through the cracked door. The old sage stood patiently in the dim light.

"Are you the one I've been waiting for?" she asked with a trace of awe in her voice.

Michelle studied the old man, as though searching his soul for some miraculous answer to her secret hopes. A gentle light appeared in the eyes of the sage.

"I have come . . . "

"At whose request?"

"Yours."

The old man smiled gently beneath his forest of beard. Michelle opened the door wider.

"Do I know you?"

They stared into each other's eyes as a deep silence filled the room. For a moment, the outside world utterly vanished beneath the intensity of their gaze. Soul opened to soul, penetrating the solitary regions of that invisible landscape where their true natures dwelt.

"Why are you so familiar to me, old man?"

"We have met in your dreams."

The night visions which had haunted Michelle's sleep for years suddenly flashed before her inner eye. Each was weighed down by an overpowering presence which seemed to watch and guide them. It was that presence which had a familiar quality to it. It was that presence which she recognized in the old sage.

"How can this be?" she let out in a terrified whisper.

The old man stepped forward.

"There is nothing to fear, Michelle."

"This is sorcery!"

"No!" the strange man cried out in outrage.

The old man's voice was at once filled with implacable power. His imperative reply silenced all her thoughts. Her fear disappeared like morning mist in the heat of the rising sun.

"This is your destiny," the sage announced solemnly.

Michelle opened the door wider and let the strange man into the motel room. As his aged eyes adjusted to the dark shadows, he noticed other people huddling in the corners. Among them was Juanita and her baby who smiled merrily at the newcomer. The others weren't so trusting.

"Don't be afraid," he said softly to the glistening eyes full of terror. "I'm a friend."

"We have no friends," Michelle responded, "unless you are a follower of the Prophet."

The old man turned to her and his face became radiant. His eyes vanished behind wrinkles and sparkling tears as his features lit up with warmth and a strange smile.

"Yes, I'm his follower . . . But he followed me once . . . I'm his grandfather."

Robert leapt to his feet, angered by the man's statement. "He had no family! Everybody knows that!"

The old wiseman turned a patient, melancholic look upon the aggressive youth.

"Didn't he teach you to rid yourself of violence? What you say is true . . . The Prophet had no family. I became his adopted grandfather, many years ago."

Juanita approached him in awe. "You knew him when he was a boy?"

The man shook his head affirmatively, pleased to find acceptance in the girl's wide, innocent eyes. He leaned forward and gently touched her cheek.

"I gave him food, shelter, and books. But what he

learned and who he became was not my doing. That was entirely his work and that of greater powers."

"He saved me from death, me and my baby," Juanita said in a whisper of ecstatic joy and gratitude.

"I was told of this miracle. I knew long ago that he would do wonders in this world."

He straightened up painfully and turned to the others. "I also knew that he would meet a tragic end. All of you who love him are also in great danger. I was sent to help you."

"Who sent you?" Michelle asked, still uncertain of his motives.

The white-haired man pointed upward. "They did . . . In a dream. I have such dreams more and more often as I approach my departure from this plane."

"Your dream revealed to you where you would find us?" another student questioned in disbelief.

"Oh yes. It even showed me what bus to ride in order to reach this place. They are closer than ever, you know."

"Who?" Michelle asked, confused.

"Why, the messengers of course. Including the one you call the Final Prophet."

"How do you mean, closer?"

"The drama all around us has called them forth. Without them, we will be utterly destroyed. They have a stake in our survival. There are other forces who seek the opposite and the more they attempt to fulfill their wishes, the more the forces of light seek to counter them."

"How can you help us at a time like this?" another person questioned, studying his frail condition.

"I know of a safe haven . . . Besides, I'm all you've got."

"We're awaiting the return of our friends," Michelle

said with determination. "We don't go anywhere until they come back to us."

"Your friends are not coming back," the old man said sadly. "I saw that in the dream as well."

"I don't believe it!" Michelle cried out. "I don't care what your dream told you! They will return to us safely and I will die waiting for them rather than leave without them!"

"Me too!" Juanita said courageously.

The sage studied the intent faces around him, realizing that they all felt the same.

"Your friends are in grave danger. They've fallen into the hands of the evil one."

Michelle let out a gasp as others burst into tears and moans.

"But they are not alone . . . That I know with more certainty than the fact that I stand here before you! They will not be abandoned in their hour of need. Not now."

"How can you know this?" Robert inquired in a trembling voice and wiping tears from his face.

"Because the forces of light need them as much as your friends need their supernatural assistance. Without your little group, there is no hope for the accomplishment of the Prophet's mission. And that mission has ultimate importance, not only to the human race, but to the galaxy."

"How is that possible?" Michelle asked, trying desperately to find hope in his words.

"Don't you realize what you're involved with? Do you think the Prophet appeared merely to offer you a few bits of wisdom? Your awakening is necessary to the existence of the sun, and of the living being we know as the Milky Way. If we all fall under the influence of darkness, there will be no one to generate the finer energies that keep the solar system from . . . "

He felt that he was saying too much to people who were unprepared to hear his revelations.

"From what?" Robert asked eagerly.

"From being sucked into the black hole that is forming at the center of the galaxy!"

A heavy silence filled the room and his words seem to hang in the air like an ominous cloud. No one moved as the implications of his strange statement slowly sunk in.

"I've come five hundred miles to find you . . . and you know what the conditions are like out there. So I'm here to stay. I'll wait for your friends with you."

"Then let's make some tea for you," Michelle ordered as she pointed him to a chair. "What is your name?"

"Tobias Hungerman."

"Mr. Hungerman, we welcome you . . . "

"Call me Tobias," he said as he gratefully sat at the table and rested his weary limbs. The companions joined him around the table. Juanita sat next to him, holding her baby lovingly in her arms.

"Tell us about the Prophet when he was young."

"Let the man rest," someone said.

"I'd be glad to tell you about him, young lady. That story was the most beautiful period of my life. I was much younger then of course, and handsomer too. It was just before the turn of the century. Things seemed normal then, although we knew that something immense lay out with the new millennium. I had moved to a small town not very far from here, at the edge of the Sierra Nevada mountains. I'd been a lifelong student of philosophy and metaphysics. My beloved teacher had just died and I wanted to get away from the centers of culture."

"Don't you like people?" Juanita asked innocently.

"Most of them were so immersed in the foolishness that passed for culture. Even then I knew it was all headed for what the Federation's made of it—a senseless, hypnotic trick meant to deaden the human soul."

One of the students brought out a cup of steaming tea and placed it before him.

"Thank you," Tobias said gratefully. He sipped it as they all watched him. "Haven't had such good tea in decades!"

"Linda's from England," Juanita said merrily. "She really knows her teas."

"I can tell . . . Anyway, my closest neighbor in those days was a strange old lady. Everyone thought she was plain crazy. I wasn't so sure. We didn't talk much but she knew that my hobby and addiction was truth seeking. And I guess she appreciated that. One day, she showed up at my door. She looked terribly distressed so I invited her in. She told me she'd be dying soon and that she needed my help. I tried to convince her that she looked healthy to me, but she was certain of it. She told me that she did not live alone as we all thought. She had a young child with her that nobody had ever seen. It was an abandoned baby boy that she had found three years before, left to die in a wooded area in the foothills of the Sierra Nevada mountains."

"Someone just left a baby in the middle of nowhere?" Juanita asked in horror.

"She told me she always suspected that the child was a changeling . . . "

"What's that?" Juanita asked.

"There's an ancient Celtic myth that changelings are children born from the tuatha de daanan peoples, the fairy folk, and left for people to find and raise as their own. In other words, he'd come from another dimension. The woman almost had me convinced that she was indeed insane until I realized that she had loved and cared for that child at the cost of great sacrifice. She kept him hidden away because she was afraid the community would take him away from her. And she knew there was something very special about him. Even as a small infant, there was a unique healing heat in his hands. She told me he had the eyes of an old wiseman. He didn't behave at all like other children. He was thoughtful and reflective even at that early age. He seemed to understand her without words, as though he could read her mind."

The friends listened in awe as the old man told them of the early life of their beloved Prophet, the man who had changed their lives forever. The little motel room was filled with a reverence and silence worthy of a great sanctuary as the old man quietly whispered about the wondrous presence of the one called the Final Prophet.

"Was he from this world or not?" Robert asked impatiently, always the sceptic.

"I lived with him for ten years. He seemed human enough, in spite of the old soul that lived inside him. One day he looked at me and said: it's time for me to go. I nodded, knowing this time would come. Then he was out the door and I never saw him again. But I always knew he was here for a special purpose."

"You didn't answer my question," Robert said firmly.

"I think the Prophet came from the stars, that's what I think. But I'm just an old man . . . "

A stunned silence fell over the group, as though a veil was being lifted on some cosmic truth that was too vast to be grasped by the human mind. The dark motel room seemed to morph into an ancient chapel.

"But it's his teachings that matter," Tobias said in a whisper after awhile. "That's why he appeared among us. Be sure that sustained desire to make his ideas come alive within you is never lost, even in the face of such utter catastrophe."

"I feel like the external trauma around us has entered into my very soul," Michelle stated sadly, unable to hide the guilt in her tone of voice. Tobias turned luminous, compassionate eyes upon her.

"He taught you to know yourself, did he not? Surely, you remember his observation about our nature and how to begin the process of transformation. Life is indeed a constant interference with those aims. In a more natural world, people should be able to have time to be quiet, to think or reflect, to move at a slower pace. We have been aborted from a natural life and the necessary suffering resulting from this is hard to take for everyone. And yet . . . The Prophet said over and over again that life's in-your-face distractions end up being our best teachers.

"That's still a problem for me. Especially now that life is nothing but destruction," Michelle whispered.

The old man reached out and placed a warm hand on her shoulder.

"I know that you were one of his closest students. Remember his fundamental revelation to us—using negative energy for transformation means neutralizing the negative momentum that generated it and rechanneling this available energy for conscious work. If you pull the irritation out of your irritated reaction, what you have is new energy circulating within you. The effort of not going with the current, which is now drowning people by the millions, creates a sort of alchemical effect which refines that energy and may give you an intense moment of self-awareness and intensified presence to the instant of your life.

"Don't forget that the Prophet's teaching deals with awareness of and intentional uses of energy, harnessed for the aims of awakening. The "enemy" is not in the external world, not even with the Federation after you, but up close and personal—within you. It is that which becomes irritated which is your troubles, not the apparent cause of that irritation. Use it to remind you of what you are really trying to accomplish."

"Sometimes the observer within that he taught us to become forgets and sometimes the observer separates and remembers the teaching," Michelle stated as her throat tightened.

The old man took a sip of tea and looked around at the faces staring at him breathlessly. Tobias understood from a place deep within that it was his duty to feed these distraught disciples who were so lost and without direction. Though he hardly felt worthy of the task, he realized that there was no one else available to remind them of all that the Prophet had taught them at the cost of his life.

"It is more complicated and more subtle than this, although it is true that ultimately the presence of your authentic self is already behind or within your current state of consciousness. But vanity creates pictures and assumptions that provide us with other identities that are so far removed from the "One" you are that there is real fragmentation. If you truly follow the Prophet's teaching, you will become another person, and yet be more truly yourself than you have ever been. You will not be subject to the knee-jerk reactions, requirements, expectations, and concepts of reality that you are now.

"Most of you experience yourselves as your opinions, feelings, etc. But you are something else, something inescapably spiritual. Don't ever forget what the Prophet told us—we must travel the path of self-becoming in order to encounter lasting meaning and purpose.

"There is a critical part of you that is missing. It will not appear until you have conquered your weaknesses, old habits and illusions.

"We have to develop new psychological 'muscles'", a student stated with emphatic certainty.

"This is not correct," the old man said bluntly as his

shimmering eyes turned upon the man who thought he understood. "This a partial truth. We begin with new muscles of attention and awareness. But that is just the tip of the iceberg. This "iceberg" leads to the source of your being to which you must become transparent.

"The fact is that we are all shattered into many contradictory pieces and the outcome of our personal spiritual battle is still uncertain. To "know thyself" is to come face to face with the tragic and dangerous reality of this condition. Once that happens, the real journey and struggle begins."

Everyone silently absorbed what the old man with the strange glowing eyes had said. They each shared the same inner excitement, as though their beloved Prophet had returned in the shape of this ragged tramp and once again offered them life-giving wisdom.

"The ticket," Tobias continued, " to enter into this is nothing less than sacrificing everything to what is best in us. There is much old snake skin to be removed so that conscience, heart, spirit, can be unburied and bring forth the light of new understanding."

"I feel that my life runs it course and ultimately is of little significance, value or meaning. I want to know what is on the other side of the curtain," someone in the back of the room said in a faltering voice.

"This is true and not true," the old man responded. "You are seeing only partially and "through a glass darkly." This is a stage. You will move beyond this. Many seekers have stayed there and died in those feelings of emptiness and meaninglessness. You do not need to do that. You have already been given material to start peeking behind the curtain. There is more than the world of senses and even of mind. There is mystery, wonder, help, power, love, light available to you. A wiseman from the last century, whom the Prophet loved to quote, said one day to his students: 'Open the door and let yourself be found. That is the whole thing.'

"Most of our inner efforts are aimed at removing obstacles that inhibit the experience of deeper things which will answer many of your questions and transform your understanding. Having encountered the Prophet and his disciples, you are on the right track, you have been given pieces of the most important puzzle there is. Trust that you will be helped to put it together. Just remember that if you get close to the fire, it burns. But the burn can be more than pain. It can be transformation."

"The difficulty for me sometimes is the inability to find meaning or value in anything," Michelle admitted from the depths of her soul. "The feeling that our death and the uncertainty of what occurs thereafter permeates everything around me with a 'unreality'."

Tobias suddenly took hold of her chin and raised her face. Tears streamed down her cheeks as he stared fire into her eyes, sending a new force into her crushed spirit. When the tears had stopped, evaporating in the heat pulsating from the old man's aura, he spoke to her with a distant, serene calmness.

"It is urgent to your life that you begin to integrate that awareness with the "other reality" that is before you. This is a cornerstone development. The mystics speak of immanence and transcendence simultaneously, or eternity in time. Some of them were called "witnesses to eternity." At the same time, they were fully engaged in life.

"Your deepest longings are directly linked to your mundane everyday life. The Prophet wants you to translate that lofty knowledge into "being" which incorporates common sense, strength, devotion, sacrifice, self-transcendence, acceptance, forgiveness, and sometimes righteous indignation at darkness and intentional evil."

He patted her cheek with infinite gentleness, then turned to the others.

"Listen to me, all of you. Don't let the destruction of everything you've known fool you. There are ultimate, eternal realities that cannot be torn down. Believe this until you know it with every fiber of your being. An ancient saint said that you must believe before you can understand. You must open the door to the possibility of such reality before you can encounter it. Part of your soul knows there is something more. Find that part of yourself and remember it always.

"The Prophet wished with extraordinary compassion and empathy to awaken you to a reality that can change everything for you and make you who you are truly fated to be. But know that you are wandering into holy territory, dealing with sacred things. You must eventually develop a new sensitivity toward the reality of the "higher," the divine, the transcendent, the immortal. The Prophet came to remind us of our obligation to existence itself.

"What I am here to say to you is this: Be careful not to forget all that has been given to you. The Prophet's teachings have power you know not of. You can receive help from beyond the reality you know. And in fact you already are. So be humble and focused and committed to your heart's deepest longings."

The old man raised his hands, sending an energy of blessing over the group.

"Be at peace. Even now, in the midst of the Tribulation. Trust the mystery that caused your path to cross with that of the Final Prophet."

CHAPTER TWENTY-TWO

Jeremy, Lynn and their companions were forced into a steel room beneath the Federation's military headquarters. Several soldiers stood in front of the bolted door, machine guns in hand. They were still in shock from the abrupt end to the chase as helicopters had landed ahead of them and the tires were shot out from under the car.

"We're lucky to be alive . . . "Jeremy mumbled. He knew it wasn't true, now that they were all caught in the enemy's net.

"How did they manage to find us?" he asked to break the terrible silence.

Andrew shook his head trying to hold tears back. "They must have planted some kind of tracking device on us when we were in the jail. That's the only way I can figure it. We brought them straight to you. I'm so sorry!"

"Don't be," Lynn said softly. "This is all part of the play."

"What do you mean?" Andrew asked, eyes brimming with tears.

"Do you remember what the Prophet said about accepting what is and in doing so finding the traces of purpose and meaning behind the events? Even now, there's no reason to give up hope. We may be exactly where we're suppose to be."

"That doesn't make any sense!" Jeremy said. "What are the others going to do if we get executed? The Prophet's mission is over."

"The Prophet's mission is not dependent on just us. It's much bigger than that," Lynn insisted. "If we don't succeed, someone else will step forward."

"You think so?" Jeremy challenged. "I don't agree. I think we're it, we're the remnant. The others who were with the Prophet are scattered."

"Maybe we shouldn't talk about this anymore," Andrew suggested. "You know they're listening."

"It's all nonsense to them," Jeremy continued. "Military officers don't have mystical inclinations."

"I'm not so sure we're just dealing with the military, Jeremy."

"What do you mean?"

"Ask her!" Andrew replied, pointing to Oriana. She looked at them, pale as a ghost.

"What's he talking about?" Jeremy asked.

"He may be right," Oriana said in a trembling voice. "The cult has ties to the highest levels of the Federation."

At that moment, the heavy door unbolted loudly and swung open. The large silhouette of Stefan Zorn suddenly appeared in the corridor. He entered the room like a cold gust of wind, accompanied by two savage-looking bodyguards. The door slammed and bolted behind him.

He silently studied the group, walking around them as they stood in the middle of the room. He stopped in front of Jeremy and glared at him for a moment.

"So you're the Prophet's right hand man?"

"I was his friend," Jeremy said softly, showing no fear of the vicious man.

"He's dead and gone. Why are you still making a fuss about it?"

"His words came true."

"I could have told you what was going to happen just as easily!" Zorn said, his eyes sparkling with anger.

"You couldn't have told us how to endure it," Andrew called out.

Jeremy turned a look upon his friend that told him he shouldn't have made that comment.

"Told you how to endure it?" Zorn asked with a curiosity he couldn't hide. "You've got a secret anecdote to disaster? How are you going to fix the global devastation?" he asked, inches away from Andrew's face. "Tell me what you meant!" Zorn ordered.

"Just that he told us we would have to develop the moral courage to deal with these conditions."

Zorn peered into his soul silently, searching out a deeper answer. Andrew tried to still his mind so that the occult master would not steal anything from it.

"He taught you how to be in touch with another type of consciousness, didn't he?" the man growled.

Andrew turned pale but did not respond. Zorn looked at Lynn who stared back at him defiantly.

"He taught you how to resist external stimulus . . . so as to build an independent state of being. Am I right?"

He stepped in front of Lynn who didn't blink at the nearness of his repulsive presence.

"Am I right, young lady?"

"What does it matter to you? Do you need to control everyone, is that your ambition?" she responded.

"Pretty much," he retorted with a sly smile. "I don't appreciate independent souls. They aggravate me and interfere with my plans. You can understand that, can't you?"

He stepped back and looked at the group.

"We can't have people thinking for themselves when we need cohesion and obedience at a time like this."

"Do you expect to brainwash the entire population?" Tom blurted out angrily.

"Yes, I do! Starting with you."

"Go ahead and try!" Tom said with foolhardy courage.

"I take it you're not one of the Prophet's followers," Zorn observed as he approached him.

"I didn't know him," Tom answered with a new uneasiness, surprised that the man knew this.

"You didn't learn from him like the others did. You're just blowing your horn out of sheer arrogance, aren't you? You don't know what you're talking about or who you're dealing with."

Zorn's features darkened while a strange light seemed to emanate from his eyes. Tom let out a shout and fell to his knees as though a bolt of electricity had gone through him. He trembled in near convulsions.

"Don't fool with things you know nothing about, boy. Next time, I'll fry your brains."

He turned to Jeremy. "You need to teach him some manners. If the rest of your group are as stupid as he is, this is going to be a piece of cake."

"Why are we such a threat to you?" Lynn asked, hoping to save Tom from any further torment.

"What if I told you I just disliked your kind?" Zorn replied disdainfully.

"It wouldn't be worth this much trouble," Lynn continued. "I'll tell you why we're a threat to you."

"You will?" Zorn retorted merrily, enjoying her courageous nature.

"You can't control us, no matter what you do! You can't have power over us."

"You might be surprised, young lady," Zorn grumbled.

"You think pain is a form of control? You can break someone, but you'll never win their souls over."

"I don't give a damn about your soul!" Zorn suddenly shouted in a rage.

"Maybe you don't want people to know about your

plans," Jeremy stated, calling the wild man's attention on him.

"You don't have any idea what my plan is, even with the traitor among you," Zorn said as he pointed at Oriana. She turned away from him in revulsion and fear. He turned back to Lynn and looked deeply into her eyes.

"Do you want to live?"

"Of course," she answered simply.

"You love this man," he said pointing to Jeremy, "and you want to have a long life with him in spite of the hardship out there."

She nodded and looked over at her beloved who sent her his love silently.

"And you also know that I have the power to end it all for you right here and now. One click of my fingers and these soldiers will fill your body with holes, toss you into a mass grave, and that'll be the end of that."

He let the words sink in for a moment and walked among them, looking down at them disdainfully.

"General MacDaniel once gave you a choice," he continued, "to ease the people's fears instilled by your pesky prophet. That didn't work out so well. I'm willing to give you another chance."

He peered into each one's eyes, except for Oriana who kept her head turned away from him.

"Come work for me. Help the people understand that their only chance is to fall into line with the new world order which will take us out of this free fall."

"You must be insane!" Lynn said coldly.

Zorn raised his bushy eyebrows in mock surprise. "That's not very nice. I'm offering you your life."

"You want us to support you?" Jeremy cried out. "We are devoted to the other side!"

"What makes you so sure that I'm evil?"

"The Prophet told us," Jeremy said defiantly.

"Aah, and he knows all . . . But the fact is that you don't know anything about me. Maybe I'm devoted to the cause of the human race and my aim is to get us through this cataclysmic time."

Oriana could take no more. She turned around to speak up and reveal what she knew about this man. At the same moment, Zorn turned his glimmering eyes upon her and deadened her voice. Her vocal chords became paralyzed beneath his fiery gaze. With all her might she tried to speak, but nothing came out.

Zorn turned back to the others. It had happened so fast that they noticed nothing. Zorn had merely turned away for an instant.

"I can use people who want to sacrifice themselves for the betterment of their fellow humans. I know your motives are pure. I can give you the opportunity to help humanity."

Jeremy stepped forward, wanting to get the man away from his loved one. "How can you do that?"

"I am interested in power, this is true," Zorn said more gently. "But it's not merely personal power. It's for the sake of the big picture—the welfare of this planet and its inhabitants. It should be clear to you that under these conditions there must be a new kind of control or we will disintegrate completely into dark ages and never rise again. Ultimately, my plans are benevolent even though they may not look that way."

"What are you asking of us, then?" Jeremy demanded.

Lynn took his hand. "Don't bargain with him, Jeremy!"

"You shouldn't listen to the little lady all the time, Mr. Wilkes. You should make your own decisions. I'm giving you the chance to find fulfillment in caring for the needs of desperate people on a large scale. I'll put you in charge of our food distribution and medical services. Think about it. In the blink of an eye, you would go from penniless vagabonds to people with the ability to touch millions of lives."

"We don't have the same goals," Jeremy protested.

"It doesn't matter what our differences are!" Zorn insisted. "We have to journey on the same road for awhile. I'm telling you that I need people who mean well to do the kind of work I need done. I'll put others who do a different kind of work in other positions."

"You mean like the death squads out in the streets?" Andrew stated bitterly.

"We call them cleanup crews. How would you handle it? You got some better ideas?"

"It seems to me that murdering people on street corners doesn't qualify as an idea at all!"

"Well, I'm a common sense sort of fellow. We have to do what we have to do. I'm also a very busy man so I will end this conversation and leave you with this opportunity. Think about it. I'm handing you charitable work on a silver platter. Take it or leave it. Makes no difference to me. Either way, I will win. You'd better accept that."

He turned around dramatically and looked at Oriana.

"You, however, are another matter! You're gonna have to come with me."

"No!" Tom cried out.

"You haven't learn your lesson yet, son?" Zorn said angrily. He waved his hand and Tom's body was thrown back against the wall with full force. The crack of his bones echoed through the room. "Doesn't pay to be so hardheaded."

He turned to the soldiers. "Take her!"

The soldiers grabbed her as she screamed. "Please help me!" she managed to cry out as they dragged her across the room.

Lynn jumped between Oriana and the soldiers.

"Wait!"

One of the soldiers raised the butt of his rifle to strike her. Zorn held up his hand.

"Just a moment! Do you have something you want to say to me?" he asked, careful to hide a victorious smile.

"Don't take her," Lynn begged. "I'll convince the others to consider your offer seriously."

"What is she to you?" Zorn wondered, looking with disgust at Oriana.

"A treasured human life."

"Are you telling me that you'll change your position completely for her safety?"

Lynn nodded with difficulty.

"Then you can keep her for now. Your cooperation is more important to me than her punishment."

With that he turned and walked out the door swiftly.

Oriana hurried over to Lynn and hugged her.

"You can't do this. He'll only use you."

"We're not going to let him take you away to some dreadful fate."

"What am I to you?" Oriana asked in tears. "We haven't known each other twenty-four hours. My life was doomed from the beginning. I was born to this."

"No one's life is doomed like that! In this short time with us, you've heard the Voice. You know that there is another force in the world."

"I do! But for the moment, it's the dark one that's winning. I know he will eventually destroy me. I have too much information. And he hates disloyalty more than he does goodness of heart."

"What about those things he said about charitable work?" Jeremy asked.

"Believe me, Stefan Zorn is evil to the core. He has no interest in humanity's welfare. His kind have been preparing all these centuries for the manifestation of forces that use humanity for their own dark purposes. These purposes have nothing to do with our welfare. He's not about to change. I may have seen a new light, but he never will. He's offended against it too often."

"So what is his mission?" Andrew questioned impatiently.

"He's right that it's a secret I was never privy too. But I can tell you this. There's an intent to use human beings as organic transmuters of energies to feed certain needs of the cosmos. The wars that have been fought were not really for conquest or defense, but for the generation of certain emanations that are nutrition for another world, the one that Stefan Zorn works for. That world thrives on human suffering and death."

"Maybe we can do some good in spite of him . . . play along with him for awhile," Tom suggested, rubbing his bruised shoulder.

"Once he's accomplished his aims, you'll be done for. He'll never forgive the Prophet for humiliating him," Oriana stated sadly.

"Our first priority is to safeguard the lives of the people around us," Lynn said with determination. "If we can't do that, we're of no use to anyone."

"I don't understand," Oriana retorted. "You told me you were charged with a mission to reawaken the human spirit."

"That's right and in order to do that we must exemplify that in our own lives, which begins with the things and people closest to us. There were plenty of helpers of humanity who worked for the larger good and disregarded those nearest to them. That's not what the Prophet taught us. If we're devoid of that kind of authentic care and love, we can't do anybody any good."

"I'm not worth all this!"

Lynn took Oriana by the arms. "Even if you did sacrifice yourself, we'd be stuck in this situation. We must make the best of where we are now. And if we're butchered at the hands of Stefan Zorn, then so be it. We will not sell our souls to him for our own safety. Besides, there are too many clues that we are receiving help. Andrew and Tom were pulled out from their clutches once before. It could happen again."

"I think you're fooling yourself!" Andrew said angrily. "How can we possibly do anything useful when the evil ones have all the power. Now that we know that Zorn is in tight with the highest echelons of the Federation, it means that he'll control everything. The rebuilding process is already a lost cause."

A loud noise announced the unbolting of the door. They all turned to see the gruesome figure of Dr. Tagore appear in the dim light. They reacted in revulsion to the spectral figure. He looked at them haughtily. But his eyes didn't carry the glint of fierce hate that was his typical expression. A deep melancholy darkened his features. His usually erect posture was slightly stooped beneath its weight.

"Are you looking for me again?" Andrew said, hoping that the demon would focus his evil intent on him rather than on his friends.

"Where's Oriana?" the man said in a hoarse whisper.

"I'm here," she responded, stepping into the pale stream of light coming through the doorway.

"Oriana . . . How did you get yourself into this?" he asked with deep sadness.

"I had to leave. I didn't belong with you anymore."

"I've loved you since you were a little girl," the man stated, his voice quivering with rare emotion. "How could you leave me?"

"You loved me? I never saw it."

"Since the death of your parents, I've been like a father to you. Don't you remember? We use to go for walks in the park together. You liked holding my hand."

"I don't remember."

"It wasn't that long ago!"

"Why did you come here?"

"I can't let him have you. I know what he'll do to you."

"You would disobey your Master's orders?" she asked, stunned.

"I told you, you're the only being I've ever loved. The sweetness of the little girl you once were was the only joy I've known. I promised your parents I would care for you. I didn't know what it would do to me."

"So you've come to say good-bye?"

He shook his head. "I've come to take you with me."

Her mouth dropped open. "He'll roast you alive!"

"I know some safe houses."

She looked fearfully at the half dozen soldiers surrounding him and armed to the teeth.

"What about them?" she asked in terror.

"They're paid mercenaries. They do my bidding."

"He'll find you!"

"Even he doesn't know all the secret places we've established. That was my department."

"I won't leave without them."

"What?"

"You'll have to take my friends with us."

"I can't do that, Oriana."

"Then I stay!

"I came for the little girl who once called me 'papa'."

Oriana knew this was her only chance to save her friends. She swallowed hard and placed her hand on his scarred cheek.

"She's still in here, papa. I do remember your goodness to me. You were the only one who was concerned for my welfare. I'll always be grateful for that. I'll go with you, but we must bring them along. We can drop them off outside the city."

"Zorn will have my hide for sure."

"What difference does it make since you've already crossed the line?"

"You'll stay with me?"

"I will."

"It will be like it use to be, when I bought you lollipops at the fair?"

She had always known that he was disturbed. Now it was clear to her that he was completely insane.

"I'll hold your hand like before."

"No time to waste, then!" Dr. Tagore growled as he motioned for the companions to join them.

Stunned by the turn of events, the friends hurried behind the soldiers as they rushed down the hall to the docks below. A dark van awaited them. The friends were ordered into the back and told to hide under blankets and behind boxes that littered the vehicle. The soldiers piled in and the van headed toward a heavily-guarded post.

A soldier peered into the vehicle. Dr. Tagore held up an official pass. The officer saluted him and waved them on.

The van hurried through the smoldering city. Crowds wandered the streets in a daze. Sirens and loudspeakers filled the air with confused sounds that intensified the chaos. Inside the van, an eerie silence contrasted with the outside noise. Everyone was mute, except for an occasional order from Dr. Tagore to the driver. Oriana sat next to the grim occult leader who held onto her hand like a drowning man. She did her best to hide her disgust and thought of her friends hidden behind her. Their breathing kept her sane as he caressed the back of her hand. She turned to him and looked into his freakish features. Buried behind the scars and decades of encrusted dark energy was the faded light of a fatherly love. She was his only link to his human side. She sensed that he would be good to her . . . until his mind went completely over the deep end.

Soon they reached the boundaries of the ruined city. Trees and grass appeared as a reminder that life could start again, even after the worst catastrophes. The van turned onto a dirt road and came to halt in the middle of nowhere.

"Get out!" Dr. Tagore roared at the companions.

Lynn took Oriana's hand. "Come with us," she whispered.

Oriana turned a look of terror upon her. She was too frozen to respond.

"Get out before I change my mind!" Tagore shouted in a frenzy.

Jeremy pulled Lynn out of the van as the others followed.

"We can't leave her with him!" she murmured in horror.

"We've got no choice," Jeremy said, trying to comfort her.

Lynn leaned back in the van to say good-bye to her new friend. Dr. Tagore turned to slam the door in her face. In doing so, his coat opened, revealing the butt of a revolver protruding from his belt. Without thinking, Oriana grabbed for it and tore it free. Tagore turned around to find the gun cocked and aimed at his forehead. His wild eyes turned dark with anger.

"How dare you turn on me? I took care of you . . . "

One of the soldiers moved abruptly, trying to raise his weapon. Oriana fired the gun at him and the man slammed against the van, hit in the shoulder. She turned back and aimed the smoking pistol directly between Tagore's eyes.

"You're next . . . "

"Oriana," the man begged, "why don't you love me?"

"Because you're a beast, not a human being."

"I'm human! If you shoot me, I will bleed."

"Shall we find out?"

"I put my life in danger to save you . . . I don't understand."

"Tell your soldiers to put down their weapons and step out of the van."

"Have you no gratitude?" he asked cynically, his face turning hard and losing all warmth toward her.

"For what? For being tutored in your dark ways and brainwashed into thinking that what you did was right?"

"I took you to the fair . . . . " he muttered between his teeth.

"You're the one who molested me!" she blurted out suddenly.

Tagore's face turned red. "What are you talking about?"

"I've had nightmares for years and a vague memory . . . The silhouette of a man . . . colored lights behind him!"

She prepared to shoot.

"Wait!" Lynn cried out. "Don't kill him. It won't help us."

She motioned for the others to disarm the soldiers as Oriana held the gun in a tight grip. Andrew and Tom pushed the soldiers out and checked them for additional weapons. Jeremy took hold of Dr. Tagore and helped him out of the vehicle. Oriana followed, the weapon still ready to fire.

"You'll regret this!" the freakish man warned. "I swear you'll regret this!"

The companions got into the van as Tagore and his men watched helplessly.

"Maybe she ought to shoot him," Tom suggested. "That'll keep him from coming after us."

"What are you saying?" Lynn retorted angrily. She

placed her hand gently on Oriana's shoulder. "You don't want to be like them, remember?"

Oriana looked into Lynn's eyes and became aware of the violence and hatred polluting her heart. She handed the weapon to her and turned away, ashamed. Lynn quickly closed the van's door.

"Let's get out of here!" she called out to Jeremy who put the vehicle in gear and tore off in a cloud of smoke which covered the grim men left behind with dust and humiliation. Tagore's eyes beamed with evil intent as he watched the van disappear.

"I'll find you!" he muttered hatefully. "I'll find you wherever you go."

* * * * *

The Federation's armies amassed over the most devastated areas of the world, where populations were decimated by the catastrophes. In one terrible day, a thousand planes roared back and forth across the wreckage, bombing it into oblivion. There was no way to help the wounded and the world's resources would be toppled over trying to salvage what the typhoons and earthquakes had left alive.

In the Middle East, squadrons filled the skies over territories where revolution was anticipated. Religious fundamentalists were sure to make the most of the devastation. They were already organized to force the starving, confused and desperate hordes to do their bidding. Their agenda was power, not care for the masses they controlled. On the same day as the bombs fell over the last shreds of southeast Asia, so did they rain upon Iran and Iraq until the populated lands were as inanimate as the surrounding deserts.

The Federation forces then turned upon Africa. Smart bombs hit refugee camps where survivors were gathered by the hundreds of thousands. In a few hours there would be no one left to carry contagious diseases across the borders. Nor was there anyone to interfere with the military raids. No one was organized enough to shoot back or to create a renegade army. This was indeed the moment to strike, just as Stefan Zorn had advised. Hundreds of special forces lived in the skies, refueling in midair, flying from place to place according to the high command's urgent orders. Wherever surveillance or espionage had warned of rebellious action, the planes would break the sound barrier overhead and drop their deadly cargo upon the suspects. The plan was simple—to keep the world population on its knees until it was completely at the mercy of the dominating forces.

Military installations and nuclear plants were guarded by carpet bombing their surroundings so that nothing within a hundred miles could come near them. Only the Federation's jets could descend out of the skies into the precious locations. It was a novel plan, to destroy the enemy before he even appeared on the horizon. At the same time, satellites sent messages twenty-four hours a day to huddled masses living in the ruins. The messages were designed to bring some measure of hope for normalcy's return. The makeshift studios in the Federation's various headquarters uplinked images of stability and strength to a world where no such thing existed, except on the flickering screens of the remaining television sets.

Staged presentations of food shelters created in cavernous warehouses were beamed across the world, making it seem that the benevolent dictators were solving the famine problem. People were fed with pictures of other people being fed and given the illusion that they were next. Every so often, wanted posters would appear on the screens, faces of individuals who were on the short list for execution. The Federation's expectation was that desperate people would turn them in for the reward and just as important would stay away from these hunted persons who were doomed to be caught eventually.

Certain politicians, major criminals, serial killers who were out of control even for these times, were shown several times of day. Every few hours, the photos of Jeremy, Lynn, Andrew, Michelle, Tom and Oriana would appear in the ghostly light of some TV screen in all parts of the globe with a resonant base voice warning all to beware of these persons and promising large stores of food and money for those who would provide information leading to their arrest.

The world was on fire. Nothing was left of decency, kindness, compassion. All power was in the hands of dominators who knew how to keep the people in absolute need and terror. The human spirit had reached its darkest hour. Only those who had learned to stay alive inwardly despite their circumstances according to the great teachers of wisdom could hang onto their sanity.

Ideas that had taken centuries to develop—freedom of the individual, democratic government, religious liberty—had vanished like dust in the fierce winds that howled across the planet. As the ancient prophecy had warned, the sun no longer gave its light, neither the cosmic sun shrouded in clouds that would linger for years, nor the sun of the human spirit. As in the days of the holocaust in the previous millennium, all sense of a benevolent force in the universe had crumbled beneath the trauma of the moment. Humans were reduced to the most basic survival instincts and like sheep led to the slaughter accepted the Federation's stranglehold over their lives.

Reconstructing the structures of the world would take immense labor but rebuilding the human soul seemed like an impossible task. New generations brought up in this devastation, parented by people long devoid of depth and meaning, would become little more than two legged animals without conscience, without learning, living from sensation to sensation. Their lives would be brief and focused on finding the next meal. If the inherent nobility of the human race was to be salvaged, it would have to be with help from beyond. As never before in history, the time was at hand for the return of the messengers of light . . . before it was too late.

THE END

In preparation

THE ABOMINATION

Book 3
of
The Messiah Chronicles

Humanity is enslaved by forces of darkness in an age of monstrous destruction as a remnant seeks to salvage the future against all odds.

THE MESSIAH CHRONICLES SERIES

THE FINAL PROPHET
Book 1
THE TRIBULATION
Book 2
THE ABOMINATION
Book 3
THE MESSENGERS OF LIGHT
Book 4

About the Author

Theodore J. Nottingham has authored, edited and translated a dozen books, ranging from metaphysical and historical fiction to humor and non-fiction works on spirituality. He is also a television and video producer whose productions have been broadcast on national network and cable television. He lives in the United States with his wife and daughter and is working on future books in the *Messiah Chronicles* series and other novels. He can be reached at tnottingham@usa.net

Other books available from Nottingham Publishing

- The Color of the Wind; Fables for a New Age
- Coming Soon The Holy Man's War:
  Book One of the Mystic Isle Legends

For information, contact Nottingham Publishing
tnottingham@usa.net http://tedn.hypermart.net